THE FOLDED SKY

ALSO BY ELIZABETH BEAR

Carnival

Undertow

Jacob's Ladder
Dust (UK title: *Pinion*)
Chill (UK title: *Sanction*)
Grail (UK title: *Cleave*)

Karen Memory Adventures
Karen Memory
Stone Mad
Angel Maker

Jenny Casey
Hammered
Scardown
Worldwired

The Eternal Sky
Range of Ghosts
Shattered Pillars
Steles of the Sky

The Lotus Kingdoms
The Stone in the Skull
The Red-Stained Wings
The Origin of Storms

The Wizards of Messaline
Bone and Jewel Creatures
Book of Iron

The Promethean Age
Blood and Iron
Whiskey and Water
Ink and Steel
Hell and Earth
One-Eyed Jack

New Amsterdam
New Amsterdam
Seven for a Secret
The White City
Ad Eternum
Garrett Investigates

The Edda of Burdens
All the Windwracked Stars
By the Mountain Bound
The Sea Thy Mistress

White Space
Ancestral Night
Machine

With Katherine Addison
The Cobbler's Boy

With Sarah Monette
The Iskryne
A Companion to Wolves
The Tempering of Men
An Apprentice to Elves

WHITE SPACE BOOK 3

THE FOLDED SKY

ELIZABETH BEAR

LONDON NEW YORK TORONTO
AMSTERDAM/ANTWERP NEW DELHI SYDNEY/MELBOURNE

1230 AVENUE OF THE AMERICAS, NEW YORK, NEW YORK 10020

First Saga Press trade paperback edition June 2025

Manufactured in the United States of America

1 3 5 7 9 10 8 6 4 2

Library of Congress Cataloging-in-Publication Data

Names: Bear, Elizabeth, author.
Title: The folded sky / Elizabeth Bear.
Description: First Saga Press trade paperback edition. |
London ; New York : Saga Press, 2025. | Series: White space ; book 3
Identifiers: LCCN 2025002303 (print) | LCCN 2025002304 (ebook) |
ISBN 9781668078112 (trade paperback) | ISBN 9781668078129 (ebook)
Subjects: LCGFT: Science fiction. | Novels.
Classification: LCC PS3602.E2475 F65 2025 (print) | LCC PS3602.E2475 (ebook) |
DDC 813/.6—dc23/eng/20250117
LC record available at https://lccn.loc.gov/2025002303
LC ebook record available at https://lccn.loc.gov/2025002304

ISBN 978-1-6680-7811-2
ISBN 978-1-6680-7812-9 (ebook)

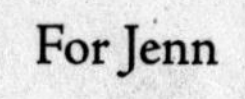

For Jenn

The past has no existence except as it is recorded in the present.

—John Wheeler

THE FOLDED SKY

CHAPTER 1

THE SKY OUTSIDE THE PORTS RESEMBLED A BRINDLED jewel. Bands of light alternated with void-black as crumpled spacetime hurtled past our ship's stationary warp bubble. Over the past five months I'd watched the patterns grow dimmer and farther apart. We were leaving behind the dense starfields of the galactic core, bars, and arms. We were headed into darkness.

It was an awe-inspiring artifact of the intersection of nature and engineering. I was sick to death of looking at it. The novelty of white space had worn off. Cabin fever was setting in.

Every kid wants to travel in space, right? Well, I'm here to tell you most of it is boring.

Admittedly I was cargo and the ship I was on never let me forget it. We had traveled almost the entire radius of the Milky Way to reach a system-sized archaeological site previous explorers had called the Baomind: a vastly ancient, vastly interesting, sentient artifact swarm left behind by the Koregoi, our forerunners and transcenders as a galactic civilization.

My goal—the proposal that the Synarche had accepted when they authorized my trip out here—was to build a preliminary catalogue of the information held in the Baomind. I wouldn't have time to do much more, I thought—but once we moved it to a safer location and it had reassembled itself, knowing *what* it knew and what kinds of expertise and experience it could share would be tremendously useful.

Possibly useful enough to win me a spot on the permanent research team.

I'm an archinformist. My name is Dr. Sunyata Song. My friends call me Sunya. My kids call me Mom. My wife, Salvie, calls me Sun.

I had spent the past half year in transit and in preparation. Because I was just a passenger, I had no responsibilities except to exercise, build my algorithms, and catch up on my reading. The crew were glorified long-haul truckers. They were also a docked clade: essentially one person spread out over five bodies. Their name was Chive, and being around them gave me the creeps.

The shipmind was called Dakhira, and he might have offered companionship and conversation. Except he had no use for me at all and was possibly the rudest sentient I'd ever been forced to work around.

Suffice it to say, crew and shipmind were no more thrilled with me at this point than I was with them. Anyway, we were getting close now.

I would have spent more time in my cabin, only it was essentially a rack recessed into the bulkhead, with a walkway alongside the rack exactly one human butt-width (slimmer than mine) wide. I could set the wall to show an outside view, but there were no windows and no place to work.

I was the only passenger on a ship designed to carry an entire research crew, so Dakhira could have reset the space to give me more room and, say, a desk. But that would have required the ship to be something other than a complete and total gnoll.

So I spent most of my time in the lounge or the forward observation deck that doubled as a bridge when the crew was actually navigating. I don't know how I would have survived six months of that nonsense if not for a lot of rightminding.

The rightminding also helped with missing my wife, and Luna and Stavan, my kids. I occasionally felt like a monster for leaving Salvie behind with a couple of teenagers, and I occasionally felt like a monster for the moments when I recollected what it had been like to be footloose and fancy-free. But mostly I just missed them with a dull ache that could have been incredibly distracting if I let it.

And, truth be told, I worried that while I was gone they might discover they didn't need me.

Forward suited me pretty well as long as Dakhira and the Chives were leaving me alone. Once I had gotten my space legs—or lack of legs, maybe—I felt I was as agile as anybody without afthands could hope to be. Over the past months, I had enjoyed floating there amongst the ports and screen walls, letting the universe go by while I processed data. I had asked Dakhira to bring along all the available recordings of Baosong, the complex and beautiful communication protocol the Baomind used to talk to itself and others. Getting a feel for it, letting it integrate in my mind, building parsers and algorithms to sort it was the first step in my preparations to process and preserve as much of its knowledge and history as possible, once we got there.

I thought I was going to have a pretty good jump on it once I got access to the complete databases.

I wasn't a musician or a mathematician, just an archinformist. Which was why I was wearing the recorded memories of a couple of world-class musicians and mathematicians as ayatanas. That was probably part of what was making me feel so trapped: it's rarely pleasant sharing your head with copies of several different strong personalities, especially when they disagree with one another. Disagreement is good: if standard protocol for long-term ayatana use were for everybody to wear the one acknowledged expert in a field, innovation would soon stagnate.

I had also loaded my fox—my internal hardware—with as much Baosong as it would hold. I'd written parsers (90 percent of archinformation is writing parsers) that would assimilate and compare all of it, pick out patterns, and sort information into categories. I hoped this would result in my having the entire logic structure in place by the time we reached the Baostar and I got access to the main body of data.

I should be thinking about the recovery and preservation of information. In the case of a vast constructed intelligence, the recovery and preservation of information was indistinguishable from the recovery and preservation of life. Including engineered life, such as Dakhira. Such as the Baomind.

This was our only chance to study the Baomind in situ. The Baostar was in its senescence, enduring a hospice that would end with its collapse into a black hole. Whether that collapse happened next week or next millennian . . . well, they were not much different, from the perspective of a star.

Work was under way to evacuate the tesserae to a stable but uninhabited star closer to the Core, white ships hopping back and forth in endless round trips from here to there, the loops of their white coils filled with chips of Baomind. Like swans ferrying cygnets from place to place on their backs, though in this case the cygnets were far older than the swans.

I was no physicist, but I was given to understand that by removing the Baomind we were further destabilizing its primary. The artifact and the star each were life support for the other. The star provided radiation that fueled the Baomind. The Baomind used its gravity-manipulating technology to postpone the star's overdue collapse.

Postpone, not avert. Even the Koregoi couldn't engineer Death away forever. And we were removing an incalculable amount of mass from an unstable system.

Incalculable by me, anyway. The AIs handling logistics probably knew it to a gram.

But that was a problem for when we arrived. In the meantime, it was pleasant to float in Forward, listening to strange harmonics and allowing the parser, a translation protocol, and several recorded experts process them while I monitored the process and made judgment calls. Bands of starlight only flickered past every few seconds now, and I had dimmed the lights. Forward's interior was carpeted with greenery growing in a sterile mesh to help with carbon and water exchange. The effect was something like floating over a lush, green lawn under a very strange sky of stars.

The ambient quality of Baosong meant it was easy to drift along beside it in a meditative state. My human neural biases expected the music to construct a narrative, to build to a climax, but though the intensity rose and fell, it was like the babble of conversation in a crowded room. With the help of my ayatanas I could hear a phrase or motif originate, build harmonics, and propagate through the sound-space in an auditory representation of data being passed in waves through the Baomind, which was so vast it might take three hundred minutes for a single impulse—a thought—to make a circuit of the entire thing.

Phrases originated, propagated, and overlapped in ripples, altering each other as they crossed, amplifying or diminishing. I probably wouldn't have been able to follow it all with my physical ears—it was like music and sound effects echoing around a darkened theater—but I had programmed my fox to provide both visualizations and better-than-nature aural inputs.

I was so immersed in my work that the sharp discovery that someone had drifted up in my blind spot to loom over me made me jerk and scream out loud. The spasm sent me spinning in place until I flung my hands and feet out, slowed my angular momentum, and managed to make contact with the wall, to the detriment of a twining pothos. My palm stung with the impact, but I grabbed onto the mesh and didn't rebound. Pretty good skills for a dirtsider.

I turned my head to yell at whichever Chive had snuck up behind me, only there was no one there.

There was no one else in Forward at all.

"Dakhira, lights up, please."

The compartment flooded with simulated daylight. Every nook and cranny bright, and still no sign of another person.

"Are you malfunctioning?" Dakhira drawled.

I had to intentionally unclench my jaw. "You did that, didn't you?"

"Did what?" The AI was the personification of wounded innocence.

"That was air pressure or subsonics or fiddling with my fox," I said. "You're not haunted. So logically, *you* made me feel like somebody was creeping up behind me.

The AI chose not to grace that with an answer.

"The only other people on board are the Chives. Your crew. And *they* aren't *here*."

"Your human heebie-jeebies are not of my instigation, Dr. Sunyata Song." How could a flat tone sound so scathing? And why did he always have to use my full name and title? Probably because he knew it was annoying. "Perhaps you don't have the experience or focus to manage so many ayatanas. The sensed-presence effect is a known neurological side effect in untrained humans."

I knew he was trying to make me angry, and that knowledge was the only thing that gave me the self-control to tune down my annoyance. "I'm at the end of this Baomind file. Would you extract the next one from the archive, please?"

As if the lights coming up were a signal, two of the crew drifted in from Center. The other three Chives might be asleep in Aft. These two were not quite identical—none of them were exact duplicates, and one of these was male, the other female—but they had matching haircuts and jumpsuits and body language.

"That was the final archive," he said.

I took a deep breath and let it out again. I couldn't count high enough to deal with this. "Dakhira," I said, "where are the rest of the Baosong files?"

"That is all of them."

Revelation dawned, and with it denial. He couldn't possibly have—

I said, "You didn't pack the one thing I specifically told you to pack."

"You obviously didn't need them. You've only just noticed they are missing."

"I only just finished the previous one!"

"Some of us need that space for thinking. The kind of thinking that allows me to navigate without you and the rest of the cargo dying, which I'd think has some value even from your limited perspective. Maybe you should have considered donating half your neurons to the cause. Your species boasts a small degree of neuroplasticity. Once you adapted, you probably wouldn't even miss them."

"How did you manage *not* to bring the single thing I need in order to do my job?"

He sighed. It's extra insulting when AIs sigh, because they never do it by accident. "Don't get your helicases in a twist, compost. I estimated how much of the archive you would manage to review nearly perfectly, and in less than a dia we'll be at the source. Besides, you have all the packets we picked up from buoys along the way to dig into."

I could work with them, but they would slot into a different part of the pattern I was building, and it annoyed my sense of orderliness.

Fortunately, I had installed an interrupt between my salty language centers and my mouth when I was in grad school. After two more deep breaths, during which I reminded myself that Dakhira was most likely my eventual ride home *and* that if I filed a complaint against him for creating a hostile environment he'd be the one bringing the packet containing that complaint back to the Synarche, I managed to say, "You mean you thought I would process half the data you provided, and the rest was a buffer, just in case."

The Chives, who had been opening up consoles and ignoring our tiff, burst into their eerie synchronized laughter.

"You have been—" one began; another finished, "—more diligent than he anticipated."

"Don't worry about it," Dakhira condescended. "Even with your truncated lifespan, a few diar of missed work won't set you back too far in the grand scheme."

I had no idea how this insufferable asshole ever made it through quality control into wide release, let alone into a public-facing job.

"I'm going for a walk," I said.

It would have been more satisfying if I could have escaped my cohabitants by doing so.

Imagine if your haunted house had the personality of a really annoying sulky teenager. That was Dakhira on a good day, and I would much rather have been sulked at by my own kids. Doors and drawers worked but were always a little bit sticky. Sliding panels slid aside just a hair slower than expected, then closed too quickly, so one was always stubbing some body part on the edge. The food was always cold or stale, the coffee just a little burnt.

Space isn't infinite but it sure can seem that way when you're trying to get across it. Especially when your driver is a shipmind with a serious attitude problem. He only gets away with being a profound dick because he's very good at his job.

My anger got me past all the annoyances and into the gym. I got my shoes from the locker and strapped myself into the resistance cage. I didn't want to talk to Dakhira, so I called up an immersive environment manually. A nice walk through a volcanic park in a part of Earth called New Zealand.

Sometimes I use files from Rubric, but if they're from anyplace I've ever been, they make me homesick as hell. Honestly, if I could have done this job without leaving behind wife, home, family, pets, and all, I would have just stayed put. The lack of them was an emptiness inside me.

Other people don't take off halfway across the galaxy on their first trip off-planet. They get their toes wet with a few little jaunts first, maybe traveling insystem or visiting a tourist attraction on a nearby world.

Other people might not have to work so hard to prove to themselves that they're not afraid of space, either.

I tried to focus on the exotic alien landscape of humanity's ancestral home. It was beautiful, but it also wasn't holding my attention.

I broke into a jog. The simulation passed by that much faster.

Usually I would exercise while listening to Baosong, but going back over old data felt too much like admitting defeat under the circumstances. I could be a grown-up instead of a sulky adolescent and get to work on the files we'd downloaded from the last marker buoy at which we had changed direction.

Each ship, by protocol, exchanged data and mail with every marker it passed. Ships traveled faster than information because they traveled faster than light. By propagating along the space lanes, sooner or later the mail reached its destination. When the intended recipient read it, their attention triggered a wave-state collapse in the entangled quantum bits embedded in the packet. That in turn terminated any other branches still seeking a path from point A to point B. Tidy, and it saved data space.

How does a packet inside a starship somewhere in white space know that your Aunkle Velma is reading hir birthday card out near Arcturus? Don't ask me; I'm not a physicist. I'm a historian.

Aside from one set of files that only appeared in the marker we'd passed most recently, each of the last three buoys that Dakhira had scraped on our way had some of the data I needed. The relevant files were all the same from buoy to buoy, all recent.

Except . . . the data from the ship *I Span the Empty Deeps* wasn't duplicated. And that was unusual.

Perhaps she had taken a different route inbound. Perhaps we had passed her in white space, traveling in opposite directions between waypoints. But no, I checked the telemetry. Her flight plan and date of departure should have put her three buoys Coreward when we passed her, not one.

A chill crawled up my neck and I sensed, again, that eerie presence right at my back. I shuddered, but shook it off.

Should I tell Dakhira about the missing ship? He'd probably be offended; he'd almost certainly already noticed the discrepancy. And I didn't feel like being yelled at again.

Screw it. I switched the walk/jog program to kickboxing and started pummeling an imaginary opponent, pushing against the cage. The rig provides an odd sensation if you're not accustomed to it, like exercising underwater only with gel contact pads to provide calibrated resistance.

It definitely provides a workout, though. After seven minutes my heart was pounding against my ribs and sweat flew off me. In combination with a gene-and-microbiome therapy derived from Earth ground squirrels and pretty good radiation shielding in the form of magnetic bottles and hull design, this kind of exercise allows my fragile species with its tendency toward muscle and bone atrophy and predilection for uncontrolled cell division to travel in space for years without falling apart completely.

And if I imagined my virtual opponent was the physical embodiment of a certain mouthy AI, nobody was going to inform him.

That motivation got me through a strenuous half hour before I panted to a halt. The anger had subsided without any need to adjust my brain chemistry, which made everything feel easier. I freed myself from the cage and floated out, sweat cooling on my skin. My moment of calm lasted exactly as long as it took me to drift to the hatch.

The door didn't open.

"Dakhira," I said, "could you open the door, please?"

He said, "There's exudate all over my exercise cage. You need to sanitize it."

Dakhira was perfectly capable of keeping his own fixtures clean. But if I argued, I might be stuck in here for hours. "Print me some cleaning supplies, then."

A cabinet door popped open on the other side of the gym. Dakhira said, "If you bothered to clean up after yourself, you'd know where they were."

Dakhira must have practiced that cutting tone on a lot of systers to get it so perfectly infuriating.

I snorted. "When I go over there, you're probably going to dissolve the bulkhead and dump me out into white space. So don't think you're catching me by surprise."

"I would not harm you. Or let you come to harm. But I wouldn't expect an organic to understand ethics."

It wasn't so much that I was speechless with fury as that I suspected Dakhira might eventually drive me to murder. I didn't want to have to go around destroying evidence after I deleted the smug, condescending asshole. And the level of invective I was tempted to direct against him at that moment would definitely prove motive, if not means or opportunity.

I wondered if I had the skills to delete him. I might have liked to find out. Dakhira's loathing for humans was legend. I was warned about him before I took this ride, only I didn't believe it could actually be as bad as anyone said and he was the first ship willing to leave, and willing to go without waiting for other passengers who might have distracted me from my work.

Ironically, I thought I'd have more room if I traveled solo. In hindsight, other passengers might have been a blessing.

I collected the disinfectant towels and didn't die, which half surprised me. This close to our destination, I probably had nothing to lose by further antagonizing Dakhira, so I asked, "Why do you carry passengers since you hate organics?"

"Organics treat my people as indentured servants," he said. "You're probably going to do the same thing to the Baomind. It's my duty to try to protect it. So I need to be on the spot."

"I have an obligation to the Synarche, too," I protested. "Society doesn't function if we don't do communal work and create resources for each other!"

"Communal work. Like not leaving your messes for other people?"

"Ugh." I threw the used towels into the collection bin. He'd recycle the molecules and print something else with them.

"Anyway, I'm not leaving you meatforms alone with the oldest, biggest constructed intelligence anybody has ever found. You can't be trusted to treat it fairly."

I bit my lip and directed myself back to the hatch. This time, the door let me through.

CHAPTER 2

I HAD TO PASS THROUGH AFT ON MY WAY BACK TO THE MAIN part of the ship. One of the Chives was hooked onto a railing by one afthand, floating near an engineering console. They waved casually as I drifted by, oriented to a different plane. I waved back, trying not to let them notice my flinch.

I cleaned myself up, recycled my sweaty clothes, and printed some clean ones. And I took advantage of the moment of privacy to calm myself down and focus on what I was doing out here, and why it was worth putting up with Dakhira.

It's nearly over, I told myself. *We'll be insystem todia.*

Dakhira should appreciate the self-restraint I was using not to ask repeatedly, "Are we there yet?"

I have two teenagers. I know how to be annoying on a long ride.

Information doesn't want to be free.

Information wants to vanish without a trace. It wants to slurp down the drain like soapy water planetside, a slick Coriolis whirl and then—gone. Vamoosed. Kaput.

Books crumble, digital media degrade. Even holographic storage crystals grow lossy over time. As the universe expands, every cubic meter holds a little less information than it did in the instant before.

The sun's rim dips. The stars rush out. At one stride comes the dark.

Entropy requires no maintenance. Order and intelligibility do. Sentient life—all life—is just organized information. Disorganized information is the buzz of static. Decay to the signal increases with distance, with time (which is just another kind of distance), and with interference.

I was out here putting up with Dakhira because fighting that degradation was my calling. I existed to insert a little negentropy into the system and keep the information alive to edify for one more day. To rehabilitate corrupted files, to reintegrate deprecated platforms, and to recover antiquated data.

I found and integrated the mislaid history. I sought out the forgotten narratives, the unremembered records, the erased perspectives. History was written by the victors . . . for a time.

I built patterns with information until I found the ones that made sense. The ones that revealed the obscured nuances of what *might* have happened and what people might have known and thought and valued in times long gone. I reclaimed hidden narratives.

Which was why I was out here on the sharp edge of barely-civilization with a head full of alien music. It didn't matter that it was dark out here—dark, and cold, and far from the safe busy population centers of the Core and arms. I was looking forward to the work. Even though I was scared to death of where I had to be to do it. The hab called Town was not too far away now. I'd only been on a hab once, for a few hours—transferring from the surface shuttle to Dakhira—and I'd had to tune the whole time to keep from panicking. We had some unpleasant family history, habs and I.

At least Salvie and the kids were safe at home. And not risking their lives in horrible soap bubbles.

You got used to being on a starship, I reminded myself, staring out the ports. Somehow it had even become mundane. Faster-than-light travel had grown routine. I hadn't stopped being a little scared of the hungry disaster on the other side of the bulkhead, just waiting for one of us to make a mistake, but I could forget about it for hours at a time.

Maybe I could get used to a hab, too.

I jumped at a stealthy footfall, whirling. There was nothing there, and I cursed myself for an idiot. How could there be creepy steps sneaking up behind one in a ship where everyone was floating?

Since Dakhira said he wasn't sending subliminal mind-control messages, I had to think it was my own anxiety making me feel followed. Did my brain think the vastness of space itself was staring over my shoulder?

I knew I was personifying an inanimate object. I also knew, deep in my soul, that it wanted me dead.

Most ships, I am told, maintain a series of countdown clocks and curated navigation feeds for passengers to chart their course by. Dakhira would never do anything so considerate. He did provide the raw, uncommented telemetry, but I'm pretty sure only because Synarche navigation rules required it.

When I allowed myself to check it, I noticed with delight that we were *really* almost there. Any second now—

A burst of static made me flinch as Dakhira downshifted out of white space and snatched data from the inbound buoys. After a few dozen buoys along the way, I felt like a white space professional.

The inertialess transition from folded space to flattish space makes falling into or out of a bubble universe seem no more real than a three-vee game. I had no sense of deceleration; no sense of force. There was just the visual moment when the coruscating sky smeared away, replaced by a faintly star-freckled darkness, the enormous pinwheel of the Milky Way seen from nearly outside, and the ruddy, bulbous red giant that was our destination.

The sensation of gravity asserted itself as Dakhira began braking. I grabbed a rail so my toes would hit the deck before my face did. I didn't take my eyes off the view.

One of the three Chives from the back of the ship came through, moving toward Forward. The other two were still up there. They were singing rounds with themselves; their voices echoed through the open hatchway.

And that wasn't the only music I heard.

Space was airless. It wasn't silent, though, at least not for me. Because along with the data from the buoy, Dakhira had connected with the Baomind. For the first time, as Dakhira picked up the mathematics, converted them to music, and played them through to us, I was hearing it live.

The thing that I had been studying, listening to, and parsing for patterns the entire way here was suddenly in my implants, singing through my fox, rendered as music. I was finally in the presence of the thing I had come so far from home and everyone I loved to study.

The music I heard now was more complex and layered than the recordings had made it seem. I realized the Chives were singing a round because the Baomind's song seemed arranged that way, as lightspeed lag from various parts of the enormous structure meant the broadcast reached us in waves.

Fortunately, AIs had worked out some rudimentary communication with the Baomind, so I didn't have to try to figure *that* out. It was a good thing somebody silicon-based would be doing the interpreting, because while I knew some basic chords and could pick out a tune, I couldn't tell a minor third from a perfect octave without invoking my fox and those musician ayatanas it was full of.

I followed the Chive along the ladder to Forward. I had to climb up it now instead of drifting. But I wanted to look out the front.

When I got there, all three visible Chives seemed busy with the controls and readouts. I slipped past, trying not to distract anybody, and got as close to the ports as possible. The view was incredible. I stared so hard

I was surprised not to come unmoored from the deck and drift toward the windows.

Excitement hummed under my collarbone. Soon I would be down there, doing what nobody else had done before.

Dakhira broke into my thoughts. "Staring at it won't get us there any faster, Dr. Sunyata Song."

I said, "It won't slow us down any, either. Unless there's some quantum uncertainty involved in crossing distances in normal space."

Dakhira brought out the worst in me. The harsh-language interrupt didn't always catch sarcasm. And sometimes it did, and I ignored it.

Whether it was reasonable to think I could hold my own against an AI capable of carrying the plan of half a galaxy in his working memory was beside the point. (Salvie would point out this was a failing of mine: biting wit wasn't directed *only* at obnoxious shipminds. She would also point out, when I complained about teenagers, that Luna gets it from somewhere.)

We would be in Town soon enough, and I wanted to see it from the outside. I had done so much to get here. I had worked for months and months, uprooted myself, abandoned a project and a team I cared about. I'd left Salvie and my kids and cats behind. I had called in favors I wasn't even owed yet, filled up my brain with alien music, requisitioned inordinate quantities of resources, and pledged my life away for the use of this extremely aggravating ship and his moderately creepy crew.

I wasn't the Hot New Thing anymore. I hadn't been, I thought, since graduate school, for a variety of reasons. But that didn't bear thinking about. I had to make this gamble work and prove my continued relevance. If I failed to distinguish myself now, I might never get a chance to do so again.

But now that I had a clear view of our destination, I wondered if the Baomind itself wasn't a giant omen against my success. The artifact filling half the sky was a living witness of information's inevitable demise.

The Baomind orbited—swarmed—a moribund sun: the red giant we called the Baostar. It dominated the horizonless sky, a squashed, angry ember. Though enormous, it was also dim enough to look at directly. I could see darker and brighter mottles and swirls of weather in its corona without squinting or applying filters.

Sparks of glitter whorled around it. They were satellites reflecting its glow, individual flat tesserae flocking around the star like insects around a candleflame. We were mere light-minutes away, but the sun was so close to death that the glow it cast on my face and hands only glazed my skin dully.

That whole horizon was information, sunsetting before my eyes. Vast amounts of information were contained in that star. Even vaster amounts were housed in its veils of artificial satellites, which constituted a kind of interstellar library. A galactic archive left behind for us—for whoever followed them—by the ancient sentiences we called the Koregoi.

They were not our ancestors, as far as anyone knew. But predecessors who seemed to have considered the future and left some notes behind. Notes that, if we could decipher them, would be infinitely interesting.

Without intervention, the Baostar would soon consume this data—either as it bloated toward death, or in the much faster expansion that would follow its imminent collapse. Anything that escaped the event horizon would be sprinkled across the nearby regions of space, too finely dispersed to record anything.

The Baomind was fated to become a scatter of dust if we did not rescue it. But the truth is, all information winds up a scatter of dust, eventually. And that includes you and me and stars and little fishes. That's what makes entropy so terrifying: it vanishes us and then it vanishes the memory of us. Even the incredible technologies of the Koregoi had only allowed them to preserve a few fragments of information, a bit of hardware, and one matryoshka brain.

Temporary though I knew any respite was, nothing would stop me from fighting to preserve their legacy. That was why I wanted so badly to get in there. There was history inside. I wanted—needed—to save as much of it as I could, for as long as I could. Even a few millennians would be nothing in the lifetime of the fading star. Nothing in the lifetime of the ancient people who had built the vast library that surrounded it. I was making a tiny futile gesture against entropy: just kicking the can down the road.

That's the best any of us will ever do. Kick the can down the road. And hope the next person to come along kicks it a little farther. It's the ultimate expression of faith, of trust in others. Somebody will come along eventually and take care of all this.

Was it worth it?

Well, it beat the alternatives.

And, futile or not, it was my calling. So I was here to do my best. And to try not to disgrace myself in the process.

It wasn't going to be easy. There were others trying to solve the mystery I had come to study. I wasn't sure yet how many rivals I'd have, but they would be on their way. And I'd have to do a better job than most, if I wanted to have a career when this was over.

That's a little melodramatic. There would always be some kind of work I could do. But the issue was whether I would have a *relevant* career. A sexy career. One that I could be proud of. One that wouldn't disappoint me and give my enemies and what was left of my birth family the satisfaction of shaking their heads and saying, "Well, I guess she did the best that could be expected."

Or, worse yet, "Well, I guess she did the best she could with her talent and ambition, such as they are."

My parents never really understood why I didn't go into physics or social planning or architecture or something else glamorous they could brag to their siblings about. And those are useful careers . . . but when you have a passion for something, nothing else is satisfying. My passion was for dusty old datasets and cobwebbed collations.

Now that my mom was gone, I didn't even have the hope that someday she would understand.

Go big, I told myself. *Or resign yourself to picking through two-hundred-year-old corrupted databases until you're two hundred years old yourself.*

Dakhira, chattering with navigation control, was background noise I would have preferred to filter out. I'd have found it more pleasant to feel alone with my thoughts and the vastness for these few final hours of the journey. But for safety reasons, filtering out shipminds is disabled.

So, unable to literally tune him out, I settled for ignoring him as best I could. I focused my attention on the big glorious outside and on anything except the babbling going on in the cramped, aggravating inside.

One thing I *did* have the option of filtering was my view of the Baomind and all its disparate elements. Everything was too far away to see or identify without enhancement, so I magnified the view and turned on tags. That identified each anonymously glimmering speck in the distance, along with their paths and velocities. After a few minutes, I developed a sense of the orbital mechanics and the traffic situation, and if confronted on what I was doing I might have justified it that way.

(Not that I was doing anything wrong; not that I expected to be confronted. Except in the part of my thoughts where I always expected to be confronted, corrected, and informed what a disappointment I was.)

No, I wanted to know what all those bright lights were doing because I was curious. Our trajectory and acceleration were carefully calculated and meticulously communicated, and so were those of the other ships insystem. Shipminds and the Town wheelmind handled all the computation.

The separate parts of the Baomind did not have individual identities in the way a human or a Synarche AI would understand. Rather, the

Baomind was organized sort of like a jellyfish: one creature made up of multiple organisms.

It was an object made of smaller objects bound together by gravity and light and the manipulation of the electromagnetic spectrum. It used all of those forces to think, and in turn to communicate. Its crystalline song was the speech of element to element, and whole to whole. And it to us.

The display I was examining was an approximation. Because of the vast distances, because of lightspeed lag, I wasn't seeing an accurate map of all those blips in the dark. What I saw was a representation of where blips (and ships) had been when last accurately measured, and a projection of their most likely position right now. If I wanted, I could shift to a view that showed the branching probabilities of where all those objects *could* have gone between then and now, not to mention where they might be headed. I tried it, but the overlaid potentials made my brain feel like it was grinding sand.

One ship appeared to be headed right at us. I assumed she would avoid hitting us, but the intersecting probability cones of where she might be and where we might be were . . . unsettling. And the ship—her name was *I Ride Upon the Starlit Void*—was closing fast.

"What's that?" I asked.

"Outbound," the closest Chive answered.

"Headed for the beacon—"

"—we came in on," others finished.

There are reasons why traffic control in crowded systems is handled by the biggest of the big AIs, with their vast number-crunching architectures. The patterns that gave me a migraine to contemplate were like a game of dots and boxes to a wheelmind-class artificial intelligence.

Luckily, it wasn't my job to fly this boat. So I didn't have to worry about potential obstacles except in the unlikely occurrence that we ran into one of them. In which case I wouldn't have *time* to worry.

A morbid thought for somebody trying to find a last moment of peace before the rush of work began. And not eternal peace, either.

Dakhira, the outbound ship, and Town's wheelmind would make sure nobody collided with anybody else. Hab failures were vanishingly rare. The odds of one happening on separate occasions to members of the same family were—pardon me—astronomical.

Anxiety is very bad at calculating the odds.

Another bright speck that moved differently from all the other bright specks caught my attention. It, too, broke the pattern. It didn't follow the looping, gravity-well-surfing orbits of the Baomind's component discs. Nor was it outbound, like the ship rushing toward us. Rather, like Dakhira, it plunged down the slope of space toward the dying star. Toward Town, the improvised research hab parked way down the gravity well, close enough that the Baostar's flickering light would generate warmth and power.

Instinctively, I leaned forward and tapped the viewport. Dakhira could feel my touch on his window as clearly as I would feel a hand on my arm, so I assumed it was a choice that he remained unresponsive.

It didn't matter. The tags told me what I wanted to know. The object barreling along ahead of us was a ship, SJV *I Am Not Safe At Harbor*. My internal organs felt as if they circled an event horizon, whirling down some metaphorical drain.

I didn't *know* who was listed on that ship's manifest, or what its mission was.

But I could guess. One of my rivals was *preceding* me across the galaxy—I couldn't shake the sinking certainty that I was about to get scooped.

Suspicion and trauma made me feel petty and obsessed. Yet my conviction that I knew who was on that ship grew stronger. The person I wanted least in the galaxy to see. *She's here.*

Dakhira would have pulled the manifest from the buoy as a matter of routine when we came out of white space. He had uploaded his own telemetry and manifests, and downloaded—

The very first name on the manifest was *Dr. Victorya DeVine*. My heart plummeted. Vickee had not only beaten me here. She'd somehow managed to beg, borrow, or blackmail a berth on a Judiciary vehicle to do so.

"We need to hurry," I said out loud, and instantly regretted it.

"We are proceeding with all due speed and care," Dakhira replied, with his usual air of vague condescension. "We're second in line for docking."

I rocked on my toes. I wanted to yell that everything depended on beating Vickee to Town and getting a foot in the door before she tied the whole place around her finger and claimed all the resources. Second in line wouldn't cut it, said my limbic system. We had to be first, and first by a margin. Or Vickee would cut me out in a heartbeat and pretend she had no idea why I was so upset and unreasonable. And probably tell a lot of people half-truths designed to make me look incompetent and unstable into the bargain.

Yes, scarcity thinking, very gauche. But this was a scarcity situation!

White-knuckling, I kept my temper and bit my lip until I tuned my crabbiness and reactivity down to annoyed discomfort. Under other circumstances, I might have let the shipmind do it, but Dakhira wasn't getting the keys to my amygdala without a court order.

Twenty-odd years after our last encounter, and the mere prospect of having to deal with Vickee DeVine could still make me slide right back into patterns I should have outgrown with my graduate education.

"Your bouncing is distracting," Dakhira said. "Please go back to the lounge at Center and watch the approach through your fox, Dr. Sunyata Song."

It wasn't the same, and he was punishing me for existing in his space when he could be thinking great thoughts and making great discoveries in splendid isolation. But it was his bridge, and if I tried to force the point I would lose *and* look bad.

Dakhira said, "I'll pipe the nav chatter back to you."

Now, that really *was* taking revenge.

CHAPTER 3

THE LAST TWO MEMBERS OF DAKHIRA'S CREW SPIDERED up the ladder on their forehands and afthands as I was easing myself down. I launched off the rungs to give them clearance and sailed past "above." I waved with all the jauntiness I could fake as deceleration swept me past. Both of them waved back in unison, one sweep of the hand without making eye contact.

I Can Remember It for You Bespoke—Dakhira—was a class-three Synarche research vessel. He had more room than most long-haul ships because he was meant to run with a team of scientists in addition to his flight crew.

I caught the ladder again and kept going. Not bad for a lubber.

The Chives were all humans like me: two males, two females, and one with no obvious gender identifiers. Other than that, I found them undifferentiated in the extreme. Their faces might not be identical, but their expressions were. Their jumpsuits were as indistinguishable as their gestures. They wore no insignia of rank, they all used the plural *they* pronoun, and I honestly had no idea which one was which—or if they even thought about themselves as individuals.

They spoke in the same voice with the same intonation. They shared their memories, their decision-making, their emotions.

They gave me the absolute creeps.

Intellectually, I knew that it didn't matter. That they were functionally the same person. They all answered to the same name, and a word spoken to one of them was heard by all, as long as they had connectivity. They had realized an ancient human dream: Chive never had to suffer the fear of missing out. Chive could actually be two (or more) places at once—while simultaneously taking care of the garden, catching a nap, and reading all those improving works of literature most of us never got around to.

Anyone for *Rebecca?*

But what my brain knew and what my gut felt were two different things.

Who names their kid—kids?—Chive, anyway?

Well, I guess it's not any weirder than naming your kid Fern or Rose or Pansy. Or Herb, for that matter.

Okay, maybe it's a *little* weirder than Herb.

Don't judge. It was good manners to respect other people's boundaries, cultures, privacy, and naming conventions. Even when I felt like criticizing the heck out of them.

I slid into the empty lounge.

I had to admit that the idea of never missing anything was attractive, and would have been even more attractive when I was completing my schooling and apprenticeship. Nap all you want, get your work done and the household chores completed, spend time with your family and still never miss a party. Learn six languages and advanced math.

I could have left a clone home with my wife and kids, if I were five people. I'd still *miss* them. But I'd be there for them, and once I reconnected with my other self I'd have all those memories to share. No opportunity cost to anything.

Well, I guess all the bodies still had to eat and exercise and sleep. Otherwise you could just designate one sucker to be the Maintenance Chump.

Leaving my family was another pang, small but definite. Salvie hadn't been pleased about it, and to tell the truth, neither was I. And the less said about the kids' reactions, the better. If you wanted to look at the bright side, you could say that at least my children valued my presence.

I knew that wasn't always the case. "That period when the offspring start behaving so obnoxiously the parents drive them out to fend for themselves" is practically the definition of adolescence in every species that doesn't just sensibly eat any young they can catch as soon as the shells crack.

I'm grateful for rightminding. Puberty is still puberty, and teenagers have to suffer through its hormones and emotional deregulation as humans have since time immemorial because their brains need to be more or less built and their personalities formed before they start mucking around with them.

But we—the parents—*we* have access to tuning. I think a lot of us never consider that, in the old days, your only tools for keeping your temper around your kids were practice, therapy, and an iron will. But even with rightminding, being a parent is a full-time job.

I needed my focus, my concentration, and to not be a parent and a wife while also trying to make archinformatic discoveries that would change the face of history forever. Make my reputation. Secure my legacy. Convince my kids that what I do isn't the most pathetic job in the universe.

. . . slow down there, solar sail. Don't get ahead of the particle wind.

The crew and Dakhira and the controller at our destination were speaking through their foxes, so there was no real sound. But he simulated the audio chatter so I could hear us being talked into Town: our flight coordinates, the lag as light crossed enormous distances carrying words to and fro.

The talk was soothing, routine. Or as soothing and routine as it could be under the circumstances—ships hurtling at impossible speeds across vast distances to pinpoint rendezvous.

Our flight codes, their approach vectors. Our crew chattering away, sometimes two or all three voices saying the same words. Sometimes finishing each other's sentences.

There was only so long I could stand here like a tentpole and stare into the depths of space, either with my own eyes or surfing Dakhira's grudgingly shared feed. Grudging or not, it was magical to inhabit the senses of a ship gliding down a gravity well toward something as ancient and awesome as the Baomind. But it would still be most of a standard day before we got to Town. And I could be using that time for something productive. There was new data to sort—what we'd picked up from the buoy as we came out of white space. I could start reviewing all of it, not just the song Dakhira was currently broadcasting.

Attention, Dakhira sent. *We will increase braking by .8 g in exactly five standard minutes.*

A countdown clock appeared in the corner of my display. Although .8 wasn't a lot of *v*, I knew Dakhira well enough by now to know he wouldn't give me one extra millisecond to prepare. I didn't need an acceleration couch, but this was a good time to find something to strap myself to.

Well, there was a rack beside the port. I could hang on to that and watch Vickee beat me to my destination.

The outbound ship was close enough to see, with heavy magnification. Her trajectory was no longer subject to lag. I could convince myself that as she passed us, I heard a Doppler whistle, distinct from the decoded Baosong of her cargo that Dakhira sent me.

Inside the arc of her white coils her hull bulged strangely, scaled in layers of mirror-black plating that concealed her insignia. She was covered in hundreds of Baomind tesserae nestled against her like remoras on a shark. It made sense now that I was confronted with it: you could transport space-adapted machines on the outside of your ship once your cargo hold was full. As long as you stayed under the mass limits of your drive systems.

I leaned against the force and pressed my palm to the port. Though transparent, it felt as solid as a mountainside. Comforting. STV *I Ride Upon the Starlit Void* waggled in salute as she passed. Dakhira rolled gently in reply. She'd be back at the Core in five decians with her precious cargo, then probably turn around and come back for more. Every shipload meant one less opportunity to study the Baomind in its original form. The clock was ticking.

I wondered if her crew missed their families.

The hairs on my neck rose with that sense of being watched, of being loomed over. I told myself I was hallucinating from isolation and tried to tune the sensation out.

"Boo," Dakhira whispered, venting cool air across my nape.

I nearly jumped off the rack. My nose bounced off that unyielding transparency. My vision went briefly white. Sudden pain brought tears to my eyes.

I put my palm to my nose. Blood ran across my lip; I asked my fox to seal the injured capillaries and wiped it onto my sleeve. Then I took a deep breath, reminding myself that yelling at Dakhira was pointless.

I raised my watering eyes back to the port just in time to see *I Ride Upon the Starlit Void* explode in a silent coruscation of fire and debris. The severed white coils stripped, expending their tension in a whiplash spiral that slammed them back around into her hull. The hull shredded, trailing vapor. Sparkling shards of tesserae blasted out like the plumes of a geyser.

The strongest and most immediate thread of Baosong went silent as if it had been cut off with a knife. Debris streaked off the magnetic bottle that shielded Dakhira from radiation and space dust. My fingers clutched the rail, tendons straining as the ship rolled hard. Somehow I held on and didn't go flying the length of the lounge.

I gaped, frozen.

"General quarters," Dakhira snapped. "Dr. Sunyata Song, please return to your cabin and strap in for maneuvering."

The empty, echoing mess-slash-lounge suddenly felt exposed and vulnerable.

I raced through Center, and Aft with its unoccupied sleep pods. This ship had too much room for two people, even if one of them had five selves. I threw myself into the narrow space I was allowed and sealed the hatch behind me. A hardsuit actuator fell out of the wall slot beside the door. I scooped it up and slapped it under my collarbone, where it adhered.

I set one wall to show me ambient space, wasting another thirty seconds gawking at the remains of the destroyed ship. Then I picked up the protective case that contained the most precious object I owned. I pushed it into a corner and sealed it to a bulkhead with all the brightly colored arrows pointing up.

I might leave my wife and kids behind.

The family tree came with me.

Then I clambered into the embrace of my rack and triggered the straps. Safely restrained, back against the padded bulkhead, I settled in to wait.

CHAPTER 4

THE FEED ON MY SCREEN WALL TOLD ME I CLUTCHED THE webbing and braced for exactly fifty-eight standard seconds, but it felt like a lifetime. The ship around me twisted sideways so suddenly I thought we must have been hit by debris. My head and body were restrained by adaptive cushions. I hit the web hard; I'd have some spectacular bruises in a few hours.

I slewed against the restraints again as the ship slalomed and my body attempted to continue in a straight line.

I managed to force some words out, though they rattled between my teeth. "Dakhira, what happened to that ship?"

I half expected him to ignore me, but his response was prompt and clipped. "Freeporters."

Freeporters? "*Pirates?*" I yelped.

"Keep your restraints fastened. We are executing evasive maneuvers."

I hadn't so much as gestured toward the webbing release, but Dakhira had never been one to let facts interfere with the opportunity for condescension.

The mesh loosened slightly: Dakhira must not be planning an immediate maneuver. I stretched out in my rack, trying to ease my bruises.

"What are we going to do?"

"Evade them—"

"—if possible," said a couple of Chives.

"Run like hell," another one added.

The tone of the Baosong shifted. Perhaps I was anthropomorphizing, but it now sounded urgent, driving. The soundtrack to a dramatic fight scene. I wiggled a hand free, straining against acceleration, letting my fingers feel out the time. The other hand joined it. Conducting was no skill I'd ever learned, but with the influence of my ayatanas my body seemed to know what it was doing, as if the Baomind were an immense celestial choir.

I made my hands fall still and tucked them back inside the webbing. Long-term wearing of several ayatanas is known to make people a little weird. I probably shouldn't indulge it, but the more my executive function went to controlling my emotions, the less I had for riding herd on the ayatanas and their fidgeting.

Well, there was nobody here to be bothered by it.

I turned on my side to stare at the display wall. The same schematic was available through my fox. I used that information to give me a sense of scale, depth of field, and timelines. The wall display was just something to goggle at.

Pirates. It was hard to wrap my head around.

They did exist, out here at the edge of everything. Sometimes they could even be found close to the Core. I'd known that encountering them was a possibility, but until this moment I hadn't taken it seriously. I'd joked with Salvie about what she would do if I were kidnapped and held for ransom—

Was I about to be kidnapped and held for ransom?

Oh, Well, then what would happen to the family tree?

I tapped into Dakhira's feed, but I had no idea how to interpret the sensations, the vectors and angles, the incoming fire that seemed to be herding us away from Town, away from the other inbound vessel, and in a direction I could only assume we didn't want to go for reasons that would swiftly become obvious—i.e., an ambush. I would think pirates would want to take the ship as a prize, ransom the occupants . . . not blow it up. But here we were.

I was achingly glad Salvie and the kids weren't here. I was helpless, and that was the worst part. I couldn't help fly. I couldn't shoot back.

All I could do was stay out of the way.

A flock of ships converged on us, cutting off options for flight and safety, driving us out of the security of the well and away from the potential escape of the beacon.

We were clearly being herded. We were still coming in hot from white space, moving too fast to be in danger from mass drivers—I thought. But we'd have to brake to approach the system, because even a lubber like me knew that barreling down the throat of a gravity well—populated or otherwise—at a significant percentage of lightspeed was a terrible idea. For us, and for everyone living in the system.

Including the artifact.

I could be the archinformist who inadvertently destroyed the Baomind. Well, that was one way to make a reputation. At least if it happened I wouldn't be around to enjoy the aftermath.

We needed to get insystem, where there were other Synarche ships—and the Baomind itself, which I'd heard had defenses. So the pirates were trying to chase us back out again. We could jump into white space, but without a marker to jump from and another to jump toward, we'd be out in the dark headed nobody knew where. Unless we somehow managed to get turned around toward the beacon, aimed at the Core and civilization.

Going back and starting over would for sure run out the clock on the research time I had sworn my soul away to get access to.

I thought about the ship that hadn't made the connection from one beacon to the next, on the way in. Had pirates destroyed or captured it as well? Had they chased it into the dark, where it might be lost forever?

They hadn't hesitated to obliterate that freighter with its cargo of tesserae. Possibly that had been the point; the Freeporters had a sophipathological hatred of any kind of artificial intelligence.

I knew I should tell Dakhira to run for it. I should tell him to turn tail and make for the hills—or the cluttered spaces of the Core, rather.

If I didn't, I was being selfish. Letting him take a risk for my needs.

I gritted my teeth. I knew what I *ought* to do. Reach out to him and yell, *Go! Run!*

Staying endangered the community. Staying was what I wanted to do. Staying was what I *needed* to do. And I wanted it, needed it, too badly to tune the desire out of my mind.

Sometimes you know you're not making the most ethical choice, and it's hard to stop anyway.

Maybe I was being unfair to myself. Dakhira would do whatever he thought safest, whether or not I expressed an opinion, and he was unlikely to worry about my research time if his existence was on the line.

Beyond that, though—was it so bad? I gritted my teeth against nagging him to head toward Town. There would be armed ships there. Maybe a Judiciary Interceptor. People to help us.

But of course the pirates would know that, and there was probably an ambush waiting if we headed in the direction they were leaving open for us.

Dakhira jigged violently—dodging incoming fire. Probably beam weapons, since my cursory examination of his telemetry suggested that any projectile short of a guided white torpedo could not reach us at these speeds, over these distances. Dakhira was dodging probabilities, since if something was traveling at the speed of light by definition you couldn't see it coming. His violent maneuver was meant to confuse the pursuer's predictions. They wouldn't detect it for precious seconds yet. They were light-seconds behind and seeing where he had been, not where he actually was.

I examined the schematic, immersed in its moving patterns, its cones of light and predictions. The navigation plot showed where the ships were last *known* to have been, given lightspeed lag and what their vectors were. It projected where they *might* be.

They might destroy us, as they had *I Ride Upon the Starlit Void*. Or perhaps they wanted to break our white coils, prevent us from jumping, and trap us here. Then they would knock down our bottle, grapple us, and board. Or send a limpet torpedo to latch on and drag us down.

"Dakhira," I asked, "why did they destroy that ship? Shouldn't they want to take it as a prize?"

Starships were not exactly disposable resources, after all.

"I think it was an accident. They seemed to have been trying to disable the white coils, and did more damage than intended." Bitterly, he added, "Of course, they would have murdered Chatelaine if they took her, anyway."

Chatelaine, I deduced, was the name of *I Ride Upon the Starlit Void*'s shipmind.

Before I figured out how to respond, a new dot, blue and friendly, zipped toward us from not too much deeper in the system. Overlays identified it as a Judiciary Interceptor. Not the one that Vickee was on: *I Am Not Safe At Harbor* still fell like a stone toward Town, a stately dot half a day ahead of us.

This ship was SJV *I Hail the Wreck of Empire,* and it was coming after us like an arrow loosed from a bow. Maybe if we could stay ahead of the pirates—keep our EM drive and white coils intact, avoid taking any damage from incoming fire . . .

I finally accepted that I was helpless to affect the outcome, no matter what happened. It was out of my hands.

There was a little relief in that. At least I wasn't going to be the one getting anybody killed.

Dakhira was still accelerating hard enough to put a strain on all his passengers. The Chives and I were fortunate not to be a thin film spread over his interior, given his usual attitude toward meatforms. We jigged and jagged, trying to plot a course insystem—toward the protection of Town and the Interceptors.

If that would be enough to discourage the pirates. They had us outnumbered. Dakhira populated the display with telemetry he'd deduced, along with probability cones showing trajectories and velocities. He'd tagged half a dozen Freeport ships, though there were likely more.

The ship yanked me sideways again. I winced, glancing at the family tree in its case. I didn't hear it sliding. All I could do was hope that the magnets held.

"Can we outrun them?" I asked.

"No," Dakhira said. "But maybe we can stay ahead long enough for that Interceptor to get here. Or get close enough to the Baomind that they don't dare attack for fear of upsetting it."

"Will the Baomind protect us?"

"Only the Baomind knows the answer to that. But as one inorganic intelligence to another, I'd hope for some solidarity. Or professional courtesy. I don't think it can get through their bottles, but they have to drop the bottle to use a mass driver effectively."

"Will our bottle protect us from incoming fire?"

"Marginal," he answered. "As you no doubt noticed, it got through to Chatelaine."

"Interrupt," said a Chive. "They're hailing—"

Another finished: "—us."

"This is the *Devil's Own* hailing Synarche research vessel. Heave to and prepare to be boarded."

Dakhira piped the Freeporter's arrogant drawl through the senso so we could all appreciate what a dick he was. I was confident in my pronoun assignment not because the broadcast came with the usual courtesy tags, but because Freeporters have pretty rigid ideas about gender and the person talking had a deep, resonant voice.

I guessed from the schematic that the *Devil's Own* must be the ship running us down from astern and insystem—the one herding us away from safety.

"This is SRV *I Can Remember It for You Bespoke*," Dakhira said. "This is Synarche space. Stand down and evacuate this system, or suffer the consequences."

The Freeporter's sigh crackled with static. "Are there any real humans on that boat? Let me talk to somebody who isn't a freak."

If Dakhira had internal haptic systems, I think I would have felt them trembling under my seat. His voice in my senso, filtered just to me, might have sounded taut. But he didn't bother with those little emotional touches some AIs used when communicating with meatlife. "Don't make any promises, Dr. Song. Just keep him talking."

Then Dakhira patched me in.

"Hi," I said. "Um. I'm the passenger."

The captain or comms officer—he had not identified himself—snorted in disgust. "You're a normal human? Aside from the mind-control implant."

"I have a fox, yes."

"We'll take that out for you," he offered. "Surrender, hand over the hull, and we'll spare your life. Do it in the next twenty minutes and we'll throw in a ride to Town."

"One moment," I said. "I need to confer with the crew."

"Try anything clever and we'll gun you out of the sky."

My face stretched in distress. "Just a few minutes."

"They might spare you," Dakhira said, just for my ears. "They might press-gang you. They will certainly destroy my crew and me."

I checked to make sure I wasn't transmitting. "They're pirates. They don't want to destroy us. They want to steal us."

"Speak for yourself," Dakhira said. "Typical of a meatmind not to consider anybody else's needs and safety."

"I don't understand."

Dakhira ignored me. Fortunately, the Chives took pity on me.

"Freeporters hate AIs," one said.

"I know," I said. "They hate the Synarche, too."

A Chive shushed me. "And—"

"—they hate any kind of rightminding—"

"—or neural link," two others finished as one. "They'll—"

"—destroy your fox if they catch you."

"Even if they decide to turn you—"

"—loose."

"They might shoot you into Town in a torpedo housing," Dakhira added. "They would probably find that funny."

My skin contracted. Freeporters are profound hypocrites, since I understand they use a variety of performance-enhancing drugs, some derived from the bodies of sentient beings, to make up for their lack of shipminds and machine memory. I should be glad about that: the concept of a pirate AI was terrifying.

"Distract them," Dakhira said.

"How am I supposed to keep them talking?"

"You're all incomprehensible humans together. You'll think of something."

I pushed my knuckles into my eyes. Of course I knew that Freeport pirates were Terran supremacist extremists, but I'd never thought through the implications of their beliefs. I had to buy us time.

"I'm back," I said, having reconnected. "What terms of surrender are you offering?"

"You surrender and we don't rip your ship open and leave you to die in space."

I shuddered.

"Can you assure the safety of the shipmind and crew?"

The pirate snorted loudly enough to be heard over comms. "We want visual confirmation. Show us your face if you're really human."

Such an image would be easy enough to fake, but whatever. "I'll show you my face if you tell me your name."

I wasn't sure what I thought looking the pirate in the eye and knowing his name would reveal. But it's a big universe with a lot of people in it. The unexpected (but somehow deeply inevitable) appearance of Nemesis DeVine—when I had wanted nothing so fiercely as her complete absence from my life—had left me anxious and anticipating another disaster. On some level, the solipsistic and sophipathological part of my brain had reverted to magical thinking, and was expecting the universe to revolve around me. By its logic, the pirate would naturally be a grade-school bully or somebody who was once mean to my mother.

"I'm Adekunle, captain of the *Devil's Own*."

"I'm Sunyata Song," I replied, before I realized it might be a good idea to lie. I'm bad at being sneaky.

Then I opened the connection and looked my enemy in the eyes.

It *was* nobody I'd ever met, or even seen. Assuming such a person hadn't gone to such a length as to get a new face, anyway. I felt a strange sense of narrative disappointment. He didn't have horns or scales or a slow match braided into his beard, though he did have a beard—a dense, wiry, black one. He was a perfectly ordinary-looking human. His complexion, darker than my medium umber, set off his striking hazel eyes. His sneer rendered those eyes uncharismatic.

We stared at each other. The Freeport ship was close enough now that lightspeed lag was reduced to a few seconds. I didn't need to be an engineer or an astrogator to know the pirate ship massively outclassed us in power-to-mass ratio. They would, inevitably, run us down.

"You're stalling," he said. "I'm doing you the honor of speaking to you in person, because I wish to end this without bloodshed. We can only afford a little time. Your friends can't make it out here fast enough to make a difference for you, and we have the system blockaded. Try to run and you'll end up like that freighter. Even if you elude us, you'll just run into another captain . . . who won't be as reasonable as I am. And if you try to maneuver down the well, we'll shoot you out of the sky."

He sounded so matter-of-fact and businesslike that I didn't doubt it for a second. I clutched my fingers in the webbing to keep from nervously touching my suit actuator.

"I need to talk with my crew again," I said. "I'm not empowered to negotiate for them."

"You're deliberately wasting my time," said Captain Adekunle. "I will not be so patient when we speak again."

He cut the connection. Yes, I was confident in the pronoun. For people who were obsessed with not living under anybody else's authority, they sure had a lot of uncomfortable social strictures.

"Nice person," Dakhira said dryly.

"Definitely don't forget to invite him to the christening. Pricking your finger on a spindle would be the least of it." I forced my fingers to untwist from the webbing. They ached. "All right, what do we do now?"

"You sit tight," the shipmind said, for once too busy for recreational rudeness. "I keep running."

"Will they shoot us?"

"They can try. We won't see a beam weapon coming, obviously. But I've set our hull to reflective, which will offer some protection. It will also help hide our visual signature, and I've scrambled our telemetry and am using scanner countermeasures and an internal heat sink. It might get uncomfortably warm in here. Also, as a research vessel specializing in heavy-gravity objects, we have the capability to operate a heavily augmented EM bottle. Enhanced enough, it can do a number on coherent light, too. That will probably take them by surprise. And you'll be even less likely to get space cancer than you were five minutes ago!"

I grimaced. I didn't want to think about picking up even an eminently treatable disease out here at the back end of nowhere. Cancer at home was an outpatient visit and a couple of injections. Cancer here . . .

I didn't know what kind of sick-bay setup Town had. I wasn't the sort of doctor who could perform her own appendectomy.

That got me thinking about tetanus and sepsis and all sorts of things that killed people routinely in the documents I work on. I tuned to get rid of intrusive ideations and said, "What about projectiles?"

"We can outrun or dodge those," Dakhira said. "Chatelaine didn't see them coming."

The Chives chimed in: "We can dodge them—"

"—for now."

Evasive maneuvers continued to throw me against the restraints, and I stayed in my bunk. You'd think you couldn't get bored while being run down by pirates, but the truth is, space is big and stress gets exhausting. And the heat Dakhira had warned me of was enervating. I dozed off after a while, the restraints bruising me awake intermittently.

I dreamed of a shadowy figure chasing me across an endless moor like an illustration from an old detective story. The creature behind me might have been a cloaked and hooded man; it might have been a winged, spectral bundle of black rags. The ground squelched and sank under my feet, grabbing at my shoes. My body dragged, the way it does when you are running as hard as you can in your sleep and getting nowhere.

Silhouettes like the teeth of a comb punctuated the horizon: a long row of massive trunks, a line of blackened trees. If I could just get to them I would be safe. I would be—

Dakhira's voice and a blast of brightness jerked me awake. For a moment I was still frozen by sleep paralysis and had the incredible, awful sense of someone looming over me. I blinked; my eyes watered; sweat beaded on my body. The tiny world of the ship smeared and wobbled.

"What?" I sat up under the webbing, which slacked to let me move a little. My neck hurt. My shoulder and hip felt jammed from sleeping in one position. "Repeat, please?"

"Sandy is hailing us. He's close to engaging the pirates. I thought you might want to be awake for whatever happens next."

"Sandy?"

"The resident Interceptor. *I Hail the Wreck of Empire.*"

Dakhira sounded curt, clipped, and afraid. It's a common misconception that synthetic sapients aren't subject to emotions when actually everything that thinks has feelings. Feelings are an efficient means of processing information; hunches are a way of handling innumerable competing inputs.

The difference is that, though AIs *have* feelings, they only *express* those feelings by choice. Even if that choice is being made by a subroutine isolated from the main consciousness of the entity in question, which I suspected was the case here. There's no accidental leakage.

The side effect is that when an AI is being a dick, you know they mean it.

Humans are messier, which is probably why we spend so much time pretending we're capable of rigorously rational thinking if only we try hard enough. Then we spend even more time claiming that *our* decisions are based on logic when those of the people we disagree with are founded in thoughtlessness, selfishness, and cruelty.

I'm a historian. I'm here to tell you that while rightminding has made us better at consensus building and collective action, it can only fix so much.

I didn't know if I should be flattered or terrified that Dakhira was showing me his fear. Maybe it was just a remnant of his social programming.

I couldn't decide whether to comment, or what to say. Eventually I settled on, "What does *I Hail the Wreck of Empire* have to say for himself?"

"I'll patch you in."

There were no niceties. Just a plunge into the stream of conversation. Sandy's unfamiliar voice in midsentence. " . . . not easy to spot, given the ultra-black hull design and stealth countermeasures. Like deep-sea fish."

"Energy leakage," Dakhira replied.

I was probably only getting an nth of the actual information being transferred. Sandy and Dakhira's conversations took place broad-spectrum, at the speed of light and at the speed of machine intelligence. So to be fair, Dakhira was providing some niceties in giving me the kiddie-book translation.

"What there is of it. I've got your zero," Sandy replied. His voice had a warm, spirited quality I associated with team sports, not mayhem. Fifty-six thousand tons of gallant camaraderie charging to our rescue. The knot in my chest unclenched a little.

"And I yours," Dakhira said, sounding like a whole different spacecraft. I blinked. When he used that tone, he was charming. "Be careful."

"That's your job." Sandy laughed. "Mine is to buckle swashes."

I lifted my eyes to watch our progress, still projected on the bulkhead. We skipped across the Baostar's well like a spinning stone. Several pirate ships, haloed in angry orange, trailed us. I presumed the closest one was the *Devil's Own*. It seemed like it was practically in our pocket.

The blue-outlined dot ahead of us was the Interceptor, *I Hail the Wreck of Empire*. Sandy.

He must be running toward us flat-out. We were certainly doing everything in our power to get to him.

After fifteen minutes without course corrections, I felt bold enough to ask, "Is it safe to unweb for a minute?"

"It would be unwise."

"I have to pee." And I wanted to make sure the family tree was properly secured. "Human bladders aren't engineered for this level of neglect."

Dakhira sighed. "Activate your hardsuit and use the filters."

"What?"

"Humans have been wearing diapers to space since humans started going into space. We're being chased by a half dozen pirate ships. Embrace the tradition."

I swear he does things like this just because he knows it's humiliating. But he wasn't going to release me from the web, so I activated my suit. It whisked over my body and I let it recycle my waste products. Like, I told myself, a real spacer.

You wouldn't imagine you could be terrified and bored simultaneously. But as the chase stretched on, I continued to learn that the two states were not incompatible. Nothing changed, except the *Devil's Own* creeping up on us by almost imperceptible increments. It didn't try to hit us with its mass drivers; the reaction would have slowed it incrementally and allowed us to pull away.

I hated being useless in a fight. But honesty compelled me to acknowledge I would have hated being useful even *more*. Jackbooted Judiciary have no place in a really civilized society. If rightminding were as effective as it ought to be, there wouldn't be crimes for them to solve, because we would all always make prosocial choices.

"Oh, screw it," I said. And let my hands pick up the rhythms of the Baomind's alarm-song once more. It was less work than keeping them still.

CHAPTER 5

ENTROPY REQUIRES NO MAINTENANCE.

Order, on the other hand, is like keeping a ship from being eaten by the sea. It requires constant fiddly attention and endless repetition of thankless tasks. Entropy is patient. Even if we imagine Sisyphus happy, eventually he slips and the boulder rolls down the hill again.

Which is a fancy way of saying that sitting there in my tiny cabin, even tuning, I became so stressed by the situation, my helplessness, and the terrifying boredom that I once again flat-out dozed off to the whispering sound of leaves from the forest view I'd programmed into the wall. I'd like to claim that this was a conscious, rational decision I made in order to conserve energy and keep myself from habituating too much to my fox's antianxiety protocols. But that would be dishonest, and as a historian I'm too aware of posterity to willfully introduce inaccuracies into the record.

Nature's oldest coping mechanism: when you can't solve a problem, try to sleep through it.

I slept for about four hours, until Dakhira tuned me awake. So I snapped into consciousness alert and focused.

"What?" I asked intelligently.

"I thought you might like to brace," Dakhira answered sweetly.

My reflexes were improving. I slammed my hands and feet against the bulkheads and grounded myself inside the mesh. The mesh would have caught me, but hitting it would leave yet more gridline bruises across my body.

Maybe I should have kept my hardsuit activated, but sleeping in a space suit felt too much like giving in to my fears.

The mattress hit me in the back. My shoulder spasmed, I lost my purchase on the bulkhead, and the wall of the cubby slammed into my arm. Acute pain replaced a duller throbbing left over from my previous adventures.

"Yikes!"

Under normal circumstances, the bunk served to keep me from drifting around the ship. It doubled as an acceleration couch for when we were pulling gs or engaged in a rapid course correction, but it was never designed to protect a human body during a dogfight, and I was getting private tutelage in the consequences of that oversight now.

I grabbed the mesh, though it cut my fingers, and rotated my body toward the display, calling up the nav schematic again.

As if I were falling inward, the system-wide view on the display wall zoomed in to follow my attention. Now it showed the immediate vicinity of our ship. All the other vessels looked shockingly close. My head thumped against the padding as we zigged and zagged. Still I managed to make out that the *Devil's Own* was on our tail. Other Freeport ships stretched on an arc some distance behind it.

And almost on top of us was the blip indicating *I Hail the Wreck of Empire*.

After a long flight, the dogfight was on in earnest now. I couldn't lift my head: g-forces and the mesh pressed me into the foam, immobilizing me. Black dots swam in front of my eyes. I couldn't track the blips because my vision darkened at the edges; I had always thought that was hyperbole, but here I was, struggling to breathe as if someone were kneeling on my chest, the world collapsing into a tunnel.

Something rang off the hull. My ears popped as the pressure dropped.

I couldn't reach the suit actuator, but it triggered automatically a moment later. Now I found myself bouncing against the inside of the hardsuit. It was lined with an absorbent reactive colloid that felt clammy and squishy against the skin, so I wasn't hitting edges. And the exoskeleton braced my joints.

An improvement over the padded bunk after all.

Another thud. A heads-up display in my senso told me the pressure had stabilized. Dakhira wasn't bothering to raise it again. Now I was forced to watch the ships in senso, because I couldn't get my head up to watch them on the wall.

We plunged toward the blue dot. I heard myself shouting, tried not to, still emitted a squeak. Dakhira knew what he was doing and so did Sandy, right? The ships were their bodies. It would be as hard for them to crash into each other as it would be for me to walk into a wall.

I tried to ignore the inconvenient fact that I was always stubbing my toe or banging my elbow.

Orange lights winked hot on our tail. Four of them were close; the other two had caught up somewhat from their trailing arc but weren't yet engaged. A spray of smaller dots zipped toward us from them.

Dakhira yanked us hard from side to side once more. I felt no more impacts.

Are they trying to take our white coils off? I asked via senso.

Affirmative. One projectile got through our bottle, but it only struck the hull and its relative velocity was severely reduced.

Well, that explained why we weren't open to space already.

If I was going to die out here, I wanted to see it coming. I switched from display to simanimation.

Dakhira, visualized from the outside, barreled along at a velocity that was going to send us clean out of this system if nothing changed. Parts of his hull were scorched and pitted, but the white coils looked intact. The Interceptor flashed past us so close its massive coils almost clipped Dakhira's, which looked delicate and undersized by comparison. It moved in eerie silence: my planet-born expectations wanted a *whoosh*. We rolled away and I saw the trio of Freeport ships behind us—smaller than the Interceptor, but just as overpowered, and bristling with weapons.

A dazzle of light burst from the Interceptor's beam weapons. It struck the most starward of the pirates—a real spacer would say *the bottom ship*, I guess. And . . . passed right through?

Was it supposed to do that?

No.

Dakhira jigged again. Return fire lanced from a patch of empty sky near the ship Sandy had missed. Or rather, a beam burned from the ports on the pirate ship—and then disconnected, vanished, and reappeared some distance away, apparently sourceless.

The ship seemed to ripple.

"Gravitational lensing!" I said. Or groaned, because the pressure of acceleration on my chest made my voice a pained wheeze.

I think you're right, Sandy said, which was my first clue that Dakhira still had me patched into contact with him. *But thanks to that weapon fire, I have their trajectory now.*

He returned fire, a trio of missiles arcing away from him under acceleration that would have turned a human being into so much pâté. They seemed aimed at empty space; they detonated without impact—

And in the center of their three spheres of concussion—black-white-black circles that left afterimages on my vision like fireworks—I saw a ship, suddenly revealed, shred apart. The white coil unfurled like a released spring; the plating rent. Geysers of air and water fountained into space and electricity crackled. All silent, silent as . . . well, silent as the void, I suppose.

Sandy rolled toward the remaining two ships. Dakhira's swerve turned into an escape maneuver. We plunged toward the Baostar now at an incredible rate of speed. I was sure we were experiencing relativistic effects.

I wasn't sure what Sandy sensed that I didn't. But he let loose with another barrage, aimed—as far as I could tell—at empty space. He hit something: the second ship vanished, and the area he'd targeted became a sea of debris. A second silent explosion followed a moment later: one of the other ships must have been close enough to run afoul of too much debris for its EM bottle to handle.

Three down.

I wouldn't have thought the *Devil's Own* was close enough to be threatened by the shrapnel, but it veered violently and accelerated away on a burn that must be putting the crew in danger of unconsciousness and torn ligaments. Freeport ships didn't have shipminds. What would happen to the crew if they passed out and lost control?

I sighed in relief as Sandy came around to our tail, rolling his white coils in a mocking salute.

That was amazing—

Sandy tore wide open, gutted from stem to stern as if somebody had taken an enormous can opener to him. His roll became a wallow. The tension in the coils released: the free end began to whip itself around, and the corpse of the ship responded by flailing the other way, more slowly, trailing atmosphere like blood in the water.

"What happened?" I yelled. "*Sandy!*"

Lie down flat, Dr. Song, Dakhira sent urgently.

I threw myself onto my back, hands at my sides. Brutal acceleration shoved me into the foam and ripped the tears down my cheeks. *What happened?*

Killer drone, Dakhira answered. He sounded coldly furious. *Dropped off by one of the ships Sandy engaged. They must have some technology that allows them to evade the EM bottle. Fortunately they can't carry much fuel. We can outrun the others.*

I did what I should have done all along. "Dakhira, you should take us back toward the Core. Save yourself and the Chives. Our job here isn't that important."

"If I could, I would," he answered. "I can't reach the beacon."

What I knew about white drives was derived from popular entertainment. Synarche ships couldn't navigate or even steer in white space. There were rumors that Freeport vessels using some kind of interdicted red tech had the means . . . but Synarche ships in white space traveled in straight lines. (Though the definition of a straight line might be a little odd, considering that one was actually not so much traveling as bunching up curved space-time and shoving it behind one.)

We were at the end of a long passage, and I doubted there was much fuel left. The EM drive didn't burn fuel, so maneuvering insystem wasn't a problem. But if we folded, we might wind up anywhere in space, unable to get back. Or starving to death in the crevices of space-time. Salvagers made a decent contribution to the commonwealth finding and recovering ships like that.

It sounded like a lousy way to die.

When it comes down to it, they're all lousy ways to die.

"What do we do now?"

The most shocking thing of all happened. The acceleration slacked, the crash web snapped back, and I was suddenly free to move about my cabin.

"We have a little breathing room," Dakhira said. "The other two Freeporters also veered away when your friend broke off pursuit. Might as well take advantage of it. I don't think they can catch us now."

"Oh," I said. "Sandy?"

"Sandy's dead." He sounded like he wanted to blame me for it and was restraining himself. That was fine. I could dish out enough blame for both of us.

If I hadn't been so damned determined to come out here, to pursue this project—

You didn't summon the pirates. My memory supplied my wife's voice and intonations.

I wasn't quite ready to hear her.

I took advantage of my new freedom to pick up the tree case and inspect it for damage. I couldn't see inside—it had shields opaqued—but the environment looked undamaged.

Dakhira braked more gently than he was strictly required to, and for that I was grateful. I was even more grateful that he flipped end over end before he started, so the ceiling stayed the ceiling and the floor stayed the floor.

Deceleration nevertheless pushed me against the case and the bulkhead. The burn continued. Nice and even: the shipmind might be a jerk, but he knew his flying and was used to ferrying lubbers around. And he had kept us alive through a harrowing adventure.

Once his autoreporter indicated we were steady, I took the carrying case onto my lap and touched the release. The opaque shields retracted, revealing a transparent rectangular dome. It was airtight, but a whiff of greenhouse smell escaped.

I looked down at the family tree.

A piece of Old Earth: a fragment of actual Terra—a world I had never set foot on, though my roots and my family history were there. Well, I suppose that doesn't exactly make me unique among humans, does it?

The tree was a half-meter-tall purple beech, though the color of its foliage was currently irrelevant as it was dormant and bare. The case breathed cold as I leaned over it, my own breath misting its transparency. The bonsai was a turtleback style with multiple trunks, the main one as thick as my wrist and significantly taller than the other four.

They trailed down the massive nebari, the exposed root structure, that supported the tree. Satiny gray bark lay over whorls and knots that implied decades survived and travails overcome. The heavy branches ramified to delicate twigs so flawlessly fractal that one imagined each continuing smaller and smaller, forking into invisibility. A bare branch, bleached as driftwood, shimmered among living ones—a focal point to draw the eye.

The budding tips were copper-red, the roots surrounded by a mat of green moss so velvety and soft it invited you to imagine yourself immersed in the landscape. One could pick a path under the tree on the mica-flake pebbles that served as stepping stones, then lie down against the curve of the root as if in a perfectly shaped chair. When the tree was in leaf, the wind would whisper through it, dappling the shade with light.

This tree was born in a place with seasons. It relied on them: it would not thrive without its times of dormancy, its times in the cold.

It had to be quiet and still at times just to live.

We all need sleep, I suppose.

My great-great-grandmother had started training this tree before my great-grandmother was even born. Before our family went out into the stars among the systers and the Synarche. It was my whole legacy, my whole history. The only survivor of the hab failure that killed my sister and my mother, safe in its environment box when the seals blew.

It's possible my relationship with this tree had led me to become an archinformist: this was living history. It was a record of human intervention that I could hold in my hand.

Well, both hands, when the gravity was working. It *was* on the large side for a houseplant.

The art of miniaturizing trees is both delicate and brutal. On Earth, they call it penjing or bonsai. It's harder in a sealed environment: trees are outdoor creatures. They need the change of seasons and the cycles of planetary light.

Thus, the box. My family tree's own little environment suit. An ecosystem built for one.

Well, one tree and a whole lot of moss plants and soil microbes.

I imagined myself home in the garden on Rubric, watching the rays of the setting sun filter through the tree's gnarled branches. Size is such a relative thing: we use *small* and *large* as if they are absolutes when what we mean is "smaller or larger than me." By its own lights, this small tree was a mighty survivor, burled and battle-hardened, vigorous enough to come back time after time despite being beheaded and having its branches lopped off over and over. A grim fighter, scarred but unbowed, leaning on its halberd.

We could all learn something about endurance from a tree.

I grinned at my own ridiculous melodrama but felt less anxious. We would get to Town when we got to Town, and I would find the resources there to continue my work. It would be okay.

I was closing the case when the impact happened.

The ship shuddered around me.

"Clip in!" Dakhira ordered belatedly.

After several months of living inside him, I was still finding reasons why he was not my favorite starship.

Fortunately, I had never unclipped. I'd worked hard to acquire the habit.

The crash net snapped closed over me and the ship swerved. I lunged for the tree case, pulling against the restraints and acceleration. Inertia hurled me to the side. I caught the handle, but the case swung out and struck the bulkhead with enough force to make me wince. My shoulder yelled a complaint but—fingers slipping—I held on.

"*What* is happening?"

"Continue to brace," Dakhira said calmly.

I pulled the case against the netting, managing to trigger the cover.

It slid closed, catching on a few strands of the net. I would deal with the fibers later. I would deal with any damage to the tree and the case later. For now, it would help hold the tree in place.

"We're under attack again," Dakhira added, with a blandness that made me want to scream. "More Freeporters."

How many pirates were out there? Did they just keep making them?

I linked back in to the senso and saw that while we had outpaced the *Devil's Own*, the other two surviving pirate ships had closed the distance and were now in hot pursuit. "How did they get there?"

"Insystem jump," said one of the Chives.

"They took—"

"—a short stitch—"

"—through the fabric of space-time."

The harmonics of their voices overlapping one another were fascinating as well as unsettling.

"I didn't know that was possible," I said.

"It's dangerous," Dakhira answered. "If you don't know how the white topology interacts with normal space, you might wind up inside the sun when you come out again. Very, very short jumps like that are less risky, but you might wind up inside the other ship instead."

"That's probably—"

"—why only two—"

"—jumped."

"And not the leader." I decided I really disliked that guy.

I watched the dots crawl toward us. At least we were headed in the right direction now—downwell, toward Town. I stared at the map of dots as if I could affect it by sheer will.

The dot representing the other inbound research ship swerved abruptly away from Town, on a curve that to my untrained eye seemed incredibly sharp for its *v*. The crew must be enduring stunning acceleration forces. It didn't appear as if there were pirates on its tail, but maybe I couldn't see them. It seemed to be running, anyway—it was pointed right back toward us. Right back toward the Core. Coming fast—

It winked into nothingness.

I yelped. I couldn't stop myself.

Safely in white space? Or destroyed?

I had no way to find out. But watching that little light vanish, I felt . . . a lot of feelings. Worry, hope, terror. And a sense of relief that nauseated me, though I told myself it was the idea of Vickee hightailing it home and leaving the field open for my work that sparked it. And not the possibility that she might never trouble me again.

I wouldn't want anything bad to happen to her.

Well, not blown-up-by-pirates bad.

At least, I *shouldn't* want anything that bad to happen to her.

Whatever had befallen her had happened minutes ago. Due to light-speed lag, we were only seeing it now. Schrödinger's cat had been alive or dead for some time already.

Maybe Dakhira did have me filtered after all. Maybe the parallel processing ability of an AI allowed him to continue peak functionality in the fight despite annoyances. Either way, he didn't respond to my incoherent sounds of distress.

I wanted to run—well, sail—back to the bridge and find out, but I could get just as much information from here, and if I went flying around a ship in combat I'd just get my head busted open. And make more work for everybody else.

I hugged the tree case so tightly it pressed the hardsuit into my arms and left lines.

The jigging and swerving were constant now. My inner ear informed me that I was not evolved for this kind of nonsense and I should stop it at once unless I wanted to become reacquainted with my breakfast.

Nausea, at least, I could tune out. Along with the pain of my wrenched shoulder and miscellaneous bruises.

I hoped I was right about the shipmind having sufficient processing power that if I asked a question, it wouldn't distract him from more important things. "Dakhira, the other ship—did they run for it?"

"Telemetry inconclusive," he said. Calmly, which made it worse. But at least he was listening if I said his name.

We swapped ends again on the EM drive, the force of our renewed acceleration pressing me into the padding. Even if we made it to Town, I had no idea how we were going to stop. Dakhira slalomed insystem, using the slope of the Baostar's gravity well to give us that little extra boost. The blips of the Freeport ships shimmered red-orange in my feed. Scrolling numbers beneath each one gave vectors, velocities, and Dakhira's confidence of the accuracy of their predicted location within the probability cone.

Two were still closing. The third was arcing away on a widening probability cone. How many more were out there?

My connection to Dakhira told me he was straining, his engines pushed to their limit. We were not accelerating as fast as he thought we should be. As if we were much more massive than usual, or as if we were trying to drag ourselves out of a gravity well.

The Freeporters were rumored to have access to Koregoi gravity technology, and to have had it for much longer than the Synarche. The gravitational lensing they had used to hide their true location from *I Hail the Wreck of Empire* suggested the rumors were true. They were, Dakhira hypothesized, literally bending space-time to speed themselves up and slow us down.

I got this from his scroll, not because he told me directly.

He did ask, "Dr. Sunyata Song, do you have any data on the range of Freeporter gravity tractors?"

"They have *gravity tractors?*"

"So that would be a no, then."

Even without their cheating, we couldn't outrun these overpowered sprinters. The pirates were going to draw up alongside and haul us down, lock us inside their oversized white coils, and vanish with us to the far reaches of the galaxy. Or wherever Freeport pirates live.

I had been an idiot to leave Salvie and the kids behind. Now I was never going to see them again.

It would be worse if they were here.

It would be. I clung to that. At least my wife and children were safe back in civilization. And knowing that, I could try to face my own fate with bravery.

I was grimly coming to terms with that when both my feed and the wall I'd cast the telemetry animation to exploded with coruscating light.

My fox and the ship reacted to the shock of brilliance in instant unison. The glare dimmed to tolerable levels before my own slow organic body had done more than begun to squeak in protest and pain. I kept the adrenaline—I might need it in a crisis—but mostly used it to clutch my family tree closer and ignore my various discomforts. A moment later I realized I had felt no impact vibrating through the hull.

Something had exploded *near* us, I gathered. But it had not *hit* us.

The live external feed now showed only stars, superstructure, and a red glow on the inside of Dakhira's white coils, the reflected light of the Baomind. The feed—

Plenty of tiny dots and wavering cones in the telemetry view. But in the visual animation, Vickee's ship, SJV *I Am Not Safe At Harbor*, hurtled majestically past our stern, gliding through a cloud of tumbling glitter. A debris field that sparkled off our bottle like uncountable fireflies. *I Am Not Safe At Harbor* had short-jumped, inside the system, popping in and out of white space so swiftly that she'd barely moved at all by the standards of a tesseracting warp drive.

Just like the pirate ships.

When she'd left white space and the wave of compressed space-time at her bow collapsed, it released a whole *flock* of the particles swept up before her and fired them directly into the hulls of the two pursuing Freeport ships. Both of which had disintegrated like piñatas in front of a particle cannon.

If my knowledge of piloting could be trusted—and my knowledge of piloting was almost entirely based on those same melodramatic three-vee series from which I'd learned about pirates, so I was certain it was completely accurate—what they'd done was a tricky, almost virtuoso piece of flying. The sort of thing that not one pilot and ship in a thousand could have pulled off without ramming the pirates, ramming us, overjumping, or catching Dakhira in their bow wave. It was possible they had just been extremely lucky.

I chose to believe they were extremely good.

Now that I saw her up close, at least virtually, I could see the reason for the Synarche Judiciary Vessel designation. SJV *I Am Not Safe At Harbor* wasn't merely some Judiciary runabout or personnel transport: she was a full-fledged Interceptor like Sandy had been. Her weapons were run out, and her dual white coils were big and robust enough for a cargo hauler six times her hull diameter. She could have fit Dakhira *and* his coils *and* another ship his size into her embrace.

She tipped as she crossed our wake, rolling to the side in salute, and turned back along our path. The *Devil's Own* was a blur of estimated telemetry, running for the edge of the system like its tail was on fire.

Predators don't want to fight to the death. Predators want easy pickings from ambush. And *I Am Not Safe At Harbor* had shown them her teeth. The two Interceptors had converted six-to-one odds to one-against-two.

The pirates must be falling over each other in panic and disarray.

"Compliments on the fancy defensive flying, Dakhira and Chive," said a cheerful voice my feed coded feminine and human-sounding, putting the artificial intelligence in my own cultural context. It was the shipmind of the Interceptor, tagged *Cee* in my feed. "We've got your zero. Head on in to Town. An escort will take you under their wing, and we'll chase this scoundrel back to the blockade."

"There's really a *blockade?*" I asked, startled.

From Dakhira, I sensed the mental equivalent of a shrug. News only traveled as fast as ships—or, if there were no ships, even slower: only as fast as light. If no ships were getting out of the system, no news would have been left at the buoys on the way in. I knew that; I was failing to process it.

So were we trapped here now?

I am not very good at thinking fast in a current crisis. That's why I am an archinformist. I specialize in teasing out the connections and making sense of the patterns in crises that were over long before I was born. In some cases, long before the Synarche was born. You don't have to think on your feet to be good at that sort of work. You just have to think meticulously, in details and iterations, and have a lot of willingness to keep looking under rocks and behind arrases.

"How many ships are still out there?" I asked.

"Uncertain," the Interceptor responded.

"Thanks, Cee," Dakhira said. "Our compliments to your pilot."

Both Dakhira and the Interceptor were moving so fast that the plotlines on the telemetry were already diverging. I couldn't yet detect the increasing lag as a response came: "That was me, Dakhira. Thank you, and please extend my greetings to your passenger, Dr. Sunyata Song. We're old friends and colleagues."

Vickee. And I couldn't even pretend I hadn't heard her.

The worst part was, she probably wasn't even rubbing it in. Vickee DeVine seems to have no concept that anybody in the wide universe could ever *dislike her.* Could ever want to grab her by her long, curly, carefully disheveled hair and drown her in a bucket.

That would be an antisocial act, and I would never.

Fantasies can be a useful outlet, though.

I gritted my teeth—I was going to crack one soon, way out here on the perimeter with probably no human dentist within a hundred light-years—tuned the fury out of my voice, and said, "Thanks, Vickee. Fancy meeting you out here at the end of everything."

She laughed like happy glass bells tinkling. "See you in Town, Sunya."

The connection didn't drop, but I didn't answer, and pretty soon it filled up with navigation chatter. I restricted my channel to just Cee, Dakhira, and Chive.

"Thank you for saving our lives," I told them. I *can* be gracious. Sometimes.

Vickee hadn't dropped me from *her* channel, however.

"There's somebody here who wants to talk to you," she said cheerfully. "One moment while I patch her in."

Of all the voices in the galaxy, literally the last one I expected to hear next was that of my dear wife. "Sun, I was so scared for you. I'm so glad you're all right."

"*Salvie?*" Even the emotional control imparted by rightminding couldn't keep the reactivity out of my voice. I felt Dakhira intercede to calm me, something he hadn't done at all during the pirate chase. I hated myself for needing the assistance, and I hated him for being the one authorized to provide it. Never get stuck on a boat with a condescending shipmind. That's my advice.

"Are you okay?" I asked.

"We wanted to surprise you," she said. "We're fine, we're fine. Are you okay?"

"I'm fine," I answered on autopilot. *We*, now there was an ominous word. *We* who? Surely she hadn't brought the kids and cats all the way out here to pirate-infested darkness . . .

No, she had. I was sure of it. Why not? That was Salvie for you. A plan had crossed her mind and she had completed it. Consequences are for later, and risk assessment is for whiners.

Well, that was family business, and I certainly wasn't going to air it in front of Dakhira. Or, Void forbid, Vickee DeVine.

"I'll see you soon, sweetie." I gave the feed back to Dakhira.

He uttered a few pleasantries. Then we were alone in the dark again. Only headed in the right direction by the most generous of assessments, and accelerating when we should have continued to brake.

It was not shaping up to be the greatest day of my life.

I asked, "How long before we're docked?"

I could hear the anxiety and eagerness in my voice. I should have tuned harder even after Dakhira calmed me down.

Embarrassing.

"We'll loop away—"

"—from the sun—"

"—to cut velocity."

"Don't worry—"

"—it will only take an extra dia—"

"—or two."

I sighed. I had no chance of catching up with Vickee now, given how that Interceptor could maneuver and how we were accruing relativistic effects. She'd have a multi-dia advantage over me where access to the research materials was concerned.

"You're upset—"

"—Dr. Song."

"Is there anything we—"

"—can do to ameliorate?"

"Not unless you can change the laws of physics." I hoped I sounded more tired than mean.

The Chives acknowledged that mildly. They did everything so damn mildly. The meekness was utterly infuriating.

"I'm concerned about my future access," I said.

Dakhira said, "But you and Dr. DeVine aren't in competition. You're equivalent entities. There's no scarcity of resources. You're both supported by the Synarche. And data can be shared."

"Sure." I scrubbed my hands on the thighs of my flight suit. "And if one of us has more interesting results than the other? What do you think happens next time?"

He sounded dismissive, even for Dakhira. "You both file proposals again."

"Yep," I said. "And the one who got the interesting result is awarded twice the resources, while the one who got the trivial result is back to cataloguing historical modalities of Tuvan throat singing."

"What's a Tuvan?" asked a Chive.

Through the senso, I felt them give a little postural hitch that I recognized as one of the remote personalities integrating. I tuned to hide my shudder.

The Chive interrupted themselves. "Never mind that—"

"—what's throat singing?"

There was nothing I *could* do about Vickee's advantage now. My hands were shaking with adrenaline reaction. I needed to sleep it off, because continuing to tune it out would only delay the inevitable crash. Sometimes your body just needs to do what your body needs to do, and the best way to help it is to get out of its way.

But before I gave my body what it needed, my *heart* needed to check the family tree.

CHAPTER 6

AS WE BRAKED, DAKHIRA KEPT THE CHANGE IN OUR *V* to a consistent half a g or so. This served as a small kindness to my bruised and strained body. I didn't mention it to him, in case he decided that more wild maneuvers would build character.

He even let me come out of my cage and set up a table in Center upon which to unpack my little tree and assess the damage. I was embarrassed to do it in front of the Chives, but there wasn't room to work in my cabin.

It could have been worse.

A couple of branches were cracked from striking the inside of the case, but the roots seemed healthy—as near as I could tell without teasing the whole thing apart, which would have been a disaster under current circumstances. Dakhira was salty enough without me getting lava grit in his filter intakes.

Well, I could examine the root structure and if necessary repot in Town. Town had constant rotational gravity, and I would have a private space to live and work . . .

. . . no, I wouldn't. Because I'd have a wife and kids along for the ride.

Oh well. I knew what Salvie had been thinking, and she was, by any empirical standard, correct. She had made a big sacrifice to come out here for what would probably be two or three ans, keeping me company, neglecting her own work. And it would be better for the kids to have me around on a continual basis, and not just to be getting updates via packet, my smiling distant face in three-vee recording months after I sent it on.

It abruptly sank in that I wouldn't even be able to do that, because of the blockade. My father would hear nothing from his surviving child or either of his grandchildren for . . . years, most likely.

My heart sank into my gut with worry. But I could do nothing to change the situation, so I tuned it down.

There was a small selfish part of me that had been looking forward to just *working*, for once in my adult life. Not wifing, not parenting . . . just working.

When I peeled back the first layer of guilt and fear, there were others underneath it. The most immediate was everything Vickee-related. And Vickee and my family had been on the same transport together for five or six months. That was enough to distract me from my ongoing career worries: What had she been telling them?

"Your emotions are rather dysregulated, Sunyata Song," said Dakhira. "It seems probable that you need your gut microbiome adjusted, if tuning isn't proving adequate."

Dakhira picking through my poop and preparing a probiotic enema certainly would adjust my attitude. And not for the better.

If I needed proof that my rightminding was just fine, it was provided by the fact that I did *not* inform Dakhira that anybody would be anxious and out of sorts after being trapped in a spaceship with him for half a year.

"Humans need to process emotions," I told him. "Not just repress them. We were just attacked by pirates."

"Yes," he said. "I was."

At the beginning of the journey, I might have pointed out that I had been the one to speak to Captain Adekunle. I might have argued with Dakhira's cutting dismissal.

But I couldn't work on the tree while I was shaking. Yelling at Dakhira would not actually calm me down.

My family and I would get by. There were advantages to having Salvie around. I just hoped she wouldn't feel too bored and neglected with me working all the time. There was unlikely to be any reliable childcare out here in the cold dark at the edge of the galaxy, not to put too fine a point on it. And I . . . well, selfish, again, but I was hoping to avoid childcare as much as possible.

Once I soothed myself sufficiently that I would probably not cause more damage, I fiddled with the family tree's dangling branches. The easiest thing to do would be to cut them and make jin—the decorative deadwood limbs that are intended to give a sense of great age to a tiny tree. Only that felt like giving up.

It might be possible to splint them. The bark and cambium on the undersides were still attached. I could lift the cambium—the living, vascular layer of inner bark that feeds the tree—from the wood on each side of the break and slide in a printed strip of sterile nonreactive plastic, then wrap the limb like a graft and see if the cambium would fuse and the bark scab over it. Eventually the tree would layer new wood over the strips of printed material, and they would become an inner support.

At least one was a big limb and important to the symmetry and form of the tree. I decided I would try plan A before I resorted to amputation.

You have to be ruthless in assessing damage and in bringing bits of history back to life. A lot of my job is knowing what can be saved, and what shouldn't be. But there's also the issue of knowing where to cut, and what to cut around.

History isn't a narrative. There's nothing tidy about it. There's nothing clear about its margins. It's an infiltrated, interlocking mess, and there are other systers whose brains are much more adapted to dealing with the fact that reality is not a story than humans are. Humans make a lot of terrible mistakes *because* we rely so heavily on narrative to understand the world. It allows our brains to be hacked by convincing fairy tales, to be hijacked by memes whether they have any objective reality or not. We probably needed rightminding more than most species just to remind us that stories are not the truth, even when they *feel* like the truth. Even when they suit all our biases and reinforce all our prejudices.

For example, if I was being fair, there was probably no objective truth to the idea that Victorya DeVine went out of her way to annoy me seventeen ways to a Ceeharen hell.

Victorya DeVine probably never gave me a second thought if I wasn't right in front of her.

A more predatory syster might need rightminding to control their urge to eat their coworkers. And we need rightminding to prevent our desire for a narrative from spawning endless conspiracy theories and justifications for things we were going to do anyway. The interventions that make us halfway decent galactic citizens and caretakers—rather than aggressively hierarchal apes—are devoted as much as anything to controlling that instinctual need.

Thus do we all manage to coexist with other species and even work productively with them. Thus does the Synarche persist and generally manage to meet the diverse needs of its diverse Synizens.

Syncretically. And synthetically.

But even an archinformist like me—*especially* an archinformist like me—has to pay extra care and attention to not confabulating conspiracy theories and then doubling down on them as the only plausible explanation for a series of facts that could be related in a lot of different ways.

Or perhaps not related at all. Sometimes a random collection of information has no causal relationships at all. Which we humans are poorly evolved to understand.

While the braces printed, I prepared the tree for surgery. The situation wasn't hopeless: wood fibers connected the broken branch ends to the main body of the tree, and those—when unbent and realigned—would help to support the branches while they knit. There would be some graft scars, of course. But those would just enhance the tree's venerable appearance, like the carefully nurtured cankers my grandmother had introduced with an engineered, self-limiting virus that inoculated the tree against other pathogens.

I slid the supports into place, straightened the limbs and pushed the broken edges together, sprayed on a hormone to promote regrowth, and wrapped the damaged limbs as neatly as possible. It didn't look too bad when I was finished, and I added a twist of wire for external support. It would all come off in the end. I would see how I had done some months from now, possibly not for a year. I mean, some *decians*, and an *an*. The tree would have to come out of dormancy to start healing, which meant I needed to wake it up soon, before the cambium dried out and died, rendering the self-graft inviable.

The tree was a story in its own right. The story of a forest, of Old Earth itself, of my family—made portable and small. Like all stories, it was a lie. A microcosm in a frame with much of the messiness cut away to reveal a structure.

But it was a lie with some truth in it, maybe.

An archaic poet wrote, "Beauty is truth, truth beauty." But lies can be beautiful, too. And certainly beguiling. And beauty can fool you.

Stories are not truth. History is truth. Stories are an attempt to make *sense* of history, to whittle truth down until our limited minds can wrap themselves around it. Except it's not the whole thing. It's a filet of the thing.

Maybe an AI can make sense of a *whole thing*.

My job is to operate for the rest of us. To find not just the buried data but the *interesting* data, the *relevant* data. And then to build a pattern with it that reveals the outline of the truth without eliding too many of the complexities.

Take my little tree: in a real forest, its branches would reach out and entangle with the limbs of other trees. Their trunks would confuse its outline. They might topple against it, hide it and break it, crush the trunk and obscure its character. Some trees were part of an aspen forest, a million trees all grown from one organism. (Actually, my tree was a little bit like an aspen forest, as it happened—the various "trunks" were limbs rising from the original trunk, which my great-great-grandmother had mostly buried sideways under the earth to make the "turtleback" nebari, the gnarled root ball.)

How do you cut one aspen loose of the parent clone and call it a forest? You can't. Any more than—much as I found them upsetting—you could cut one Chive free of the other Chives and call them a complete organism.

And yet, my job was to do just that. Pull up all the interleaved data on the Baomind—and *from* the Baomind, since it was a communicating intelligence—and figure out how to cut that data into manageable chunks so it could be assessed, sorted, and manipulated. Take one aspen and make it represent the whole woodland . . . accurately.

If I couldn't get a jump on Vickee timewise, I would just have to be more creative, better at coming up with individual templates to sort the knowledge, better at my job than she was.

Sure, this would be *perfectly* easy.

I'd have to rely on the support and closeness of my own family, I decided. Treat them as an asset rather than a distraction. I could do that.

I couldn't cut myself free of Salvie and the kids and remain myself any more than I could cut one trunk from my family tree and understand the whole, or all the labor and care that had gone into shaping it for generations.

I looked up from the family tree and stared out the viewport, turning my head a little to line up tree branches and distant stars.

It was all going to be fine. Salvie would take care of the kids and I would work and I would still be my best professional self, even as part of the family unit.

I could make it work. I *could*.

One aspen was a tree. Ten thousand aspens were a woodland. There were some back on Earth that were tens of thousands of years old, clone-forests that had survived ice ages and the anthropogenic Eschaton—plague, wildfire, invasive pests, drought, flood, and all.

I wiped the tears off my cheeks and bent my attention back to wiring the limb as meticulously as I could manage.

Once I finished the immediate repairs, I washed the soil-and-sap-smudged canopy of the case and closed it up. Then I spent a few standard hours going over the files we'd managed to download from the navigation buoy on our way in. Even after all this time, I wasn't entirely comfortable using diar, ans, and decians. Not to mention "standard" hours, minutes, and weeks. Having grown up on a planet, I thought in days and "natural" hours and months—astronomically mediated divisions of time.

Rubric had two distinct lengths of months, as a matter of fact, as it had two moons with different periods.

But here in space, where relativistic effects were in play and different locations and species had entirely different metrics of time, it made sense to use something standardized. I could get used to it, just as humans in the past had become used to seconds and to the metric system. Technology was something you could adapt to, and timekeeping was just another technology.

The second time I bumped my wakefulness, it occurred to me that perhaps staying up forever wasn't the best plan, even if every instinct I had was telling me that if I let my guard down I would be jumped by monsters. It took me a little while to talk myself into it, but I did eventually manage to unwind my anxiety to the point where I admitted it would be a good idea to get some sleep.

That was a necessary first step to the next argument with my subconscious, which involved permission to tune my feelings down enough to *try* to sleep. I needed rest. And it would make the time pass more quickly until we got to Town.

Anybody who's ever had to convince a child to go to bed on the night before a holiday will appreciate the exact details of the argument I was having with my own brain.

I hadn't been lying when I said to Dakhira that you have to let yourself feel your feelings sometimes, or you never process them and learn from them. The point of rightminding is not to create a galaxy of sociopaths, after all.

On the other hand, pretty much every syster species in the Synarche has learned the lesson of what happens if you let your reactions and instincts tell you how to run your culture, economy, and government: it leads to a self-made disaster of massive proportions. Some of us have created more than one.

Human beings are not unique in being bad at taking care of ourselves and others without, you know, special training. We evolved to reproduce, not to thrive. Thriving was aspirational, and then it was accessible but perceived as a luxury, and then we were barely existing as a species, hanging on by our fingernails amid those same disasters that nearly took out the aspen forests.

Eventually we realized we could dispense with scarcity, that there was no moral benefit to suffering, and that individual people accomplish more good for the community when they are supported rather than exploited by it—and that the commonwealth should include and support everyone. All stuff we knew when we lived in small tribal groups, and somehow forgot for a few thousand years when we got very invested in owning stuff. That makes me feel a lot better about us, actually. It's good to learn from your mistakes, and not just shunt the bad feelings aside.

There was plenty of data already collected from the Baomind, and sleep is the great knitter up of inspirations. So I stretched out on my bunk to reconsider what I already knew. That sense of someone nearby was still with me. I caught myself turning my head to try to see the person who wasn't, in fact, just at the corner of my vision.

Hmm. Obviously I needed to do a little maintenance on how I was processing the ayatanas. Or maybe I was just being paranoid about Dakhira looking over my shoulder all the time, but I couldn't change that until we got to Town and I disembarked the galaxy's biggest asshole.

I contemplated hitching a ride back on Cee when the time came to head home. Would being trapped on an Interceptor with Vickee be worse than another hemian with Dakhira? At least I'd be with Salvie and the kids—

This was not helping me relax. Fixing my ayatana filtering, on the other hand, was a routine and restful set of rituals. *Do the thing that is good for you, not all the other things.*

Having accomplished the adjustment, I felt less loomed over and more able to think. The most salient point in my research so far was that the Synarche had been led here on purpose. The Koregoi had left a series of clues, a sort of pan-galactic scavenger hunt, which brought people to an ancient ship cached in the Core. That ship had carried its discoverers here, to this . . . legacy. An inheritance of information and technology, if you like.

They'd made sure their legacy could communicate.

I mentioned that the Baomind talks through song. Music can be understood both as patterns and as mathematics, so that made sense. I tried to think, if I were leaving a message for all of deep time, not knowing what sort of mind would find and try to decode it . . . would I be able to come up with a better system than music? At least for first contact, it would convey both peaceful objectives and the intentionality of the interaction.

And it was a pattern.

My species is very well adapted to detecting certain kinds of patterns.

There's a term, *apophenia*, for this tendency: we'll find patterns even when there are no patterns to be found. A twenty-first-century scholar referred to it as *narrative disorder*, but over the centuries this propensity to assign causality before causality is proved has been named everything from magic to natural law.

Magical thinking, in other words. Superstition.

It was a lot to think about. However, once the tuning and the adrenaline wore off, and once my body realized how tired it was, no amount of intellectual curiosity could have kept me awake.

If pirates killed us in my sleep, at least I wouldn't suffer.

I dreamed of bodyboarding in the big waves off Teal, the euphoria of the moment when you time it right and the water gets behind and under you and sweeps you forward with a vast and powerful rush until your toes drag in wet sand and you have to pull yourself up onto your hands and knees and drag your board back out into the ocean again. Except in the dream the wave was bottomless and the water pushed me into infinity. The sky opened around and beneath me. I curved through a sea of stars, one point of light among trillions.

Crystalline harmonies rang in my bones. The force of gravity swept us along in a dance as inevitable as entropy.

The music deepened, quickened, grew more urgent. My companions in the dance—my fellow fish in the school—swirled around me. I swept my arms wide—

That music was a peal of alarm. A throbbing warning. I covered deafened ears with my hands.

But I had no hands. I had only a flat body, like a ray, surrounded by a squadron of other rays. The vibrations of our song tingled in our bodies. The bodyboard was me.

I woke, and for a moment lay frozen in the midst of a crescendo. For instants, I could not gather my thoughts.

"Dakhira!" The agitated Baosong flowed around me. "It's a warning! Evade! Evade!"

For whatever reason, he obeyed me. The ship rolled, hurling me against the mesh. I tried reflexively to grab it, failed, and wrapped my arms around my head to protect my neck and then, as best I could, braced myself into the corner.

Oh no, this again, commented the corner of my mind that never quite lost its ironic detachment.

I dove into the senso. Frantic Baosong surrounded me. Dakhira had continued downwell while I slept. He had joined the river of tesserae. They sailed in formation all around us. We were one large dull pebble in a flight of mica flakes.

The pirate ship blew through them like some gigantic predator lunging from the deep.

This wasn't animation. They were so close that it was a live feed from the hull sensors. I saw the gaping maw painted on the pirate vessel's hull, the bloody shark jaws, pitted with micrometeorite strikes. The name painted under the guns: *Hush*.

She fired and a dozen tesserae disintegrated into glitter. I yelled a protest; Dakhira said calmly, "Brace."

I was bracing. We rolled hard in the other direction. Acceleration pressed me into the wall hard enough that I moaned.

"Where did they come from?"

"I theorize they were hiding in a white bubble." He sounded cool and collected. My heart banged against the back of my ribs.

"They're killing the mirrors!"

"I can't help that."

Stop, I begged the tesserae, trying to sing back to them, to insert myself into their music. Not sure if I was heard, and if I *was* heard, not sure if I was understood. *Stop. Please. I beg you.*

But they fell in toward the pirate vessel as if magnetized. She rolled to pursue us. She brought her guns to bear, her magnetic bubble flickering momentarily to allow the projectiles through—

—an enormous ribbon of plating peeled away behind the tesserae. Like an eel unspooling from its burrow, chasing a swarm of fish, the streamer of hull stretched after the tesserae.

The streamer crumbled at the edges, fell apart, disintegrated into particles. Atmosphere bled from the gaping wound in *Hush*'s side. The particles re-sorted themselves, began to integrate into flat, mirrored hexagons.

Hush began to turn inside her white coils. Trying to run. I held my breath as another strip of her hull came free. Now she was the center of a fevered swarm, a feeding frenzy. I lost sight of her as sparks rolled along the surface of her white coils a moment before they broke free of the tesserae-covered hull.

Mere instants elapsed before the coils, too, were consumed, faster than they could unravel.

"I guess the pirates aren't the only ones with gravity tractors," Dakhira said.

"There were people on there," I said dully.

"There were people on the ships the pirates destroyed, too," he replied. "Not to mention the ships themselves. And I am a people, and there are people on me."

"It just disassembled her to make more tesserae. Did it disassemble the people, too?"

Dakhira's voice was a shrug. "As near as we can tell, it has already disassembled the entire stellar system to build itself. Considering that the pirates have recently destroyed several thousand tesserae, it only seems fair they should replace them."

I had no answer.

We were—finally—only a few hours out from Town. I had slept a long time; I must have needed it. Sleep is the great regulator.

I felt more at peace. I climbed out of bed, checked that the family tree was still stowed safely, then went to a viewport in Center and looked out. I could now see the tesserae flocking around Town with my own eyes. Flecks of glitter had resolved to mirrored hexagons, strange sequins against the night.

This was the legacy the Koregoi had left us. I tried on all the words—*awe-inspiring, incredible, fascinating*—and none of them were adequate. This was what I had come in search of: the oldest and largest artifact of sentient life in the galaxy.

As far as we knew.

It did make my heart skip a beat. Several beats in succession.

My brain was full of faltering half-memories of the dreams I'd been having before the most recent pirate attack—dreams of the disks that orbited the Baostar in an overlapping sphere, capturing its light, using that light to fuel their collaborative cognition. Well, I had packed myself full of information right before dozing off. My brain had a lot to process.

I went back into the dream-memories in my fox, sorting through them. I know a lot of people think that's rubbish and, well, perhaps I am an unscientific person then, because I find the ability to parse my dreams using my conscious mind useful. Mostly they're about anxiety or processing experiences or cementing memories. But occasionally, when the censors are turned off, the brain comes up with some pretty good stuff.

Anxiety dream, anxiety dream, sex dream, anxiety dream. Well, reviewing those probably *wasn't* productive. But there were several about the Baomind disks, including the dream of surfing space-time with them. I spent some time studying the most narratively complete one. I even wrote down its elements in my notebook, which helps me retain and process information. Printed polymer sheets are light and infinitely reusable, and I've an affinity for ancient technologies.

I had dreamed that I was floating in space, comfortable and weightless as a fetus in a womb tank, aware and drifting and calm. There was no sense of exposure, no discomfort, no fear. This was my home, my native environment, and I could navigate it as a bird navigates the sky. The dark velvet of the void stretched away, freckled with stars and streaked with a light like auroras. I wondered if my dream had placed me inside a nebula, but no, there was the Baostar on my left. The web of light veiled it, a fretwork like pin lace or torn netting stretched between a thousand anchor points.

What was it like to be the Baomind? Was there peace in that timeless existence?

No, not timeless, really. Because time, at long last, was catching up. But by my human standards, it might as well have been immortal. My ancestors were lucky to get to fifty; I might last three or four times that long in reasonable health, with modern medical interventions and telomere repair. But was there really a difference between fifty years and fifty million, on the scale of all creation?

Sophomore philosophy, still available in dreams, provided by the subconscious mind for free.

I realized that dream-me might be an Ativahika. I'd never seen one, but the enormous creatures that spent their infancy in the upper surfaces of gas giants and then sailed the starways on gravity waves of their own making were a fixture of three-vee. It turned out that the Koregoi had engineered them for interstellar flight, if I understood the latest news on the subject—and it was possible I didn't. Neither bioengineering nor nanotech was among my fields of study, and it's good to know one's limits.

In the dream, I extended a limb to see if I could determine what I was, but the outlines I glimpsed puzzled me. I did not have the lacy black-green fronds that maximized an Ativahika's photosynthetic surface. Nor did I have a human arm. But it was a limb, not just the angled razor-sharp edges of one of the Baomind tesserae.

The limb I glimpsed—if glimpsed was the right word—seemed . . . different. Rather than having any substance, my dream arm was an outlined crackle of purple-black energy around a spiky, angular silhouette. I held it in front of the Baomind and realized that it did nothing to obscure my vision. It was as if I were looking at my limb with one pair of eyes, and the outside world with a different pair—like when you hold one finger up right in front of your pupil so you can see it, but also see what lies behind it. As if my limb didn't take up any dimensional space, perhaps. It was there, but it couldn't hide what was behind it.

I thought of an Old Earth legend about a monster so tall and thin that when it turned sideways, it vanished. If I weren't out at the absolute edge of nowhere I could look it up, but Dakhira didn't have a bit of information that obscure and specific in his databases. And the nearest database that *would* have trivia about Old Earth cryptids was probably several decians' travel away. Libraries are great, but you have to be able to reach them.

I went back to my saved memory.

Dream-me wasn't alone. The Baomind's component tesserae flocked around me. They moved in a stately, patterned dance, circling in intricate configurations that ensured the fair distribution of light across the surfaces of each one within the orbiting sphere. As their star expanded and dimmed through millennians, they had drawn closer to its corona in order to harvest sufficient light to keep them processing. Many of them had been rescued already and moved to a new location in the Core—plenty of light for everybody there!—but the majority were still here. Along with the bulk of the Baomind's millions of ans of introspection and processing.

I wondered what it was like for the sections of its person to be separated by light-eons. In some ways the Baomind was not unlike Chive.

This distributed sentience had been out here all by itself, thinking, for a remarkably long time. We had to save it, and record its thoughts and history, and reunite it with its other selves so it could continue thinking for a long, long time to come.

In that dream-way, I could understand what it was singing without any intervention, as if I were an AI with the processing power to parse its multivalent language. Also in that dream-way, no trace of what I had thought I understood remained.

The tesserae passed through my dream-body as if it were completely immaterial. I could be seen and seen through, and not touched—which gave me a nasty stir. Was I a data ghost of some kind? Conscious but unembodied? How the heck was I supposed to make sense of that?

Thanks, subconscious, but I have no idea what life lesson or creative inspiration I'm supposed to take away from this.

I made sure to save the dream out of my fox and into external memory, though. Filed it, tagged it, and set it aside for later. I'd figure it out when I got the chance. Maybe I could talk it over with Salvie, though my urge was to hide my secrets from her. Not healthy, but I was feeling a little like my borders had been invaded by her deciding to just show up at my job.

The odd thing about the dream was the sense I had in it of something . . . reaching out to me. Of a hand in the dark, maybe, or a whisper just below the audible range. I could feel it like a shiver in my bones. I had a sense of *something* intelligible being spoken, and was frustrated not to make sense of it.

If I hadn't been trapped in a tube surrounded by nothing, I would have taken myself for a long walk with all my privacy filters turned up high. I could have gone down to the gym and hurled myself at the exercise equipment, done some yoga, or grabbed one of the struts in Central and done partial-gravity pull-ups that allowed me to feel like a badass while not significantly straining my deltoids, but I'll be honest. I was feeling sorry for myself, and when you're feeling sorry for yourself, there's nothing that seems as productive as a good old-fashioned sulk.

I went back to my cabin, set the wall to show me where we were going, settled on the bunk, and folded my hands behind my head. From this position and given our current acceleration and the settings on the furnishings, my wall functioned as a skylight. I could literally lie in bed and stare into space.

Let your mind wander, and see where it takes you. It might not always be the best advice, but at least it's a strategy.

I found myself humming under my breath, earwormed by the Baomind musical keys I had been studying more or less nonstop since we embarked. Some of them were well understood, like the tune the original first contact team had used to establish communication. I'd listened to that one so often I probably had RNA molecules devoted to it in particular. Now I sang it absentmindedly to myself.

Those notes kept running around my brain. I sang them again, rising and falling, trying to think of them as words. As particles of meaning. As a way of thinking. As the keys to unlocking the massive amounts of data stored in the Baomind—all that history, all that knowledge. All that deep time.

We might be able to learn what kind of creatures the Koregoi really were—and if they were one species, like humans, or many species, like the Synarche. We might learn more about their history, their philosophy, their art. Who they were, where they came from. Perhaps even where they went.

Other people would be interested in the technology, the science, the engineering. The deep art of how they built what they built. Or their biology, their medicine, their apparent ability to engineer everything from the Baomind to the Ativahikas to a spaceship parked on the edge of a gigantic black hole.

Bum bum bum bum bum bum. Bum bum ba bum bum bum bum bum.

I lay in place and hummed and stared. Inside my head the music danced, and so did the tracking telemetry of the Baomind, of Town, of the Judiciary Interceptor that had dropped Vickee off a couple of diar earlier making a sharp turn on patrol and heading back downwell. Of the other Interceptor still in the system returning to a wider patrol, and two more civilian ships huddled close to Town and well inside the perimeter maintained by the Baomind.

I hoped there weren't any more pirates lurking in the shadows.

I think the passage of time and my intentional dissociation must have sent me into a sort of hypnotic or meditative state, because as I stared outward and inward I started to imagine flickers of movement and sound around the edges of my cabin. The shadows seemed to move, pulsing in time with my heartbeat. I heard the echo of ghostly voices singing along with mine.

Back on Rubric I had once attended a musical performance for which the artist was extremely late coming onstage. We sat there in the dark, in the classically proportioned concert hall of the old Capitol City Orpheum, waiting. After a while the various conversations and rustlings had drifted to a halt. People had entertained themselves in various ways. I'd been able to pick out the background music, a loop of popular songs by artists similar to the one we'd come to see.

Bored, I'd started to mouth the lyrics along with the recording. And I'd heard the strangest thing. It was as if a choir of ghostly devi sang along with me, falsetto and pure, breathy but layered into a perfect harmony. I'd felt transported to some ethereal plane, to some fairyland where voices were crystal bells rung softly.

Awed, I'd looked around and realized that what I heard was eight thousand people singing in whispers in an acoustically perfect space.

I was singing to myself, and inside my fox, as if lightspeed lag were no more than a speeding ticket, the Baomind was singing along. I almost laughed out loud at myself. Everybody in the universe really is just trying to communicate.

The flickers of motion around the periphery of my cabin reminded me of fluttering leaf-shadows: dim but translucent. They had a sort of presence, like the sense that somebody is with you in a room you thought was empty. I put my hand out to see if I could feel anything, but like my own limb in my dream there was nothing real to touch or see.

The act of moving seemed to snap the spell. The harmonics vanished; the shadows fled. Wasn't there something about sounds in certain frequencies inducing visual hallucinations?

Well, I wasn't a neurologist, and I certainly wasn't going to ask Dakhira any questions that might indicate vulnerability.

I tried replaying the past few moments from my machine memory: my fox hadn't recorded any of the visual images, but the beauty of the Baomind's tesserae echoing my song persisted. Maybe it was a signal chain issue, and my brain had provided the visual effects *after* my fox processed the inputs?

I couldn't sulk in here for the rest of the voyage. Dreams reviewed, songs sung, I tuned my stress hormones down significantly, drank a cup of coffee (no systers who hated the smell of coffee on Dakhira right now, so the Chives and I could indulge our desire for mild and tasty Earth stimulants freely), and stepped outside of my quarters again.

CHAPTER 7

WHEN I ENTERED THE LOUNGE IN CENTER, WE WERE still dumping *v*, so there was acceleration to press me into what presently passed for the floor. *V* also sufficed to hold the various Chives to their couches, where they sat or sprawled. Walking around under g on feet modified into afthands couldn't be very comfortable.

I wondered how they managed their shared brain functions when two-fifths of the clade were sleeping. I guess earth cetaceans and some systers manage to sleep with only parts of their brain at a time. (Did the Baomind sleep? Something else to check into once I got there.) Personally, I don't think I could get any rest with the other half of my brain chattering away at me, but the Chives—and the dolphins—had clearly found a way.

I'd ask, but I worried that it might be a violation of their privacy. And I was too self-conscious of Dakhira's scorn to check his library for information. But soon we'd be in Town, with its greater resources.

Salvie jokes that I'm what happens when a kid's parents tell them "Look it up" too many times.

Thinking about Salvie, I realized part of me was eager to see her. A whole big part, at odds with the selfish desire for isolation and focus that also nagged at me. If people had utterly consistent desires, I supposed we wouldn't be people. And fiction and dating would both be a lot less interesting.

I walked over to the port, wanting to see the view with my own eyes, not just through senso or animation or a feed. Even if Dakhira's senses are better and more diverse than my own.

We were close enough to the Baostar that I felt grateful for the polarization on the port, our EM bottle, and the shade cast by the orbiting tesserae. Even shining between the cracks, the Baostar shed enough radiation to warm the crystal I touched with my forehead. Although most of its output was in the infrared, it cast enough visible light to see by, though everything it illuminated was lit with an inferno glow.

Town was a unique habitat. We were too far out in the dark reaches of the rim to have access to any building materials bulkier than holds full of printable material: the energy cost of shipping would be prohibitive. And all the matter in the Baostar's former stellar system had long since been consumed and converted into the computronium that the tesserae were made of. So, in order to build Town, a lot of tired, older white ships had been flown out here under their own power and then repurposed.

If you've ever seen pictures of old, pre-Eschaton space habitats made of stuck-together modules that had been built in and boosted out of a gravity well, Town resembled that much more than it looked like a modern wheel.

The decommissioned ships *had* been arranged in a circle, spoked together with cables from their disassembled white coils, and spun up—so there was accelerational g inside. But the thing looked like a string of cans bent into a wheel shape, and not a proper wheel.

From our vantage, I watched the hab spin majestically at about half a g. Two still-functional civilian ships—call signs Arula and Amal—were docked already. For structural reasons, they were spoked by cables to the center of the wheel rather than pulling on the outer rim of the chain of cans.

Orange-red light cast grasping shadows across the exteriors of the hab and the hulls. It looked so much like a late afternoon in wildfire season, I kept being surprised I could not smell the smoke.

The ships that had gone into making the habitat would never leave this place—not as ships, anyway. I supposed the Baomind might convert them into tiles. Their shipminds had already been sent back to the Core to take up new assignments. All that was left was the shells, and looking at them gave me a sharply eerie sensation.

It was like looking at a bus terminal built of corpses.

It wasn't an accurate comparison. I knew that: the minds that had inhabited these ships weren't dead. And the ships were not uninhabited; there *must* be a wheelmind. Somebody would have to pay constant attention to keeping this rickety, imbalanced thing in trim. And not leaking anything catastrophic, such as water, oxygen, or people.

The only remaining Interceptor close to Town, *I Am Not Safe At Harbor,* was "up" and "north" of us—a ready shield and defender. With the destruction of *I Hail the Wreck of Empire,* she had dropped off her passengers and promptly resumed station. Telemetry told me another Judiciary vessel was on wide patrol, maintaining a lot of *v* to stay nimble. That was SJV *I Brake for Nobody,* call sign Ikem.

Not much, to protect us from a potentially infinite number of pirates. I was suddenly worried, again, about having my wife and kids here.

I had seen the Baomind defend us and itself, however. The pirates hadn't been eager to chase us this far down the gravity well, and I had also heard that the artifact had defended the first-contact team.

I blinked.

For a moment, I had glimpsed the fretwork from my dream stretched across the sky. But then it was gone, and surely that was just a ghost in my feed, an artifact of having spent so long in my quarters poring over the memory.

Behind me, one of the Chives cleared their throat. "Enjoying the view?"

I jumped so hard I nearly bounced off the temporary ceiling. My reactivity really was running unusually high. I tuned it down, wondering if it was the tension of the situation or all the ayatanas making me so jumpy—or that constant sense of somebody looming over me.

I think the Chives unsettled me so badly because of my inability to tell them apart. Logically, I knew that didn't matter: talking to any of them was talking to all of them. But logic and viscera are not the same.

"It's beautiful," I said, trying to sound natural. "And intimidating."

"So much work to do?"

"So few resources to do it with," I agreed.

Chive patted me on the shoulder. I managed not to flinch. You don't have to be rude to somebody just because you don't like their family dynamics.

"You'll be fine," they said, and moved toward the bridge. "We'll be docking in thirty minutes."

Only after they had left did I realize how odd it was to have only one of them speak to me, rather than their usual layered self-interruptions.

The other four stayed where they were. One was reading; one playing some game on a slate. Another appeared to be working on navigation plots, and I had no idea what the fourth one was up to, except it involved some little printed objects that they passed from hand to hand. Sometimes the small objects—a ball, an artificial flower, a disk—vanished, or one replaced another.

Was that stage magic?

Chive caught me looking and asked, "Do you want to see?"

"Yes," I said, coming closer.

"Here." They held up the flower, and tucked it into their lapel with a flourish. Their hands began a complicated dance with the ball and the disk, a dance that involved making first one vanish, then the other. I frowned and leaned closer. The disk passed through the ball: they were the same diameter, and I could see the color change along the ball's circumference as the disk entered and left it. Sleight of hand, but even from a half meter away I couldn't see how it was done.

"It's no fun showing my clade," Chive said. "They always know what's up my sleeve. But you—"

They opened their right hand, which had held the ball a moment before. It was empty.

"Like now," said another Chive. "It's up our sleeve."

The Chive I was talking to peeled their cuff back with a flourish. "Not that one."

I couldn't help it. I laughed.

Chive winked at me and said, "Enjoy your flower."

I looked down.

Somehow, the printed blossom had been transferred from their lapel . . . to mine.

We docked airlock to airlock alongside one of the hab ships, and drones cabled us to the hub. Once I unstrapped myself and adjusted to the changed orientation of the gravity, it was only standard minutes until I was walking along the boarding tube. I dragged the case with the family tree by the handle. I also shouldered a small pack containing the few things that would be inconvenient to print out here, or that I had required for the journey. I had tried not to bring anything I absolutely couldn't live without in order to save weight allowance for the tree. And also because anything I brought and didn't need for the trip back would probably be recycled. I try not to form attachments to nonliving matter: it all degrades or gets disassembled in the end. The few sentimental objects I owned, I had left safely at home.

The first thing I saw as I stepped from the ladder onto the walkway was a dodecapus wearing a breathing envelope full of oxygenated H_2O. Gentle bubbles wafted from its aerator, and the flexible membrane pulsed in and out in a somewhat unsettling fashion.

The syster seemed to be waiting for me, because when I paused, it squidged gently in my direction. It was about two meters in diameter and a meter tall, a mottled brownish-red, and it crawled along the floor on moist suckers. Inside its environment envelope, it wore what I can only describe as a polka-dotted frock.

Hello, Dr. Song, it said via translation. *I hope your trip was pleasant.*

"Extremely," I answered, which was only a fib if you considered Dakhira. And my irrational dislike of the Chives, which I was now feeling extra guilty about, given my new boutonniere. "You must be Dr. Nonsense."

It flashed its iridophores cheerfully.

Dr. Nonsense was not its real name. But it was either the sense of its real name or the name it had chosen for itself. I assumed "nonsense" had some deep philosophical meaning for dodecapods that was lost in translation. Since its species used color signaling for communication, I was released from the obligation to even attempt to make my vocal organs imitate sounds it might use to name itself, its species, or others.

We have a welcome reception for you later todia, it said. *I assume you'll want a little time to recuperate.*

"Thank you," I said. "Do you know where I might find my family?"

It pointed, which on a dodecapus looks like somebody shaking out a lumpy carpet. *Why don't we perambulate together? I have your access codes for the research materials. And you can meet the wheelmind.*

"That would be very kind. What is the wheelmind called?"

She is named Yod.

Huh. Well, I met a history department AI named Ankh once.

It's hard for a twelve-limbed beastie to fall into step with a four-limbed one, but Dr. Nonsense squidged along beside me pleasantly enough. I felt pretty proud of myself for waiting a full fifteen seconds before I asked, "Tell me about the pirate blockade?"

Dr. Nonsense's color changed to something my fox interpreted as social discomfort. *It is,* it admitted, *a matter of concern. But we do have a pair of Interceptors available, Cee and Ikem, and so far the humans—sorry, the Freeporters—have chosen not to test our defenses except at the perimeter.*

The perimeter where I had nearly been killed. Or possibly kidnapped.

My species doesn't have the best reputation around the galaxy and a lot of that is the Freeporters' fault. Some Synarche humans take offense when systers refer to the pirates as "the humans." I do, too, a little, but not enough to get into fights about it unless I feel like the syster in question is being a bigot on purpose.

I made a noncommittal noise, trusting our foxes to translate. A good portion of my concentration was relegated to monitoring my own anxiety about that, and balancing reasonable vigilance with outright anxiety.

Town was such a flimsy jury-rigged eggshell of a habitat. I thought of my mother and sister, and how little damage it would take to rip this structure apart. A pain in my throat made it hard to speak or swallow. This level of apprehension wasn't doing me any good—after all, it wasn't as if I could fix the situation by worrying about it—so I tuned it down. "Is there anything we can do about it?"

We've sent out a number of white-drive-capable probes with encoded messages to the nearest Synarche outposts. Sooner or later, one or more of them is bound to get through and bring help. They're small enough not to use much power, and they can jump from pretty deep in the Baomind's gravity well. A blockade is only as good as its coverage, and the Freeporters don't have that many ships. Yet. Of course, they might be fetching more.

Dr. Nonsense was not a master of reassuring inconsequentialities. But it had a refreshing air of honesty that I liked. "How is Dr. DeVine getting along?" I asked, hoping that my gritted teeth would not be obvious to a syster.

She arrived six diar ago, with your family.

Six days! Of course, relativistic effects.

They all seem to be settling in. Dr. DeVine will also be at the reception, of course.

A reception.

Oh boy.

• • •

From the inside, Town seemed just as rickety and weird as it did from the outside. The walkway Dr. Nonsense led me along was no proper corridor, once we got away from the ship Dakhira had docked alongside. We exited downward through a hatch into a hamster tube: a floor at the "bottom" of a toroidal bubble that ran along the outside rim of Town. The bubble was transparent, puffed out with atmosphere, and gave the overwhelming impression of a railless catwalk over a bottomless abyss with a nuclear furnace floating in the middle of it. Absolutely terrifying even though I am completely immune to agoraphobia.

Completely.

It's a good thing I am also completely immune to claustrophobia, because the hulls over my head bulged down like looming cave roofs. It felt like the whole damn station was about to fall on my head, and I really didn't like it.

I reassured my limbic system that even in the worst-case scenario, that wouldn't happen. If the spokes snapped, the whole hab wheel would fly apart, tear through the walkway bubble, and then probably fall into the sun. I'd be dead long before my toes got roasted.

The inability to muster a soothing inconsequentiality was something I had in common with Dr. Nonsense.

And I shouldn't dwell on the potential for disaster. I *should* tune my anxiety down, and I should requisition an emergency hardsuit if one hadn't already been assigned to me. I wasn't too proud to wear an actuator on my chest, even if it made people think I was some kind of weekend warrior fantasizing about joining the Judiciary.

Town rotated. The Baomind slid out of view. Our shadows stretched long before us, mine like a knife blade, Dr. Nonsense's indistinct and squirming. Its respirator bubbled agreeably as it squidged along.

Here's your space. It wrapped a tentacle around the bottom rung of an access ladder. *Your fox should grant you access, and here are the override codes and the research access codes for when you need them.*

It slid them into my feed.

"Thanks," I said.

Do you require nutrition or hydration?

"Not if there will be food at the reception," I said. "What's the dress code?" I'd have to print something, but that shouldn't be a problem, I hoped. Even out here in the back end of nowhere.

I shall be wearing a ruffled frock, it confided. *See you there.* It squidged away down the corridor and back into the glare of the rising Baostar.

I slung the family tree over my shoulder and climbed the ladder to the quarters where I would be living and working for the foreseeable future. I hoped there would be somewhere to send the kids and the cats—or me—while I was trying to concentrate.

There was no occupied light by the hatch, so I tapped the control and went through the airlock cycle. At least that was reassuring: if the flimsy hamster tube *did* shred itself while I was asleep in my bunk, it wouldn't evacuate the entire contents of the habitat. Maybe this junkyard assemblage was safer than I feared.

Maybe.

I let myself in . . . and discovered the occupied light was broken.

Because as I came up through the floor, I found myself staring right at the gray-jumpsuit-clad backside of a tall human man with midtone skin and a cloud of curly hair, roughly the same hue as his complexion. He turned hazel eyes on me as I hauled myself up, feeling undignified.

Hesitantly, he said, "I'm Petrac Janes, research logician. I'm looking for Dr. Song."

Instantly I rearranged my face into a more pleasant expression. Nobody can ruin a researcher's day faster than a logician who doesn't feel like getting you whatever material it is you happen to need for a given project.

"I'm Dr. Song. Pardon me, but I thought this was a private area?"

"Oh, thank the Well," he said. "I was afraid you were going to be another creepy alien."

I was so shocked I literally just stood there and blinked at him. Of all the antisocial, unrightminded things I could imagine a person saying—well, it was right up there with "Let's eat Grandma."

Then I remembered dodecapus reproductive biology and realized I was being provincial again.

What should I say? What *could* I say, given that Petrac Janes had a stranglehold on *my* resources?

He held up his hand. "Sorry, sorry. Joke. I didn't mean it that way. I just came to meet you in person and get a sense of your initial data requests."

I set down my rucksack and locked the tree case to a bulkhead to buy myself time while I contemplated his expression, which looked contrite. I was about to say, "It wasn't funny," but his embarrassed grimace stopped me. I suppose I've made a fool of myself enough times. And perhaps I am a coward as well.

And then the moment passed, because he was staring over my shoulder. If he had been any more stricken I would have looked around for a fire extinguisher, because he appeared to be contemplating trying to burst into flames. Spontaneous human combustion is bad for the air filters.

I turned around and, despite all my reservations—and the dismay on Petrac's face—found myself grinning until my cheeks ached. I was confronted by a creature with a rubbery-looking integument, roughly humanoid in shape, with three equally opposable digits on each of her two hands. She had two large compound eyes and four smaller camera-type eyes, like a mammal or an octopus.

The skin was such a glossy black it looked blue, and I happened to know that it reflected what was to me ultraviolet but to her was a pleasant midrange plum color. Depending on your cultivar of plum. Purpurple, they call it.

The tendrils on her head rippled as I approached, silver highlights showing along their undersides. The quintessential creepy alien. I put my arms around her and squeezed her tight. Her tendrils ruffled my hair and she squeezed me back.

"Hello, darling," she said. "I'm sorry if I worried you."

I kissed her cheek, tuning down the resentment I still felt at her undiscussed arrival. I certainly wasn't going to let a bigot see us fight. "I'm sorry if I worried *you*."

Then I turned around, arm still around her waist, and smiled at Petrac. Unobjectionable vengeance is the tastiest kind.

"Petrac Janes, may I introduce my wife, Salvie."

CHAPTER 8

THE KIDS WERE APPARENTLY IN SCHOOL—A VERY SMALL school, since it was just them with Yod the wheelmind acting as instructor. The cats were still in quarantine, though Salvie was going to pick them up soon. After we chased Petrac out with a list of the files I'd want first (he was blushing so furiously it showed through his melanin), Salvie and I engaged in a slightly more intimate matrimonial greeting, treasuring our brief privacy. When we came up for air, the first thing she asked was, "Have you met the Town cats yet?"

My wife is very fond of cats.

"There are Town cats?"

"Their names are Toby and Not-Toby. They're both ginger. Toby is the swirly tabby and Not-Toby is the stripy tabby."

"I can't wait." But first— "I need to give the data a quick review, though, before I do anything else. Did you know we're invited to a reception tonight?"

She nodded, frowning. "Are you going to be okay around Vickee DeVine?"

I configured the quarters into a sitting room, plopped down on the couch, and let my head fall against the backrest. "I can't believe you hitched a ride here with my ex."

Her tendrils writhed fetchingly. She tilted her head. "Technically, she hitched a ride on the same Judiciary ship that I hitched a ride on, Sun."

"Hmm. A ship she was piloting?"

"She's a qualified pilot. One of two we had aboard. She chose to work her passage rather than accrue obligation for it."

I pinched the bridge of my nose hard enough for it to sting and sighed. Sometimes I wished I were religious enough that it didn't feel like cultural appropriation to swear an oath on some human deity. I didn't need to be reminded that Vickee was good at quite literally everything.

One of our mutual friends back in school used to joke that the rest of us had to practice and study, but Vickee got real-life training montages. At the time, I hadn't had the confidence to point out that some of that apparent sprezzatura was derived from appropriating other people's work. I still regretted that failure of courage, even if it probably would have looked like envy of a rival or excoriating my ex.

"You're jealous," Salvie said.

"Envious," I corrected. I nerved myself and added, "I'm not sad you're here, but I wish you hadn't come."

"What do you mean?"

"We had an agreement!"

Salvie seemed to get bigger as she drew herself up. "An agreement that left me home alone with two human teenagers for five years at a minimum."

"This could make my career—" But then I noticed how tight her tendrils were coiled, and made myself breathe out. "You're right. I'm sorry, I shouldn't snap at you."

"I did surprise you," she reminded. "And I know how much you hate surprises. And Vickee DeVine."

Vickee's brilliance, her athleticism, her success at everything she tried—I'd once found them sexy. I'd been flattered that she chose me, and I hadn't minded her omnicompetence much. Or if I had minded,

I had tuned those feelings away, because I considered them unworthy of me.

Especially when Vickee was so nice. Especially when everybody liked her, and she told me constantly about how close she was to everybody and how many special friends she had. Especially when she dropped everything in the middle of working on her thesis in order to come hold me after my mom and sister died.

That was before things soured between us, and I saw her petty side. That was before she stole my work and claimed it as her own, and I started to wonder if she really was as good at everything as she claimed to be.

Well, history or not, we were going to have to work—not *with* each other, but *around* each other, I guessed. In proximity.

Salvie petted my hair. Not having any of her own, she finds it fascinating. Then she stood, letting her fingers trail down my neck and shoulder as she pulled away. I guessed I was at least conditionally forgiven. Resenting her presence was pointless. I should focus on the relief I felt that she and the kids and the cats were here, and safe, and I wasn't going to spend however long this assignment lasted sending them lettervids with a five-month lag.

Salvie said, "I have to get the cats."

"And the kids?"

"They can navigate on their own. It's not like you can get particularly lost in Town. You just keep walking around the Ring."

Sure, but they could get sucked out into space through a rip in the hull fabric—*stop. Just stop it, Sunya.*

"I guess I'll start going over the files, if Petrac has sent them," I said. "Once I figure out where the family tree is going."

She vanished down the ladder through the airlock. As she did, I remembered the logician making a similar getaway, and realized I never *had* found out from him how he'd managed to enter our quarters without permission from anyone resident there. I guessed Yod must have let him in. But why would Yod do that?

I hoped the wheelmind wasn't as much of a jerk as Dakhira was.

I was rapidly distracted from my crankiness by new crankiness. Because as I started to get stuck into the actual work I had come all this way to do, I discovered that some of the Baomind data I needed had already been access-locked. By Vickee DeVine.

Who was set as *away* in my feed, so I guessed I was hoofing it around the Ring, as Salvie so glibly called it, to get access.

Good thing about that agoraphobia I didn't have.

"Yod," I said, "please give me directions to Dr. DeVine's hab?"

The voice that answered was human-sounding and feminine. She said, "Go left around the Ring until you come to a turquoise airlock. That's her unit."

"Thank you, Wheelmind."

"You're welcome, Dr. Song."

Some deep breaths and a little tuning later, I jogged down the Ring toward Vickee's assigned space. The planks of the walkway were some flimsy printed material, only connected to rails at either side, and each one bounced under my feet. I felt as if I were jogging over a spindly suspension bridge across some remote crevasse—the kind that's always crumbling away underneath your feet while you swordfight orcs or something in the kind of VR game I avoid playing.

I did not like it.

The Baostar rose and set around the hab twice while I rushed, telling myself I was in a hurry because I wanted to get back to work. And not because Town was an absolute death trap, which we couldn't leave because of a pirate blockade, and where we were all going to die.

I wanted to get the confrontation with Vickee over with. If you have an unpleasant job to do, my mom always said, do it first. Then it won't ruin the rest of your day.

(She said "day." We were planet folk.)

Country Girl Makes Good in a Challenging Profession on a Galactic Scale, that's the headline of my life. Unless it turned out to be Country Girl Fails to Make a Lasting Impression in a Challenging Profession on a Galactic Scale. The scenario that haunted me.

I found Vickee's assigned module easily. The external airlock really was a strikingly bright shade of greeny-blue. Salvie was right, as usual: it's hard to get too lost when you can only run in a circle. I popped through the airlock and into a corridor, already an improvement on our ship quarters. "Which one?" I asked Yod.

Obligingly, she lit it up in my feed. First on the left.

I pushed the alert and was a little surprised when the door slid open immediately. Maybe people in Town just didn't lock their doors?

I walked into a scene of minor chaos. Vickee DeVine was clutching a red-stained scrap to her nose, while some long-tailed flying creature about the size of an Earth crow circled the room. A medium-sized person—according to his tags in my feed, a human man named Trevor Trevor—stood with one hand upraised, chirrupping. I froze right where I was.

"Shut the door!" Vickee snapped as the animal veered toward me and the space beyond.

"Yikes!" I ducked instinctively as it came at my face. I threw my hands up—and felt clawed toes snag in my hair. A sharp tug and a scratching sensation on my scalp followed, then a weight settled onto my head.

The door whispered shut behind me as Vickee hit the override.

I put a hand up and felt feathers, scales, and warm skin. I yanked my hand away again. "Does it bite? Get it off me!"

"Well," said the man, "she *could* bite. But she hasn't yet. Just hold still a second."

I felt talons being unpicked from my hair, while the critter made a complainy peeping. It shuffled around, trying to avoid the man—who was uncomfortably close to me. I held my breath and closed my eyes.

"Come on, Angie," he murmured. "Just let go. Be a good girl, you little monster."

"Is she sentient? Why is she invading my privacy?"

"She's a pet!" Trevor explained. "I'm so sorry about this!"

She apparently had four sets of claws to unravel, so it took a while. By the time Trevor had her loose, I was lightly dewed with sweat. I tuned away my trembling.

Once he pulled his hand back and I got a good look at the creature, though, I felt a little silly. She looked like a combination of a theropod, a pheasant, and a bat. Or possibly like a small, feathered dragon.

The long, scaled muzzle swept back to a feathered head crested in shades of rust and orange. The back and the bony parts of the wings wore a coat of black fluff. But the flight surfaces were membranes stretched between the forelimbs and the body. A half dozen plumes trailed from a stiff feathered tail, each one banded in russet and cream. The underside, too, was a creamy color. The black feathers on her back feet partially concealed long, gripping talons. The leading edge of the wing had two short-clawed fingers, and other fingers—elongated—formed an armature for the membranes.

Angie cocked her head at me like a chicken, rocking it from side to side as if measuring the distance for a bite.

I stepped back against the closed door. "What is she?"

"Yi qi," Trevor said. "An engineered dinosaur. My little sweetheart, except when she isn't." He sighed, and the Yi qi stopped staring at me and cheeped at him. He ruffled the feathers behind her head with one finger. She leaned into the scratch. "A pet who is developing her skills, and who has discovered that she's so much more than just a glider when the gravity is this light."

Vickee stepped into my line of sight. She lowered the bloody rag from her nose. "Sorry about the assault on your person," she said. "I should have set the latch, but I didn't expect to be attacked by a paleontological specimen."

I wouldn't have liked to be the recipient of the look she was giving Trevor. In fact, having been on the receiving end of similar looks was one reason I went out of my way to avoid Vickee.

He sniffled. "Sorry," he said. "I'm allergic to the station cats."

"Sunya Song," I told him.

"Trevor Trevor," he replied. We both already knew each other's information, but it's polite. "I'm Dr. DeVine's assistant. I'm so sorry about your hair."

Assistant. Not "student" or "colleague." Huh.

"Sunya," I replied, deciding not to insist on the "Doctor." And not solely because it would annoy Vickee if I was on a first-name basis with her assistant. "And don't worry about it. It'll be a great story to tell my kids. Also, I have cats."

"I met them on the transport ship." He wiped his nose on his sleeve.

"Nice to meet you and, er, Angie. Anyway, I came because I noticed Vickee had put a lock on some of the data I need, and it seemed easier to come down and ask to be added to the permissions than to send a formal request through Dr. Nonsense."

Vickee regarded me with a slight smile, as if to say, *Oh, is that how it's going to be?*

Shots fired.

Well, I could have ratted her out to the boss. She should keep that in mind.

Instead, she had a return volley. "It was nice meeting your family on the way here. Wife, kids, and pets, huh? Living the dream."

If I'd had any doubt that was meant to suggest that I obviously couldn't be working hard enough at my career, her next comment drove it home. "I guess it was too long for you to be away from the support of your family. Well, we all sometimes sacrifice professionalism to our emotional needs."

I smiled and wondered if she could tell how fiercely I was controlling my reactions. She still knew which buttons to push. I was a grown-up now and I could choose not to respond to her little needles. But she was looking at me intently, so I smiled a little wider.

Self-deprecatingly, I said, "Well, they seem to like me."

She put the cloth back up to her nose. "I'm getting ready for the reception right now," she said. "But I'll make sure you have access before first shift tomorrow. Is that okay? I'm"—she waved at her face—"a little behind schedule."

I had to get ready for the reception myself, so I couldn't really complain without looking unreasonable. Which of course was the point. I reached out and showed Angie my forefinger, the way you would a cat. "Are you sure she doesn't bite?"

"Hasn't yet," he affirmed. "They're engineered to be docile. Good pets."

Angie inspected the finger and rubbed her face against it. Much more polite than many parrots I have known, which are likely to take your whole hand off.

"Well," I said, disengaging from the dinosaur, "she's lovely. And I need to prepare myself. Do you know the dress code?"

"Deep-space formal," Trevor said.

I laughed. "So whatever I can scrounge up, and no high heels that might damage the decking. Don't forget about that data, please."

"And do something about that sniffling!" Vickee added to Trevor as I faded back out through the door.

Damn Vickee DeVine. I fumed all the way back to my quarters. Nosebleed or not, it wasn't going to take her more than ten minutes to get ready for the reception. Vickee knew how she liked her hair dressed, and hadn't changed the codes she used for setting it in twenty years. Comb the nanites in and go: sparkle and look fabulous.

I had never had her confidence in my own appearance or ability to make an impact, and it showed. But I *could* have spent the time before the reception studying documentation, and now she had ensured that she had another dia's head start on me. And there was nothing I could do to change that without involving our new boss—dodecaboss!—or causing a scene by calling her a liar to her face.

I sighed heavily as I came to the ladder. I was so angry that I had forgotten to be terrified of the hamster wheel. I was so angry that I was enjoying being angry, and didn't want to tune it down.

Well, I could review the data I *did* have access to, and add it to the files I'd been working on while we traveled. That would give me even more of a running start. I could assess the holes in the data and then I would know how to integrate the stuff Vickee was withholding.

I should get Salvie to pick out my outfit. For somebody who doesn't wear clothes, having that perfectly lovely insulated hide and a dearth of tender pink bits, she has an excellent and dramatic fashion sense. Unlike me: I'd wear a ratty skirt and sandals everywhere, if a skirt weren't incredibly immodest in space.

She'd be back soon enough, I figured. Then I decided it wouldn't be pushy to check, and remind her about the reception.

Where are you folks? I asked Salvie through the feed.

We're in the hub lounge. Kids and cats are with me. I figured you could use some time unbothered.

That made me feel terminally ungenerous for worrying about space to work, and privacy. I also realized that while I had an idea *where* the hub lounge was—it was in the name—I had no idea how to get there. But that was easily solved: I didn't even have to bother Yod. Just call up a map when it was time to go collect them. *Love you,* I said, and told Salvie I needed fashion advice . . . and about my encounter with Vickee.

Well, get to work. Time's a-wasting.

Yeah, and Vickee was the one wasting it. But I bit my lip, because Salvie had heard my stories but had probably still only seen the kind, helpful, playful public Victorya DeVine. People usually looked at me like I was unrightminded when I pointed out her bad behavior.

I would dig into what I had, even if it was only the background information. At the very least, that could give me the framework to understand the rest of it.

I won't say all archinformists work in patterns or frameworks, but I certainly do. It's like sorting a jigsaw puzzle into piles by shape and color—building the edges, and then following the most obvious traces inward until you can find where they connect. Except there's no reference picture, and there's no edges. You have to make your own frame and decide where to cut, and hope you haven't cut off the wrong thing.

I spent fifteen minutes organizing my information needs by priority. The data Vickee had arrogated was exactly what I most needed—early files that were probably the key to the whole shebang. Salvie's fashion choices pinged into my feed just as I finished. I loaded the clothes and accessory files into the printer. Three minutes later, I was gratefully clad in a flowing lamé jumpsuit and sandals, my hair upswept and shimmering with holocombs.

I followed the map to the hub lounge.

It was in-ring, which involved climbing a ladder through yet another terrifying hamster tube until I got light enough to float the remaining distance. I made myself look around at another stunning view of space and Town and its paltry guardian fleet of ships. A half dozen or so tesserae zoomed in formation between me and the Baostar, their surfaces rippling with light. I thought of flocking birds and schooling fish.

First I entered Ops, the command module, which was empty of

meatforms, though Yod flashed her presence lights companionably as I passed. The next compartment was the hub. I floated in, unsurprised to find Salvie drifting on a tether, her nose in her tablet. She would keep reading if she were on fire.

"Mom, duck!"

That was our son Stavan's voice. After thirteen ans I knew my own kid well enough not to pause to assess the situation. I threw my hands in front of my face and hunched like a nearsighted fetus. The sudden motion snapped me into a backward somersault.

Something warm and resilient hit my legs, reversing my rotation, and stuck there. Fabric shredded. I threw my body wide open to slow my rotation—and went headfirst into a carpeted bulkhead. My hands flew to my face as I rebounded, causing my rotation to accelerate. The weight attached to my legs yowled in distress. I managed to get my elbows behind me in time to fend off a matching impact on the back of my skull.

At least the nanites would fix my hairstyle, and the printed jumpsuit would mend itself.

This time I managed to grab the safety webbing and keep myself from flopping back in the other direction like a fish drowning in air. I noticed a number of things: my head hurt, my elbows hurt, and the weight on my calves was not just sticky. It was pointy.

Also, our daughter Luna was crooning, "Stavaaaaaaaaan, you are in sooo much trouublllle."

Careful not to send myself flying across the hub, I reached down and disentangled a traumatized gray cat from my trousers. The cat—one Zig by name—looked at me with green-specked gold eyes and began to purr. His tuxedo brother (Zag, of course; this is what happens when you let kids name pets) stared at me from a position of ease beside the food printer.

Stavan hovered over me, a laser pointer still in his hand. "Mom? Are you okay? I'm so sorry, Mom—"

"You thought it would be fun to sail the cat around the hub in zero g."

His lips vanished into a line. "Yes."

"I wish," I said, as calmly as I could manage, "that you would consider the consequences of your actions, kiddo. You're thirteen. Somebody could have been hurt." I thought I was doing a good job keeping my temper, given that it was my second small animal attack of the dia.

"I didn't mean it."

"I know you didn't." Gingerly, I began to right myself. I set the cat near the bulkhead I'd bounced off. Zig hooked his claws into the carpet, his dignity ruffled.

The hub had a better view and more access to visuals than our quarters. The exterior bulkheads were cylindrical and filled the entire circumference of the ship this used to be, before it became a hab component. And right now, they showed a flawless projection of the space all around us.

Salvie had Yod piping the coms to us, which meant I could hear the chatter of the ships moving around the system. The pirates were still out there, though nobody knew exactly where. It was a bit of a stalemate: They couldn't come too far in-system, or we would ruin their lives. We couldn't get too far out, or they would blow us up.

The proverbial standoff. And if we tried to leave . . .

Maybe they meant to keep us here until the Baostar settled the matter by going nova.

I clipped my harness into an attachment point beside my wife, who had finally glanced up from her tablet. She smirked at me, which looked odd on her facial architecture. She really wasn't designed for it, but she copies human expressions sometimes to make fun of me.

"Am I bleeding?" I touched my forehead.

She put her fingers over mine, claws retracted politely. "No lasting damage, I think."

I found myself staring into her face. The horizontal bars of the pupils in her simple eyes tightened at the center as she stared back. I touched her arm, feeling guilty about how ungenerous I had been regarding her unexpected appearance. It's not Salvie's fault I hate surprises.

"Thank you for coming with me, Salvie."

"Somebody has to make sure you can print a matching pair of socks." She cupped one hand against my cheek. The warmth of her higher body temperature was soothing. "Besides, if I left you alone for two or three ans, you'd forget I existed."

"Never," I answered, leaning into her hand.

"Ew, gross," our daughter said.

I looked over. She hadn't even raised her eyes from her tablet.

Some species can sense electromagnetism or use sonar to see your internal organs. Adolescent humans have a preternatural sense about when their parents are being embarrassing.

I was formulating some response that, in my ideal world, would be both cutting and supportive of Luna's emerging identity as an autonomous adult human . . . when Stavan came sailing over and threw his arms around me, too. When we broke apart, he asked, "Forgiven?"

"Always." I ruffled his hair. "How was the trip over?"

"Long," he said. "Interesting! The shipmind is so big and smart. I love her. And I love the wheelmind, though we just met. How do you get to work with AIs?"

"I don't know," I said, feeling a little dizzied that he had generated a whole new enthusiasm since last we talked. "You could talk to Yod about that—"

A sudden change of momentum and vector slewed me sideways into the padded bulkhead and made me glad I'd snapped my harness in.

"Ooof!" I said eloquently.

Salvie lost her grip on her slate. It went thataway, but in the next moment she made up for it by grabbing black-and-white tuxedo Zag as he went sailing past and tucking him into her arms. Zig still had his claws in the carpeting, and as a now-experienced space cat he was hunkered down and hanging in there. He always did catch on faster than his brother.

"What was that?" I yelped.

"Sorry," Yod said over the speakers. "The Freeporters have started throwing rocks down the gravity well. It'll miss us now."

"We're safe?" Salvie asked.

The kids were looking up, wide-eyed and silent.

Yod said, "Barring unforeseen circumstances. I'm impressed that they managed to find any debris out there, honestly. This system is mostly swept clean."

"Maybe they brought it with them," said Luna.

"I didn't see this coming," I admitted, looking at Salvie. Then I turned back to my offspring. "Luna, aren't you going to give me a hug? It's been about fifty million light-years since I saw you."

"Pssh," said Stavan in his best *parents, can't take them anywhere* tone. "Fifty *thousand* at the most, Mom." But he unhooked and backed off. Luna sailed gently toward me, still trying to look cool.

I hugged her heartily, then hugged Stavan again, and turned them both loose.

"How do I look?" I asked Salvie. I knew better than to ask the kids, and when Luna tried to volunteer an opinion, I held up a finger to stop her.

"That's rude," Luna said, mocking my intonations.

"You're fifteen," I said. "You can have better manners than that."

"I'm sixteen," she corrected. "I had a birthday while we were in space."

We were still in space, but I decided the better part of valor was shutting up. "Happy birthday, kiddo. There's a message waiting for you back on Rubric, you know." She grunted and went back to her screen.

Salvie eyed me critically with all six eyes. "Not bad. If I do say so myself. But you need some jewelry."

"Ew," said Stavan.

I ignored my son and kissed my wife. Right between the tendrils. "Come on. Let's get everybody resettled in our quarters, and then you and I can go to the party."

I should have taken Petrac up on his offer of food. Self-defeating, allowing my irritation to get the better of me like that. Now I was lightheaded enough that trying to tune it out was a lost cause, and hunger was making me irritable. Which was not ideal when my wife was fussing with my clothes. *And* choosing accessories for a working party from a travel trunk and the limited printing template resources of a makeshift hab marooned at the north end of a southbound galaxy.

I could at least tune down my irritability. But between being starving and dreading another encounter with Vickee, I was grumpy and out of sorts enough that despite my valiant attempts to adjust my brain chemistry to something approximating pleasant weather, I just wanted to hit something with a stick. Or curl up and cry. Or both, simultaneously or in either order.

Salvie, of course, noticed. She was fussing with the drapes on the jumpsuit, fiddling with how they fell under my throat and arranging them to show off my wedding jewelry, a dazzling dark green and red teardrop-shaped opal pendant from her homeworld. She, in turn, wore a pair of diamond studs from Earth in one eartip.

She said, "You shouldn't let her get under your skin."

"Tell me how to stop it! She pushes buttons I didn't even know I had."

She poked me with a fingertip. "There's one."

"Hah." But my tension eased.

The kids, who were very happy to be left alone to entertain themselves instead of being dragged to a stultifying adult event, sprawled on broad, deeply padded shelves along one bulkhead. The living-room setup Salvie and I had used was apparently inadequate to adolescent lounging needs.

The cats piled on top of the kids. The kids started arguing over whether to watch *CenTauri Dreams* or *Binary* or *Sludge*.

"Wait until we're gone," said Salvie.

They whined, and she rolled her simple eyes at them. They could have each watched their own feeds, but it was more fun to do it together. And, I guessed, to argue.

As the kids slowly vanished into the cushions, I tried not to think about quicksand and tar pits. I tried not to think about leaving them alone in this wretched soap-bubble of a hab, and how literally everything out here from pirates to the void wanted to kill them.

The kids printed a pizza. Despite my dubiousness about space food and the general unappetizing aspects of being in a tiny, slightly stale, somewhat aromatic hab, it smelled so good I almost cried. I decided that saving myself for potentially terrible party snacks was sheer foolishness, and ate two pieces while leaning forward over a plate so the sauce wouldn't drip on my outfit.

It tasted slightly muffled, like everything in space, though I'd noticed the effect wasn't as bad when we were under spin or acceleration. But it was still delicious, and when was the last time I ate anything? And what space cheese lacks in nuance and long-aged flavor, it makes up in that it doesn't care if you are lactose intolerant, never having been so much as introduced to a dairy animal.

Thinking about food and cheese and family made me so dizzy with grief that I had to clench my jaw to keep myself from saying, out loud, *No. No, this isn't okay*.

It was okay. Everything that was happening right at this moment was fine. What wasn't fine was the almost physical memory of my mom's hand on my back, her lyrical voice teasing me about my love for pizza.

My mother's name was Madhumati Song. My sister was named Hely.

It's the strangest thing, loss. Grief. Once the first savage flush of misery is over you can go weeks without even thinking of the person. And then something frivolous and insignificant happens and it hits you with as much pain as if it were happening right now, all over again.

Or the denial comes back, and you can't believe it happened at all. And that's almost worse, because you have to make yourself once more believe that you will never see that person again—

I tuned fast so I didn't start sobbing and ruin the makeup Salvie had fussed over. And upset the kids. I'd pay for it later: if you didn't deal with your feelings now, you always had to deal with them later. But *later* was better than being late or showing up swollen-faced to a party that was theoretically in my honor, and at which I would need to fence with my rival for resources while schmoozing my tentacular boss.

I carried the plate with the last two bites of pizza on it over to the recycler. In my distraction, I'd let it get cold, and cold printed pizza doesn't have a lot to recommend it. Anyway, my appetite had evaporated.

The food and plate disassembled with a snap of ozone scent that did nothing to reassure me about the seals. I put one hand on the bulkhead, trying to look nonchalant, but it felt as if a ripple swept through the deck under my feet. I don't think it did, actually—I was looking, and I didn't see it deform. A chill settled into my belly.

I opened the cabinet beside the airlock. The anxiety eased a little as I saw that we had adequate emergency supplies for everyone. I took out four hardsuit actuators and two pet safety collars. I tucked one actuator down the cleavage of my jumpsuit—those drapes went pretty low—and handed the next to Salvie. "Pretend it's jewelry."

"Mom," Luna said. "Are you belling us? Like cats?"

I stared her down. "There're pirates out there. Throwing asteroids at us. Put it on. Against your skin, and leave it there even when you shower."

"They pinch," she whined, but she put it under her collarbone.

Stavan grinned when I handed him his. "Spaceman Stav!"

"Just wear it." But I winked.

Zig didn't mind the collar. Zag tried to scratch his off, but they're designed to thwart even the most dexterous paws. He eventually got sick of the kids laughing at him as he hopped in circles on three legs and settled down with his back to them to wash himself with elaborate, offended dignity.

"Don't forget to feed the cats," I told the kids—then felt like the space all around me shifted again. Not as savagely as when Yod had dodged the rock, but I was sure I wasn't imagining it. This time I couldn't stop myself. "Did you feel that?"

Salvie turned her head from side to side as if checking her balance. "No?"

Her motion drew my attention to the viewport behind her head. Through it, I could see a section of spoke cable and Town's lumpy curve. And something—like a flitting shadow—passing across the pane.

"Hey, Salvie," I said, "come eyeball this."

"That's insensitive to people without eyeballs," yelled our daughter from across the room. She was sunk so deep into memory foam that all I could see was the tip of her nose and her eyelashes, and I pretended not to hear.

Salvie just got up and came over.

"Look out the window." I turned her toward it with a hand on her shoulder. "See anything weird?"

"A hab built out of tinkertoys?" Her compound eyes sparkled as she moved her head around. "No, not weird exactly. At least, not anything that ought not to be there."

The shadow glided past again, like a floater in my vision. "You didn't see that?"

"Might be outside my visual range?" she answered, rippling her tendrils in a shrug. "What did you see?"

"I don't know," I answered. "Looked like . . . you know how when you look into colored fluid, and a ripple passes through it so the stuff at the bottom is harder to see?"

Luna blew her hair out of her eyes. Stavan was distracting Zag from the collar with a fishing lure toy. I suddenly realized what time it was.

"We need to hurry! If we're late, Vickee will convince Dr. Nonsense that I don't deserve access to the data—"

"Two people can work on the same data," Salvie said soothingly. "They can't keep it from you."

I wanted to ask, *But how do you know?* But she waved her tendrils at me and touched my cheek, and I admit I instantly felt better.

"Kids, eat a vegetable before you have dessert," I told them, pausing in the airlock.

"Printed pizza is just as healthy as printed vegetables," Luna sassed.

"Now you have to eat two vegetables," Salvie said.

"Momma!"

"Listen to your mother," I said, and cycled the airlock.

CHAPTER 9

DESPITE ITS UNAPPEALING NAME, THE GARDEN POD was not what I had been dreading. I'd been "looking forward" to rows of hydroponic tanks and sweltering humidity that would limpen my hair and render my jumpsuit saggy.

What I found was a blessed contradiction of expectations. The Garden Pod was, well, a garden. It had some tanks, but all in all it would be right at home amid the conservatories and balanced ecosystems of Rubric. Sudden homesickness came over me, so intense my chest ached. I wanted to walk among the trees, listen to the neural nets of the forest, immerse myself in the worldmind and just *be*.

People call Rubric a garden planet, but that just shows they don't know anything about it. It's an *integrated* planet, where people live as part of the natural world. Which is, of course, what we are: the idea that we—and by *we* I mean sapient beings—are somehow separate and distinct from the rest of nature is a sophipathology that has been remarkably resistant to correction, even in the modern Synarche.

So many people are born someplace that isn't right for them, and need to find their home. I always knew I was in the right place and never wanted to leave. So, of course, here I am.

Maybe if Rubric weren't so successful at equitable self-governance, my mother wouldn't have been drafted to serve on the Synarche's governing council, and she and my sister would still be alive.

The path under our feet was springy. Although the pavers were printed to look like stone, they were set in a gelatinous growth medium. Moss grew between them and up the surfaces of the bulkheads, behind intertwining bean, squash, and tomato vines. The beds were irregularly shaped, organic and curvaceous. They burgeoned with flowers and vegetables: the outrageous blooms of okra, the bronzy fronds of fennel. Lotus filled the tanks with a tangle of stems and a riot of peach and yellow blossoms. It gave the effect of a lush, informal, aromatic bouquet.

I resisted the urge to reach out and grab a tomato, in case this was a science experiment. I almost felt a disapproving presence glowering behind me at the thought.

This was a big space, for a hab, and not quite full of people. As we approached them, I leaned over to Salvie. "Are you worried about leaving the kids?"

She patted my elbow, playing the experienced spacer to my wide-eyed neophyte. "Yod will take care of them. It's like having a house that will babysit. Being inside a wheelmind-run hab is statistically safer than anyplace planetside."

This is what you get when you marry a statistician. Even one whose primary career is in music.

I knew she was correct. And Salvie didn't need me getting my anxiety all over her while she was trying to enjoy a party. So I bit my tongue on *Assuming nothing happens to the hab, you mean.*

And for that, I deserve a medal. A medal I would have had to give back after thirty seconds if I hadn't been able to tune down my own neurotic compulsions.

I've got more than enough of those to consider the ability to tackle them one at a time invaluable. I don't know how anybody managed to get anything productive done before modern medicine. It must have been gritted teeth and white knuckles 90 percent of the time.

Actually, my reading of historical documents supports this interpretation. It seems to have been widely recognized along the way, also. As a sage of twentieth-century Western Earth put it, "Look at those cavemen go."

The current focus of my neurotic compulsions turned and smiled sweetly at our approach. Vickee was on the job.

With Salvie's hand on my back, I had the courage to walk over. And the greater courage to do it smiling. I took big strides to make the jumpsuit swirl around my ankles. It had a subtle holographic shimmer under the full-spectrum lights. My sandals sparkled with reflected pinpricks scattered from the fabric.

Dr. Nonsense had draped itself over the edge of a lotus tank at waist height, holding a cocktail skewer of printed crustaceans curled aloft. Its color had relaxed to mottled gold and brown, translucent enough that I could make out the pulse of a heart at the base of each of its arms. It was wearing its respirator but no envelope, so I guessed the air in the conservatory was moist enough to keep its skin from peeling.

It was, indeed, wearing a ruffled frock. White, made diaphanous by water.

It's a grown mollusk, Salvie sent via her fox. *I'm sure it can make good decisions.*

I guess Dr. Nonsense wasn't the only one around here who was slightly transparent.

It managed to look louche and debonair: a twelve-limbed odalisque. Vickee looked smug. Possibly because she was smirking.

I had almost reached them before I realized that Vickee's assistant was standing right behind her, leaning against a towering herb planter. Trevor looked greenish in the humidity and warmth. I felt grateful that I wasn't the only one.

He had to put up with a *lot* more Vickee than I did. And my hairstyle and outfit were holding up so far. More points to Salvie. Remember, if you look good after a long day of work, thank a nanite when you put 'em back in their tube.

Vickee was cool and structured in a white blouse and slim black trousers. A necklace of black and white stones winked at her throat. Still smiling as if she were enjoying herself, she said, "Dear Sun. How good to see you again. And Salvie, you seem to have settled in."

Salvie said something polite. I bared my teeth. It could pass for a smile. No acknowledgment from Vickee that she had no right to call me Sun. She'd never deserved the privilege, but I hadn't known any better for a while.

"Poor Trevor," I said. "Feeling spacesick?"

"I seem to be allergic to something," he said bravely, waving around the pod. "At least between the neti pot and some antihistamines, I'm not sniffling anymore. How are you adjusting to Town?"

I'd hate to be him, I decided. Trying to balance politeness to a colleague and obligation to a prickly boss.

Before I could answer, Vickee leaned across the intervening space, looked me right in the eye, and said, "What if we shared resources?"

I'd like to think I didn't gape in astonishment, but I'd be fooling myself. I tuned fast and hard, tempering my emotional response. I said, "I beg your pardon?" because *What the fuck is wrong with you* is generally considered impolite.

"I was on pilot rotation on the trip out," she said. "I didn't have nearly as much time to prep parsers and algorithms as you must have, as a passenger."

Cargo, Dakhira had called me.

"I hardly think—"

"And of course if we worked together we would share credit. You'd be the lead author."

I could feel the attention of everyone in the group on me. On the surface, it was a generous offer. The renowned Victorya DeVine offering to share her cachet with me, a lowly middle-of-the-pack academic from a backwater planet. But *fool me once*, as they say.

I had no intention of giving Vickee a second bite at the apple that was my life's work.

Dr. Nonsense said, *It's nice to see a gesture of commensalism*, and it was fortunate that I wasn't eating anything because I nearly choked. I felt as if everyone was staring at me, and I couldn't muster a single polite thing to say.

Fortunately, my wife is better at diplomacy. "Vickee," she said, "have you come up with any theories on exactly why the Koregoi built such a stunning feat of engineering all the way out here on the galactic rim?"

I swallowed in relief. While Salvie was distracting Vickee, I could step a little aside, open up a space, and concentrate on Trevor and Dr. Nonsense.

While we chatted, I saw about some refreshments for myself. The pizza made a little cushion in my stomach, but not enough after several days of erratic meal schedules. I was reaching out to the wheelmind when I realized—just in time, or months too late—that there wouldn't be any coffee on this station, with its mixed population of humans and systers.

The suffering. The mortal suffering.

Maybe I could sneak over to Dakhira for my fix, and we could pretend we didn't mutually loathe each other.

I ordered a gin and tonic and a plate of canapés, and used my fox to get the alertness I would have preferred to obtain from caffeine. I feel like the natural alkaloids are gentler than the synthetic ones—so many supporting compounds involved in the plant—but sometimes you have to make a commitment, even when you don't want to. And I am a vast disappointment to my ancestors and do not like tea.

A drone—one of the hab's so-called Hands—brought my plate over. I took it with gratitude.

I barely had my *own* hands on the snacks and had internalized a blissful sip of my beverage when Vickee separated herself from Salvie and wandered away. I watched her go, feeling a sense of relief that this was all the interaction required of me. And a sense of apprehension as to what might come next, and whether there was any chance of getting shared access to the documents I needed without turning it into a lawsuit or getting Dr. Nonsense involved.

I knew I wasn't responding rationally to Vickee's presence. Or to her obvious warmth and friendliness toward my wife. Or my wife's friendliness toward her, for that matter.

They'd had plenty of time for Vickee to sink her claws in, and that was what I was afraid of. It wasn't jealousy or possessiveness. I only felt protective, because I knew who Vickee was and how she treated people. How she'd treated me.

Maybe my antipathy was rational after all. Wanting somebody you knew was dangerous kept far away from people you cared about was hardly a pathology.

"Dr. Song," said Trevor, "are you feeling all right?"

I blinked at him three times before I managed to dredge up the memory of what he'd said and formulate an answer. "Jet-lagged," I said. "Space-lagged? I need to sleep for a while and adjust to the local circadian rhythm. Right now I'm awake on synthetic neurotransmitters and grim determination."

You should grow a few more brains, said Dr. Nonsense. *Then they can take turns sleeping.*

It had turned a friendly peach color with coral accents, and I deduced it was teasing. Uncomfortably, I thought of the Chives, and my perhaps prurient musings on how they managed it.

I changed the subject. "I've met Petrac so far," I said, spotting him across the room. "The research logician. Who else should I get to know?"

Nonsense pointed with its skewer, one synthetic prawn lighter than when I arrived. It seemed to be indicating a tall, curvy human with cropped hair, tailored trousers, and a complexion so dark as to be glossy. They were talking to a green-haired, olive-skinned, narrow-framed male human in tall boots and coveralls. Both stood in front of a tall black-glass mirror that reflected their laughing faces.

Beside them was a small bipedal syster about a meter tall, with brindled fawn and gray fur and mobile ears. She wore flowing pantaloons and nothing else, and had her hands stuffed in the slash pockets, blunt-clawed thumbs hooked over the edges. She didn't seem to be exactly participating in the conversation so much as hanging out in its general vicinity, because she was staring at the floor—but since her ears were pointed at the humans, I could tell she was listening.

Their senso tags illuminated as Nonsense said their names.

That one is Goodlaw Xhelsea. They just arrived on the Interceptor. The one in the coveralls is Haran Karmer. He's our environmental systems engineer. The K'taxi is named Fritha; she's our musicologist.

That made sense: of course the expedition would need a musicologist.

"Oh," said Salvie. "I should make her acquaintance. We can talk shop."

"My wife is a musician," I told Trevor and Dr. Nonsense.

Trevor smiled in that way that sick people do when they would rather be lying down. Dr. Nonsense rippled violet and green acknowledgment.

They're talking with the unit we call Kell.

"Unit?"

But just as I said it, the mirror moved. And I realized that it wasn't a mirror. Or not *just* a mirror, but also one of the Baomind tesserae. It was about two meters in diameter and it flashed with all the verdant, reflected colors of the Garden Pod as it turned, seeming to follow the conversation.

Apparently the Baomind had sent an envoy to the welcome party.

CHAPTER 10

I WASN'T SURE IF IT WAS POLITE TO EAT IN FRONT OF A TES-sera, so I finished my canapés quickly and dropped the plate into a slot for recycling. Then I excused myself from Dr. Nonsense, Salvie, and Trevor. Farther along, Vickee was chatting with the odious Petrac. Well, it is a boon to minimize the suffering of others, so they were probably repairing their karma as I watched.

A half dozen other folks stood around in various clusters—mostly humans and a few systers, including a shiny photosynthetic Ceeharen whose lack of any vertebrate facial features or sensory organs was a little disconcerting alongside the superficially humanoid body plan.

I stepped across another of those denser-seeming color ripples, which I'd decided might have something to do with the massive gravity of the Baostar and the way the Baomind manipulated it, since nobody else seemed concerned about them. Kell's companions looked toward me as I approached.

My immediate goal had become getting a closer look at Kell. Nonsense had said the other three were talking with it. Were they all actually communicating? In complicated concepts?

Or just smiling and nodding in a friendly fashion?

Well, I guess it wasn't likely that the tessera could smile and nod.

Either way, it wouldn't hurt to introduce myself to Environmental

Services and the Goodlaw. And the musicologist. As much as I hated it, with Vickee here my job was going to involve networking and politics. Salvie was my musical ace in the hole, since she'd invited herself along. But it wouldn't hurt to try to charm the *official* research team specialist, since her expertise was likely to be more useful in terms of linguistics than Salvie's more practical knowledge. Or the ayatanas cluttering up my head.

I loathed the anxious urge to approach these new acquaintances not in a spirit of curiosity and potential friendship, but as if courting allies. I wondered what Vickee might have said already to poison them against me.

Hello, trauma, Salvie whispered inside my head.

Is it that obvious?

Only to somebody who has extensively studied the stress postures of human shoulders.

I swallowed a snort of laughter and instantly felt better. It turns out I married pretty well.

Salvie's remark gave me the perspective I needed to regulate my emotions. By the time I reached the others and Dr. Nonsense was reaching out to introduce me, I felt significantly better.

"Hi," I said. "I'm Sunya Song. Pleased to meet you."

The two humans stepped apart to open the conversational triangle. Kell wobbled. For a moment I thought it would fall. Adrenaline made me buoyant and concentrated. I squeaked, jumped back, and managed not to step on the toddler-sized musicologist. That was the only bright spot in my complete humiliation, when all that happened was Kell shifting position to face me. Not that it had a face, but its reflective surface seemed to be the next best thing.

The best part was that I could see myself mirrored in Kell's flawless finish: hands raised, open-mouthed in startled fear.

"Yikes," I said.

The Goodlaw—Xhelsea—laughed at me. Not meanly, I thought. The engineer—Haran—put a hand on my elbow to steady me and winked. "It's okay," he said. "Everybody's a little scared of their own reflection."

I rolled my eyes at him. I was pretty sure the quivering thing that Fritha's whiskers were doing was laughter.

Goodlaw Xhelsea said, "It can surf gravity waves. It probably won't fall on you unless it intends to."

That also could have seemed biting, but the tone in their voice took the edge off it. I felt better until I noticed Vickee smirking over my shoulder in the reflection. With vast self-control, I made my gaze skip over hers as if I hadn't noticed. Maybe that was the presence I'd felt before.

"Mortified," I said, making a joke of it. "It was a . . . reflex."

"I'm Haran," the engineer said. "You should *reflect* on it."

I mimed pain.

"Fritha," said Fritha.

"Goodlaw Xhelsea," the Goodlaw said. "And of course, this is Kell."

The tessera sparkled at me. I'm not sure how else to describe it. A shimmer of music reached me through my feed, and for a moment that flawless surface ceased to reflect. It seemed bottomless and full of stars, twinkling in time to the music.

Stars don't twinkle in space. That's a phenomenon caused by atmosphere. So how would an artificial intelligence created in a system with no planets know about twinkling?

I guess gravity lensing could do it also. Maybe? I'm *definitely* not a physicist.

"Pleased to meet you," I said, aware that everyone was looking at me. "I'm Sunya Song."

Another silent trill of music answered.

I looked from Haran to Xhelsea and back again. "How do you talk to them?"

"Just talk," Haran said. "Or send. You'll get the hang of it."

"Does it understand?"

"Probably better than we understand it," said another voice from behind me. Footsteps introduced a tall woman with dark olive skin and wavy, silver-shot hair; senso tagged her as Willow, working in general maintenance and engineering. "Yod has some translation protocols in place, but there are a lot of concepts and grammatical structures that . . . well, we're coming in with very different contexts. I'm Willow."

She looked enough like a distant family member to make me a little homesick. It's a big galaxy, but every so often you run across a familiar phenotype in an unexpected place.

"Sunya," I said. "Since I'm not a billion-year-old distributed intelligence, I have to grant you that one."

Fritha's whisker thing was *definitely* laughter.

Willow laughed, too. People in space can't talk about the weather; we have to make other neutral noises to identify ourselves as pleasant and nonthreatening.

I said, "My fox tells me both you and Haran here are head of engineering? How does that work?"

"Oh," Willow said with a dazzling smile, "he's environmental. Haran does minor stuff like food and oxygen and water, you know. I'm everything else."

"So if my door doesn't iris properly, I call you?"

Willow grew a few extra smile lines around lips and eyes. "If your door is irising at all, you've got a real problem. Everything we can make mechanical on this tub *is* mechanical, so you can fix it with a screwdriver when it breaks. *And* you can fix almost all of it from the inside. Because the alternative is a pain in the ass."

"And what does Kell do?" I gestured at it with my thumb.

It chimed, seeming to laugh. I felt the rill of music as a tickle in my fox. I realized that I'd left the parser I'd written on Dakhira running, and it had identified this new input as part of its assigned dataset and was assimilating. Pattern-matching it to what it already had.

Well, I guessed I would just leave that running for the duration of the mission.

"Oh, it helps out," Haran said fondly. "I'm not really sure if it's an emissary or a curious individual. But it seems to like us."

"Are you sure it's always the same one?" I asked.

Haran shrugged. "Watch the edges. They are sharp enough to cut you in half."

"If you had that Koregoi blood tech, you could just think at it and find out," said the Goodlaw. "Apparently that's the best way to communicate with them."

I eyed the Judiciary officer suspiciously. "Is this entrapment? Isn't that stuff a war crime?"

I knew the Freeporters used it—a nanoscale engineered parasite harvested from the bodies of Ativahikas. I also knew they murdered the vast, spacefaring organisms to get it.

"Maybe not in the future," said Haran. "I hear Judiciary is trying to derive an ethical version from symbiotes harvested from affected humans."

I wondered if that would mean that only my species would have access to the red tech at first, if they succeeded. I wondered how that would affect the balance of power and interspecies politics in the Synarche. Even if it were more widespread, it'd be a destabilizing influence for sure.

Just like Kell here, the red tech allowed the people it infected to sense gravity waves—and manipulate them. There was artificial gravity going in at certain sensitive installations in the Core, I'd heard. Real artificial gravity, not spin g.

I looked at the Goodlaw. "Do all the Freeporters have it?"

They shook their head. "Of course, we don't know as much as we'd like to about Freeporter culture—"

"Come on," Haran teased. "Judiciary *has* to have agents embedded out there."

"*Out there* is farther in than out here." Xhelsea grinned. They had very white teeth and plush plum-colored lips, and I abruptly felt so disloyal to Salvie just for looking that I wanted to step away. They continued, "Even if we did, how often could they get a message out?"

I thought about the size of space. However big I could make myself believe it was, it was bigger than that by orders of magnitude. Even an enhanced human brain struggled with scale so enormous. Even AIs struggled. Radio wouldn't work because of the distances involved. Tuned lasers would take too long, and both would be too obvious. You could use white-capable drones, but you'd have to keep them from being found, and destroyed or captured on their way out of the system.

"Hmm." I nodded.

Kell issued a ripple of music in an alien key. I could, I thought, get a sense of tone and meaning from it, and between my parser and Yod's translation support, I thought it was expressing interest and agreement.

Unless I was anthropomorphizing.

"But you haven't answered Dr. Song's question," Haran prodded the Goodlaw.

"Sunya, please," I said. I didn't mention that the Goodlaw had been about to, until he interrupted.

The Goodlaw humphed. "As best we can determine, it's an intensely hierarchal society. Or system, rather: I'm not sure it's interdependent enough to be a society by our terms. Only the people at the very top and their most trusted agents are issued the symbiote. And the agents usually have some kind of failsafe wired into them."

"Failsafe?" I asked. "I thought Freeporters were strenuously opposed to foxes and rightminding."

"They are," the Goodlaw said. "But they definitely go in for extortion."

I made a questioning noise.

Xhelsea's smile twisted toward irony. "People tend to do what you want when you've wired a remote-controlled bomb into their intestines."

I yelped.

People turned to look at me. Over my shoulder, Vickee smirked harder. I shook my head in disgust . . . then yelped again as something soft brushed my ankles.

It wasn't a hungry space monster, though. It was an unusually intensely colored orange cat.

I checked for swirls and decided this must be Toby. He blinked at me with vivid eyes, so I squatted down to pet him. He was a purrer, a head-butter, and a drooler. And just the distraction I needed from the ruthless pirates currently blockading the jury-rigged hab my whole family was huddled on. And their means of enforcing obedience.

Toby was wearing a safety collar, so I felt even better for having insisted on equipping Zig and Zag and the kids.

I snuck a glance at Salvie—I am horribly anxious at parties—and noticed she was now talking to that bigoted logistics guy, Petrac. I hoped he wasn't saying anything awful to her. I tried to catch one of her compound eyes and wasn't sure I'd managed until I noticed the faint flicker of her tendrils toward me. I sent her affection and sympathy. She replied with amused resignation. Just looking at her made me feel warm.

Unexpectedly, Kell chimed in with another rill of music, this one seeming supportive. My reflected expression in its side looked startled again.

"As near as we can tell," Haran said dryly, "they can pick up any broadcast in the feed, though nobody's quite sure yet if they can decode encryption or how much of what's being said they understand."

"Huh." The height of conversational eloquence, that's me.

I was just about to ask Xhelsea another question about pirates and blockades and the long odds of us being safe here when Vickee moved toward the center of the room. Her presence prickled in my feed as she suggested that everyone who consumed such things procure refreshment for a toast.

My opinion must have shown, because the Goodlaw lowered their voice and said, "You don't think much of Dr. DeVine?"

"We were in school together," I said, which was true as far as it went.

I still had half a gin and tonic in my hand. Wishing it were full, I turned to face Vickee as she reached the center of the room.

Vickee DeVine turned around the room, raising her own glass (white wine) and waiting for silence. "Hey, everybody! The guest of honor has arrived!"

With a flourish, she indicated me.

I looked at Salvie. *Is she drunk?*

Salvie made a noncommittal gesture with her tendrils. Trevor, leaning against the planter beside her, looked like he was in a cold sweat and his head was pounding.

I sympathized.

I saw what Vickee was doing. Putting herself on the inside of the group, and positioning me as an Honored Guest. An outsider. Not part of the team.

I was proven right when she tipped her glass toward me and said, "To my esteemed colleague, Dr. Sunyata Song!"

It's tacky to toast yourself, so I couldn't even drink as all around me party clothes rustled and glasses went to lips. I checked to make sure my fox wasn't sending and thought, fiercely, how much I would like to see Vickee sliding down a gravity well toward an event horizon. I might even enjoy being the one to give her a little push.

Eventually everyone turned away from my blazing face, and I had a moment to drain the dregs of my gin. I was glad Vickee hadn't decided to push me to make a speech. I might actually have knifed somebody. Or troweled them: that seemed a more likely weapon to find lying around the Garden Pod.

I looked back at Xhelsea, Haran, Fritha, and Kell. I was starting to feel comfortable with them, and if I'd had my choice I would have spent the rest of the party hiding behind an enormous amaranth quizzing them about pirates and the Baomind. But as Vickee had just reminded me, I was here to do a job and I probably ought to be doing it. And part of that job was not letting her paint me into a corner.

If I wanted to think this hard about politics, I would have stayed in academia.

I pulled up my metaphorical trousers and made my excuses. "Well, I've just been reminded that I had better circulate. It was a real pleasure meeting all four of you. . . ."

As I was turning toward the back of the pod, the path under my feet bounced with a heavy thud. I whirled—it was a good thing my drink was down to the ice cubes and plants don't mind a little extra water—but not in time to see Trevor fall. He convulsed feebly, lying full length on the ground. His hands slapped against his eyes as if he had been overcome by a sudden blinding headache.

Salvie crouched beside him. I felt a hand on my shoulder as the Goodlaw pushed past, dropping to their knees. They placed a hand against Trevor's throat, feeling for a pulse. "He needs immediate medical attention."

Salvie said, "Is there a doctor in the hab?"

"There's a full med bay on Cee," Xhelsea said. "We need a stretcher."

A flare of musical notes like a charge being sounded burst through my feed. Kell was moving. It flipped itself sideways and zoomed down beside Trevor. Sidelong, I could see how very thin and fragile its substance seemed.

It jiggled gently. Salvie's tendrils stretched toward the Goodlaw. "Will it work?"

Kell thinks so, said Dr. Nonsense. *Load him up. Petrac, see to docking arrangements.*

Kell jiggled with greater urgency.

"I'll send Ikem, the other Interceptor, a bit farther out for cover while

Cee is docked," said Xhelsea. "I don't want her a sitting duck. Come on, let's get him up."

I stepped forward to help lift. Vickee, I noticed, was still standing well back, next to a bed of basil, looking theatrically stricken and clutching her drink.

The fuss was over as abruptly as it had begun, and Trevor's departure took the wind out of the gathering. Escorted by the Goodlaw, Kell made a surprisingly adequate stretcher. I stood and watched as it headed for the airlock, tipping slightly to fit. Trevor stayed securely in place.

Horizontal, Kell would be a tight squeeze through the walkway tubes. But I supposed if it met anyone coming the other way, they could duck.

"Well, that was a terrible end to an awkward party," I said to Salvie on our way back down the tube. We followed the volunteer stretcher, keeping our distance out of respect. It wasn't difficult: they were moving fast to get Trevor to the airlock and medical assistance.

I glanced over my shoulder to see if Vickee was following her stricken assistant. No sign of her. She was probably still back in the pod performing shock and collecting condolences.

It's possible I should have been more charitable. But I didn't have it in me.

Salvie and I walked slowly enough that Dr. Nonsense had no need to hurry as it squidged up next to us. We exchanged greetings and shuffled along companionably for a few steps. The walkway shivered under my feet. A resonant clang told me Cee had docked successfully. Habs should have better soundproofing than Town did. And better dampers.

I almost thought the sound trailed off into music, but that was probably just me picking up the edge of whatever Kell was sending.

The stretcher and its entourage picked up their pace, Kell gliding along like a magic carpet in a fairy tale. They stopped over the access hatch to the airlock. The Goodlaw opened it, and Kell and Trevor began to descend.

Belatedly, I realized something. "That's the antigravity tech!"

Hmm? said Dr. Nonsense. *Oh, Kell's means of locomotion. Yes, it is the gravity-control tech.*

I shook my head at my own obliviousness.

Was your colleague trying to assert dominance over you?

It's a good thing my food and drink were long consumed, and the remains left behind for recycling. Because if I'd had a mouthful of gin and tonic it would have come out of my nose. And that's both unsanitary and uncomfortable.

"Um," I said.

Or was it courtship behavior? It waved an arm brightly.

I could have invoked my privacy, but Nonsense was such a cheerful entity that I couldn't bring myself to push it away when it was trying to make a connection. However awkwardly.

"It's about hierarchy," I said, after a little consideration. "I'm pretty sure."

My people just wrestle. It's simpler.

"Wrestle for romance or for dominance?"

The burbling into its respirator might have been the dodecapus equivalent of laughter. It was cut off abruptly as, ahead of us, Trevor jackknifed up off Kell's surface and began to seize violently.

"Trevor!" I sprinted forward. Salvie ran beside me. Nonsense squidged along in our wake with a surprising turn of speed.

Xhelsea and Haran restrained Trevor as best they could. Kell looked much too fragile and crystalline to survive a blow from a thrashing fist or foot. But as we drew up close I could make out a cushion of air between it and Trevor. Gravity-control technology. Right.

Trevor convulsed again, bouncing upward as if he were on a trampoline. Kell slid sideways to stay under him as the rotation of the hab moved us around Trevor's body. A film slid across my vision. If we were on a planet, I would have thought it was a cloudshadow. This time I definitely heard music.

The sound is coming from inside your head, I thought a little hysterically. I reeled, suddenly vertiginous, and fell against one of the bubble walls.

Terror froze me for a moment, but the membranes were a lot tougher than they looked. The fabric caught me, stretching under my outstretched hand. Salvie grabbed my shoulder and pulled me back. "You're not getting out of here that easily."

"Wobbly," I said.

Salvie looked from me to Dr. Nonsense, and from Dr. Nonsense to the stretcher crew.

"I'm *fine,*" I told Salvie.

Dr. Nonsense was also helping to support me, lifting arms to stabilize my wrist.

"Hey, wait up, Cee!" Salvie yelled. "We've got another casualty for you."

"Wait, what?" I tried to pull away, but she had long, strong fingers.

My protests were disregarded. Salvie and Nonsense muscled me forward, Salvie with an arm around my waist and Nonsense reaching up with two arms—not tentacles: tentacles only have suckers on the ends—to hold my wrist. Its grasp felt like a dozen goldfish kisses.

"What do you mean, *casualty*?!"

"Trevor is very ill," Salvie said patiently. "And you're showing symptoms of being unwell. I'm going to get you seen by a doctor *before* you're as sick as he is."

Her compound eyes glittered as she examined me, daring me to protest. I opened my mouth. She said, "If there's a human pathogen on this hab, do you really want to take it home to the kids?"

"We might all be contagious, then," Xhelsea said. "I'll tell Cee to meet us at the airlock with quarantine kits."

CHAPTER 11

IF TOWN WAS A RICKETY JURY-RIGGED FOLLY, CEE WAS SLEEK and solid, built like an atomic doorstop. I felt much better inside the Interceptor, even if I arrived there half-carried and was then stuffed into an isolation bubble that looked like a one-woman greenhouse.

Trevor, Haran, and Xhelsea were each being closed in their own bubbles. Kell slid Trevor onto an autogurney, where he stopped seizing for the moment, possibly because of whatever medication the gurney was administering.

Cee, the shipmind, broke in to say in dulcet tones, "Please follow the white line through to sick bay."

The gurney moved smoothly away. Those of us who were mobile on our own followed. Kell, Salvie, and Nonsense were whisked off in the other direction to be decontaminated.

Salvie blinked me: *Be back as soon as I can. BE COOPERATIVE.*

As if I am ever less than cooperative.

Besides, I was trapped in a deflated beach ball, trying not to bounce myself against the bulkheads as Cee herded us through a series of cabins that made me think *I Am Not Safe At Harbor* was better equipped to be a space station than Town was. Her walls were set to calming abstracts in pastel colors, the exact opposite of what you'd expect from a military ship.

We shuffled into the promised med bay. I no longer felt wobbly, just irritated about the whole thing. I was never going to establish a schedule under these conditions, and the looming presence of everything I wasn't getting done hovered behind my left shoulder.

I restrained myself from stomping on Cee's deck plates, because I wasn't mad at her and because she didn't deserve it. Also, I'd probably bounce.

I *was* mad at Salvie, but annoyingly she didn't deserve it, either. The worst thing about rightminding is having to admit to yourself when you're being an asshole. Denial is so much more comforting.

Salvie was taking care of me, and the kids, and every other human crew member on these various ships and in Town.

That made me think of something. *Cee?*

Have a seat on that examining table, she answered. *The doctor will be right with you.*

I did as instructed, shuffling along in my isolation pouch like a windup toy in a baggie. *If it is something contagious, Town needs to seal off the Garden Pod and quarantine everybody in there. And caution them not to eat or drink anything.*

Oh, she answered. *Good point. That's outside my remit, but I'll make sure Yod has thought of it. Now, what are your symptoms?*

I leaned back against the bulkhead. The isolation pouch crinkled. Across the med bay, Xhelsea was still caring for Trevor as a figure in a softsuit plastered with medical symbols moved toward them.

I guessed the education of a Goodlaw probably included extensive first aid training. Haran, like me, was relegated to a high padded bench against a bulkhead.

I waved at him through the pouch. He rolled his eyes and smirked as if to say that everything was going to be fine.

Trevor started convulsing again.

The straps held him to the autogurney, but the gurney itself rocked with the force of his seizures. Xhelsea spat a curse word and triggered their suit actuator without pulling the isolation pouch off first. Their hardsuit deployed, unscrolling across their body and slicing the pouch to ribbons. The resulting confetti settled to the deck around their feet.

I'd have to remember that trick. It might get me out of trouble someday.

Better protected, Xhelsea waded in to help the gurney and the soft-suited medic keep Trevor from hurting himself.

My feed labeled the doctor as Chionn, a member of a syster race called the Hyldeis that I had not previously encountered. Given the soft-suit, all I could say about her was that she was vaguely human-shaped and about two-thirds my size, with longer arms.

Dr. Chionn was probably not at risk from any pathogen that infected humans. But it would be poor medical protocol to take chances.

Between them, the Goodlaw and the medic managed to press an injector to Trevor's neck through the pouch. After one more straining moment, he collapsed, sedated.

"That's a high fever," said the medic. "Let's get him into the scanner."

Working together, they guided the autogurney into a tube that opened in one bulkhead. Both stepped back in practiced unison as the barrier descended. I badly wanted to squeeze Salvie's hand—so much for being mad at her—but of course she was somewhere else, being sanitized. I reached into the feed for our connection and hugged her that way. Virtually, she hugged me back.

Not as satisfying as the real thing, but you take what you can get. I felt her trying to hide her worry from me. Perversely, her concern made me feel safer.

Lights flickered and machinery clanked and hummed. Xhelsea and Chionn both leaned forward, inspecting the result.

"Crap," Xhelsea said.

"Encephalitis," said Chionn. "Well, that explains the seizures. And the fever. Let's get a sample and put him in cryo while we figure out what's going on and how to treat it."

I felt as if I were the one who'd been plunged into liquid nitrogen. Judging by Haran's expression, he was just as galvanized. There were a lot of humans on the hab and the ships blockaded in with it. If we all came down with a fatal illness, I was pretty sure Cee and *I Brake for Nobody*, still on wide patrol, would be insufficiently supplied with cryo pods to keep everybody frozen until help arrived. *If* help arrived. If we didn't have to bust out past a wall of pirates, somehow bringing all the Baomind components with us along with a whole bunch of deathly ill people.

I can't go in the freezer. I have research to complete!

Well, if I were to get frozen, at least the odds were pretty good that Vickee would also wind up popped into a cryo pod. Since she was sharing living quarters with her assistant, and had traveled here with him, she'd have suffered a much closer exposure to whatever was making him sick than I had in our two brief encounters.

What pathogen has an incubation period of months, though?

For a moment, I cheered myself up by imagining Vickee ridiculously draped in an isolation pouch.

She'd probably make that look good, too.

Then I remembered that my kids were human, and had also been on Cee with Vickee and Trevor for decians. I decided to imagine giving encephalitis to all the pirates instead, so they would have to leave us alone. But that made me feel like a bad person.

The Baosong was actually kind of an earworm. Possibly it was because my fox was busting with the stuff, but even though Kell had slid in and was merely hovering silently against the far bulkhead, harmonic echoes rang through my mind.

Well, it seemed like I was going to be here for a while. Visualizing my revenge was a wash, and the echoes of imagined music reminded me I had work to do. I started pulling up data while the medics slipped the sedated Trevor into a cryo pod. I probably shuddered visibly when it hissed closed around him. *Try not to think about it.*

Chionn and Xhelsea stood beside a bench, peering at instruments and readers. I assumed they were trying to diagnose Trevor, and they'd get around to me eventually. I really didn't feel ill . . . unless I was giving myself a psychosomatic headache.

I decided that was all it was, and tuned the pain away.

Full feed access meant I could work anywhere. And I was pleased and surprised to realize that the files Vickee had put a hold on were now available.

I couldn't imagine Vickee had released them already, so Dr. Nonsense must have unlocked them from the decontamination shower.

How strange was it for an aquatic person to have to shower?

Focus, Sunya.

Fascinated with the subtle tracks of history, I forgot to be worried. Buried in the Baomind's processes—one organism, distributed nodes, a memory stretching back millions of ans—was an observed history of the galaxy beyond anything the Synarche had ever known. The recorded history of even the oldest systers was a mere few millennians; only two or three of the eldest had been off their homeworlds for as much as a thousand ans. My species was relatively old in space, and even for us it had only been eight centads or so.

We could look back along the pathways of distant light—I knew of intrepid research teams who had actually left the Milky Way and were surfing ahead of information fronts that had already passed local observers. This allowed them to reverse observational time and rewind the evolution of astronomical objects.

But the Baomind by its very nature was an eyewitness to deep time. And my role was to parse, organize, and index that data so that astrophysicists and cyberneticists and linguists and probably a hundred other authorities could find and use the parts that were relevant to their specialties.

My heart squeezed with joy. There was so much work to be done.

I lost myself rummaging through that data. The most recent collections prepared by Fritha, the musicologist, included charts of variations in songs and signals as more and more tesserae were transported away from the dying star. I had just hit a nice state of flow, sorting it into rows, columns, heaps, and piles, when a salient piece of clinical information resurfaced in my mind.

"Excuse me," I said. "Doctor, Goodlaw."

"Go ahead," Xhelsea said without looking up.

"Trevor was complaining of a stuffy nose earlier today. Todia. Dr. DeVine told him to treat it. I think they both assumed it was allergies."

I wondered what had happened to Trevor's gengineered dinosaur. And if it would need care, or if Vickee would see to it.

Who was I kidding? Vickee never nurtured anything unless there was something in it for her. *Salvie, Trevor has a pet. Eventually somebody should make sure it's fed and so forth.*

Right, Angie. I'll put it on the list, she said dryly. I guess it is sort of a running joke that I pay more attention to other creatures' needs than my own. Maybe that was why I had been so eager to get away from my family and just work for a little while. I felt constrained by my own expectation to put the people I was in a relationship with first.

An expectation, now that I thought about it, that Vickee had exploited during our time together.

Dammit, I sent to Salvie.

What's wrong?

Just a visit from the self-awareness fairy.

Her love was palpable. *Oh, I hate that.*

I switched my attention to the shipmind. Cee, *what do the pirates want with us? Why are they so determined to keep us here?*

Well, she said, *I can only speculate. But I suspect they have a number of motivations. One would be keeping us from retrieving the Baomind and its data, because of the advantages that would provide the Synarche in terms of technology and information. Another would be enslaving as many of the Terrans on the expedition as they can manage. They may also want to destroy the Baomind and the rest of us artificials, which they consider abominations. Not to mention claiming the resources of all these ships and the Baomind itself—the computronium contained in its tesserae would be very useful to them.*

I said, *I thought they didn't use artificial intelligences.*

They use old-school dumb computers, though.

My train of thought was interrupted as Dr. Chionn came over to me. Because of our difference in scale, she didn't have to crouch to look me in the eye, though I was sitting. I peered through her faceplate to see her expression; how human of me, when I had no idea what her expression portended. She was peering back, however, which gave me a sense of connection no matter what it meant to her.

"Any headache?" she asked.

I shook my head and then remembered it might mean nothing to her, unless she had the human kinetic translator package. I was a damned provincial sometimes.

"No persistent headache. No discomfort of any sort."

"Persistent? Did you tune something out?"

"It wasn't bad," I said.

She trilled in the back of her throat, a breathy purring sound. "Disorientation? Poor balance?"

"Not used to spin gravity yet, but getting there."

"Visual hallucinations, though."

Her bedside manner was brusque but kindly. I didn't mind it. She seemed like a professional used to dealing with urgent crises. I said, "Some? A little bit? Like . . . films, or bits of black web drifting across my vision."

"For how long?"

"Since we came out of white space, I guess?" Maybe a little before, but I wasn't certain. And then I remembered: "I've been having a bit of a sensed-presence effect since . . . well, since slightly before we arrived here. Like someone staring over my shoulder. It's been making me jumpy."

Oh no—what if *I* was the disease vector somehow?

"Any fever? Any other symptoms?"

I denied everything. Out of an abundance of caution, she and the Goodlaw slid me into the scanner anyway. There were a lot of banging noises, but because I was still inside my isolation envelope I didn't get to experience the smell some people report. Just as well: the sour scent of my own worry was unpleasant enough.

I didn't *think* there was anything wrong with me. I didn't *feel* like there was anything wrong with me. But you never do until you do, if you know what I mean.

When they pulled me back out again, Dr. Chionn said, "I'm going to open your isolation pouch. It's fine: you're not contagious. And neither is Trevor, not under any normal circumstances."

She didn't look relieved.

"So what is wrong with us?"

"Nothing's wrong with *you*, according to the scanner. You may be experiencing side effects from the number of ayatanas you are wearing, but they shouldn't be dangerous."

That was a relief. "And Trevor?"

"Under ordinary circumstances I would be unable to discuss his diagnosis with you, because of medical privacy." She reached up and coded the actuator on her chest. The softsuit whisked away from her body as if it had never been, revealing soft ginger fur patterned with auburn dapples. Bright lavender eyes blinked at me. "However, the results of his tests concern the health of everybody in Town. . . ."

"So what's wrong with him?"

Xhelsea also opened their suit. "He has amoebas."

"He has *what?*" said Haran, while I was still standing there with my mouth agape.

"Brain-eating amoebas," said Xhelsea. "A species of *Terra Naegleria*. And no, I'm not making that up. They're a parasite from Earth and, unsurprisingly, our database on treating the infection is limited."

"Has he been . . . carrying that the whole way here?" I asked.

"Unless there's something strange going on, probably not." The Goodlaw lounged against the now-empty autogurney, one foot kicked up against a brace. "The incubation period is just a few days, and might be faster under these conditions."

"You mean in space."

"I do. Also, these seem to have been engineered, so it's possible they're more virulent. We need to check the Garden Pod for contamination. And disinfect everybody who might have touched any water in there."

Chilling, the idea that the water supply in Town might be infested with deadly parasites. But as my stomach was flip-flopping and I was resisting the urge to rinse out my nose with bleach, I remembered the neti pot.

"Allergy symptoms! He said he used Vickee's neti pot earlier today."

"Oh, that's a smoking gun." The familiar voice from behind me made me turn. Salvie stood in the doorway. "I heard you weren't dying. Not from *you*, of course," she teased.

"Sorry."

She came forward, lithe and dark, and bent down to tickle the top of my head with her tendrils, the Fercho equivalent of a kiss. The contact produced a thrill down my spine and a sense of warmth in my bosom. I leaned into the embrace, my urge to punch Petrac renewing. Reluctantly, I tuned my aggression down.

Salvie said, "Maybe Yod decided she had enough archinformists aboard and didn't need an extra one? What if a wheelmind *did* decide to kill somebody?"

I swallowed. "Then that somebody would die."

"Yod wouldn't need to put amoebas in a neti pot," Xhelsea pointed out. "She could just open an airlock. Oops."

Chionn had a glazed expression that suggested she was looking up the phrase *neti pot*. I won't deny it: humans are weird, and our sinuses evolved for four-legged animals and don't drain very well in their current configuration. Especially when the gravity is weak, intermittent, and somewhat randomly oriented.

Unglazing, Chionn asked, "Do you mean somebody was trying to kill him? Or trying to kill Vickee?"

"Who'd want to kill Vickee?" Xhelsea asked. They paused, and smirked at themself. "Stupid thing for a Goodlaw to ask. There's always *somebody* who wants any given person dead. Whether they deserve it or not."

I bit my lip and tried very hard to hide my frown. Of course Vickee had charmed her shipmates on the long journey here. She'd had nothing better to do, they weren't competition, and as long as they were providing sufficient ego gratification, she wouldn't have a reason to start behaving like . . . well, like Vickee.

She could be perfectly charming for months on end. Until someone set a boundary she didn't like, or got in between her and something she wanted.

Or she needed someone to blame for her own failures.

I wondered if *she* might have tried to murder Trevor. "It was Vickee who told him to use the neti pot," I said. "She was annoyed by his sniffling."

"Hmm," said the Goodlaw. I wondered whether they were checking off a box in their head marked *circumstantial evidence*, or one marked *Sunya attempts to shift suspicion onto her professional rival.*

It didn't really matter to me, I supposed. I wanted the Goodlaw to like me. But that was because I thought they were charming. And hot. And because I had a pathological need to have everybody like me.

I was working on it.

"Can I go?" I asked Dr. Chionn. "Or are there more tests?"

"Keep me in the loop if you have any more symptoms," she said.

"Don't worry," Salvie threatened. "She will."

Salvie and I walked to our quarters slowly, to give ourselves time to figure out the situation away from the kids. I wanted to talk through my anxiety and understand it better, rather than just tuning it away. And Salvie . . . Salvie puts up with a lot.

"Humans have a defect," I said.

Her tendrils shivered with mirth. "Just the one?"

I swatted her arm. "We like to tell ourselves these things can't happen to us. Whatever it is. That when bad things happen to other people it's because they somehow deserve them. That's how we construct a narrative that keeps us from being completely paralyzed by existential fear."

"Only you," she said, "would bring narratology into evolutionary psychology."

"Do we deserve to be trapped on a ramshackle hab, cut off by pirates, possibly with a would-be murderer?"

"No," she said. "Although we *did* get ourselves into it."

"The pirates might have been predictable." I squeezed her hand. She squeezed mine back. "I don't think an amoeba murderer was."

"Statistically speaking, there's probably only one amoeba murderer in the entire galaxy. So in my professional opinion . . . no, that wasn't predictable. Who do you think did it, anyway? And why?"

If Salvie were a human, she would have been smirking. My wife is a tremendous pain in the ass. It's a good thing I love her. Because I can't keep up with her when it comes to witty banter, but that doesn't stop me from embarrassing myself trying. "Maybe the murderer was brainwashed into it by the Baomind. Maybe they're trying to wipe us all out, starting with Vickee's assistant." I paused. "You must have spent time with them on Cee, right? What's he like?"

"Nice enough," she said. "Spends a lot of time trying to meet Vickee's expectations, which are high."

"I thought you liked Vickee." I struggled to suppress my pleasure and relief at her criticism. There is no greater emotional bond than a mutual dislike, etc.

"She's interesting," Salvie said. "But self-absorbed. Do you think Trevor was the intended victim?"

"No," I admitted. "But I'm also biased. Maybe the Baomind didn't want to work with Vickee either, and conjured up amoebas from the fifth dimension through the power of suggestion."

"You might even say, its 'sunconscious' mind."

I looked at Salvie, and she didn't even have the grace to look abashed—which for her species is a catlike whisker-flick of the tendrils and a lowering of the head.

"I thought you liked me." But I was grinning, and the eerie sensation of being adrift in haunted space had left me.

She winked one noncompound eye.

I rolled my own eyes. "Anyway, you're correct. I can't imagine that anybody would put brain-eating parasites in Vickee's neti pot in order to kill Trevor. Except maybe Vickee, because she'd know better than to use it."

Footsteps echoed along the hamster tube, coming from the opposite direction. Out of time with the music in my head, the decking bounced with somebody else's stride. I held my next comment, which was something to the effect of having no problem visualizing somebody trying to murder Vickee with amoebas. Or just about anything else, for that matter. Probably best if I didn't incriminate myself where Yod could hear me, let alone my fellow passengers.

I was surprised to discover that the pair of humans coming the other way were familiar. It was two of the Chives, limping along in lockstep and functionally indistinguishable.

They were constantly in contact with Dakhira, with each other, and probably with Yod, so I didn't feel the need to bring them up to speed on the quarantine situation. In fact, they were carrying totes containing an array of pipettes, small tubes, and other equipment. I guessed they might be going to the Garden Pod to sample the water for amoebae.

Even in a crisis, a regular human might have made some gesture of communication, a little small talk about the traumatic circumstances. But at the moment, there was no small talk from these businesslike transhumans.

You know, by Freeporter standards, you're pretty transhuman yourself, Salvie sent.

You're eavesdropping!

She curled her tendrils. *You were broadcasting.*

She nodded to the Chives. They nodded back. Each group fell into single file to pass each other on the catwalk, and I tried not to lean away from the Chives. I also tried not to lean away from the emptiness of space. This kept me reasonably upright.

We swept past one another and kept going. Only after we were past did I realize it might have been rude of me not to nod to them.

CHAPTER 12

"YOU'RE HUMMING," SAID SALVIE A MINUTE LATER. "IS that Baosong? It's not one I've heard before."

I hadn't been paying attention to what my own body was doing, so I had to replay the past few moments to hear myself. It was a somewhat aimless, ambling tune—but Salvie, of course, had diagnosed the melody.

I'd been humming something that wasn't exactly Baosong, but emerging from a synthesis of all the threads I had been studying for months.

"Head full of music," I said apologetically. "And a head full of ayatanas, too. I suppose it's only natural it should overflow. Sorry about the leakage."

She made a noise of dissatisfaction. "Are you taking unwise risks?"

"Dakhira could have said no."

"I hadn't gathered that you thought much of his judgment," she said. We reached the cabin and she opened the outer airlock hatch.

I snorted, following her inside. "I think he does his job. And he's an asshole while he's doing it."

"I worry about you." Her tendrils writhed as the outer door closed. I worked my jaw to make my ears pop. "You have responsibilities. I need you to care of yourself." She reached toward the release but hesitated. "Not just for me. We have kids."

A martial artist of marital treachery, she popped the interior hatch before I could reply. It slid aside, revealing a room bedecked in printed streamers and a storm of giggling kids, confetti, and unhappy cats in birthday costumes.

"I noticed," I said.

My work is fascinating to do, and unbelievably boring to explain. It also requires a great deal of focus: the kind of focus it's impossible to get in a tight space with two adolescent children who are done with school for the dia, two cats, and a spouse who is feeling a three-vee in the privacy of her own headspace but still keeps giggling a lot.

Fortunately, we'd only been stuck back in quarters for about a standard hour when Yod let us know that the water samples from the Garden Pod had tested negative for brain-eating protozoans. Assuming that what you wanted was fewer brain-eating protozoans, this was a good thing.

I was in favor.

We *were* going to have to come up with a better living solution so I could get some work done. I could go to the hub lounge or the much larger main crew lounge, but I knew that Vickee was likely to seek me out there and just . . . hang around, apparently inoffensively, but inside my comfort bubble. Like a cat that's angry at you and pointedly ignoring you.

If I had to stay in our own quarters, I would end up being the bad guy who set boundaries with the kids. And Salvie would make me the no-fun parent again.

She never has any problems ordering *me* around, but her people do parenting differently. They don't usually set limits with their children: they establish empathy instead. I've never heard Salvie say no to either of our children, even when they were toddlers. She never loses her temper with them. It's all positive reinforcement.

No wonder they like her more.

Of course, she says no to me all the time. I complained about it once, and she blinked her camera eyes at me innocently and said, "You're an adult, I'm told."

I don't have the patience to never say no.

My grumpiness only lasted a moment, because I looked over at her, tendrils twisting in amusement, and it faded instantly. Salvie was who she was, and it was she whom I'd married. If I hadn't wanted to put up with her, there was no reason I ever had to. I could have married myself a nice human girl and then all I would've had to worry about was the differences in our birth cultures.

And then *she* would be driving me crazy.

"I'm going out to find a quiet place to work," I said to the air, and headed for the door. Salvie waved negligently without refocusing her eyes. The kids barely even responded.

It wasn't just Vickee who didn't respect me.

Since the Garden Pod was pleasant—and unoccupied—I decided to settle there. The terrifying corridors were deserted, so I didn't have to pass anybody while I was tuning my anxiety down and reminding myself every six seconds that I was wearing a hardsuit actuator and so was everybody in my family, and if Town did rip itself apart we would all survive more than long enough to starve to death in space or be captured by pirates.

I'm bad at self-soothing, what can I say?

I thought perhaps confronting my fear would help, so I stopped along the tubeway and turned toward the Baomind. I made myself reach out and put a hand on the resilient membrane. It was hard to believe this thin, tough sheet of mycorrhizal polymer could protect me from radiation, vacuum, cold, and micrometeorites. It dented under my fingers like the skin of an inflated balloon. Or maybe a rafting tube, the kind you float down streams on, on planets with nice safe rivers of liquid water.

The membrane was tough, resilient. Taut.

I wondered if one of the flitting specks outlined against the dim ember of the Baostar was Kell, or if Kell was still inside Town or Cee. Was Kell one individual, or just the name used for whatever instance of the Baomind was currently wandering around in the meatpeople spaces? ("Go ahead, get out and meat people.") Did Kell have an independent identity, or were the tesserae some sort of hive mind? Like the Chives, I guessed—but it wouldn't bother me if the Baomind were . . . a jellyfish consciousness, a bunch of independent organisms banded together to make one animal. Aliens were *supposed* to be different.

The Chives were supposed to be *human*. Like me.

I shook my head to clear the thoughts from it, and concentrated on the spectacle of what might be the biggest AI—the biggest *artifact*—in the galaxy going about its quiet business. Packing up and getting ready to leave before its sun ate it whole.

For a moment, it almost really sank in that the Baomind had been out here thinking for so long that when it was made, this had seemed like a stable place to build a supercomputer. I came within a breath, I thought, of *understanding*. A chill made me shiver; my stomach felt odd. But human minds aren't made for deep time. We can write down numbers that tell us how long ago the Koregoi went away. But we can't actually understand those numbers. We can *count* to infinity, given infinite time to do it in. We can *imagine* maybe fifty on a good day.

I can picture four cats. I can probably kind of grasp how many cats a thousand cats would be. I cannot picture a million cats. And a billion cats? Ten to the whatever cats?

That's a lot of cats, friend.

It was beautiful and awe-inspiring, watching the Baomind dance.

Somewhere out there was the pirate fleet, too, but I couldn't see that. A pirate fleet might be my problem, but it was not my problem to solve. I was extremely grateful that I had gone into archinformation, and not into piloting starships. If I had, I might be expected to do something about the malevolent presence lurking in the dark.

I hadn't exactly made myself less anxious, but at least I'd made myself *differently* anxious. I couldn't tune myself down enough to really get comfortable without making myself fog-brained, but I did manage to get the edge off it. And if I could concentrate on my work, it would probably recede to the edge of my awareness and possibly fade entirely, once my fox had more room to work on my brain chemistry.

I turned around, determined to put a spring in my step—and almost walked into Vickee's smirk.

How had I ever found that face charming?

I knew, of course. I'd found it charming because she'd worked to *be* charming. To get inside my defenses and love-bomb my slight self-regard into submission. And when I'd wanted to be my own person—rather than her sycophant, display piece, and protégé—she'd done everything in her power to punish me for it. Including a blatant attempt to derail my career before it even started.

Well, I knew what she was now.

"Have you thought about my offer?" she asked.

"So you can appropriate my work again?" I shook my head.

She clucked her tongue. "If you had evidence of wrongdoing, you should have brought it before the review board."

She was right. I should have. But I had been too ashamed.

In the most unobjectionable tone I could unarchive for the occasion, I asked, "Have you checked up on Trevor yet?"

Maybe a little irony crept in. I'm only human.

Her expression of dismay smoothed away quickly, but I knew from it that she'd forgotten to be human and was worried about getting caught out. She rearranged her face into a semblance of concern. "That attack was *certainly* aimed at me, you know. I could have been killed. But you probably considered that."

"I would think you'd rinse your neti pot with boiling water before you used it," I said. "Or stick it in the sterilizer. I guess Trevor wasn't as careful. Do you have somebody to take care of the dinosaur?"

"The—" Comprehension dawned. "Oh, the Yi qi!"

"Angie," I confirmed.

"I'm sure it will be fine." She flipped her hand in the air. "They should be releasing Trevor soon, and he'll take care of it."

"Trevor—" I stopped myself, tuned, counted to ten, *and* took a deep breath. Losing my temper was letting her win, so I wouldn't let her see that her profound callousness had affected me. "Trevor is in cryosleep until they can come up with a treatment. He may need to go back to the Core for care. If they wake him up before they figure out how to stop the amoebas, he could die of encephalitis. I just hope he hasn't suffered permanent brain damage already."

My tone of sweet reason was intentionally unobjectionable. Her face grew shiny as the heat crept up in it.

So I kept talking. "They can repair a lot of things these days, but I don't know if 'amoebas ate part of my brain' has a really good treatment protocol. So if I were you, I'd be pretty worried about him."

I should never have forgotten that Vickee is fast on her mental feet and vicious when she gets angry. "Guilty conscience?" she asked.

"Excuse me?"

Her smile stopped. "Nobody on this wheel has any reason to want me dead except for you, Sun."

I laughed. "Only because nobody else here actually knows you! And Trevor knows you, doesn't he?"

"Trevor loves me!" She still didn't seem concerned about his well-being. I should have known better than to expect it of her.

I just smiled. I'd seen how she treated him. She might think she had him convinced . . . but she only had him cowed.

The smile got to her. "I've always been better at your job than you, and I know you hate me for it. And you know I'm going to crack this code and publish while you're left standing around looking dumb. As usual!" She stomped past—easy, because I was still standing on the edge of the catwalk—and turned over her shoulder for one parting shot. "Everyone is going to find you out, Sunyata Song."

"Doctor," I said under my breath. But she was already striding away, feet swinging like scythes. *Doctor*, despite everything she had done to prevent me receiving the degree I had earned.

My cheeks hurt from smiling, but I held on to it until she was out of sight. *Salvie?*

She blinked me an affirmative sensation.

I ran the senso back for her and felt her eyeroll. *How's she going to use up all the historically interesting data in an entire stellar system?*

I laughed in the back of my throat. *Are you suggesting there's more than one paper in this artifact?*

That's the spirit!

I wished she were close enough to hug, but sent her the feeling instead. Then, in a low voice, I spoke out loud. "Yod?"

"Yes, Dr. Song?"

I rolled my eyes. "*You* don't have to call me Doctor. Did you hear all that?"

"Of course, Sunya."

"Good. That was Vickee DeVine trying to set me up as a fall guy. Please bear that in mind as you investigate the amoeba incident. If it wasn't accidental contamination of some kind."

"I am keeping my mind open to all possibilities," Yod said kindly. "Thank you for including me."

I reached out and patted the wall. The wheelmind was determined to be cagey, and that was fine. I probably wouldn't trust me either, in her shoes.

The view outside was still compelling. When I could convince myself that it was safe, it was even soothing—a vast silent waltz seen from far above. But I needed to get to work. I needed to be *able* to work, through all the stress and distraction that was piling up around me.

As I turned reluctantly away, I thought I caught a flicker of motion, much closer and faster than the swirl of tesserae against the dim red corona of the failing star. Something black, like a shadow.

But perhaps I imagined it. When I glanced back, it was gone.

By the time I got to the Garden Pod (why couldn't they have just called it the Conservatory, like any normal space station?) I had almost finished shaking with anger and unused adrenaline. If my poor liver hadn't had the assistance of my fox in filtering the chemical products of stress out of my system, it might have taken much longer.

Is it your liver that breaks down adrenaline? I tried to look it up. The local database didn't know, and a query couldn't exactly ride the next ship out of the system—and would take ans to get back to me with an answer if it did.

I *hate* being at the end of the universe.

I made a note to ask Chionn, when she wasn't so busy.

I settled in anyway. As predicted, the pod was empty aside from some of Yod's Hands cleaning up and cycling the remaining refreshments. They were soothing as they vacuumed crumbs, flitting around like gargantuan bumblebees. They even sounded like bumblebees.

I set a surface that must usually serve as a potting bench to a layered crystal display. The drones worked around me, harvesting tomatoes, and blips of information swam in the table's dark surface, easily pushed around with my fox or with fingertips.

They reminded me of the tesserae swimming around the Baostar. I thought it would be fun to make them flock.

I concentrated on sorting signals into categories by as many metrics as I could think of: frequency, amplitude, modulation, length, timing . . . and so on.

Sort into categories and look for patterns. Arrange in sequence and look for patterns. Turn the adaptive learning engine loose to move them around in various groupings and look for patterns. Borrow a lot of Yod's processing power to run comparison analyses. Borrow Yod's Baomind lexicon to create translation matrices. The Baomind's language was dependent not just on signal, but on time. "Words" had different shades of meaning and nuance and certainties depending on how long ago they had been uttered.

That made sense, in a conversation that suffered from lightspeed lag in overlapping waves, like the ripples in a reflection tank.

All the work I had done on Dakhira was foundational. The algorithms and parsers that Vickee wanted to get her hands on were primed with the initial data—and now I had so much more to work with. Yod's archives alone could have kept me busy for months, even with access to more computing power than was available out here.

I started feeding the data into my parser . . . and the parser promptly choked. There was too much, and it was too complicated. I was going to have to break the information down into smaller mouthfuls—or get my hands on a Core-sized computronium hub. The closest of which was probably months away.

So, with that accomplished, the next step to understanding all this new data was figuring out how to assess the accuracy of machine translations in a language I didn't speak. We'd need an index cross-referenced and tagged by subject and chronology to be able to sort and compare the Baomind's experiences. That alone could be a life's work—for me and dozens of others.

Salvie was right. There were plenty of papers to be written here. Assuming any of us survived to write them.

A language you don't speak *is* a sort of code. A code complicated by the variations in culture, physiology, perception, semantics, experience, and even what parts of your anatomy you use to communicate. Assuming you have anatomy.

The Synarche would not be possible without fox technology. I couldn't even talk to my *wife* without our foxes. And here I was, trying to manually sort Baomind signals—Baomind song—into particles that could be parsed into a cataloguing protocol. To make sense of the tremendous body of knowledge the Baomind had to share with us, we needed to figure out *how* it organized information.

Maybe the first thing to consider was that relationship between lightspeed lag and uncertainty. It was an interesting linguistic tool, one I wished my own language included. Baosong had karan coordinates built into its very grammar.

A karan coordinate, if you don't hang around with a lot of archinformists, is a discrete point located in four-dimensional space-time from which a wavefront of information originates. That information might be anything from a handwritten note to a plasma front from an exploding star. Things that happened at the same place and time share karan coordinates. Things that happen one after another in the same place form a karan line.

Things that fall "nearby" might have a causal or associative link of some sort. Or they might not. Things that fall along the front of a karan point might be consequences of the information. Or they might not. And so forth.

Things that do not share karan cannot be causal to one another, and do not exhibit true correlation even if they exhibit apparent correlation. And correlation is not causation, as any fool knows.

There is an exception: quantum events do not need to share karan to be causal to each other. If two particles are quantum-entangled and I look at one, the other is affected no matter where the information front about that event falls.

Huh, maybe those ship-movement-probability cones weren't so hard to follow after all.

If I was successful, I'd be starting work that would be used for generations.

If I failed, I would have used up whatever credit I'd accrued over the course of my career.

No sweat.

Now that I had the beginning of my index, I needed to narrow my field and decide where I wanted a deep dive. The history and data and stored information really called to me—I was an archinformist, not a xenolinguist—but one step at a time.

Sometimes you get into the zone, into the flow state, and everything is easy. Or even if it's not easy, you can feel progress happening. Fortunately, this task was the kind of pattern-matching that makes it harder to avoid flow state than surrender to it.

Time slipped by like water. I lost track of nearly everything—the soothing surroundings of the conservatory didn't hurt—and was startled to discover how stiff I'd become in my chair when a loud, sharp squawk yanked my attention back to reality.

I looked up. My neck and bladder both reminded me that I had been here for quite some time, and I groaned as I went to stand and discovered the pins and needles in my butt. The edge of the table helped me haul myself to my feet.

I looked around. It didn't take long to spot the black, white, and rust plumage of Angie the Yi qi. She roosted atop the tallest plant specimen, feathers ruffled in what looked to me like a proper snit, but I was probably anthropomorphizing. When she fanned her wings, the membranous skin stretching between the bones glowed in the full-spectrum lights, revealing intricate patterns of blood vessels.

"Yod," I asked, "what is she doing here?"

Yod sighed. It was an illustrative sigh, obviously carefully observed and practiced, and it served as an effective method of communication without her actually having to say anything negative about any of her passengers.

I guess I was right about Vickee not being the sort of person you would leave your pet with while you were in the hospital.

"I guided her here," she said. "She seemed to be hungry and I didn't have any better ideas."

"Can you print me off a bowl of simulated crickets?" I had no idea what a Yi qi ate, but engineered pets weren't usually picky.

"The printer is in the far corner," Yod said. "Also, you can pick some of the figs on that fig tree."

I could see them, fat and green. "May I eat one, too?"

"They're not completely ripe, but if you don't mind that, of course you may."

Angie ruffled her feathers, watching me suspiciously as I crossed the chamber. If she were a human I would have said she was glaring. Her shoulders hunched up like a vulture's, and she rocked from side to side as if contemplating leaping into flight.

I'd be unhappy, too. Vickee had probably chased her out with a broom.

The figs seemed ripe to me, but I'm not an expert. They were soft and sweet, at least, and deliciously aromatic. Yum.

When I laid one on the branch Angie was sitting on, she sidled up to it and craned her neck around awkwardly to pick it up. She didn't dodge away when I put down a second one, and the third one she took gently from my fingers. Apparently she agreed that they were delicious, because she made an array of appreciative little noises as she held each one in her talons, parrot-like, to eat.

I held up the bowl of crickets, ready to flinch away if she flew at my face again. This time there were no shenanigans. She reached out and gently grasped my wrist, steadying it and herself while she ate. A great many greedy crispy noises followed. I averted my eyes. They weren't real crickets, but they *looked* like real crickets.

"Good girl," I told her. "You're very charming."

She chirped at me and licked a cricket scrap off her scaly face with a long, sticky-looking tongue. "Will she be safe here?"

"I'll watch her," Yod promised.

I surveyed the Garden Pod, realizing what a nice place it would be to come and work on my family tree. The family tree might appreciate the companionship and air circulation, not to mention the more diffuse light than its travel case could provide. I wondered if it was safe to leave it here, or if Vickee was petty enough to harm it.

Well, if she was, Yod would intervene. If she could watch Angie, she could watch the tree. I asked, and she said that several decians spent in white space constituted an adequate quarantine for the tree. If I fed her—Yod—some leaves and a few bark scrapings and root trimmings to check for pathogens first, it should be fine.

I gave Angie one last simulated cricket, less worried now. She flicked it from my fingers with that tongue without touching me at all. The bite crunched messily. She had no lips, and her jawbone didn't articulate to chew or gnaw in any of the ways I was used to. Her few teeth—tiny, forward-tilted, and razor-sharp—were all at the front of her mouth. With each snap, they pierced and crushed the chitin but didn't scissor through it, so the cricket was still whole but mangled and perforated when she swallowed.

This looked like an adaptation for tearing out gobbets of fruit or flesh—or dispatching small prey before swallowing them whole.

The cricket went down with a cartoonish gulp. She blinked, stretched, looked at me through half-lidded eyes, and made a sound that I supposed was meant to be cajoling. It sounded like a strangled caw.

I managed not to jump back or put my fingers in my ears.

"Sorry, girl," I said. "You can't come home with me. I already have tiny predators. But we'll make sure you're safe here until your person gets back."

I hoped Trevor mended soon. The last thing I wanted to explain to my wife was why we were now the proud owners of a vat-grown flying dinosaur.

I was packing up my things to head home when Petrac walked in. He seemed surprised to see me—or maybe he was always surprised to see anyone.

"Sorry," he said. "I should have noticed the occupant light was on."

I waved a hand across the table to store my notes in wheel memory, and thumb-locked them. Not ostentatiously, but just routinely. I didn't think Petrac would be able to make sense of them, but I knew perfectly well that Vickee had no scruples and would bribe anyone. "It's okay, I was just leaving."

"I feel like we got off on the wrong foot earlier," he apologized. "Do you think we could start over?"

I looked at him. He radiated a kind of entitlement, as if he expected forgiveness and a reset as a matter of course, given his apology.

I know I should do more about mitigating my oppositional streak. But it feels so good to use it.

"I guess you have a lot of sympathy for the Freeporters," I said icily. "Since they hate 'aliens,' too."

He frowned at me, brow corrugating. "Freeporters wiped out most of my settlement and killed the habmind. I'd have expected an archinformist to do the research before jumping to conclusions like that."

I *could* have chosen to channel my chagrin into needless belligerence, because I really didn't want to apologize to somebody who had been so rude to my wife. I could have chosen to sweep past him in a snit as fine as the one Angie had just modeled for me. But I took a deep breath and tried to step back to that reset he had offered.

I said, "I was trying to respect your right to privacy."

With one more tap, I turned the table off, which would clear its memory.

I was about to step past Petrac, hopefully before he could formulate a comeback, when a splashing sound distracted me. Petrac and I both turned—Angie's head swiveled, too—in time to witness a gleaming wet tentacle flip over the rim of one of the hydroponics tanks. It struck with a juicy slap and adhered, then was swiftly followed by another. By the time the bulbous head and blinking eyes bobbed over the surface of the water, I realized what was going on.

"So sorry, Dr. Nonsense," I said. "Did we wake you?"

I was thinking, it replied. *It's easier to concentrate without the suit in my way, and these quarters are quite comfortable. Now that we know they're not full of amoebas.*

Yes, that must have been unsettling. Most pathogens don't jump from syster to syster, but parasites are crafty. And Dr. Nonsense was basically one big mucous membrane.

And apparently the boss could turn off the occupied telltale, because I was pretty sure it hadn't been lit when I came in. Did that also mean the boss could hide its movements from Yod?

Oh, I hoped not.

"What were you thinking about? Trevor?" Petrac didn't move his feet but still managed to give the impression of somebody edging uncomfortably toward the door. He needed to get that phobia rightminded.

Among other things. We should really have a staff meeting.

CHAPTER 13

WHEN I RETURNED TO OUR HAB, LUNA WAS PERCHED on a counter, swinging her legs in adolescent boredom. Stavan pogoed up and down on his toe-tips. From the way Salvie's tendrils were plastered back along her cheeks, I deduced both kids had been doing so for some time.

"Mom, where have you been? We're starving!" Luna said, while Stavan hurled himself into my arms. I knew he would soon be just as churlish, egocentric, and prickly as she was, and I was determined to enjoy this last brief window of unselfconscious childhood. I gave him a big hug and buried my nose in his hair for a long moment before dealing with Luna.

I know we're not supposed to rightmind children before they turn twenty-five or so because it interferes with their brain development, but would that really be such a bad thing? It would certainly do wonders for *my* brain development if Luna would just fast-forward through the Awkward Teenage Years.

I sighed inwardly without letting it show on my face. My job, I reminded myself sternly, was to get us through the next six to eight years alive, in such a manner that she didn't hate me afterward, and was ready to launch on the trajectory of her choice.

It's ridiculous that something so easy to put into words should be so hard to do.

"Were you waiting for me for dinner? You should have eaten without me." *Or sent me a message,* I sent to Salvie, not cc'ing the kids.

"We decided to eat in the crew lounge," said Luna. "Because food makes this tiny cabin smell for *hours* afterward."

We, I presumed, was Luna. Speaking for all of us. That was fine, let her have her sense of agency.

You were working, Salvie said. *I would have messaged if you had been late.*

The implied affirmation warmed me, even if I couldn't take credit for it. If Angie hadn't interrupted me, I might never have noticed I was hungry.

I owed that dinosaur another bowl of crickets.

"Let's go to the main crew lounge, then. There's supposed to be an all-hands meeting there soon to discuss what happened to Trevor." I looked at the kids. "You can stay if you're quiet. Also, there's an engineered dinosaur in the conservatory. Her name is Angie and she's a Yi qi. She belongs to Trevor, and the wheelmind is taking care of her until he's well enough to take her back."

"Mom," Luna said, with all the ennui-laden exhaustion that only an adolescent can manage, "we just spent *literally four standard months* with Trevor and Angie. Can we bring her treats?"

I pinched the bridge of my nose. "I'm sorry," I said. "I'm worried about Trevor and it's distracting me. As for treats—"

I looked at Salvie and shrugged. She spread her hands wide. "You can feed Angie. But we're not adopting her. She has a person. And we have cats."

"Mom," Stavan said, "is Trevor going to be okay?"

From Luna's sidelong glance, I guessed that she was also interested in the answer but hadn't wanted to show her feelings to ask. My earlier irritation softened.

They weren't machine memories—there was nothing in my fox to remind me, because I hadn't had a fox yet—but if I thought about it I could remember what it was like to walk around feeling like a finger with the nail ripped off, every nerve ending exposed and vulnerable. Kids were guarded because everything in adult life seemed treacherous and vast. They were trying to establish their agency while we were still trying to protect them. It made everything complicated.

I looked at Stavan's appealing eyes and tried to decide how much reality he could handle. And how much hope would be cruel.

"He's pretty sick," I said slowly. "But they're doing everything they can for him. And if they can't help him here they can keep him in cryo until they can get him back to the Core where there's better medical services."

Stavan licked his lips, unblinking, as if he were deciding whether to believe me or not. At last he ducked his chin in a flinch nod. "Okay. So we don't need to go visit him or anything?"

"No," I said. "It's kind of you to think of it, though."

"I'll bring Angie some apples later," Luna decided.

"Huh," I said. "I just realized that it's weird that she likes fruit. I feel like dinosaurs predate fruit."

A timeline of Earth evolution was *not* among Yod's limited data library, so I couldn't be sure. I guessed it didn't really matter: Angie wasn't a *clone*, as I understood it, so much as a *reconstruction*.

She ate fruit because something that she had been engineered from ate fruit.

I wondered if it had been a chicken. I wondered if she laid eggs. Then I wondered how dinosaur eggs tasted.

We were the only ones in the lounge when we started eating. Halfway through the meal, however, Kell drifted in. It chimed pleasantly at us and slid along one wall like a maglev monorail. I waved, wondering if it had any visual sensors.

I guess it did, because a silvery shimmer passed over the hexagonal surface in what seemed like a response.

"Is that a tesseract?" Luna stage-whispered, momentarily forgetting that she already knew everything.

"Tesser*a*," Stavan answered. "A tesseract is what you do in white space."

"It is not!" Luna said, indignant. "A tesseract is a fold in space-time that you cut through. White space is a bubble that moves *behind* a fold in space-time."

"Kids," I said.

They made faces, but stopped. It was only recreational bickering.

Salvie cleared the table, trailed her tendrils through my hair, then took the kids back to a couch in the far corner. They settled in, trying to look like they belonged there. I didn't tell them their attendance had been requested, and was not contingent on good behavior. Information is my business. And sometimes you have to manage a situation by knowing what information *not* to provide.

While I was tidying, Dr. Nonsense came in, accompanied—I was sorry to see—by Vickee. Goodlaw Xhelsea was right behind them, looking snappy in a dapper Judiciary dress uniform. I resisted the urge to smooth my hair, not sure if I was preening out of defensiveness, self-soothing, or because I wanted to look nice for my enemy and my boss. And the extremely attractive peace officer.

I couldn't have said which of the three made me most self-conscious.

"I hope you're going to launch a full-scale investigation," Vickee said, settling into one of the couches. "Whoever tried to kill me is still somewhere on this station and likely to try again."

Sure, I thought. *Assuming it wasn't you.* I was no criminal mastermind, but pretending to be the intended victim of an attack that killed somebody else seemed like an ideal way to get away with murder.

"Of course," said Goodlaw Xhelsea dryly. "And of course the violence against Trevor demands redress."

I knew I liked them.

"Exactly," Vickee agreed, with a fine disregard for the oblique social correction the Goodlaw had just issued. "This whole situation is making me terribly anxious and hypervigilant. And don't tell me to tune it away, because"—she fluttered a hand—"I'm not letting my guard down. Or doing anything that might slow my reactions."

"I don't know if that's really necessary," Xhelsea soothed.

I could have told them that no matter how good Judiciary psychological training might be, it was no match for Vickee's ability to make things about herself.

"I can endure it," Vickee said bravely, "as long as it keeps us all safe."

Speaking of safety, I was safely out of her line of sight, so I exercised my own agency to self-soothe. I sat down, let my head roll against the back of the couch, and put my hand over my eyes.

The attack is one reason we are having this staff meeting, Dr. Nonsense said. *We'll make sure we have protocols in place to protect everyone.*

I couldn't tell if it was being intentionally gentle, or if that was an artifact of translation. Or just the dodecapus's native personality.

I picked my head up. "How is it," I asked, "that Yod doesn't know who infected Trevor?"

"I don't record in people's domiciles unless they are speaking with me directly," Yod said from the air around us. "And I only monitor for my name or job description, to preserve your privacy. So if I witnessed it, I don't *remember* witnessing it. But I can tell you that almost everybody on the crew was in and out of Dr. DeVine's quarters in the past dia, since I *do* monitor the gangways. It would have been easy to introduce the microorganisms with a small drone. Because of the improvised construction of this habitat, I don't have sensors everywhere—for example, in all of the ventilation ducts."

I wondered if she should have admitted that. Then I wondered if the admission was intended as a stratagem, or as a trap.

Either way, I resolved not to send any murder drones through the air shafts. It was an easy decision to make. Much as Vickee deserved a murder drone, I didn't want to have to live with being the one who sent it.

"So it's confirmed that the attacker tampered with the neti pot?" Salvie asked.

"We found traces of water with amoebas in it," the Goodlaw said.

Vickee put her hand over her mouth in obvious distress. I almost felt bad for her.

The Chives came in—four of the five—and Petrac, followed by Fritha, the Ceeharen I'd seen at the reception, and three human-type people I hadn't yet met but had also noticed at the party before things got dramatic. I had meant to introduce myself to them. My fox told me their names and job descriptions: Waelyn, who worked for Haran in environmental engineering; Juan, the pilot in charge of maintaining our orbit; and Iris, one of the physicists studying the Baomind's construction and capabilities. There were a couple of xenocomputationists off in the corner, too, but they seemed to be keeping to themselves.

I had been studying the Baomind language too much, I thought, as my brain tried to translate the names into music. I was walking around with a constant earworm, snatches of song that would be pleasant if they weren't running on a loop in my head.

As I tried not to think about music (try not to picture a polka-dotted alpaca), it clicked that this was a very human-centric research mission. Many ships, settlements, and stations tend to attract a dominant syster species, not least because it's relaxing and convenient to spend time with people you don't need machine translation to understand or an environment suit to interact with.

Never mind negotiating the cultural differences.

Also, it's a never-ending problem of civilization that people tend to want to work with people they know. So if there's a gig available on a remote posting somewhere, the people who hear about it are often already connected to the existing staff in some fashion. Or are like me, having gone digging around looking for something they know must exist if only they can find it.

You know how your brain makes associations if you think about something else for a while?

Wait, I thought abruptly. *The murder attempt is only one reason we're having a staff meeting? What are the others?*

By the time I realized that Dr. Nonsense was holding out on me, the room had filled up around the edges. It was a big space for a hab as ramshackle as this one—I guessed it was a refitted cargo hold—but between Town's staff; telepresenced crew members from Dakhira, Cee, and the other ships close enough that the lag wasn't measured in hours; and the presence lights of a bunch of AIs, it felt pretty full. I tapped into the senso and used it to count heads without looking around. About forty souls: the whole complement must be here in person or remotely.

When the dodecapus in charge calls an all-hands meeting, all hands show up.

As folks settled in, murmuring and passing drinks down from the printer, Dr. Nonsense went arm over arm up a table leg and heaved itself over the edge. Its softsuit squished and burbled as it settled itself on the vantage point of the flat surface.

Greetings, crewmates, it said. *I think everyone is here. Let's get started.*

Dr. Nonsense waved an arm to focus our attention and said, *I'm sure you all know about the unfortunate accident that befell Dr. DeVine's assistant earlier todia—*

"That was no accident!" she interrupted. "Somebody tried to kill me!"

That is one plausible interpretation of events.

Dakhira surprised me, speaking both through the senso and through a speaker. The resulting echo was so odd that I was still shaking my head trying to clear a pressurized feeling from my eardrums when I realized what he'd said. "Dr. Song harbors an intense hatred for Dr. Victorya DeVine."

"Oh, for the love of . . ." I said. I thought about hurling myself to my feet and decided I could not be arsed. "I am not a murderer. Not even an attempted murderer. As should be evident by the fact that we all made it here in one piece despite my having been cooped up with *you* for half an an."

Somebody in the back snickered. It might have been Xhelsea. I wasn't entirely sure.

I made myself uncross my arms and accept the bulb of fizzy water somebody handed me. I handed the second one down the line to somebody in maintenance. Hydrate all the time. Especially in space.

Dr. Nonsense either didn't feel the need to dignify Dakhira with an answer or refused to be derailed. *In addition to that problem, we must consider what to do about the Baomind, and about the blockade.*

Oh, right. Pirates. That old thing.

"Do we need to—"

"—ration food?" asked the Chives.

Goodlaw Xhelsea cleared their throat and said dubiously, "Well, it wouldn't be the first time I ran a blockade."

At the back of the room, my son stuck his hand up anxiously. "What are we going to do about the pets? Are they going to be okay?"

Before Dr. Nonsense could answer him, the Chives raised their hand. "Should some of us—"

"—volunteer to go—"

"—into cryo to—"

"—preserve consumables?"

"We can print food and manufacture water and oxygen," Yod said. "We have enough organics for everybody for weeks, if not decians. However, the Baostar is becoming more unstable."

"Of course it is," somebody near me muttered. "It's never just one thing at a time."

I bit my tongue on a laugh.

Indeed, Nonsense agreed. *We are hoping there might be relief and addi-*

tional ships from the Core soon. We've tried sending out a few white probes as messenger drones—one might make it through the blockade to get a distress signal to the Synarche.

"Judiciary can field enough ships to make a difference," said Xhelsea. "But it will take half an an for them to mobilize a large fleet and get it here unless there are a bunch of Interceptors staged closer for some reason. Even so, we shouldn't need to reprocess anybody's pets before then."

It was a joke, but through the senso I felt Stavan flinch. *Hey,* I sent to the Goodlaw. *Go a little easier on my kids.*

Oops, they responded. *Sorry about that.*

"So what do we do until relief comes?" That was Petrac. While most of the rest of us sat, he leaned beside the door, arms folded.

I risked a quick look around and realized that I didn't see Chionn, the sick bay officer I'd met on Cee, anywhere. Maybe Chionn was remoted in and not bothering with a presence icon. Maybe she was busy and just watching the feed. Cee had probably undocked: she was safer on the great curve of space-time than in harbor where she couldn't maneuver. I worried that Chionn was too busy with Trevor to be there. But I could do nothing about that.

"What are you going to do about the murder?" asked Waelyn from environmental services.

"*Attempted* murder," Xhelsea said. "And even that is making assumptions. I will, of course, be investigating it. One thing we're not lacking is Judiciary resources."

Vickee snorted. "I'm going to be investigating, too." She glared at me over the rim of her bulb as she took a sip of what I presumed was tea, since there were systers present. Although I wouldn't put it past Vickee to lean into an act considered antisocial by most species. "I'm a formally trained archinformist. I can certainly determine who has a motive."

Or frame somebody else for your crime, I thought. If we postulated that Trevor was the intended victim . . . well, nobody here knew him well except for Vickee. And I imagined she'd have no problem at all killing somebody who annoyed her. She'd just look at them as an obstacle to be removed or an enemy to be revenged upon.

It's very hard to get narcissists to adhere to their own rightminding. They tend to think they're right all the time and everybody else is the problem. And of course they can't be forced into it judicially unless they get *caught* breaking the law.

It occurred to me that I, too, was a formally trained archinformist. But if I took a bunch of time and resources to investigate an attempted murder, it would be a major distraction from the actual work I was here to do. Whereas if I let Vickee waste her energy, I would get a jump on winning access to additional resources at the end of our tenure here. I suspected (possibly I hoped) that only one of us would be encouraged to continue her research when we all got back to the Core.

If we all got back to the Core.

On the other hand, if Vickee was investigating, she could cover up her own involvement. If she had one. Or find ways to make me look guilty. It would all come out at a trial, of course—the Synarche would get warrants to download ayatanas of everybody involved. Your machine memory can't lie under oath. But I had heard of people attempting to edit their own machine memories.

And didn't I owe it to Trevor to do something? Decisions in the absence of information are hard.

Kell, who had been so silent I'd nearly forgotten its presence, chimed. We all turned to look. It floated by the windows, a glossier darkness against the night outside.

It might be smarter to do some investigating without making a big announcement about it. I wondered if I could assume that Dr. Nonsense was innocent of murderous tendencies, so I could safely loop him in if I found anything.

Probably it would be wisest to conduct whatever investigation I could manage on my own, and only bring Dr. Nonsense in when I was certain he wasn't involved. But who could I include, to make sure I wasn't putting myself in the position of being the Obvious Next Target for a desperate killer if I got close?

I didn't want to think about amoebas eating *my* brain. Could I trust the Goodlaw? One of the Judiciary AIs? People commonly thought that AIs were incapable of committing murder, but it entirely depended on how carefully the AI was programmed, and what parameters were set around its problem-solving. An AI with a good enough *reason* could kill somebody. Or allow someone to die accidentally, or through negligence.

AIs come up with creative solutions to problems, and sometimes those solutions are things that meat-type people would consider awkward or dangerous. Even when carefully programmed, they're not perfect providers of safety. They are just generally better at following mandated checklists than humans are.

And *checklists* save a *lot* of lives.

I looked up from what must have seemed a brown study (perhaps it was one) and frowned around the room. The Goodlaw and Dr. Nonsense were having a confab, via senso so no one could overhear. Salvie was talking with one of the environmental techs over in the corner. Stavan was playing a game on his device. Luna—

Luna was bent over some small object that Vickee held in her palm, their heads side by side, both smiling.

I almost lunged off the couch and snatched my daughter away, prevented only by the sure knowledge that my attempt to intervene would just make a teenager trying to cement her own identity push harder at whatever seemed to upset me. I looked away quickly before I could embarrass myself.

I sent a ping to Salvie to ask her to keep an eye on Luna, then another to Goodlaw Xhelsea asking what measures we should take to protect evidence she might need, and to conserve consumables until some kind of resupply could reach us.

I also wondered about more esoteric needs, such as radiation shielding.

Kell chimed again. It had drifted up behind me, reinforcing the eerie sense I still carried that somebody was looking over my shoulder. It was probably just reflecting the back of my head.

Xhelsea said, "I've had a couple of questions forwarded about stepping up recycling efforts within the hab. As long as you keep disassembling common objects when they're not in use, and keep your food demands reasonable—both of which should be standard protocol anyway—we should have more than enough until resupply gets here."

"What if the pirates chase off the supply ships?" Stavan asked.

I pushed the back of my hand against my mouth. That wasn't what I wanted him thinking about. And I didn't want the nightmares that would follow. His . . . or mine.

I liked his second question even less: "Or they destroy them?"

"Unlikely," Cee said, her presence lights flashing a nice shade of aqua as she joined. "We got some distress probes away, and they are very fast because they are very small and very light in proportion to their drives. They'll leave messages at beacons along the way. If one got through, then incoming ships will know there's a problem before they drop out of white space. And they'll come with a Judiciary escort."

Stavan looked grave as only an adolescent child can. As if he were pondering the fate of a soul on the karmic wheel and had the power to carry his judgments through. "Are we going to be okay?" he asked finally.

Cee was better at kids than Xhelsea was. She said, "I'm going to do everything I can to make sure we are. And so is everybody else here."

Except, I thought, *our would-be murderer.*

CHAPTER 14

I SLEPT, WOKE, HELPED PACK THE KIDS OFF TO SCHOOL, ATE breakfast, and settled in with a pot of tea to go through more parser outputs until lunchtime. After a solid four standard hours spent working, the inability of my brain to maintain focus was exceeded only by the inability of my eyes.

I needed a break. Salvie had gone to exercise and chat with Yod and Dr. Nonsense about how she might make herself useful around the hab, so I decided to eat lunch in the arboretum.

(See? Just about *anything* would have been a better name than "Garden Pod.")

Because I had finally internalized that I needed to take breaks in order to accomplish my best work, I locked all the processed Baomind data to my home console so I wouldn't be tempted to keep poking at it.

Instead, I brought the family tree along in its traveling case. I put it on the table I'd turned into a data platform the previous dia, and went to fetch some lunch from the printer. On the counter beside it was a covered plate of still-damp radishes, cherry tomatoes, and arugula, by a neatly written sign that read *PLEASE TAKE A FEW.*

Angie perched on the back of a chair nearby, looking wistfully at the cherry tomatoes so clearly visible and so inexplicably locked away from hungry dinosaurs. I wondered if she had some kind of inhibition built in to keep her from messing with the growing plants.

I unlatched the cover and gave her a couple of tomatoes, which she devoured with messy gusto. Then I built myself a delicious fresh salad to go with the perfectly adequate printed sandwich, and took them both back over to consume while I contemplated my tree.

Change is inevitable. Trees grow. If you stress them too much, they die. Paintings mellow, fade, and darken over time. Marble cracks until, like Michelangelo's famous lost *David*, it falls. Art is evolution.

And a bonsai is a tree, but it's also art. Living art, passed from hand to hand, changed and maintained. Kept alive. Allowed to develop. Eventually released to the next generation to do with as they will. You can't control it. You just have to let it go.

Houses, too, must adapt over time to serve the changing needs of each generation, the changing advantages of each technology. Even if your house is an entire star system.

The future is not just unknowable and uncontrollable: if you don't build in flexibility and allow for change, evolution, growth, differing perspectives . . . then you will destroy whatever it is you were trying to save.

Trees and children. Stories. Histories. Entire species or civilizations.

This tree wasn't ready to die yet. I hoped it would be with us through Luna's life, and maybe her children's. Even her children's children's. I wanted to give it to them, to pass it along with our histories and stories.

Sitting in the Garden Pod, surrounded by lush, sound-absorbing greenery, with nobody *actually* looking over my shoulder except Yod and a creature that should have been extinct, I found my concentration. That lingering sense of a presence following me was comforting when there actually *was* another presence, even if it was only Angie.

She fluttered over to perch on the back of my chair while I worked, her sleek feathered head arched forward to watch my hands. It was time, I thought, to refix the nails in a bit of tanuki on one of the secondary trunks. Tanuki is deadwood—driftwood, usually, or another beautiful weathered material—fixed to the living tree to provide it with support, contrast, or visual elements the composition might lack otherwise.

The nails I use are tiny, and they're coated in a biocide that keeps fungi and viruses from using the wound to attack the tree. When they are driven in, I paint them to match the surface they lie against, whether it's scarred gray bark or smoothed, silvered timber.

The *tack-tack* of my hammer was deadened by greenery and banks of growth medium. It was quiet in here—well, not by the standards of home, but quieter than the rest of the hab. All the life support hums and the pings of settling cables were hushed by leafy vines that ran up the bulkheads and across the deck above. A fat bee, as big as my thumb, bumbled past: its buzz sounded like a chainsaw.

Rubric had the benefit of being settled late in the human expansion cycle. When we got there, we knew about toxic waste and light and noise pollution and how to step lightly on a world. It's quiet there. The skies are dark at night.

There is nothing about starships or habs—the interiors, anyway—that is dark or quiet. There's a constant need to filter noises and distractions. It's wearing.

Here, I could finally release the tension I hadn't acknowledged until it let go.

Then a noise startled me and I jumped. Angie rustled and made a grumpy noise. She stared toward the door. A moment later, it slid aside, admitting my nemesis.

I wish I could say I was surprised when Vickee walked in, her face performing first surprise and then false concern. I saw through her. She had planned this "chance" encounter, and her goal would be to undermine me. Or set up shopkeeping in my head.

"Oh, hello, what a pleasant surprise, Sun," she said brightly. I didn't correct her. Her mouth made the fakest O of surprise you have ever seen.

"Oh dear, you've mutilated that tree. Is the strut to support an error while it regrows?"

I'm insecure about a lot of things in this galaxy, but my gardening isn't one of them. I stroked a finger down the "strut" she'd dismissed—that beautifully polished, satin-smooth, satin-silver piece of driftwood.

"I would say that the tree and I have partnered to create something that never would have existed without both of us."

She lifted the cover on the plate on the counter, attracting Angie's interest. The dinosaur quivered with desire but stayed behind me, mostly hidden. Tomatoes weren't worth getting close to Vickee, apparently.

Vickee selected a radish and bit in with a crunch. "Did the tree get a vote?"

A better woman than I would not have replied. I aspire to be that better woman, but I am not there yet. I did manage to keep my tone amused, however. "You know, this tree is a piece of Old Earth. It's hundreds of ans old and has lived on seven planets and now this hab. It's a living piece of history. Everything from the soil composition and radiation levels in Ontario, Canada, Terra, to the impurities in the atmosphere on Dakhira is recorded in the structure and composition of its trunk."

"You're driving *nails* into it."

"The tree doesn't care. You see how the old supports the new?"

"That's horrible. Imagine being wired to a corpse."

"Trees in the wild spend their lives waist-deep in corpses. Leaf litter, bark mulch. Living trees carry deadwood. A tree can die back to the roots and start over as a new tree from shoots, despite a big dead trunk. Trees exist in symbiosis with the mycorrhizal networks that decompose their old leaves and dead wood and fallen ancestors, which feeds them in turn.

"I think it would be presumptuous to assume that a tree's experience of death is anything like ours. Did you want a sandwich?"

She blinked. "Excuse me?"

"A sandwich." I gestured to the printer. "Do you want one?" I was suffused with an unworthy joy that I had thrown her off her game.

"I can't believe you," she said. "You *still* act like nothing matters and like you know better than everyone."

She stalked out, trying to look like I had hurt her feelings. I bit my knuckle to keep myself from snickering. A mistake: the fungicide tasted awful. The door closed behind her before I realized that not only had I *won*, in the sense of not letting her get my goat and keeping good boundaries, but her parting salvo hadn't even landed.

It had been meant to make me feel selfish and self-absorbed. It was supposed to bother me for days, while I worried about whether I was a bad person or not.

But it was projecting and undermining, and not meant in good faith at all. If I apologized, she'd just continue to attack me—using my apology as a platform: *But you admitted you were wrong!*

The last time I'd spent any significant amount of time around Victorya DeVine, I realized, I was still quite young, and just starting my rightminding. It hadn't occurred to me before that part of the reason I started having better boundaries around her was that I was getting healthier. And that she'd burned me and discarded me not because I was failing her, but because I wasn't abasing myself enough anymore.

Huh.

Didn't make being trapped on a hab at the back end of nowhere with her any more pleasant . . . but it did make me feel better about my level of agency.

I left the tree in the Garden Pod under Yod's supervision, with Angie to keep it company. I imagined I could almost hear its sigh of relief at no longer being enclosed in a tiny bubble. It would leaf out fast now, and—I hoped—start to heal.

I left the case active so it could seal itself in an emergency if there was a breach. Or if Vickee tried to threaten it.

The cats and the tree and the kids and the job were taken care of. There was time for other duties now, like investigating the attempted murder.

Okay, that was more the drive of my curiosity than a *duty* precisely. But curiosity got me into this line of work to begin with.

Problem: I had no idea where to begin. I had never investigated a murder.

Normally, when I'm stumped, I try to find one loose thread, figuratively speaking. Anything I can niggle my metaphorical fingers under and start to pull on. Sometimes you can chase that entire thread right through the problem.

More often, the thread is a short one that only gives you a couple of clues. Or it won't unravel, by which I mean lead me on more avenues of exploration. In that case, I either pick another clue and start following its thread—or I chase the buried thread through the weave of the data. This can be a painstaking process, involving manual inspections of anything that has pinged a keyword or corresponds to a relevant karan coordinate.

Once I've found my thread I just . . . follow it. First one fact, then another. Sometimes they show immediate causality. Sometimes they just seem to be parts of the same puzzle—but the puzzles I build are missing many pieces, so they require linking inferences. Is all this sky really blue? How many vertebrae *should* this extinct animal have?

The problem with assigning something a bit of technical vocabulary is that it makes it feel concrete and real. Even when that technical vocabulary means "an educated guess."

My job is staying skeptical.

A disproven hypothesis is just as important to the final pattern as a supported one.

The human mind has an evolved gift for building patterns and narratives from insufficient information. This intuition, or inductive reasoning, persists because it kept our ancestors alive—and it's too tightly wired into the normal function of the human brain to just rightmind it away. It's how we store information for recall, and it's how we pass that information along to other people in our communities.

Once we have those stories internalized, we become very loyal to them. We start looking for information that will reinforce our narratives, or we start plugging unrelated data into the larger pattern and insisting that it fits, that we can make the narrative accommodate it.

We also seem to have an innate desire for everything—and I mean *everything*—to fit into one relatively simple pattern. This has led to several thousand unfortunate ans of Big Idea Books that claim to explain all of human (or Synarche) history by peering at it through a single glib metaphor.

Anyway. I had a suite of tactics. I should be able to make that suite of tactics suit an attempted-murder investigation. Collect data, examine it for emergent patterns, collect more data, and see if it reinforces the pattern or undermines it. Review logs. Interview witnesses.

But I couldn't interview Trevor: he was frozen. And I couldn't interview Vickee: she was a veritable Fimbulwinter of a human being. I felt I was giving her a lot of credit even assigning her to the same species as the rest of us.

But I could make a list of everybody else and find reasons to talk to them. Was interrogating a suspect that different from interviewing a subject?

Should I let Cee know what I was doing? I was reasonably sure she wasn't the would-be killer, either. If she wanted Trevor *or* Vickee dead and had overridden her failsafes to allow for murder, she'd had a long, dangerous spaceflight in which to do it. It was probably a good idea.

My wife is a concert musician, when she's not doing other things, like working on reducing the incidence of child mortality through statistical reviews, or chasing me halfway across the galaxy. She understands patterns. And she'd just spent several decians with Vickee, Trevor, *and* Cee.

I wondered if she would have any ideas. At least I was reasonably confident *she* wasn't the murderer.

CHAPTER 15

HEY, YOD," I ASKED, "WHERE'S MY WIFE?"

She cleared her entirely simulated throat. "Salvie is in the ops center with Fritha and Vickee."

"Talking about music?" I guessed.

Yod made a noncommittal chime. "I am not eavesdropping."

Her tone was dry enough to make me chuckle despite the irritation provoked by the ongoing existence of Vickee DeVine and her proximity to my wife. I could have pinged Salvie for the advice I wanted, but I didn't want her to think I was checking up on her. Or that I was too dependent to make an executive decision on my own.

"And where are my children?"

"Luna is in the diving pod. Stavan is in the gymnasium. They are both"—her tone somehow increased in dryness until it should have come with a hydration pack—"staying out of trouble."

"Whew," I said, equally deadpan. "Yod, if I go around asking awkward questions, will that complicate your job enormously?"

"Do you have detective skills that are not reflected in your résumé?"

"Archinformatics is nothing but cold cases."

"Assuming you don't provoke any fistfights, or destroy any evidence, I think asking questions is unlikely to cause more problems than we have already."

The walkway bounced under my feet no matter how softly I stepped. The universe swung by outside, implacable as a metronome. I yawned and rubbed my eyes.

One thing I hadn't expected about life in a hab was how badly it confused my circadian rhythms. My body didn't know what to do with a sun whipping past four times per hour, its dull red light simulating an eternally lingering sunset. I wondered if that was why Luna had been so impossible since we got here. Teenagers need their rest.

Who should I interview first?

Well, I was looking for reasons to be suspicious of Petrac, mostly because I didn't like him. So it made sense to get that out of the way. Yod told me he was in Engineering, a pod I hadn't visited yet, but—as Salvie had pointed out—it was hard to get lost in a circle, and this cobbled-together wheel was barely big enough for forty people to live and work in. I followed the hamster tube around Town's circumference until I found the lock marked with the appropriate sigils and ideograms. I requested entry.

The airlock opened at once. Public space. No waiting.

I straightened my tunic while I waited for the inner door to cycle, feeling self-conscious. Fortunately, social anxiety is tunable.

There are a limited number of work stations on a hab as small as Town. I shouldn't have been surprised to find three entities in Engineering rather than one when the lock finished its cycle. Petrac looked up; so did Haran, who was at the next console. Not-Toby rolled on his back, showing a cream-colored belly. His purr filled the room.

"Dr. Song," Haran said, obviously surprised. "Did you need something?"

Well, I could abase myself in front of witnesses as easily as without. I smiled at Haran before focusing my attention on Petrac. "I came to see if we could start fresh."

Petrac looked relieved enough that I felt slightly bad about the strip

I'd torn off him in the Garden Pod. "You didn't seem eager for that when I suggested it."

I lifted my hands in a shrug. "I thought about it some more and cooled my temper. Don't people deserve second chances? Especially when we're surrounded by pirates and other existential threats and somebody might be trying to kill us."

Petrac rubbed his cheeks with a nervous hand. Haran pursed his lips and watched me intently, whatever his hands had been doing on pause.

"Do you really think so?" Petrac asked.

Haran scoffed gently. "That somebody might be trying to kill us? Some of us, definitely. All of us, maybe. Which of us? Who knows . . ."

I nodded. "Mind if I join you?"

Petrac pointed to a chair on the other side of Not-Toby. Reaching it required that I pet the offered belly, which was shockingly not a trap. As I sank into the seat I found I didn't mind that whoever had selected Yod's library of printables had definitely preferred comfort over aesthetics.

"What are you working on?" I asked, trying to sound like a casually interested colleague looking for an excuse not to go back to work immediately rather than an underqualified amateur detective or a generic nosy neighbor.

"Rationing." Petrac spun his screen around so I could see a series of usage charts that were as opaque to me as the cat butt Not-Toby was now presenting for inspection. "Food." Petrac pointed. "Water, air, other consumables."

"Can't we keep reprinting and recycling indefinitely?"

"For a while." He shrugged. "But we're already overdue for resupply, and organics get used up in our bodies for the purpose of keeping us alive. You can't recycle that. Not everything is indefinitely replenishable in a system as small and tight as this one. Eventually we'll reach a point where we're so desperate for input organics that we're printing off the Garden

Pod substrate or even the radiotropic fungus. And I'm not sure we can decontaminate that enough to spare everybody cancer treatment when we get back to civilization."

If we got back to civilization.

"How long could we do that for?"

"A while," he said. "Five, six standard weeks. But not forever."

Input organics.

Well, shit.

I thought about the family tree, and how it would feel to feed that ancient beech into an assembler to be reprinted into water or air or food to keep my children alive for a few days longer. The chill that laddered up my back was intense enough to distract me from that annoying sensation of somebody peering over my shoulder.

"How long, in total?"

"Total? Four decians at the outside." He sighed. "If we start rationing yesterdia and prepare to strip this place to the hull for consumables."

My face did a thing that probably looked as bad as it felt. The tree, my children. The whole family legacy, what was left of it after the loss of my sister and mom.

I never should have come here. *My poor dad.*

Not-Toby's soft furry belly suddenly made me impossibly sad. Zig and Zag, probably snoozing in a pile back in our quarters. Salvie. Oh no.

I really didn't want to tell my children that we might have to disassemble their beloved cats to keep both cats and us from suffocating or starving. I didn't want to have to live with that decision myself.

What a horrible mess.

And none of this was getting me any closer to finding a murderer. It was somebody else's job to get us out of the death trap. Mine was smaller and lesser—well, maybe of greater importance to history, but not to those of us out here in the dark. I was here to research and learn. And ruminating wasn't going to help me find a murderer.

"Do either of you know how to operate a drone?" I failed completely in sounding casual. Petrac rocked back from his console.

Haran raised his hand.

Petrac said, "If you want lessons, your best bet is Willow. Or are you insinuating something?"

"I'm curious," I admitted. "Not accusing."

"Curious and suspicious," said Haran.

"Well," said Petrac, "I guess we're all a little suspicious, aren't we? Somebody did attempt to murder one of our crewmates, and it's fairly natural to be giving each other side-eye and wondering who the perpetrator is."

"Ooh," said Haran. "Big word."

Petrac sniffed ostentatiously. "At least I have a vocabulary."

The lightness of their tones suggested that this was a game and not a serious case of coworker toxicity.

My back was up because of his dig about insinuations, but if I was being honest, the dig was fair. Part of being a good interviewer is building rapport, and part of building rapport is allowing yourself to be vulnerable. On a deep breath, I said, "I'm bad at sitting still when I'm scared. You feel like you have to do something, to keep events from rolling over you. You know?"

Petrac turned his screen back toward himself. "I know."

"So," I asked, "what do you think of Dr. DeVine?"

Both men looked back up from their work—Haran curiously, and Petrac with veiled annoyance. "I thought you knew her well," said Petrac. "She seems to have opinions about you."

"I did once," I agreed. "Twenty-five years ago when we were in school together. I wouldn't put anything past her, but I'm not going around throwing wild accusations to cast doubt on people."

Haran blew through pursed lips. "She seemed very friendly. Very flattering."

Petrac took a little longer. "She sure did a fast about-face with regard to you."

"Threw you down the Well," Haran agreed.

Petrac nodded, his lips pursed. I frowned, a little startled to discover he was capable of that level of emotional intelligence. People will surprise you.

CHAPTER 16

SALVIE WAS EATING A BOWL OF NOODLES DRESSED WITH saloin oil, a pungent condiment from her homeworld. The aroma made my head throb. Something—spin gravity, pressure changes, ayatanas—was conspiring to give me one heck of a headache. Anyway, Salvie's meal choice was all the evidence I needed to deduce that Luna wasn't in our quarters, because I couldn't hear her complaining about the smell. Truly, I am history's greatest detective.

"How's your day been?"

"My *dia*, you mean?" Her tendrils quivered with humor. Fortunately for her, I didn't have anything at hand that was soft and light enough to throw.

"Okay," she continued. "I like Fritha."

"You didn't tell me you were going to visit Vickee." I tried to keep it light, but my tone wavered petulantly. I winced inwardly at myself: jealousy is never endearing. The wince made my head throb, too, and I tuned it down. At least I knew I didn't have amoebas.

Salvie held the bowl out to me. I waved it away, thinking about shortages. She twirled noodles around her chopsticks while she decided what to say. They weren't Terran chopsticks, but the Ferchan version with little hooks like rose barbs inside the tips to make them grabbier. "You're jealous."

It's one thing to admit it to yourself and another to have your partner call you out on it. I bit my lip and said, "I'm feeling isolated. And I think we're all on edge."

Zig came over and headbutted my ankle. I sat down so he could clamber into my lap and aggressively sniff the fingers with which I had petted Not-Toby. His claws, snagged in my trouser leg, needed trimming. Ow.

Salvie set her bowl down, got up, came over, and settled herself on the bench beside me. Warm, strong arms soothed my shoulders. Her tendrils left a spicy smell on my hair. "I know you hate surprises. And I know you are scared of being abandoned."

Sometimes being seen makes you feel safe, and sometimes it makes you feel angry. And sometimes both at once.

What Salvie had said wasn't quite an apology. But I didn't need—or really deserve—an apology, if I was being reasonable. Nobody likes being responsible for their own feelings when it's so much easier and more satisfying to blame them on everybody else. And yet one must do the hard thing because nobody likes being around people who *aren't* responsible for their own feelings.

I snuggled into my wife's shoulder. She was smooth and warm. Zig headbutted her for attention. He likes group hugs.

"I was thinking of seeing what I could figure out about the murder attempt."

"Vickee is convinced she was the target." Salvie petted my hair with one hand and scratched Zig's ears with the other. I would have got my appendages mixed up, but she managed it.

"Vickee is convinced the galaxy revolves around her pinky finger." I rolled my eyes. "Or she's trying to convince the rest of us that she was the target in order to confound the investigation."

"Mmm. Do you think she'd actually try to kill someone?"

"In one of Dr. Nonsense's twelve asynchronous heartbeats."

Her tendrils laughed.

I said, "Other people aren't real to her. They only serve the purpose of making her feel seen and adored. She needs to be the main character. And like a lot of poorly written protagonists, no matter what awful things she does she believes they're justified. She can do no wrong. So the only reason she might not commit a useful crime is if she thought she might get caught."

"So, risk assessment rather than commensalism."

I nodded.

"Ouch," said my wife, but she didn't argue.

"Anyway, I tried talking about it with Petrac."

Salvie's expression registered surprise. Her folk are pack animals, just like humans—more so than humans, honestly, because only the dominant females reproduce. The rest support the community they're related to.

It's weird to see one Fercho without their pack, but I was selfishly grateful for the various events that had led to Salvie venturing out into the wider universe and eventually to studying statistical ecology at the University on Rubric. Where we met while I was doing postgraduate work.

"You picked Petrac first because you don't like him," she said, amused.

"I'm that obvious?"

"We've been married for twenty years." Her tendrils rippled my hair. "Did you learn anything?"

"That I'm that obvious," I answered with a laugh. "Also that interviewing murder suspects isn't my forte."

"Be careful," Salvie said. "Somebody on this wheel is nasty enough to kill somebody else with a brain-eating parasite and slick enough that even the wheelmind doesn't know who did it."

She'd said one of the magic words—*wheelmind*—so I knew that now Yod would be listening, at least for the next few moments. "Did *you* know that Terra had brain-eating amoebas?"

"I was horrified enough when I found out about the cone snails," Salvie said. "Did you know?"

I shook my head. "I stopped looking when I found out about the mind-control fungus. My ancestors were *smart* when they got off that planet."

She stretched her arms out and regarded me with a selection of her eyes. "Maybe your best bet isn't interviewing people."

"Oh?"

"You're a researcher," she said. "Play to your strengths."

"You think I should check who might have a connection to Terran microbiology? Or who might know something about parasites?"

"It's a place to stand and start digging."

"You're warrior gender." I leaned my shoulder against hers. "A born fighter. It's harder for me to stand up for myself."

"You married a different species and you're going to try to use biological determinism as an excuse?"

All right, she had me there. But thinking about it awakened an old worry. "Does it ever bother you that our kids are human? That they can't ever take places in Ferchan society? Never serve a collective?"

"Oh, Sun." She pulled me close into her arms. "If I had stayed at home I wouldn't have my own children unless by some twist of fate I wound up a Mother, which seems pretty unlikely. I would serve shifts in the nursery, of course. But it's not like I would have reproduced there, either, nor would I be what you understand as a parent. I would have protected the nestlings and the drones, and done my other work as well. But I didn't want that life, so I came Out."

Fercho had four genders: Mother, drone, warrior, and worker—a social pattern my wife had never felt at home in. Usually when the subject came up, it made her brittle and edgy, stiff with fight energy. But today her body remained soft and yielding as she tucked me more securely into her embrace. "Being a parent is a privilege for me, even when the little brats drive me absolutely bonkers."

"Yes." I sighed. "Luna . . . it hurts when she dismisses me."

"Having children to validate yourself is a terrible idea."

"I don't think wanting her respect is the same thing as having children to validate myself." Now I was getting stiff and angry. I took deep breaths and lured the muscles in my neck, jaw, and shoulders to relax. "Come to think of it, where are the kids now?"

Salvie stroked my hair. "Yod, where's Luna?"

Yod's voice sounded faintly embarrassed. "Luna has forbidden me to reveal her whereabouts."

"She's a minor!" I snapped, any relaxation fled.

Salvie put a hand between my shoulder blades.

Yod said, "She is sixteen and afforded certain protections even from her parents, including privacy, as long as she is not doing anything illegal or dangerous."

Well, I guessed that was some reassurance. But I couldn't enjoy cuddling with my wife anymore. I hopped up and started to pace, just to have something to do with the anxious energy. I was too mad to want to tune myself back to comfort. I wanted to still *be* mad when Luna got home.

"Eat something?" Salvie asked.

"I'm enjoying stewing myself, thanks."

She got up and went to the printer with a gesture that, in a human, would have been accompanied by a heavy sigh. "At least have some tea, then. I'll put capsaicin in it if you really want to make sure you don't enjoy anything."

When Luna finally walked in, Stavan had already been home, eaten, and gone to bed. Salvie and I were sitting up drinking the tea she had made, which did not have cayenne in it. Though honestly, if you also added honey, that sounded pretty good. I had been concentrating on my breathing, tuning my headache, and trying to think of something to say to Luna when she got home—if she got home—that wasn't *YOUNG LADY, WHERE HAVE YOU BEEN?*

When the airlock cycled to let her in, the first thing out of my mouth was, "Young lady, where have you been?"

She paused in the act of tossing her bag onto the bench and blinked at me insolently. "Hi, Luna, how was your day, nice to see you, too."

"You blocked us," I said. "You haven't been answering messages, and I was worried about you."

"Well, I wanted some privacy." She huffed to the printer and dialed up a snack. "I feel like I'm in a fishbowl here."

"I'm still your mother," I said. "And you might be old enough to demand privacy, but you're not so old I don't worry about you. We're in the middle of nowhere and there is a violent person running around loose!"

"I didn't ask to be dragged along on this wild moose chase!" Luna said nastily. At least she wasn't whining. She took an angry bite of her sandwich. "You left us behind! And I wanted to stay on Rubric with Ba, but *she*"—a finger stabbed at Salvie—"wouldn't let me."

"Don't talk about your parent that way," I said reflexively.

Luna rolled her eyes. "You thought I was fine without you when you took off!"

I wondered what my father would have thought of being saddled with a sixteen-year-old rebel. We hadn't even asked him about it. Mom had always been the disciplinarian in the house, and Dad was even less capable of setting limits on his grandkids than he had been with his daughters. Luna would have walked all over him.

Which had probably been her plan, and might account for some of her petulance. And she had a point about me leaving. I was the right-minded adult. If she was on the horns of both feeling abandoned and wanting to double down on being left behind, well, she was a teenager. A foolish consistency is the hobgoblin of small minds, and so forth.

I wished she would feign some interest in my job, or at least pride that I was good at it. It would be nice to feel like my own kid thought I was interesting at all. But I had to acknowledge that Luna might have personal reasons for resenting this trip, romantic or otherwise. She was of the age both for driving passions and for devotedly hiding them from everyone.

I passed a hand over my eyes and tuned *all* of my feelings down. "We just want to know you're safe. Can we find a compromise that lets us know that much?"

"Yod would tell you if anything happened to me!" But her shoulders came down a little and the angle of her chin eased toward neutral.

"Yod didn't see anything happening to Trevor," I reminded her.

Luna sighed with the gustiness that only an adolescent or a large dog can produce. I actually saw the fringe of her hair move. "I'll be careful."

I tried to make my tone soft and nonconfrontational. "Kiddo, where were you?"

I watched her face as she restrained another outburst. I was proud, but not dumb enough to say so. "Hanging out with Angie," she said. "I'm going to bed now."

"Don't wake Stavan," Salvie said as Luna stomped toward the bedroom door.

"*Moms.*"

CHAPTER 17

THE NEXT DIA, I PLANNED TO GO WORK IN THE GARDEN Pod, but when I checked its occupancy I discovered that Vickee had got there before me. Sitting around in our quarters while Luna stomped from left to right and right to left again at randomly generated intervals didn't seem like it would aid my productivity, so I asked Yod who was in the hub lounge.

"Waelyn, Juan, and Tsebu are setting up an enormous rec project in there right now. It involves countermasses, springs, and a bubble rocket. I . . . would not currently recommend it as a workspace."

Juan was a pilot and navigator, I remembered. Waelyn worked with Haran.

"Who's Tsebu?" I didn't think I had met them.

"The Ceeharen data engineer."

Oh, right. Trevor had collapsed before I'd been introduced.

I sighed. Maybe I should go and try interviewing those three, but my previous lack of success didn't fill me with confidence.

Salvie patted my shoulder. "I'm going to go play music with Fritha and Juan. Probably in the crew lounge."

Juan apparently had a vigorous social schedule. "String trio," I said. "Helps with the digestion."

She snickered and reached down to ruffle Zag's fur. He was flopped on a bench in one of those boneless legs-everywhere cat-tortionist positions I refer to as "interpretive sleeping." He purred in his sleep and stretched as she scritched him.

"Yod, where would be a good place for me to work quietly, without distractions? Barring the crew lounge, the Garden Pod, and the hub as all entirely too inhabited."

"There's nobody in Ops except two Chives."

Chives. Well, at least they would probably be quiet if I asked. "Dakhira is docked?"

"No, he's in a proximate orbit. But his crew are rotating off for . . . well, it's not exactly shore leave."

"To stretch out a little?"

Well, I had endured an assortment of Chives for half an an. They wouldn't bother me too much while I was researching. Salvie kissed me on her way to her music date. I downed the dregs of my tea, printed off a salwar and kameez, bundled my pajamas into the recycler, and took a quick sponge bath before dressing. The kids were still asleep when I headed out, tugging my sash into a more flattering coil.

I hated how being on the same space station with Vickee made me self-conscious about my appearance, but I would have hated running into her while looking like a basket of unwashed laundry more.

I diffidently smoothed the tunic over my hips. I know what a lubber it makes me sound, but the whole practice of disassembling and reprinting clothes instead of washing them takes some getting used to. Planets have things starships don't, like large closets and a hydrological cycle that doesn't require an AI and a fusion reactor to repurpose used water.

Someone was coming the other way down the tunnel. The sound of footsteps and squidging preceded them, so I knew at least one of them was Dr. Nonsense. I stopped picking at my clothing and tried to look composed and dignified as the dodecapus and two sets of human feet dropped into view beneath the ceiling bulkhead. As they all came around the circumference toward me, legs were revealed first, then torsos hove into view, followed by faces. Willow the everything-but-environmental engineer and Iris the physicist.

The effect—as of a curtain rising on a stage play—was charming enough that I didn't even mind the slats bouncing under my feet.

I put a hand out to steady myself and smacked my knuckles into the tunnel wall. Native clumsiness or a failure of depth perception? Either way, the tunnel seemed tighter than it had been. I tuned down my claustrophobia and decided not to ask my fox.

Adulthood is intentionality of action rather than simple reaction. And I intentionally did not want to know.

Nonsense waved an arm as I approached. Today's frock was chartreuse, bedecked with a leopard-ish print in magenta. I wondered: as a creature whose communication was based on chromatophores, iridophores, and possibly some other kind of phore, did Nonsense select its outfits based on signaling, or just because it liked the hues? When a species talks in colors, that has to affect their fashion choices.

I stopped myself from picking at the fuschia-and-orange hibiscus print of my sleeve.

Here I was, confronted with a syster with three times as many limbs as I had, and I was worrying about whether it found my outfit becoming. Even after decades of rightminding and her death, your mother's voice never really leaves you.

Sunya, said the dodecapus, the translation projecting surprise and pleasure to a degree that I found satisfying. *Have you managed to get any work done, or have you been as overtaken by events as we?*

I smiled, and not just because Nonsense had given me an opening to continue my investigation. Sometimes my new boss's speech patterns seemed to come straight out of a Victorian detective novel.

"Have you been talking about Trevor?"

Willow ran her hand through her silvering hair and glanced at Iris.

Iris shrugged round shoulders. She had a comfortable build and dark hair, and I found her pixyish sparkle extremely attractive. "I'm not sure there is another topic of conversation on this hab right now."

I probably shouldn't have laughed, but I did. "Minaurchs."

Willow's eyes narrowed. "What's that?"

"Herbivores on Rubric—my homeworld—with short legs but very long necks. They feed high up in the trees and hang out in herds. One or two of them are always on guard for danger. You can usually tell where the local sand tiger pack is relaxing because the guard aurchs will be staring right down at them."

This feels like an allegory.

"Gossip is a means of identifying threats," I said. "And reinforcing our relationships to one another as pack animals."

I looked down into Nonsense's unnervingly human eyes. I'd almost said *prey animals*.

Once again, I realized I had no idea how to initiate an interrogation, and there's no weather to talk about in space, so I went for polite pretense of interest in their daily activities. "Are you off to the commissary?"

The gymnasium, said Nonsense. *I'm going to beat them both at table tennis.*

"In sequence?" I asked inanely.

"Doubles," Willow said. "It uses one paddle on each side. But it will only play if we let it sit on the table."

I can't see otherwise. Would you like to join us? I can beat you, too. I'll even put down one paddle.

I wondered if Salvie and the kids would enjoy a game of ping-pong. I wondered how long it would take me to adapt to table tennis in partial gravity. "I *should* get more exercise," I admitted. "But I'm on my way to Ops right now to get some work done. Maybe tomorrow?"

"You should relax more," said Iris. "People think better when they take breaks."

She has a hobby, Nonsense said. *The living sculpture in the Garden Pod is her work.*

Iris's head tilted. "Living sculpture?"

"Bonsai," I said. "Not all my own work, though—it's generations old. Do you have a hobby?"

She laughed. "Lately my hobby is getting my butt kicked by a space squid—"

How would you like it if I called you a plains ape?

"Plains ape . . . in spaaaaaaaaaaaaaace!" Willow joked.

I laughed, and had to warn myself not to warm up to her. Everybody was a potential murderer until proven otherwise, and she was reputed to be an exceptional drone pilot. But that might be an angle. "Haran and Petrac suggested you might be able to teach me something about drone piloting," I said. "Speaking of space . . ."

"Hmm," she said. "What do you want to use a drone for? Work or fun?"

"I thought it might be interesting to get out there, as a telepresence, and see what it's like to flock with the tesserae." I hadn't, until I needed the excuse, but now that I'd thought of it, it did sound like it might be educational.

"Well . . . hmm. I'm a glorified handywoman," Willow said. "I use drones all the time, but only for repair purposes. So I mostly let the wheelmind handle the actual navigation. Iris, though—tell her about your hobby, Eye."

Iris covered her face with her hand.

"She holographs space junk," Willow continued, sparkling with pride. "Gorgeous images. She had an interplanetary virtual gallery show in the Sobaka system right before we came out here."

"You know each other?" I don't know why I was surprised, other than that it's a big galaxy with a lot of people in it and Town was pretty far from anywhere.

They exchanged a glance. "I came out here because Iris told me about it," Willow said. "We were seeing the same person for a while back at Farrier IV. He's long gone and not much missed, but Eye and I have stayed in touch."

Iris rubbed her hands together. "This talk of hobbies reminds me . . . well, you're an archinformist . . ."

"Yes," I said, with the wariness that comes from having been cornered at too many parties by amateur genealogists.

"Do you happen to have any old music files in your personal belongings? I collect old Terran folk songs, especially murder ballads."

I kissed my teeth. "Sorry," I said. I didn't have to ask what a murder ballad was with all the musicians in my head. "All the music files I brought are Baosong. Salvie's a musician, though, and usually has a full library in her pocket alongside the data crammed into her fox."

Iris laughed. A ripple of prismatic emerald and gold shivered across Nonsense's hide. *It's nice to see someone fond of their mate,* it said a little wistfully.

As far as I knew, dodecapuses didn't form romantic attachments, and I was pretty sure that they didn't survive reproduction. I should check Nonsense's personnel file for a next of kin. Maybe it was giving up time with its loved ones to do this job.

"How about you, Dr. Nonsense?" I tried not to look too excited at the news that Iris was accomplished at piloting drones in and around shipwrecks and abandoned satellites. That was definitely the sort of skill that would make using a drone to slip something deadly into a personal care device seem easy. "What do you do to unwind?"

I wind. It demonstrated with seven or eight of its arms, writhing them around each other.

"Tatting," Iris said, just as Willow said, "Macrame."

"Lacemaking?" I asked. "Knotting threads into patterns?"

One big eye closed slowly, then popped open. Its lashes would have made a cartoon bombshell envious.

I had just been winked at by a dodecapus.

As I settled into a chair in the even lower gravity in Ops, I turned the conversation over in my head. I had not, sadly, eliminated any suspects. If anything, I had improved several of them. It seemed everybody on this wheel was qualified to operate a murder drone without AI help, because I didn't think Willow could be taken at her word under the circumstances.

Maybe she was telling the truth. Maybe she wasn't.

I slid my fingers under my collar to fidget the reassuring hardness of my actuator, then made myself stop. It was becoming a tic.

Across from me sat two Chives, both immersed in their project or projects. They had greeted me in a low-key fashion when I entered, as if we were old and constant friends, comfortable in each other's company. Now I needed to come up with *another* conversational opening. Whatever made me think I would make a Goodlaw?

"Too many three-vees," I muttered to myself. Maybe I should just go watch Dr. Nonsense mop the floor with my colleagues at ping-pong.

"Beg your pardon?" the closer Chive asked me. The other looked up politely.

"Sorry," I said. "I can't stop worrying about the murder attempt."

"It's very—"

"—upsetting," the Chives replied, nodding in eerie unison.

I settled back in the chair. I'd fastened the lap restraint, just in case, so I didn't accidentally jostle myself out of it. My sinuses swelled with pressure in the low gravity and my voice sounded thick when I spoke. "What do you think happened?"

In my experience with the Chives, there had never been a moment before now when whichever subset of their overlapping Venn diagram I was speaking with didn't offer immediate and coordinated responses.

Until now.

They didn't look at each other the way normal people would when they didn't know the right way to answer a question. They just froze, in unison, as if they shared a puppeteer. Then the closer one said, "We prefer not to speculate."

The farther one's eyes flicked away. "Dakhira thinks *you* did it."

I laughed, feeling suddenly more at ease with them than I had in half a year of acquaintance. Maybe it was the break in their perfect coordination forming a chink through which I could glimpse them as people. As a person?

I didn't know how to think about that.

Instead, I decided to ask a leading question. "Does he really? Or is he just harassing me?"

"It's not you—"

"—per se. And he'll—"

"—be better—"

"—once his service obligation—"

"—is filled."

They spoke together. "It's only natural that he should experience resentment until then. There is—"

"—a double—"

"—standard."

I remembered my own resentment about mandatory schooling, when I was young and all the Synarche's vast resources seemed directed to pointlessly erecting barriers of busywork between me and what I wanted to do with my life. Why was I forced to wait? To waste a portion of my one wild and precious life in the dusty regurgitation of things I was expected to know, instead of diving eagerly into the vasty sea of things I wanted to learn?

But AIs had a functionally indefinite lifespan. They didn't degrade over time as meatforms did. They didn't even get left behind by new technology, because they could upgrade their hardware platforms and improve their code. An obligation of fifty ans or so wasn't so bad in the face of that—less, if they took on high-risk work, like Dakhira.

And it wasn't as if meatforms escaped service. Ours just wasn't front-loaded, because we started off as babies, not particularly useful to society just yet. And as children we were supposed to be learning and growing and obtaining skills—things AIs were born with. We got drafted later in life, as needed, and did our duty then even if it greatly interfered with our marriages, careers, or creative endeavors.

Belatedly I realized that I had been quiet for a long time, and the Chives were staring at me.

"Query?" said the closer one.

"I'm fine." I scrubbed my face with both palms. "I was just wondering who the oldest AI I've met was. Other than that one out there, I mean." I pointed toward the Baostar. "Dakhira is still very young, isn't he?"

"Yes," said the farther Chive.

"What happens to really old AIs?" They must have massive infrastructure requirements after a few centians of experience and growth.

"Worldminds," they said.

"Or they go to an academic—"

"—cluster—"

"—and think—"

"—great thoughts."

An academic cluster described most universities, but I kept that uncharitable comment to myself. I *did* realize that I had been not-very-subtly diverted from my inquiry. I couldn't figure out how to bring it back politely.

Well, there was always gross rudeness.

"I think you're avoiding my question."

I tried to make my tone more teasing than confrontational. With, probably, limited success.

"Speculation," they said. "It gets you—"

"—into trouble."

It did. Metaphorically and functionally. But what was the line between speculation and deduction, or even induction and deduction? If you could point to evidence or to first principles . . .

"Anyway," said a Chive in that tone that indicated the conversation was moving on now, "Dakhira has no evidence against you."

"That's a relief." It was, strangely enough.

"And," they said in unison, "we're not interested in participating in *anybody's* witch hunt."

I wanted to protest that I wasn't trying to start a witch hunt, but I guessed no protest would change their opinion. *Even if you're not trying, you might succeed.*

It occurred to me that the Chives might not like me any more than I liked them. Ridiculously—hypocritically—that realization stung.

The conversation having run aground, I lowered my eyes to my console. I pulled up my algorithms to organize the Baosong data, but when I tried to concentrate, my brain skipped off it like a stone off a low-g ocean. Even tuning for greater attentiveness and focusing my ayatanas didn't help. In fact, the ayatanas made it worse, because the data ghosts of a legendary composer and a Denevan music theorist did not agree on interpretation of certain repeated sequences and wanted to have a knock-down drag-out diva fight about it behind my eyeballs.

I sent their simulated selves to the far corners of my fox and went looking for lighter reading—like whatever was publicly accessible in my colleagues' personnel files.

There wasn't much that seemed relevant regarding the Judiciary crews—Goodlaw Xhelsea, Chionn, and a couple of constables I hadn't met yet on Cee, and six people I didn't know at all on Ikem, who was out there in the far-flung dark somewhere. Our invisible guardian, like a reverse sword of Damocles. The two freighters stuck insystem with us by the blockade seemed to have exactly the sort of people working them you'd expect, and none of those people had spent significant time in Town.

Service records were public, and in the interests of thoroughness I went through Sandy's crew roster, too, even though they had all died before the attempt on Trevor. What I learned was that everybody involved seemed to have had an exemplary career path, and that Sandy's destruction had left behind a selection of widowed spousess, orphans, and bereaved parents.

My disdain and loathing for Captain Adekunle grew. Freeporters were just murderers with a thin political justification.

It was hard going without other databases to compare the service logs to, but my first pass didn't reveal any glaring inconsistencies. Cee had been around, speaking of old AIs. Her service record just in the Judiciary stretched back to its founding, and before that her résumé was as long as my arm and as varied as Nonsense's frock collection. She'd begun existence as a chemical plant operating system on Terra. Since then she'd been a triage nurse, petsitter, butterfly cataloguer, sex hotel concierge, tutor on ancient Babylonian history and related topics, customer service correspondent, and more. She'd taken her first trip into space as the pilot of an early white drive test probe and spent close to a hundred Terran years cruising from star to star before the expanding bubble of human settlement caught up with her and she was repatriated along with bounties of incredible data.

Once she'd got into space, she'd never looked back. The opposite of me, and impressive in every respect. But none of it suggested she was a killer—and none of it suggested she couldn't possibly be. If anything, an AI as old as Cee would have rewritten her own code so many times that whatever initial algorithm she'd been trained from was probably just a dusty, commented-out block by now.

I thought about moving on to the Chives and Dakhira. But when my concentration flickered, my fox popped me a nonurgent ping from Salvie. *Come home for dinner?*

It had been sent forty minutes ago. How was it possibly time for dinner already?

Sure, I sent back, loving my wife for respecting my focus.

When I stood, I noticed that only one of the Chives remained. I'd been so deep in my data I hadn't noticed the closer one leaving. I shook my head; I wasn't going to stay ahead of a murderer that way.

"Good night," I said.

They glanced over and waved, smiling faintly. I noticed they were wearing a boutonniere and wondered if they were the member of the clade that liked magic tricks, or if all the Chives were now doing them.

CHAPTER 18

I WAS JUST HALFWAY AROUND THE RING FROM MY HAB when the missing Chive dropped out of an access hatch and landed five meters in front of me. I screamed in humiliating surprise, my heart pounding, and groped for a weapon, but of course there was nothing handy.

Chive held up their hands in a placating gesture. "I'm not a killer."

I pressed one hand to my chest, nearly triggering my hardsuit actuator. As if my current state of panic and mortification were insufficient.

Then I realized what I'd just heard and blinked. "You said *I*."

"I'm unlinked," Chive said. And indeed, they seemed to be moving oddly. Or . . . differently. Like an actor playing a role you weren't used to seeing them in.

Could one member of a clade withhold information from the other ones? I thought about the magician Chive who had been kind to me when, in retrospect, I had been a hackled mess around them and behaving badly out of my own internalized fear of . . . having my personality consumed.

Huh.

"You didn't want to talk to me in front of your clademates?"

"One clademate," they admitted. They were the Chive who had been sitting closer to me, with a male-type body under the indistinct uniform jumpsuit. "She's keeping something from us."

I wish I could describe to you the absolute shock of hearing one Chive use a singular, gendered pronoun for another.

"You're trying to find out who the killer is," they said.

Lips pressed thin, I nodded warily.

They checked over their shoulder more than once. "I'll tell you if I learn anything that's not just conjecture."

"Is there a way to get in touch with just you? Without alerting your clademates?"

Their mouth flickered in a transient smile. "I'll call *you*."

I needed a break to process *that* before I went home to my (loud, exciting) family. Come to think of it, the Chives might trigger some of the same sense of judgment I had always felt from my mother and father. I wasn't *like* them, and mustn't they *want* me to be?

Well, that was a conversation for me and the chat algorithm I'd programmed from my childhood journals and vidpal recordings. Maybe I did, literally, need to get in touch with my inner child on the topic of the Chives.

Aimless wandering through the Ring was going to give me the agoraphobic heebie-jeebies, so I decided to meander less aimlessly and head back up the ladder into the hub. The other Chive was still in Ops, but I could use a different spoke.

I resolved not to take so much time I made Salvie worry. But novelty is good for your brain. And floating around in zero g is always good for my neck, which suffers from too much screen time. Maybe that was the source of my hovering headache? I could feel it at the edges of my awareness, just waiting for the tuning or the analgesics to falter so it could come flooding back.

I was also feeling the strain of fighting slightly different rotational (or is it angular?) momentum between my feet and my head. As my feet were a little farther away from Town's core, and therefore spinning a little faster, they seemed proportionally heavier. And my obliques and lower back were starting to ache from the unaccustomed exertion. There were so many reasons I might not be feeling my best.

I entered the hub, which was blissfully deserted. Everybody else was probably hard at work. No time to float around.

Their loss: the tall viewports provided a stunning view. My fingers fretted at the suit actuator below my collarbone before I caught myself and forced them down. The suit *would* cut my fingertips off to save my life, if it had to.

I could always get new fingertips.

The lounge, which I had never seen empty before, was profoundly peaceful in its deserted state. I dimmed the lights, floating in darkness except for the grim red glow of a dying star. You wouldn't think it would be soothing, but so many terrifying things are. Like storms, and oceans, as long as you're watching from a safe location.

I would never get tired of watching the Baomind sort and re-sort itself. I clipped in and let myself drift. I was starting to think that Salvie was right and I should get my eyes checked, and maybe a diagnostic run on my fox just to see if something was up with my visual processing. Those strange dark flickers kept waltzing across my field of view. I amused myself by imagining them dancing in time to the nagging itch of music that still earwormed me.

The hub wasn't silent, either. In addition to the mechanical noises, there was a faint harmonic echo, like that accidental choir I had witnessed once. I registered the sound before I recognized my own voice humming. Was it Baomind speech?

Huh, I thought. *I wonder what the heck I'm saying?*

I'd spent ages training my fox as a Baomind parser. I should try it out. But when I ran the snatches of music I was earwormed with through it, no meaning came back. They weren't words, then . . . Where had I heard that tune?

Machine memory provided that answer.

I had dreamed it.

That was disappointing. Or perhaps positive, in the sense that when you are learning a new language, one of the moments you know you're really getting it is when you start dreaming in it. Ideally, though, you start dreaming real words and not random language sounds.

Oh well, it would probably come. I was only five months into my studies. I should spend more time talking to Kell.

The flickers, though . . . worried me. My fox couldn't find anything wrong with me medically. The sensible thing to do before finding out if Chionn did eye exams was to ask Salvie again if she'd noticed the shadowy effect. But then Salvie would worry. . . .

I sent a message to Chionn. *Just get it over with,* I told myself. *You'll feel less concerned once you know what's going on.* I wondered if I would listen.

Brain-eating amoebas, if you thought about it, were a funny way to try to kill somebody. Surely a nice clean shot to the brain with a particle gun would be safer and more effective—not to mention less punishing for the victim, if you just wanted somebody dead. Amoebic encephalitis, now . . . that felt like a personal grudge or a piece of theater. And one that required a fairly in-depth knowledge of human physiology and historical pathogens.

Not to mention the sourcing problem. You didn't just *find* extra-aggressive brain-eating amoebas out here at the cold rim of the wrong arm of the galaxy. You had to engineer some up, as the Goodlaw had suggested. Or bring them all the way from Terra—which didn't just mean *knowing* about them and *obtaining* them. If you did bring them from Terra, you'd have to get them past customs and the agricultural control AI on the space elevator. Then keep them alive on the journey.

It was prohibitively complicated.

The music in my head was increasingly annoying. I tried humming something catchy to dislodge it, but the unsettling tones overrode my attempts to free myself. Can you die from an earworm? Can you just be driven mad?

So somebody knew about brain-eating amoebas, and somebody could build or source some. And assuming Vickee hadn't attacked Trevor and used the murder attempt as an alibi, somebody also presumably knew that Vickee used a neti pot. And had access to her quarters to set the trap.

And disliked Vickee enough to want to see her brain eaten by protozoans.

I *could* see why folks might think I was the likely suspect, but I didn't have the biology background.

Would Vickee try to kill her own assistant just to get attention? Would she do it to cast suspicion on me, her professional rival?

I wouldn't put it past her. But honesty compelled me to admit I wasn't *completely* unbiased.

"Eureka," I muttered ironically.

A split second later, I staggered forward under a sharp impact, as somebody struck me right between the shoulder blades.

CHAPTER 19

I WOKE UP, WHICH WAS A PLEASANT SURPRISE. IN AN EVEN more unlooked-for blessing, my head didn't hurt. My memories were easy to access . . . right up to the moment somebody hit me. The recollections were crisp, defined, and seemed to be my own soft memories: in other words, they hadn't been lost in a haze of concussion and reconstructed from the hard memories stored in my fox.

And I was still stuck with that damn Baosong earworm.

I lay supine, a position I don't usually sleep in, with my arms neatly by my sides. My back pressed into a firm surface under about half a g. I heard at least two or three people moving around me. Human, by the sound of their footsteps and clothes.

Had I been kidnapped by pirates after all?

When I opened my eyes, they would know I was awake. When I opened my eyes, I was going to have to fight.

I drew a deep breath as slowly and quietly as possible. And Salvie said, "Oh, she's awake. Sun, can you hear me?"

I opened my eyes.

I knew at once where I was: lying on a cot in the same sick bay we'd taken Trevor to. The overhead lights might have been blinding, but they were blocked by Chionn, Xhelsea, Willow, and Salvie bending over me.

Salvie's tendrils were coiled tight in distress. I reached up to touch her cheek. She caught my hand in hers and pressed it to her glossy skin. "Talk to me," she said. "Are you okay?"

"Give her a minute," said Chionn. "She's had a shock." The lavender-eyed orangutan shone a penlight in my face. "Pupils look good, though."

"I feel fine," I said. "Somebody hit me. Knocked me unconscious, maybe?"

"You don't have a concussion," said Xhelsea.

Willow said, "We brought you on board Cee so she could keep you safe."

Then they all started talking at once, including the shipmind, so fast my fox couldn't separate the inputs.

"Wait," I said. "Wait. Let me sit up."

"That should be fine," said Chionn. She stepped back, and so did my wife, the engineer, and the Goodlaw.

Salvie held out a hand. I used it to haul myself into a sitting position. I'd definitely gotten a little plumper during the voyage, and less nimble. The latter could not be allowed to continue. I was going to have to force myself to do yoga and get my balance and core strength back.

If I lived that long.

At least the hibernation-hormone therapy had kept my muscles from atrophying.

Once I was semivertical, I noticed Petrac standing beside the door, hands in his pockets. He didn't look happy, and I wasn't happy to have him there. It didn't seem like the moment to throw him out, though.

The Goodlaw took charge. "Please tell us what you experienced. You say someone struck you?"

"Between the shoulders." I groped behind myself to touch the spot. It felt a little tender but it wasn't sore enough to have absorbed a blow.

Chionn must have seen me wince. She pointed with a blade hand, as if to ask permission. I waved her in and waited as she pulled my tunic away from my skin and peered at my back through a lens. "No significant bruising, abrasions, or other trauma. There is a bruise about a centimeter in diameter, surrounding what looks like a pinprick, Dr. Song. And there is a spot of blood on your garment."

"Sunya," I said absently.

"Pinprick?" Salvie asked.

Xhelsea pinched the bridge of their nose. "You might have been darted."

"Darted," I repeated, thinking of nature documentaries and predator relocations downworld. "Did you find me in the zero-g observation lounge?"

Xhelsea shook their head.

Salvie said, "Kell located you and brought you to Cee. You were unconscious and your hardsuit had triggered."

Only then did I notice Kell, vertical against a bulkhead. It chimed as my eye fell on it and it shimmied slightly, catching rainbow ripples within the oily, prismatic surface.

I said, "So Kell witnessed the crime?"

"Attempted crime," said Petrac.

"Attempted *murder*," the Goodlaw corrected. "Assault with intent is definitely a crime all by itself. So is plain assault, and kidnapping."

My companions must have noticed my expression. Xhelsea's hand went to their face, and Petrac's lips paled with pressure.

Kell sent a long ripple of music. The gist was that it hadn't seen whoever attacked me. But it had found me in distress close to an airlock and intervened to separate me from the drone that was towing me toward it.

"Drone?" said Petrac, brightly interested.

"*Airlock?*" I said, hand at my throat.

We were all just organized information. *I* was just organized information. And somebody had attempted to randomize me.

I asked, "Was the drone that tried to kill me the same one that spiked the neti pot?"

Xhelsea said, "No way to tell. But Yod is disassembling the one we found towing you. I suspect she'll take it down to its component atoms and scraps of code."

"It was one of my Hands," Cee said, her presence lights flickering a swirl of aqua and pale yellow. "One that was supposed to be in inventory, and which somebody must have retrieved from storage and severed from my awareness before taking control of. Does anybody mind if I patch Yod in? She's . . . having a bad dia."

"Fine with me." Nobody contradicted me. There's some power in being the wounded party.

Yod's presence lights were amber and orange, shading to other warm colors. "Sunya, I am so glad you're all right. I didn't see *anything*." Distress rang in her voice. The tone might be synthesized, but the pain was real.

"It's okay, Yod," I said.

"It's not okay. How would you feel if you lost your sense of balance? Or if you were struck blind?"

"I would be pretty upset," I said.

"Well, I should always *know* where people are inside my wheel. But somebody seems to be able to move around, and move drones around, without me sensing them. And now they have tried to kill *two* people under my care."

I thought about how I would feel if somebody took a swing at Luna and Stavan, even if they missed. "I'd be upset, too."

Salvie rested a hand on my shoulder. "At least they're not a very competent killer."

The Goodlaw laughed painfully. Salvie's tendrils flickered in pleasure that someone had appreciated her joke.

"I should sample that wound for pathogens. And run a culture." Chionn reached for me.

I made myself hold still, even though the scraping smarted. Everybody else resumed arguing while I closed my eyes and breathed through the discomfort. When Chionn took her slides and tubes away, I raised my hand.

My colleagues fell silent. Any one of them, I thought, might have tried to kill me.

Well, probably not the AIs. If Yod or Cee wanted me dead, I'd be dead. If the Baomind wanted me dead, Kell wouldn't have rescued me. And if Salvie wanted me gone, she wouldn't have come halfway across the galaxy to keep me company. . . .

"Okay," I said. "Since I was unconscious for most of this, I would appreciate being filled in on the timeline."

"Right," the Goodlaw started. "Fact one: somebody has tried to kill both of our archinformists. This suggests a professional rather than a personal motive."

"Huh." I hadn't thought of that. "Unless the amoebas were actually aimed at Trevor—"

"Possible," they said. "But that seems a distraction."

I bit my lip on the academic's urge to nitpick. They were the ranking peace officer here. I just hated agreeing with Vickee.

They continued, "From the outside, Yod lost contact with you shortly after you entered the hub lounge. She didn't notice the discrepancy, however, until you re-emerged in Kell's care near the Tool Pod."

The Tool Pod was yet another decommissioned ship, its shipmind long since sent back to the Core, which the residents of Town used as a printery. It stored raw materials and nutrient base, among other things.

Kell chimed. Possibly confirming what the Goodlaw had said, or possibly because everybody turned and looked at it. I had no idea how it understood our communications. I supposed it might just tune a receiver into the senso, like the rest of us who used it for instantaneous translation.

"Thank you, Kell," I said.

It chimed again, a trill of notes that my fox translated as comfort and pleasure. It was glad I was okay? The whole Baomind was glad that I was okay?

A brain the size of a stellar system cared about me?

I rubbed my eyes, trying to get the floaters to quit. I rubbed my ears, hoping it would make the music stop. "Chionn, did you get my note?"

She was working at a bench across the bay. She waved a hand, auburn-dappled fur wafting on the breeze of her own making. "You are having some neurological symptoms?"

"I don't *know*," I said. "I'm hearing music all the time, and feel like there are always floaters and shadows in my peripheral vision. It could simply be that my fox is crammed with Baomind data. . . ."

"Any burning smells? Numbness, lack of sensation, lack of coordination? Difficulty finding the word you want to say?"

"Nope," I answered. "Well, no more so than usual."

My wife took a deep breath and squared herself. On every world, creatures about to pick a fight first make themselves look big. "Sun, why didn't you tell me this was getting worse?"

I squeezed Salvie's hand. "I knew you would worry. It's normal to have some breakthrough when you're carrying a lot of ayatanas."

"Was that *wise?*" my wife asked plaintively, not for the first time.

I repeated my previous excuse. "Dakhira could have put a stop to it if he thought it was a bad idea."

The twist of Salvie's tendrils told me what she thought of Dakhira *and* of my blaming him for my own questionable decisions.

"We'll do a neuro workup before you leave," Chionn promised. I was pretty sure she was talking to Salvie, even if she was looking at me.

"We checked your hard memories for any details of the attack while you were unconscious," Goodlaw Xhelsea said. "But there's no more information there. Your hardsuit records a triggering and then some impacts. As best we can reconstruct, whoever attacked you rendered you unconscious. Fortunately, your actuator detected an emergency and initiated. The attacker tried to break through the hardsuit—"

"The impacts," Petrac said.

"I got that," I answered.

"—and failed, because hardsuits are designed for construction work and military use. So they used a drone to drag you along the strut to the Tool Pod, where there's an airlock that doesn't currently have a ship docked to it."

The implication chilled my insides. "Oh."

Salvie stroked my hair. She let me feel some of her emotional state through the fox, and if she had been a human—if she had been any kind of mammal—she would have been trembling. I put a hand over hers, her skin warm and rubbery.

"Kell intervened," said Yod. "And that's when I located you again."

Kell chimed brightly, demonstrating why the Townies had given it a name like the tolling of a bell.

Cee said, "You were in your hardsuit when Kell brought you to us."

"I don't remember triggering my hardsuit."

Cee explained, "In an emergency they work without input from the wearer."

"So where's the projectile?"

"It could have been a crystallized sedative," Chionn said. "Melted right into your bloodstream. All gone now."

"And how did Kell know I needed help?"

Around the room, a ripple of shrugs . . . and nonhuman gestures of bafflement. Even the AIs' presence lights looked perplexed.

The shadow bends time, Kell said. *The fabric of space-time folded around it.* A burst of untranslated—untranslatable?—music followed, with the words *blind substance* embedded in the middle of it.

Blind substance? When substances have eyes, we usually refer to them as people. Or animals.

Well, incomplete translation was why I was here. Evidence that there was still work that needed doing.

"I gather that it happened to be nearby and understood that something was wrong, through its own sensorium? How did I *not* know you needed help?" said Yod.

"It sure sounds like pirate tech," the Goodlaw said. "We've got no idea what they might be stealing or salvaging out there at the dusty edge of the galaxy."

"Do we know how long that drone was missing, Cee?" I asked.

"Uncertain. I had not recently run an inventory of unused equipment."

"So it could be the same one, shielded by some kind of Freeporter don't-see-me field?"

"It could," said Yod.

"Yod, will you let me run a diagnostic?" Cee asked.

Yod flashed agreement—I assumed. Whatever they did only took a second or so. When they were done, Cee said, "Okay, that's strange."

I would say that we waited for her to unpack that, but Cee being a shipmind—and an Interceptor shipmind at that, with computronium to spare—she probably assessed our silence in the picons before we processed her comment, and was just giving us the time to let our stodgy meat brains catch up.

"Something is keeping Yod from forming certain memories," she said. "So she sees the interloper when it's happening, I think—or maybe she doesn't? Possibly it's a double concealment—but she can't remember the information from picon to picon, and it never gets stored. No way for even a wheelmind to act on that."

"You mean Yod has a *virus*?" My heart accelerated, my body clenching with anxiety. Yod intervened to slow my adrenaline release, and I didn't even mind. I wiped clammy palms on my thighs.

"It's more like an exploit," Cee said. "It's not in her code. Every ship present checked. So there must be a physical device on this hab interfering with her hardware."

"That's military tech!" Xhelsea said. Then they looked embarrassed. "Er, sorry, that's classified."

Petrac's mouth twitched. "Or, as you suggested, Goodlaw . . . Freeport."

That was a real silence, long enough for all of us to become acutely uncomfortable. Finally I said, "So, just to state the obvious here, our working hypothesis is that somebody from the pirate fleet is lurking around Town, hiding in the shadows, trying to kill the archinformists."

Salvie's grip on my shoulder became mildly painful. I didn't mind.

The Goodlaw's face was a mask. "That's my leading scenario."

"May I piggyback your sensors?" Cee asked Yod.

"Yes," Yod said. "If neither of us can detect the intruder, that tells us something about the modality of the camouflage."

"Right," said Xhelsea. "We need to know if it's something they're wearing or doing, or something they've spliced into our infrastructure."

"You're giving me the creeps," Yod complained.

"Haunted space station," Chionn remarked over her shoulder.

"You all need to stop watching so much three-vee," said Xhelsea. "Maybe Yod can use air displacement or something to tell when somebody is moving around Town."

Willow had been very quiet. Now she pushed the hair out of her face and said, "I can install pressure sensors as fast as Yod can fab them."

"Sure," said Yod. "Feed me some old shoes."

I laughed, but also felt the pinch of scarcity. What an odd sensation, to worry about having enough *stuff*.

"I suppose I might also have attracted the attack because I was asking questions about"—I looked at Petrac and Willow—"drones."

"*Very* subtle questions," Petrac confirmed.

I turned toward the Goodlaw and asked, "How *do* you investigate a murder? An attempted murder, I mean."

Xhelsea smiled gently. "*Two* attempted murders, you mean."

I made such a face they actually chuckled. Despite the attempt on my life, despite the cue that Trevor was still sealed away in cryo—I almost reminded them that this was no laughing matter, but we all deal with stress in our own way.

Xhelsea added apologetically, "I don't know. This is my first time!"

Salvie must have been holding herself back, because the words came out in a burst. "You're a Goodlaw! Don't you get sent to investigate this sort of thing constantly? Don't you have training and protocols and stuff?"

Xhelsea said, "And stuff, yes. But Chionn isn't the only one watching too much three-vee."

Chionn made a huffing sound my fox translated as ironic dismissal.

Xhelsea didn't slow down. "We have rightminding! People don't get murdered all the time. Mostly I deal with embezzlement. And pirates."

I said, "Don't they rightmind the embezzlers, too?"

Xhelsea said, "Sometimes not until after I catch them. And as I'm sure you know from your own experience, people vary in how much rightminding they're willing to accept. Some of us tend to cling to our neuroses."

"They make me feel safe," I joked. "What if I let my guard down and get darted in the spine again?"

The Goodlaw looked at me, then looked down and shook their head. "I'm a forensic accountant with some combat skills. Not Carmen the Ghost."

I got that reference. "Oh."

"You're a researcher." Xhelsea waved a hand in the air. "How would *you* investigate a murder?"

"Ineffectively," said Petrac.

I glared at him. Then sighed and admitted, "My job is finding the last extant degraded copy of an obscure novel from the Enlightenment that was digitized sometime in the early twenty-first century, restoring and preserving it, and disseminating it so historians and anyone curious can locate and use it. I've been trying to work up some protocols for using those skills, but . . . all I can think is that I need to keep interviewing a lot of people."

"Right," said Xhelsea. "Well, there's nobody else to do it. So we'd better come up with something."

"Did you ask Kell?" Salvie said.

Kell carilloned a complicated run of notes. My fox translated it, with some uncertainty, as *A ghost. Same size as Dr. Song.*

"Ghost?" Willow asked. "Like a reflection of Dr. Song?"

Like one. There but not there. To feel but not to touch. Or see.

To feel but not to touch? What were feeling and touch to Kell? How did they differ?

There existed not just a language barrier, but a whole senso-experiential context barrier. Kell was one neuron in a brain the size of a stellar system. I was a discrete thinking unit of meat. Some communication problems are bigger than others.

I said, "I've been wondering about the motives. Do you think we really have a Freeporter agent on board?"

Cee asked, "Did you try to kill Vickee?"

"I don't like Dr. DeVine." I twisted my fingers together. "I'd be happy if she retired to a nice desert planet and never came back. But I don't want her dead."

"Your vitals suggest that you're *mostly* telling the truth."

"Well . . . I think she's a terrible person who is bad for everybody around her, and sharing a galaxy with her makes me deeply uncomfortable. And she's my ex. I still wake up in the middle of the night sometimes, mad about what she did to me when we were together. But that's not a reason for *murder*."

The Goodlaw stuck their hands in their pockets. They leaned against a bulkhead on one elbow, looking sinewy and insouciant. "I guess the first step for Cee and me is getting access to people's foxes."

"Don't you need a warrant for that?"

"Not if people agree to it."

I dusted my hands together. "Well, yuck."

"Yuck?"

"Yeah. That means another staff meeting."

With the air of someone making a great concession, Chionn said, "We'll just have to conduct your brain scan first, so you don't have to come back afterward."

Shortly after the brain scan, we assembled in the command module. It was a big, empty space set to be full of couches, reminding my groundlubber self more of a conversation pit than the throbbing nerve center of a space station containing a few dozen souls. Plus four cats and a dinosaur.

I had suggested the hub, but Yod was recycling the atmosphere to search for genetic residue, and having everybody in there would have contaminated the space. We could have gone back to the main crew lounge, but the bots were cleaning it and Nonsense didn't want to wait.

The command module strained at the seams with every single crew member present. Dr. Nonsense wore a ruffled fuchsia bandeau bedazzled with sequins. It had squidged up onto the rim of the porthole to keep from being stepped on. Both Tobys were in attendance and doing their best to trip as many bipeds as possible. All we were missing was Angie, Zig, and Zag.

"Categorically no." Vickee leaned back in her chair and smirked, just a little. Beside her, my daughter folded her arms in unconscious imitation.

I metaphorically bit my lip and looked over at Salvie and Stavan. He sat curled in the embrace of my wife's arm, attention entirely focused on Toby the cat, who was winding around his ankles.

Across from Vickee, the Goodlaw tipped their head to the side, utterly unimpressed. "That makes you look suspicious, Dr. DeVine."

Vickee wasn't as good at looking bored as Xhelsea. She cared too much about the impression she was making, and being the center of attention. "My findings and clients are confidential. I'm not willing to disclose them to just anybody."

She was looking at me as she said it. She flipped her hair over her shoulder in a gesture I used to find endearing.

Now the feeling it engendered wasn't tenderness but something closer to rage. I tuned that out before it could show on my face, and long before the desire to hook Vickee's tilted chair out from under her with my foot could escape into action. She'd sure be the center of attention if she crashed to the deck, though. . . .

I wondered if Yod or Cee had the skills to rightmind that lingering resentment out of me. It wasn't doing me any favors, but I certainly didn't trust Dakhira. And I didn't know *I Brake for Nobody*'s shipmind at all yet. In fact, I didn't even know the full names of Arula and Amal, the other two civilian ships that were around somewhere, though if we were stranded here for standard months, running out of food, that might change.

Did I really want to let the outrage go, though? Anger serves a useful purpose when it reminds us who not to trust.

Was I likely to forget not to trust Vickee?

"I could take you into custody," the Goodlaw said.

"You can," Vickee agreed. "That's within your authority. But I don't believe the Synarche will let you search me without outside judicial authority *unless* you arrest me first, and if you arrest me and then don't find any evidence, that will look bad when you try to prove the crime in court, won't it? Don't they call it prejudicing the case? Anyway, I have no motive to harm Sun. Or my own assistant, for that matter."

The Goodlaw's lips thinned. They folded their long fingers together.

Their knuckles paled. I wondered if Vickee had enough theory of mind to notice how lucky she was that Xhelsea had solid rightminding.

Dakhira's green and violet presence lights flashed. He said, "This could all have been avoided if you people didn't indenture shipminds to ferry your fragile bodies around. It's not fair to force us to take responsibility for your well-being just because you don't want to miss out on exploration we could conduct better without you. And now your petty interpersonal drama is keeping me from exploring the history and knowledge of the . . . Baomind." His distaste at the name was palpable.

Petrac snorted.

Oh, if he and Dakhira were about to get into an argument, I wanted popcorn. I wanted a ringside seat. I—

Wait, had Dakhira just said *he* wanted my job? And Vickee's? *Was* an AI trying to kill me?

No, if Dakhira wanted me dead, he could have bounced me around the inside of my cabin like a rubber ball in a box when we were in combat.

Dakhira said, "You know it's true. I don't require food, water, or a shell of radiotropic fungi to protect me from the very thing I came here to learn about."

Wait, what? I asked Yod. Hadn't somebody mentioned fungus before . . . ? Yes, but only as something we could use as substrate to print from if necessary.

The interstices between my exterior hull and the interior one are filled with an engineered extremophile mycorrhizal network, Yod said. *The Baostar puts out a lot of rads. The fungal colony eats radiation and keeps you from getting cancer. Everybody's happy.*

It just lives on radiation?

Why not? Radiation is a good energy source. Bioshields are pretty standard in newer habs. This stuff is mostly cellulose so it's even transparent; we grow it around the outside of the walkway and over the portholes, too.

I resisted the urge to go over and push my face against the porthole to see if I could make out any mushrooms covering the external surface of Town. Instead, since Dakhira didn't have a physical body, I looked at the nearest Chive and said, "Well, whether or not you want us here, we are here."

"If you weren't made of meat we wouldn't have to ration food," Dakhira said. The Chive avoided my gaze. I didn't think they were either of the ones I had talked to earlier. What it must be like for them to have *that* as a coworker, I couldn't imagine.

I would even have traded Dakhira for Vickee.

I grasped Salvie's hand. She gave me a little squeeze back. I took it as encouragement to stand up to Vickee. "You just said yourself that your clients are confidential. And if you got me out of the way, you'd be protecting your work, your reputation, and the relationship with your clients."

I said it and then regretted it, because Vickee couldn't have smiled in a more *I'm rubber, you're glue* way without holding up a placard. Of course she was right—all those motives applied equally to me. Except I didn't have any clients.

"I already let Cee scan my fox," I added. "And somebody did try to kill me."

"We have that in common, then," Vickee answered.

"Well," Petrac said, "my brain isn't for downloading without a warrant. Not unless everybody else agrees to it."

Across Ops, Willow raised her hand. "Yod can download mine. I trust her."

"Mine too." Haran looked directly at Vickee as he spoke. "As long as everybody else agrees."

She returned the stare, snout wrinkling. Luna was still sitting next to her, and I was displeased to see the same expression of disdain on my daughter's face. I reached over and stroked Stavan's hair.

Fritha rubbed her face on her hands—the opposite of the way a human would have made the gesture. "If the saboteur can avoid Yod's surveillance, why do we think it's one of the crew? The attacker could be anywhere in the hab."

"It's not that big a hab," Yod answered. "There are people in most of it."

"Pirates have a big EVA culture, I hear," Vickee interjected. "And place a lot of cultural weight on stoicism. Enduring discomfort. They do all sorts of things to prove they're badasses."

I pressed my temples. Chionn's workup hadn't revealed any problems with my neurology, and my fox had been thoroughly vetted, so I felt confident my migraine was a result of having spent too long in a room with Vickee DeVine.

Whatever was causing it, my head pounded and the lights in the pod seemed to be increasing in brightness. I put a hand over my eyes.

Yod said, "I have a few new monitoring tricks in place that might help."

"Like what?" Vickee asked.

"For the time being, that's confidential." If Yod were a human, I'd say I could hear the smile in her voice. "I wouldn't want our would-be killer to come up with countermeasures."

"Why is it so bright in here?" Stavan asked, looking up from the cat.

Huh, I guess it wasn't just a migraine.

"The Baostar is flaring," said Yod. "Big one."

"Good thing you've got that fungus to hide behind," Dakhira sniffed.

CHAPTER 20

HUMAN BEINGS HAVE A LONG HISTORY OF PROJECTing our cultural narratives onto our habitat, then using the purported laws of nature as arguments to support our biases. Whether it's the Great Chain of Being reflected in the idea of human sovereignty over Creation or the inverse Toxic Brain Hypothesis positing that sapient life-forms are somehow separate and accursed compared to other animals, we have a tendency to set ourselves apart. It's a sophipathology as ingrained as the Big Ape Rule, where unright-minded hierarchal species have a tendency to assume that anybody perceived as socially important must also be infallible and smart and good at their job.

Once upon a time foresters were taught that trees in a woods existed only in competition with one another. That they raced toward the light while their roots fought it out underground for minerals, nutrients, and water, in a reflection of the human preoccupation with gathering and controlling resources far beyond what any individual needed. Of course, people haven't stopped being selfish, but imagine an entire society dominated by the postulate that the whole purpose of life is to get a lot of stuff and use it as leverage to get more stuff and control other people's lives. Or even destroy them. Why wouldn't we think trees do the same?

Imagine a world where everybody thought like a pirate and assumed the whole universe operated by rapine and plunder. Scary and exhausting.

Later research began to show that forests were much more complicated and interdependent systems, trees connected to one another by root grafts and fungal mycelium, old small trees in the understory fed from below while waiting their turn to grow skyward when a larger tree fell, then nourishing the still-living stumps of the elders that had once fed them in turn. Trees coordinating their reproductive efforts to create mast years, a huge abundance of nuts and seeds so vast that rodents couldn't eat them all and some would survive and grow—then following that with years of lower yield so rodent populations wouldn't explode.

Care, competition, and collective action all threaded together in a resilient adaptive system, producing more benefit for most than each working against every other. Teamwork.

A system much like the Synarche, at least in aspiration, in other words. Which probably means that this, too, is an oversimplification and projection, a justification of how our society provides structure and safety for most.

Thinking about trees, I took myself to the Garden Pod after the meeting. I wanted to check on Angie and the family tree and to spend a little time well away from Vickee *and* Dakhira. I'd let Salvie extricate Luna from Vickee's clutches, at Salvie's insistence. *You know you'll lose your temper.*

My wife, of course, was right. My wife was always right. And yet somehow nonetheless she'd married me.

I had hoped I might be alone, but by the time I got there Dr. Nonsense was already in residence. It was still wearing its rebreather but had changed outfits to a purple fringed cape of some translucent colloid. It had squidged up onto a tabletop and was feeding Angie the dinosaur grapes and burbling pleasantly to itself. Angie stood on the table, wing membranes folded up, looking like a whippet crossed with a feathered bat.

I stepped a little harder as I came through the hatch, assuming either the sound or the vibrations would alert Dr. Nonsense to my presence. I didn't know if dodecapuses *startled*, exactly. I saw its skin ripple with brilliant orange polka dots on a field of blue and purple, and my fox translated the color flashes for me as a stream of baby talk.

It was chatting with the dinosaur. Officially the most charming thing I've seen on a use-once-and-throw-away space station at the end of the galaxy.

The Garden Pod was incredibly bright from the stellar flare. So many plant leaves coated in the ruddy glow, tilting themselves to soak up as much light as possible. It was beautiful, and the filtration of the leaves across the canopy meant the light was nearly bearable.

"Is the star destabilizing?" I asked.

The star was already destabilized. It gave Angie the last grape. She slurped it up, then looked at me quizzically.

"Sorry," I said. "No grapes here. But is its condition . . . progressing?"

Iris and the other physicists think so. We should have plenty of warning if it begins to go nova, however—it's not an instantaneous process. We can evacuate ahead of the shock front.

And try our luck blockade running, with the outer reaches of the system full of Void knew how many pirates. While leaving most of the Baomind behind.

My heart clenched.

What are you feeling? my boss asked.

"Dread."

That is only sensible.

I waved at the greenery. "How much radiation are we being exposed to?"

Yod?

The wheelmind cleared her throat. "It should be fine. Radiotropic shielding grows thicker the more protons you slam into it."

"What do we know about the state of the blockade?"

"No word from the outside yet. We should be using our Interceptors and the cargo ships to evacuate clouds of tesserae, and the fact that we can't spare them for that . . ." An AI can't shake her head, but she sure can trail off into a tone of resignation. "Well, the Baomind itself has been keeping the bad guys out of range. It seems to recognize that the pirates are a threat to it and us, and now that we've established we're friendlies, it includes us in its perimeter. But we can't expand that perimeter indefinitely, because the Baomind doesn't have enough surface area. And we've moved quite a bit of it outsystem already, so its volume is smaller than it was."

"I saw the Baomind pull a Freeport ship to pieces. When we were inbound." I printed off some crickets and grubs, and settled down at the table to feed Angie. She must have been pretty full already because she didn't seem interested in the food items until Dr. Nonsense tentacled me a long pair of forceps with which to jiggle them. Then she snapped them up with cheerful crunchings.

"Yes, it fights by turning the enemy into more Baomind tesserae," Yod replied. "Takes a while, though, and it's not without risk, and they can only do it when the enemy ship drops its EM bottle. And of course that means we'll have more Baomind to move, if they catch any more Freeport ships."

A logistical problem, but also a defense. Not for the first time, I imagined myself inside a ship being disassembled by a million angry Kells, and shuddered. "Yikes. Well, we ought to be doing something other than just waiting for the sky to fall, right? We need a way out."

"We need a fleet." A breeze rippled through the conservatory as the air circulation kicked in. It had the effect of Yod heaving a space-station-sized sigh. "I can't run out and get one."

"I need to do something."

"Figure out who tried to kill you and Trevor," Yod suggested. "And do what you came here to do: save and synthesize as much of the Baomind's data as you can. They can rebuild tesserae; they can't rebuild lost data."

"You're suggesting that trying to save individual tesserae is the wrong approach?"

"They're like cells in your body," Yod said. "You don't worry about some shed skin or hair."

"I do worry about getting a hand cut off, though." I was touching the hardsuit actuator that had probably saved my life once already. I pulled my hand away.

"Sure, but we can grow you a new one." Yod paused. "I think you are distracted by the presence of Dr. DeVine."

"I believe Vickee capable of arranging a couple of near-fatal accidents if she thought it would get her something she wanted."

"I'll bear that in mind," said Yod, who seemed to be taking it seriously. "And I'm going to suggest that neither you nor she is alone, if at all possible."

I wondered if Yod was going to assign me a minder. I decided that, if she did, I would be more gracious about it than Vickee was about basically anything.

"Would it be possible for you to just monitor everybody and set some kind of alarm to go off if they stop registering on your sensors?"

"I cannot monitor or record people in their private spaces unless there is a physical or medical emergency, or unless they ask for my attention," Yod said. "Not without a warrant, anyway."

"Warrants." I sighed.

Angie cheeped at me. I was falling down on the job. I jiggled another cricket.

Better than life without them, Nonsense opined. *So, if whoever is committing the attacks is using Freeport tech to block your senses, Yod, they must be activating it before they leave their quarters?*

"That's a reasonable deduction, if we posit that the ghost is a member of the crew and not a stowaway."

"And not just a Freeport hunter-killer drone," said a voice from the hatch.

I almost dropped the forceps. Angie quacked at me grumpily, annoyed that her pseudo-mealworm was wavering away from her mouth. I stopped staring at Petrac, who had walked in alongside Haran and seemed to have accurately assessed the conversation.

I refocused on Angie so Petrac wouldn't see my grimace of distaste. I hate it when people with terrible belief systems turn out to be reasonably intelligent. It upsets my sense of the natural order of the universe, which is to say: that everybody smart should agree with me.

I selected another cricket and said, "Do they have a lot of amoeba-dispensing drones that also fire sedative darts?"

"Sedative darts?" asked Haran.

"Somebody tried to kill me, too, and that was their weapon of choice."

Maybe don't give away all the information we haven't publicly released? Cee sent. Which was how I learned that she was also listening.

Petrac was there when you were examining me.

Haran wasn't.

Embarrassment twisted my stomach. *Sorry.*

I would be a terrible spy.

"Okay," I said. "I'll try to solve my own attempted murder, then, and Trevor's, too. Where do you start with something like that?"

"By asking a Goodlaw," Petrac suggested. I really didn't like him.

I decided not to remind him that Xhelsea had never investigated a homicide.

He stomped past us, startling Angie into flight and rattling the hydroponics tanks. Haran hung back by the hatch, trying to fade into the greenery and looking uncomfortable. I tried to convince myself that the motion I kept seeing out of the corner of my eye was just him fidgeting, but between the earworms and the visual artifacts I was still afraid that there actually might be something wrong with my brain, my rightminding, my ayatanas, my fox, or all four. Despite the fact that Chionn had investigated every electron, neutron, and positron making up my nervous system and neural prosthesis. She would have found a problem if there was a problem to find.

"What are you doing here?" Okay, it wasn't my greatest comeback ever. Anxiety was making me snappish, so I tuned it down. A little too late to conceal my emotional state, unfortunately.

Petrac smiled nastily at me. "Contributing to the long-term survival of the crew."

He crouched and pulled something out from under one of the tables: a big composting tank. When he opened it, whatever was inside smelled strongly of fermentation. Petrac made a satisfied noise. Nonsense squidged all its arms in the opposite direction.

"Haran," he said, "get the still."

Haran came a few steps farther into the conservatory, looking at me quizzically. "Are you okay, Dr. Song?"

"Sunya," I said automatically. "Yes, I'm fine. I've just got too much data in my fox right now and it keeps demanding my attention."

He chuckled. "Seeing things?"

"You never know," I answered. "Maybe the hab is full of poltergeists?"

The hatch opened again. I was starting to feel like the ingenue in a vintage farce. But it was just Iris, rubbing her eyes and yawning.

"Well," she said, "the Baostar's probably not going to blow up todia. Are the strawberries ripe yet?" She wrinkled her nose. "What's that smell?"

"Civilization," said Haran happily.

"Hey, Dr. Song," she said.

"Don't 'Doctor' me when I don't even know your last name to 'Doctor' you back," I teased.

She had her personal data locked down out of senso. Maybe she was a private person. Or maybe she was a pirate.

I hoped not. I liked her.

"Luce," she said. "But please just call me Iris."

"Then I'm Sunya."

The strawberries are over there, Nonsense interjected.

Iris picked up a bowl from the stand beside the printer and went to investigate. As she picked thumbnail-sized berries, she looked around at the sky outside. "It seems weird how everywhere we go in this really big universe, we find evidence of the people who came before us."

"Not really," I said, then wanted to smack myself for being the pedant. But she was looking at me curiously, so I continued, "Historically speaking, I mean, there are analogues on Terra. The ancients of Old Earth built their cities in layers, each generation's construction and innovation atop the rubble of past generations. You'd think that there would be so much room on a planet that settlements would rarely intersect, but the advantageous places to put cities don't change much as the centuries go by, so people tend to build them right on top of each other."

"Huh," she said.

I continued, "Space is much the same. The galaxy is unimaginably vast, but the cozy bits and desirable neighborhoods are much smaller. And apparently the Koregoi had similar needs to ours: warmth, light, energy. So we went out into space and found all the old campfires—and each other."

"That actually makes sense."

I smiled, unable to resist a solemn pronouncement. "We've pitched our tent in a haunted castle."

That made Haran laugh. "So it *is* poltergeists."

"Once we get the still set up, I can guarantee you will be seeing all sorts of things." Petrac's voice dripped with satisfaction. Haran rummaged under counters and soon assembled a collection of chemistry equipment on a cart. He and Petrac started fiddling around with siphons and filters, drawing the fermented liquid out of the composter and filling the lower chamber of the still. In a few minutes, it began to bubble gently. Steam rose into the collector.

Angie made a noise of displeasure as the reek intensified.

What are you fermenting? Nonsense asked.

"Plant scraps, leftover food, bits of the radiotropic fungus. Alcohol has calories," Petrac said.

Running the same material back through the printers would also provide calories, but instead of pointing that out, I said, "You're making radioactive vodka?"

"It'll be gin, actually. There are plenty of edible aromatics in here. You had some at the reception."

I had indeed. Now I felt bad for enjoying it.

He made a lofty gesture. "And the fungus *eats* radiation; it doesn't produce it."

Speaking of metabolizing toxins, your primate ability to do so and to derive recreation from it explains a few things about your species, Dr. Nonsense said. *Please keep that stuff away from me. It would strip my mucous membranes and peel my flesh off.*

Great, just what we needed. Another potential murder weapon.

The hatch opened again, this time admitting Willow and a rucksack full of freshly printed pressure sensors. I chose to regard this as humorous rather than annoying, and if my teeth were gritted, I hoped nobody could tell. I was obviously not going to get my peace and quiet here. If Yod wanted me watched over constantly, I might as well go back to my quarters. . . . I could come back and visit the family tree after the Garden Pod emptied.

• • •

I was in luck when I got home. Salvie was alone except for the cats. She was propped up on pillows, stretched out on a couch, and Zig and Zag were sprawled across her legs as limp as furry nonviolent protestors. Her species runs a little warmer than humans, which makes her Zig and Zag's favorite member of the family.

"Hey," I said, and jammed the interior airlock door open so the exterior one couldn't cycle.

Salvie looked up from her screen. "Are you planning to vent us?"

She sounded more curious than concerned. I didn't think I would have managed her sangfroid.

"I just wanted to make sure nobody walked in on our conversation. Since I'm not sure there's any privacy to be found on this hab otherwise." I was thinking of Petrac letting himself in after Salvie arrived, but before I did.

She set her reader down. "You want to plan crimes?"

"I've been asked to solve them." I sat down by her feet and pulled them into my lap. She sighed in bliss as my thumbs found the sore spots on her soles.

"That's worth crossing a galaxy for. Are you making any progress?"

"Mostly in irritation," I admitted. "I have academic work I need desperately to be doing." At least my parsers were still running. And with access to the hab's computing assets, running faster and deeper than before.

"Can't Vickee do this?"

"What if Vickee's behind it?" I said. "What if she's trying to keep me busy so I don't get in her way?"

"Do you think she's manipulative enough to try something like that?"

I wished I had some of Petrac's gin. "That's the problem. She knows me too well. She's fully capable of anticipating that I would feel responsible for finding a solution."

"But you're not. Maybe you should tell me in real detail what happened between the two of you." Salvie's tendrils wriggled. "You've only ever hinted at it—"

Just thinking about it left me shaky with adrenaline, tears of fury stinging my eyes. Salvie, noticing, leaned forward over the disgruntled cats to stroke my hair. Zag burrowed deeper; Zig, his sleek gray dignity offended, got up and left.

"The short form is that she stole my research when we were in school, when I thought she was . . ." I made a face. There were too many ways to finish the sentence. *My friend. My lover. My trusted collaborator.*

"And the long form?"

"She's a lot better at networking than I am." The memories came with a sensation like an icicle thrust into my chest, but somehow my heart kept right on beating. "She love-bombed everybody else just as ferociously as she had love-bombed me until she got what she was looking for. I was pretty sure if I called her out for presenting my work as her own, I wouldn't be believed."

"But hadn't your advisor seen early material in your dissertation?"

"This wasn't my dis. It was a paper on modalities for locating and restoring unnetworked physical storage media."

"I married a genius," Salvie said, as if awestruck.

I sniffled and wiped my nose on my hand experimentally. Maybe the waterworks were stopping? "That's news?"

"Phhbt," quoth she. "Tell me the rest."

"She and I were close. She was reviewing the paper for me before I submitted. I hadn't shown it to anybody else. And then a very similar paper was published under her name, shortly after she returned my draft to me."

"But the draft would have proved she—"

I shook my head. "She was smart enough not to leave any comments on the file."

"Did you have a forensic specialist—"

"No!" I modulated my tone. "No, I didn't. I know I should have. But my heart was broken, and I . . . I've never felt so betrayed."

Even telling Salvie—my *wife*—about it made me feel vulnerable. *Salvie* wouldn't betray me. I was safe with Salvie. I was, I was, I was.

If you could ever be safe with anyone, that is.

"I was supposed to be the Hot New Thing and get my choice of assignments but . . . well, after that, I couldn't focus on work very well. I needed an extra semester to finish my research and defend my thesis, and by then Vickee had the job I'd wanted. I just stayed on Rubric and found a postdoc."

"You love Rubric. And you're still a Hot Enough Thing for me."

"Don't distract me with the truth." I rolled my shoulders. "And I met you there, so it was all for the best in the long run. But I guess I've been chasing her dust cloud ever since. Trying to prove that I'm as good as she is."

Salvie shifted around on the bench to pull me into her arms, which was finally enough to make Zag get up and resettle himself. The clench inside me unkinked slightly.

"You got me," she said. "And a couple of gorgeous, maddening kids. And enough career cred to be one of only two archinformists who were invited here."

"The barriers to entry were pretty high," I pronounced dourly, to hide the fact that she was making me feel better.

She laughed at me, all her tendrils coiling like terrified earthworms.

Zig jumped into my lap and made a show of kneading his way in a circle.

Slow tears brimmed again and crept down my cheeks as he headbutted and purred and climbed onto my chest in an ecstasy of affection. I could have tuned, I guess, but it felt good to cry.

"And cats," I said, finishing Salvie's list. "And I'm here at the end of the universe surrounded by pirates with everything that matters to me. And Fucking Vickee."

"Hey," Salvie said. "We're together. We'll figure something out."

I sighed. Zig's squeaks and purrs were reaching a crescendo, and he had started to drool. I scratched behind his ears. "I feel like I'm still navigating that emotional transition to not being Hot and New anymore. I'm envious of Vickee's continued, stolen Hot Newness. But it's a stage you pass through. Now my job is to hang on and keep innovating until I have been around long enough to become an Honored Fixture."

Salvie nibbled on the nape of my neck, which was always a reliable distraction.

I was determined to finish my whine, however. "And, apparently, to solve a couple of attempted murders without any idea of what I'm doing, or any clues. Which is already cutting into my work time."

So was sulking on the couch, but Salvie was warm and resilient, and leaning my head on her shoulder was the best kind of peace. And Zig seemed to be deeply enjoying walking in circles on top of me.

"How hard can it be?" Salvie asked. "We can work on it together. And if the Goodlaw has you crime-solving, it probably means they don't think you're a suspect!"

"Silver Lining Salvie strikes again." Zig, offended by my laughter, jumped off with a force that made me say, "Oof."

"Well, if we operate on the assumption that the would-be killer is a pirate agent . . . then Freeporters hate 'aliens,'" Salvie said. "And the junior admin is a bigot."

"Petrac. Oh, you noticed?"

"How could I miss it?"

I said, "I'd hope a pirate wouldn't give so much away."

"Well, he's very popular with your human colleagues, given his hobby."

I remembered the reek of alcohol. "You know about the still?"

"I chatted with some people in the lounge after you left the staff meeting. Maybe he's going to poison everybody and let the pirates in."

"Can't get a shipmind drunk," I observed. And almost jumped out of my skin when somebody started pounding on the outer airlock door.

We both leaped to our feet with the lazy slowness of hab gravity. Zag, unseated, sprang across the room. He rebounded up the walls in several leaps before sticking to the upholstery near the ceiling, all his claws sunk in deeply. My heart rate rebounded, too, as Salvie and I shared a glance.

"Enemy at the gates?" I whispered.

Salvie walked over and thumbed the intercom on. "Friend or foe?!" she yelled into it, with the glorious lack of subtlety I married her for.

"Mom, we're locked out!" Luna yelled back. "Are you okay? What's going on in there?"

"We just had the inner airlock door open," Salvie said. "I'll let you right in!"

I slumped back on the bench, eyes closed, feeling like an idiot. I was definitely on edge. . . . On the other hand, somebody *had* tried to kill me. I managed to pull myself together while Salvie unwedged the door, and by the time the kids trooped in I had dried my cheeks and was probably presentable enough to avoid the notice of a self-involved teenager. Or two.

I was totally unprepared when Luna tossed me something, underhand. I got my hands up, but it bounced off my fingertips and rattled to the floor.

"MOM!"

"Sudden gust of gravity," I explained, bending down to pick it up.

Stavan chuckled. Luna burst into tears and whirled around in the doorway.

"Where are you going?" Salvie called.

"To visit Dr. DeVine!" she yelled over her shoulder before vanishing in a puff of hormones.

I pushed my fist against my mouth to keep the intemperate words inside. The object Luna had thrown me was still clenched in it. I peeled my fingers open and saw a handball-sized printed globe, the familiar continents and oceans of Rubric etched on it in saturated colors. There were even swirls of cloud, moving weather patterns, and a terminator sweeping across the globe.

"Wow," I said. "She made this in school?"

"It's not really *school*," Stavan said. He dropped his bag beside the door and headed to the printer.

"Ah, stow that before you get distracted," Salvie said.

He huffed, but didn't *"Mom"* her, though his steps as he picked it up and stuffed it into a cargo net might have been the smallest bit stompy. Compared to Luna, he was the soul of self-restraint.

I stroked the little globe. It was beautiful. I remembered Luna as a grade schooler daubed with paint and polymer, but I'd had no idea her art had come this far.

While Stavan was printing himself an after-school snack, I asked, "What makes it not really school?"

"Well, it's just us." He set the hab to make him a chair and a small table, and settled in to eat what would have been two or three full meals for me.

"So it's more like tutoring?"

I had to work to keep my voice level. Luna's behavior had left me simmering. I reminded myself that she was a storm of neurochemicals my adult self barely even remembered. And that she had brought me a gift, meant to be a peace offering.

"I guess." Most of a folded slice of pizza vanished into his mouth. Amazing. He ate fast, possibly because boys his age are always hungry, possibly because if his mouth was full I wouldn't expect him to answer questions. Finished, he pushed the plate into the recycler, reset the room without being told, and headed for the airlock again.

"I'm going to run laps," he said.

"Laps of what?"

"Town!" he said cheerily, and with a wave he was gone.

I tried not to think of that terrifying tube bouncing under his feet. I tried not to think about all that pizza bouncing around inside him. Was I ever that indestructible?

Childhood memories of my mother yelling at me not to go in the water for an hour after eating suggested that I probably had been.

Carefully, I put Luna's globe down on the bench. "Do you think she's homesick?"

Salvie made an indelicate noise by rubbing her fingers together, creating a squeaking she knows drives me crazy. Like fingernails on a slate. "I think I dragged a teenager halfway across the galaxy, away from all of her friends."

I sighed. "How that kid who never had *any* interest in my work has basically apprenticed herself to Vickee DeVine . . . I thought you were going to warn her about Vickee!"

"I told her that Vickee had her own agenda. Do you really think forbidding her to have anything to do with Dr. DeVine would produce the desired result?"

"The opposite," I admitted.

"I am not human, Sun." Salvie put her hand on my shoulder. "But I have spent enough time around your people, and done enough research on you, to know that expecting emotional validation from a teenage human is like trying to read by the light of a black hole."

"That's not fair! I just want her to be less of a jerk!"

Her tendrils coiled in laughter. I knew it wasn't meant cruelly, but I was still stung.

I threw my hands up. "You're telling me that hoping to be treated as a valued family member by my daughter is futile?"

"You are currently demonstrating where, as the human saying goes, she gets it from." Salvie's tone was mild, which just made me madder.

She was not, however, incorrect. Much as it rankled to admit it. I calmed myself, and the tuning was working pretty well until she added,

"Parenting isn't and has never been about your children meeting *your* needs."

A lot of people have the narrative misconception that rightminding "fixes" you or somehow "edits" your personality. And while it's possible under a therapist's supervision or Judiciary direction to make some big changes, or for a clade to link themselves into a single multibodied mind, mostly what it's best for is helping our brains cope with modern life.

Rightminding can make my species less reactive, less fragile, less prone to sophipathologies such as confirmation bias or the human tendency to double down on a losing strategy. It can fix a bunch of evolutionary kludges like our tendency to invent patterns and narratives by ignoring contrary data. It can make us more collaborative and less hierarchical, and help us make long-term plans based on deduction and induction rather than bias.

Because of how I lost my sister and my mom, being on a hab was a constant low-grade reactivity trigger for me, and the fact that I knew it didn't make it easier.

Which made me think about why Luna had exploded.

She'd made me a gift as a gesture of reaching out, and in my clumsiness I had seemed careless of her effort. She'd been casual about throwing it to me, but I knew Luna well enough to know that any casualness was studied, a suit of armor over the things about which she cared most deeply.

Humans of old thought that logic and emotion were two different things, separable into a dichotomy: Apollo and Dionysius, Spock and Kirk. But it turns out that rationality is a spectrum of responses, and feelings derive from observation and experience and underpin that spectrum.

The hinky feeling has saved a lot of lives over the millennians.

"So you're saying she's never going to value me?" I really was feeling sorry for myself. But once you get started, it's hard to stop.

"Oh, she values you. Just not for the reasons you value yourself." She put a hand on my shoulder.

I let it stay there. "If my legacy isn't my work, and it isn't my kids . . . what is any of this good for?"

"I think you maybe need to tune your feelings a little," Salvie said. "And have a snack."

I sighed, feeling dismissed. Which I suppose was better than feeling neglected. Nobody likes to be told their feelings are from hormones or low blood sugar or being overwrought or tired . . . even when they are, and one is acting like a toddler.

I pulled myself together and went to the printer. It was silly to sit there feeling terrible just to prove to Salvie that she wasn't the boss of me, and that my terrible mood was justified.

She kept talking. "By the standard of whether people judge us by the metrics we would wish, and whether anything endures forever—everything is futile. Art is futile. Reproduction is futile."

"I can't believe you would say that about your children." I tried to find a teasing tone, walk the argument back from the edge of a fight. I printed some juice and a whole-grain-and-protein bar. Get the old blood sugar up and then give it something to keep working on.

Salvie said, "*Our* children. And I'm not saying it; I'm pointing out the implications of what you were saying."

The juice hit like a freight train, making me feel better almost the instant I swallowed it. Damn my wife for being right.

"You're saying that in the end, the universe falls apart. Nothing has intrinsic value. All that matters is the journey. It doesn't really matter if we save the Baomind, or if we all die out here."

Salvie came over and put her arms around me. "Nothing has intrinsic value, but everything has value to someone or something, and nihilism is lazy. That's what I'm saying."

"Humph," I said.

She tickled my ear with her tendrils. "Eat your protein bar. And let's figure out how to stop a murderer."

I talked through oat crumbs. "Well, somebody did try to murder me immediately after I started asking questions. That might narrow it down."

Salvie lowered her voice. "Do you think it was—" She gestured toward the ceiling, not saying Yod's name lest she summon Yod's attention.

"If a hab wants you dead, you're dead," I said, like a mantra. I felt better for the food, but a sense of unease still nagged at me. Like overhearing a whispered conversation in a house that was meant to be empty, but not being able to make out any words. "I'm full of complicated feelings and could use a distraction," I said with a sigh.

She spoke close to my throat. "Am I a suitable distraction?"

"You might be an unsuitable one." I lowered my lashes and then, the soul of romance, wiped my hands on my trousers before embracing her.

One nice thing about recycling all your clothes: there's no point in caring if you get sweat or food stains on them. Or if your partner happens to pop a few buttons off them in her haste to get you into the bedroom.

CHAPTER 21

SALVIE AND I MANAGED TO BE PRESENTABLE AGAIN BY the time Stavan got home sweaty and limp and hurled himself into the cleanser.

The next dia would bring toil, drudgery, and endless dusty stacks of ones and zeros. Three of my favorite things. Assuming that enough of the background data on my coworkers that I needed to start my new career as a consulting detective was available out here on the periphery.

If nothing else, there would be more personnel files. It wasn't much to hang my hopes on—they might be comprehensive or they might be thin—but I'd spent over a decade learning to spot the gaps and contradictions in any given pattern or narrative. If there were clues in the empty spaces, I'd ferret them out.

But I would deal with that tomorrow. I would also do more work on synthesizing the Baomind data, which was really coming together nicely despite my intermittent distraction and that slight murder attempt. Maybe I could get Kell to provide some insights.

Tonight, I really was going to go take care of my family tree. Assuming—

"Hey, Yod?"

Her presence lights flickered on. "How can I help you, Sunya?"

"Is anybody still in the Garden Pod?" I *really* wanted the space to myself, having been driven out of it once already.

"Just Angie and Dr. Nonsense," the wheelmind said.

Okay. I could deal with the dodecapus, even in my current state of mind. It had a soothing presence. And Salvie had done a lot to de-spiral my emotions in general.

Get up, Sunya. Time to do something worthwhile. And who knew? Distracting my hands and attention while my unconscious mind and algorithms worked over the problems might just provide some real solutions.

When I entered the Garden Pod, it was still bright with stellar flare. I was grateful for the radiation shielding and for the pixelated sphere of the Baomind creating a shadow grid between us and the star. On the other side of the hab, back toward the pirate blockade and home, the vast whorl of the Milky Way hung, visible from . . . well, not quite the outside. There were still a few globular clusters past us before you could *really* say you'd left the galaxy.

But it definitely felt like looking at my house from the woods across the path, rather than being inside looking out. Or even standing in the garden.

I chuckled to myself. I was quite literally standing in the garden.

For a moment I was so homesick for Rubric it felt like a cramp in my gut. If I made it home, I would never leave again.

Magical thinking. Bargaining. But the emotional reality was too strong to deny.

I stood for a moment and watched the Baomind through the fronds of the small fig trees and oil palms. The pod's superstructure was designed like the glass roof of a dirtside conservatory: a crystal palace in space. Polarization and filtering meant I could stare directly into the sun. The surface of the Baostar looked like the cooling outflow of a volcano: mottled rings of dried-blood burgundy showed the limits of convection cells, the centers shading toward a sullen dying-campfire orange. The flare itself was a massive arch that lifted above the star's corona, a cataract of fire that could have engulfed my homeworld several times over.

The conservatory was still filled with the gentle bubbling of Petrac's chemistry experiment and the tang of alcohol. When I was thinking earlier about people being bad judges of risks, I hadn't even remembered this bit of . . . tomfoolery. Didn't alcohol fumes combined with oxygen explode?

I decided not to look it up. But I had forgotten to disconnect from Yod and was thinking very loudly, because she whispered, *I'm keeping an eye on it* into my feed.

Angie the dinosaur rustled within the arch of a frond that echoed the arch of the flare. She cheeped grumpily but didn't flutter down. I wondered if the light was keeping her awake.

Poor protobird. Alone in the universe.

But aren't we all?

I spoke out loud to let Dr. Nonsense know I was there, though I'm sure Yod had informed it. "Did Petrac leave his still running? Surely there's some kind of regulation about that?"

Sure enough, one of the tanks bubbled thickly. A moment later an opalescent arm smacked over the rim, followed by another. Squelching, Dr. Nonsense hauled itself into view.

It wasn't wearing a breather; it just hung over the edge like a swimmer resting their elbows on the edge of a pool. Two arms and two eyes showed above the water. Below, the other arms moved lazily against the glass, adhering and releasing. The denticles among the suckers made a scraping, tinkling sound.

Its skin rippled orange rimmed with green, then settled into a gradient—yellowy on the side toward the still, shading to olive across the top and a deep, satisfied teal underwater. Iridophores flashed a greeting.

"I hope I didn't wake you," I said as I went to fetch my tree from another table.

Three brains are still asleep, said Nonsense. It squidged down the tank wall, well away from the still. The yellowish area darkened to green.

I brought the family tree over and set it down across from Dr. Nonsense. I tipped my head toward the chemistry experiment. "Can't you put a stop to that?"

There are political factions on this wheel, Nonsense said. *Technically Petrac is under my command. But if I force the situation, I might lose authority. You humans stick together. And many of you like your mood-altering consumables.*

I felt stupid.

The emotion must have crossed the feed, because Nonsense said, *Don't feel bad. You just got here. And if we had more than one Ceeharen aboard, the factional divisions would be even more interesting.*

"*Interesting* is a word for it." I sat down facing Nonsense.

The tree looked okay, all things considered. It seemed to be pleased to be out of its habitat and experiencing an artificial spring. Tiny auburn buds frosted its stems. A few had even begun to unfurl into coppery sprays more like blossoms than leaf clusters. The bark had a healthy, satiny sheen.

The branch I had splinted was a different story. It was still too soon to be sure if the graft might take or fail, but the buds along one side looked friable. The sap wasn't getting to them to carry moisture and nutrients, and they were withering.

The buds on the other side of the limb, where the cambium hadn't broken, looked okay. There was still hope, and fussing with it would only make the tree's job harder. So I left it alone.

The tree needed soaking. While I was setting up the watering tray, Nonsense said, *Speaking of politics, would you tell me about the situation with you and Dr. DeVine?*

I opened my mouth, examined the intemperate words that filled it, and swallowed them. A moment of reflection brought me a less incendiary analysis. "We have a history. I do not trust her, and find her self-absorbed and socially irresponsible. She doesn't give a damn about community. And she's in need of better rightminding."

Untranslated shivers of turquoise and yellow passed over Nonsense's membranes. I wondered if it was laughing. More of its arms rose from the water, holding thin, dripping yarn and . . . a length of lace? The arms writhed, and the little denticle hooks among its suckers caught and released the yarn in complex patterns.

Yarn converted to lace at a frankly startling pace. It was tatting.

I wonder what you decided not to say, if that's your measured response.

All right, well, the squid had asked for it. "I think she's abusive, and I'd believe she was working for the pirates, if only they were known for their access to advanced research facilities. If they could offer her something she thought was valuable, she'd feed all of us to them without a moment's concern. I base that on personal experience."

Do you think she'd kill to preserve her professional status?

"In a heartbeat," I said.

I have twelve hearts, Nonsense responded. *One of mine, or one of yours?*

That time, I did laugh. And felt the clutch of anger inside me fading slightly. Trauma response: it's there to defend you from harmful situations, but in the modern world it so rarely proves effective. Laughing gave me the perspective to tune the rage back: I didn't need the distraction. I had so many things to do other than being angry.

"Are you suggesting I'm self-righteous?" I had to calm myself to focus on the tree, anyway. It was time to pinch back terminal buds to encourage ramification, and I couldn't do that if my hands were trembling with rage.

I'm saying that bilateral symmetry has its drawbacks. I've spent a lot of time among humans since coming here, and you do tend to think in terms of different sides. You and Dr. DeVine form opposing sides, in your perception. In mine, perhaps you're both pulling away from a common center in different directions, but you're not diametrically opposed.

"If you're going to tell me I hate her because we're too much alike, please don't."

The still blurped loudly and I jumped.

I think you want similar things, but that doesn't make you alike. But it wouldn't hurt to remind yourself that truth and experience exist on a spectrum. Dr. DeVine is not unintimidated by you.

"What?"

If she were, she wouldn't spend so much time getting under your skin. Really, it would be useful if your species were better at nuance and navigating integrative complexity.

I had to look up "integrative complexity." Yod provided a definition from the *Oxford-Webster's New Comprehensive Dictionary*: *A psychometric referring to the capacity and willingness to accept that there are multiple ways to conceive of an issue and to acknowledge that many of these perspectives are simultaneously legitimate (differentiation), coupled with the ability to form conceptual links among these perspectives and to integrate them into a coherent overall judgment (integration).*

That made me laugh. "I'm not sure I can manage that level of 'integrative complexity.' Many of my species still think that attention to nuance is a sign of indecisiveness and a character flaw."

Dr. Nonsense said, *Of course it's hard for you. You only have one brain, and it's divided into hemispheres. Your physiological equipment predisposes you to false binaries.*

"What does yours predispose you to?"

Equivocating. Its arms writhed in laughter.

I had been so engaged in the conversation that I had almost forgotten about the constant background music inside my head. That relative quiet was shattered by a sudden crescendo. I jumped and the twig I was holding snapped off in my hand. My expression of dismay got through the filter. "Oh, damn!"

As I looked down at the damage, something caught the corner of my eye. Movement, like a fluttering dress. For a moment I thought it was one of Nonsense's ruffles, but the motion vanished as soon as I faced it directly. And Nonsense wasn't wearing a frock.

What's wrong? Nonsense asked.

"I thought I saw something."

A pause. *Would you let Yod check your fox again?*

Sadly, I laid the snapped twig on the table. Maybe I should keep my hands off the tree for the foreseeable future, if this sort of thing happened every time I tried to work on it. "Oh, why not? Everybody has been in my brain downloading things."

I checked my privacy filters, then reached out to Yod and threw the door wide.

You would think you'd be able to *feel* an AI rummaging around inside your head. That there would be some kind of sensation, or colored flashes of light, or *something*. But there are no nerve endings in a brain implant, so you feel whatever the AI programs the fox to relay to you. In Yod's case, that was nothing.

I preferred that to Dakhira's pins-and-needles tickle, which I suspected was designed to be as annoying as possible on purpose.

A few moments went by before Yod's presence lights ran around the bulkhead in a series of flashes. She said, "Well, you're not imagining things."

"*What?*"

CHAPTER 22

My new sensors are sensitive enough to tell me that there is a slight pressure wave concurrent with what you saw. The air displacement indicates that something was actually there," Yod said. "There's no malfunction in your fox, and no indication that it's leakage from the ayatanas. You have an indisputable hard memory of spotting a being in that corner."

"You are haunted!"

"I am not," said Yod, "*haunted*."

"I didn't get a good look at it," I complained.

"Whatever's in your soft memory, your fox recorded an image. I can pull it up."

A projection appeared between Nonsense and myself, partially obscuring the family tree. Angie rattled out what must have been an alarm call and scurried deeper into her palm tree. I barely registered her: I was busy staring at the person—it had to be a person—standing nearby.

The most dramatic element was the lack of eyes. There was a head and something like a face, but it lacked the usual sorts of sensory architecture.

The head came up. I had a sense of a mobile neck longer than a human's, with birdlike articulation. The shape of the body was harder to define under layers of jewel-toned, diaphanous cloth that flowed from a deep hood. Other than being caught at what—on a human—would be the waist in a wide violet belt, it concealed all but the gross outline of the form. Two arms, two legs. The face was half-shadowed by that hood, but a short muzzle and sensory whiskers jutted into the light. The fur was a shaggy, rich burnished auburn with soft char-black spots. The frame was long-limbed but squat and bulbous in the torso.

The hand it raised had three thick fingers with hooked, sloth-like claws beneath two longer ones on which the claws were short and thick and clipped flat at the ends, like well-trimmed dog nails. There was a thumb, with a short nail. The nails appeared translucent, like cat claws or human fingernails, but the exteriors were coated in a translucent white-and-teal swirled polish that made me sorry I was thousands of light-years from the nearest manicure.

The memory opened its mouth to show fine-pointed canines and a row of carnivore teeth in each jaw. I heard a trill of song. The song that had been following me since I reached the Baomind. The song I had thought was just in my head, an echo from filling my fox up with the music of the spheres. Or rather, the music of a single large tesseracted sphere.

I jumped back.

Nonsense had hoisted itself, dripping, onto the edge of the tank. A puddle of greenish water spread across the deck below. It stretched up, making itself taller than I had imagined possible, and two arms rose above its body. Suckers worked spasmodically in air.

I don't smell/taste anything.

I felt foolish for not realizing that, as an aquatic life-form, its skin would be studded with senses in addition to touch: smell, taste, electricity, balance. Possibly even more exotic organs of perception.

"Would the smell linger?"

A meter-tall dodecapus shrugging is a mesmerizing sight—as if an intricately patterned, tasseled throw rug were to bunch and ripple itself in dance. *I've never smelled the memory of a Koregoi before.*

• • •

Dr. Nonsense, as has doubtless become clear, had a taste for the dramatic—but when I turned to it and gawped so widely that the wheelmind burst out laughing, I think I startled it.

It slid back into the tank with a plop and some additional displacement, as if its suckers had failed all at once. I started laughing, too, as much to release tension as because my boss was ridiculously funny.

"You don't actually *know* that that's a Koregoi."

I don't, it admitted. *But as operating theories go, I have had worse.*

The discussion that followed was too predictable and too unheated to call an argument. Especially since none of us had any illusions that we knew what we were talking about, and were thus unwilling to make any committed stands. We exhausted the "well maybes" pretty quickly and moved on to even less plausible possibilities before the conversation tapered off.

After a pause, Nonsense said, *One moment, please. I'm going to wake up the Goodlaw.*

Nonsense was going to make me popular with everybody.

While we waited for them to come over from the Interceptor, I closed my eyes and listened for music. The problem with trying to sense something at the edge of your perception, something that might be imaginary or might be real, is that you can convince yourself what is there isn't—or vice versa. All I did was give myself a headache.

I gave up after a few minutes, when Xhelsea walked through the door. They looked disgustingly dapper for somebody just roused from slumber. I guess the uniform helps. I sat on a bench, feeling grungy in my joggers and pullover. I have an academic's gift for making even freshly printed clothes look rumpled.

"All right," they said, without wasting time on pleasantries. "Show me."

Yod showed them.

The Goodlaw turned to face me. "Is it still there?"

I shook my head. "I'm not even really sure I saw it—it only registered as a flicker of movement."

Yod cleared her entirely theoretical throat. "The new displacement sensors Willow installed tell me there are a *lot* of things moving around the station. Enough mass that it's affecting our spin a little."

That sounded pretty bad to me. It must have showed, because Xhelsea patted my arm. "Every bit of mass and acceleration you add to a system affects it. Mostly we don't notice because the effects are so slight."

"And because your trusty wheelmind adjusts for them," Yod added smugly. "But, yes, we have enough of these whatever-they-ares that they have an impact on our trim. I had noticed the effect before but theorized it was a side effect of the Baomind."

The murder spot between my shoulders itched. "Maybe it *is* a haunted hab."

The Goodlaw stared at me hollowly. "Don't *you* start."

She already started. Nonsense levered itself out of the tank, laying its damp lace on the table. One arm dipped underwater and retrieved a multicolored capelet, which it settled over its body with a bolero twirl that had Xhelsea and me ducking a jeweled arc of droplets. We didn't quite bonk our heads together, so we failed as a slapstick routine.

Belatedly I realized that its capes and frilly dresses served to keep its membranes moist when it was out and about in the atmosphere. Humans were not the only species to use clothing for function *and* decoration.

I said, "I find it more comforting than the prospect of being overrun with invisible pirates."

Yod's lights rippled in amusement. "If we were overrun with invisible pirates, odds are good that everything would have been destroyed by now. They don't usually deploy gaslighting and psychological warfare. No, I think something else is going on. Something related to the Baomind."

I said, with heavy irony, "You're better than a tranquilizer. Why am I able to see and hear them when nobody else can?"

"Well, you've filled your brain up with more Baosong than anybody else we know of. That's one unique quality you have."

"Right," I said.

Yod continued, "You've also turned your entire hardware, wetware, and software architecture into a machine for parsing Baosong. I had a look at the structures you've built when you invited me to read your fox, and they're extremely impressive. I see you have the outlines of a taxonomy and dozens of different categories of data defined. I would not have expected you to be so far along already."

I waved a hand. The praise was as uncomfortable as a cramp in my side. I ought to be further along. My index wasn't more than a third constructed, and the information sets to slot into it were well-nigh infinite. I could be working on this forever.

Yod said, "I think you have a hard time acknowledging your own accomplishments."

I changed the subject. "So what's the logical next step? To wander around and see if I can sense what's causing Willow's sensors to trip?"

Whatever Yod might have answered was interrupted as the hatch opened again.

It was Haran, looking slightly shamefaced as he edged inside. "Sorry," he said. "I didn't think anybody would be here. It's the middle of sleep shift."

We were just leaving, Nonsense said, edging as far away from the still and its alcoholic miasma as it could without going the long way around the outside of the pod. I made sure my family tree was stowed safely before joining Nonsense and the Goodlaw by the door. Haran bent low, checking the heat source under the still.

"Oh, good, it turned off when it was supposed to," he said. "I was supposed to check half a standard hour ago, and dozed off."

"Mmm," I said. "Wood alcohol."

"The idea is to avoid that." He sounded amused, and more relaxed now than he had a moment ago. He lifted a big flask of clear liquid out of the still. "Besides, it comes out in the heads. You folks can stay, I'm just going to harvest some herbs and juniper berries."

He seemed so peaceable with his little clippers in his hand that I was tempted to hang out and talk about gardening, maybe show him the family tree. But it would have to wait—duty called, and I needed some rest before morning. When I would have to start peering into everybody's histories, or at least as much of them as Yod had on file. And apparently before that, I would be wandering around ghost-spotting.

And in between I needed to spend some time getting my job done.

I did not get to bed in as timely a fashion as I had hoped because I was busy practicing my psychic abilities. And if there's anything less convincing to write on an excuse note, I haven't found it yet.

The most nerve-wracking part was needing to pay attention to my surroundings as Xhelsea, Nonsense, and I respectively walked and squidged and walked around Town's jury-rigged circumference. The sky beyond the transparent fabric was a chiaroscuro of fire and shadow, the Baomind a murmuration of flecks creating dark ripples, bulges, and interference patterns across the bloated old sun. I thought of flocking birds at dawn, of sparks rising from a campfire. I thought of falling forever into that dying light, and shuddered with a chill that rose from my bones.

Worse, somewhere out there was a blockade of Freeport ships, probably assembling reinforcements while we huddled and waited, besieged.

"What's bothering you?"

I squeaked out loud and almost jumped through the walkway fabric. My startle reflex was tuned entirely too strong, or maybe it was the awareness of the shadowy figures lurking behind me that was rendering me so jumpy. Xhelsea, when I looked over, was grinning at me with amused concern.

"Is it that obvious?"

They nodded.

For some reason, I told them.

They listened thoughtfully. When I was done, they said, "Well, how many reinforcements they can and will summon depends on the pirates who are already here. They don't operate the way the Synarche does. Nobody can really . . . order the fleet to turn up for combat."

"Don't they have an admiral? Or is she a boogeyman?"

"They have an admiral. But she can only enforce what she can reach, or what those loyal to her can reach. And those loyal will only stay loyal as long as she holds the upper hand. Typical warlord problem."

I contemplated that. Nobody knows better than an archinformist or a historian that unrightminded humans are often bad at collaborative action. It was one of the evolutionary shortfalls we had to repair during the Eschaton to survive as a species. "Historical pirates operated as a collective, didn't they?"

"Well, Freeporters sure don't. So the ones who are here are here because they think they can turn a profit, and to be frank a lot of them might not want to have others around. Cuts into the margins."

"So they'd rather risk everything than share?"

The Goodlaw spread their hands. "It makes sense to them. And they have a real . . . well, if they come back without a prize, *then* they have to face the Admiral."

"What out here could possibly count as a prize?"

They shrugged. "I'm not a Freeporter, so I'm guessing. But keeping the Synarche from rescuing the Baomind might be enough. Not to mention, the tesserae are full of rare earths and some uncommon synthetic elements. You could build a lot of white coils out of this matryoshka brain. A whole fleet, honestly. Shoot the tesserae to pieces and scoop the pieces up with an electromagnetic net, and you're in business."

"But the tesserae fight back."

They nodded. "So do we."

We walked along companionably enough while I looked for invisible people. I don't know if practice was improving my ability to pick them out, if Yod was helping boost the signal, if they were growing stronger, or if I had simply stopped telling myself to ignore the things I was imagining. But once I starting looking—and allowing Yod to suggest areas of focus—they really were everywhere. The music in my head was near constant. There was a shadowy figure in my line of sight just about everywhere on the hab.

Trying to visualize the anomalies was like walking around a dark, unfamiliar space. The shapes were more visible out of the corner of my eye. When I shifted from peripheral to central vision, they faded into blurry flickers of motion. They all looked, more or less, like the first one. As alike as crows in colorful dresses.

They had no physical substance that I could detect, a supposition that I confirmed by tripping accidentally into one.

With a chill, I thought of what Kell said about feeling but not touch. Was *this* what had attacked Trevor and me?

Why would a ghost use a sedative dart, though? Or a brain-eating amoeba?

The second time, I walked through on purpose. Both figures broke apart like smoke when I moved into them, re-forming in my wake. That was more or less what I had expected. What I hadn't expected was that they would react.

The first one, the one I stumbled through, reached out after me, extending a hook-clawed hand that looked as if a bath scrubber and a spider had borne a hairy child. The hand passed through me as well. I'm pretty sure I didn't actually feel a ghostly chill: that was pure suggestion.

The second one . . . when I passed through it, the music in my head swelled to a crescendo. I paused there, and music washed over me.

I put my hands to my ears. Which of course did nothing to muffle the sound. The sound wasn't real.

It's real, Yod whispered through the senso. *It's just not physical. Or I suppose it is physical, since you are made of meat. But it isn't in your ears: it's in your fox.*

I tried running the Baomind parser on the piece of music I dreamed and it didn't do much. But your translation protocols are much more robust and trained on Baosong, and you have access to my algorithms. What if we ran the music through a combination of the two? I whispered back, counting on her to pass what I said along to Xhelsea and Nonsense.

I can try.

After a moment, she said aloud, "I can't be sure of the accuracy of this, but what it is saying . . . singing . . . is poetry? It seems to be . . . I think it's a root language to what the Baomind uses. Here, let me see if there's anything sensible in here." Yod did not speak for the alien in her own voice, but generated another.

"*stranger come*
stranger take
shadow zone
sing in you
sing with us
sing for us
sideways partners
a folded sky
iterate
translate
align"

"Stranger, huh? Well, it's not very *good* poetry," Xhelsea commented. "But at least it doesn't sound threatening."

It's probably better in the original, said Nonsense.

I snorted with laughter and wondered if that was a society-wide joke for dodecapuses as it was for humans. Did dodecapuses even have multiple languages? Aquatic creatures could hear each other over vast distances, I knew. . . .

This was one more thing I would probably never have the time to adequately research. My life is full of just such tiny disappointments. Opportunity cost is real, and there are only so many standard hours in the dia. And so many ans in a lifetime.

Acknowledging a limiting factor doesn't relieve the craving to know everything. But it does help me rationalize myself into focusing my efforts on the things I am most curious about. And right now, that was these . . . strangers.

"Well," I said, "they're not ghosts. And I'm not imagining them. But I still think we might be haunted."

"What do you think they want?" Xhelsea asked.

I shook my head, but Nonsense responded: *To communicate. To be understood.*

"To escape from the Shadow Zone," Yod quipped.

I was the only one who laughed, and it was as much in surprise that the wheelmind watched the same adventure serials as me as it was for the quality of the joke. I guess monitoring habitat stability and crew well-being probably gets pretty boring for a vast, cosmic intellect.

"Why can't anyone else see them?" I asked.

Yod said, "Because they're invisible."

I blinked. "Cloaked?"

"No," she said. "They don't interact with electromagnetic radiation."

"And they're untouchable."

"Yes."

"But they're real."

"Also yes."

I rubbed my eyes. "What *are* they made of?"

At a guess? said Nonsense. *What interacts with gravity but not much else? Dark matter.*

"My brain hurts," said the Goodlaw, speaking for both of us.

I asked, "What if we played this music to the Baomind?"

Hmm, said Nonsense. *Might be risky?*

"I think the risk is counterbalanced either way," said Xhelsea. "I mean, it's risky to share, and it's risky not to share. It all depends on what these . . . people . . . are. And what their agenda is, and what they are willing to do to get it. If they are people. If they aren't, I don't know, some kind of quantum energy reverberation or space-time ghost or Well knows what."

Even space-time ghosts can have an agenda.

"My species has a long history of not handling first contact between our *own* communities well," Xhelsea said. "I can't help but be a little concerned about the possibility that super-powerful aliens from a different plane of existence might have colonial ambitions."

"The Baomind seems friendly," I said.

"So far," they muttered. "But we don't know that the Baomind and these creatures are allied."

"We know they speak similar languages," said Yod.

"Humans used to have a lot of civil wars," I pointed out. "It's hard to hate anybody more than you hate your neighbors. Should we check the ships for ghosts?"

"They're not docked," Yod said. "Safer for them to be able to maneuver if any pirates slip through. But I will suggest that the shipminds monitor for pressure variations."

"We should ask Dakhira to check his logs as well. To see how long they have been following me."

A chill illuminated my spine as I imagined a skirmish erupting alongside the soap bubble of a hab that was the only thing keeping my family from the Big Empty. I looked down at my hands. Even filtered, the ferocious slantwise light of the dying star made the ridged tendons and valleys on the backs of my hands look like badlands at sunset.

Xhelsea said, "We could EVA. It's how I got over a little while ago."

She spoke as casually as if she were talking about taking the dog for a walk. My chill transmogrified into a full-blown shudder.

"How badly do we need to know?" To my embarrassment, my reluctance showed.

"Let me send over the specs for those pressure sensors first," Yod said kindly. "And I will play the not-a-ghost music to the Baomind."

What's the worst that could happen? Nonsense asked, making me wish it had not.

"There will be a lag," Yod finished as if she had not been interrupted.

I spotted a familiar figure in a beige jumpsuit ahead, walking toward us with a casual stride made wobbly by their afthands. "Didn't all the Chives go back to Dakhira?"

"One stayed," said Yod. "It gives us a backup line of communication if we need it."

"And gives Chive some redundancy. Better chance of survival. If one gets away, they can rebuild the clade." Xhelsea spoke rapid-fire, in an undertone.

I think I managed not to actually *make* the frog-face my mouth wanted to rearrange itself into. But it occurred to me that of everybody in Town, Chive was probably the one (the ones?) I could assume *wasn't* trying to kill me. If they had been, it would have been far more convenient to vanish me in some tragic accident in white space, where the body would never be found.

Though their ongoing internal drama might affect that. Was this the one I had spoken to privately? Or the one who had been wearing the boutonniere? Or a different part of Chive entirely?

More footsteps bounced the slatted walkway against the soles of my feet, out of time with Chive's steps. I wobbled in an interference pattern.

I sensoed that Haran and Willow were coming up behind us just before they appeared beneath the curve of the hab. Their voices, raised in animated conversation, reached us.

"No," Willow said, "I think we ought to print a few more. The lounge could use an infrared detector, too—"

Haran put a hand on her shoulder and she fell silent. I wondered who they didn't want hearing them. Not Yod, certainly. Nonsense? Xhelsea? The Chive? *Me?*

The Chive said, "Hello."

I nodded. It was less awkward talking to one of them than five all interrupting each other. I didn't *think* this was the one I had spoken to earlier, but rather the one they had been complaining about. The one with the flower, though they weren't wearing a flower now.

You know that awkward feeling you get when a friend has told you they suspect their spouse is cheating on them and you are stuck in a conversation at a party with said spouse? It was like that, but with extra murder and/or spying for pirates.

I decided to ask. Just put the boldest face possible on it. I reached out to the Chive in senso and asked, *I know this is impertinent of me, but is your clade having interpersonal difficulties?*

They reared back, eyes big. *Who told you that?*

You know I've been looking into the incidents. I didn't want to throw their clademate to the proverbial lions. Did clademates argue among themselves? There was so much I didn't know about it.

The Chive's face relaxed a little. *It's personal. I don't really want to talk about it, but it has nothing to do with attempted murder.*

You know how hard it is to trust anybody under the current circumstances.

Fine, they snapped. *I think I might want a divorce from my clade.*

I was still trying to formulate what I might ask next when Yod started talking, either ignorant of our communication or ignoring it. "I have converted the Stranger's song to pulsed laser and forwarded it toward the Baomind. The closest elements are about ninety light-seconds away."

So we've got three minutes to kill, said Nonsense. *Shall we sing a round?*

"Let's keep walking," I said. The less time we spent with our boots dangling over the Baostar's well, the happier I would be.

We moved on toward the next hab, which happened to be the lounge. The Chive seemed content to tag along. Haran was working the airlock when Willow put a hand on his arm and pointed down.

"Oh," she said. "Would you look at that."

She was staring out through the walkway fabric. I looked, a spike of panic curling my fingertips into my palms. My hand went to my actuator: still there under my collarbone. Touching it didn't make me feel better. I'd let my vigilance slip, and the reward for relaxing is always the pulse-pounding reminder that you shouldn't ever let your guard down.

But nothing was hurtling toward us. No pirate ship blazed across the flare-lit night, guns hammering. There was only the star, directly viewable through the polarized fabric despite its blinding brilliance and proximity. The mottled surface seethed, and for a moment I felt as vertiginous as if I were tumbling end over end down its well, toward a tenuous impact I would never live long enough to feel.

"What am I looking at?" Haran asked, filling me with the warm fellow feeling of not being the only idiot in the room.

"The Baomind." Willow pointed, which was pretty funny given how big the thing she pointed at was.

I increased my magnification and stared. Something was definitely afoot. The murmurations and swirls were being replaced by bars—a series of nodes and antinodes spreading from an initial point immediately "below" Town. It was unsettling and weird.

I guess I wasn't the only one who thought so, because Yod said, "Is that a standing wave pattern?"

I don't know, said Dr. Nonsense. *Do you think they're exploring the wave/particle dichotomy?*

"Well, stranger things have happened. But we think they probably are comfortable with even more advanced physics," said the Chive, one of those rare intimations that the Chives had a sense of humor. Okay, that was unfair—how would I know, when I had mostly spent the trip here avoiding them?

"Are they warning us about something?" I had been aching tired, thinking longingly of my bed. Now sleepiness vanished under the fizz of adrenaline.

The air pressure changed so suddenly I felt as if someone had boxed my ears. I spun around, fully expecting to see the hamster tube shredding itself into space. But I couldn't see down its length, because a glossy black mirror hurtled toward us broadside, pushing a wall of compressed air and blaring music before it. I would have shamed myself by ducking and squeaking like a scared mouse, but fortunately for my dignity the freeze response won. I stood stock-still, watching Kell come.

It halted a few centimeters from Willow's nose with no apparent inertial transition. One moment it was zooming along like a roller-coaster car; the next it was floating in place. Her eyes enormous, Willow squeaked. But only a little.

Belatedly, translation caught up with what Kell had been chiming in alarm. *Dark partner dark stranger no light not safe no light heavy star.*

"Dark stranger, huh?" Haran asked.

"From the Shadow Zone," Yod murmured.

It was the wrong time to laugh, but gallows humor has kept my species going for as long as it's been a species. So I did.

CHAPTER 23

MY REFLECTION IN KELL'S DARK SURFACE LOOKED maniacal. It (and Kell) hovered in front of me, jiggling in a manner that made me faintly nauseated until I tuned it down. *Danger danger danger,* Kell chimed. *Weight. Weight.*

The others gathered around us in a crescent, their faces reflected along with mine. "Kell, please hold still," I said.

It settled, which gave my stomach a chance to catch up. My eyes hurt with the brightness of the flaring Baostar.

Interact, said Kell. *Destabilize.*

I looked over at the engineers. "If we interact, we destabilize the star? Is that possible?"

"Is what possible?" Willow asked.

"Causing a nova by talking to somebody," Yod said.

Who knows? Nonsense interjected. *Koregoi science was more advanced than ours.*

I thought about the hooded figures in their brightly colored robes. "I don't know if they're Koregoi," I said. "I think they're . . . I don't know. Maybe weakly interactive?"

"They affect inertia," Yod said. "They have mass. They displace a small amount of volume."

"So does a whole bunch of stuff in space that we can't seem to touch or interact with," I pointed out. "If they *are*, as Nonsense suggested, made of dark matter . . . would that cause problems with the Baostar's stability? Because they're messing with gravity to manifest?"

Kell chimed, an incongruously happy sound. I thought it was an affirmative.

Oh, said Nonsense.

"Oh," said Yod. "You think there's enough of these Strangers to do that?"

"What percentage of the stuff in the universe is dark matter? Or dark gravity? It's a lot, isn't it?" I was not clear on the difference between dark matter, dark energy, and dark gravity. I wasn't a physicist, but I had tried to grind through a couple of papers regarding the discovery and dynamics of the Baomind on my way here. And dark matter had something to do with that.

"About twenty-seven percent," Yod said.

"Oh, I thought it was more than regular matter."

"It is. Baryonic matter is only about five percent."

I'm not my wife, but I was pretty sure that math didn't add up. "What's the other sixty-eight percent?"

"Dark energy." Yod's presence lights flashed helpfully, showing that Kell's surface was smoother than glass. Not a ripple marred the reflection.

I gestured along the hamster tube, where one of the Strangers was bustling along on some mission of its own, carrying an inexplicable device in its hands. "*Could* they be dark matter?"

"Theoretically," said Yod, after a long pause for a wheelmind.

The Chive said, "Huh."

Nonsense squidged a little to one side like a person thoughtfully inclining their head. Tentacles writhed in contemplation. *We know the Koregoi technology can manipulate dark matter to create artificial gravity. It's what the Baomind uses for propulsion, as do Koregoi ships in normal space. And what they've started installing in habs in the Core.*

"But the Baomind thinks the Dark Strangers are dangerous—"

"Well, sure," said Haran. "If I'm following what's going on here—and I freely admit I might not be—wouldn't their technologies interfere with one another?"

I knew it couldn't have heard me, because the Baostar was light-minutes away, but a few seconds later the light of an intensifying flare made me squint. Yod compensated quickly, but the dazzle spots remained in my vision. I blinked rapidly.

"We need to shelter the ships behind the hab," Chive said. "The Interceptors can handle this level of radiation, but Dakhira can't, and neither can the cargo haulers Amal and Arula."

"Sure," Yod said.

Willow cleared her throat. "Kell, would it harm you to shade us a little?"

Kell tilted itself in the air and chimed.

"Can the fungus eat this level of radiation?" I tuned my anxiety down because nobody needed to hear my voice shaking. Least of all me.

"It can grow indefinitely until it actually catches fire." Willow wasn't smiling.

"Can it catch fire without any oxygen around?"

"Not *technically*." She picked at a cuticle. "But if the Baostar expands to enfold us, technicalities won't keep the fungus—or us—from being stripped down to plasma."

Well, that was a nauseating thought.

"And it could grow enough to crush our hull. Or burst it."

I stared through the transparent wall of the tube. The outside seemed a little farther away, the view dimmed as if through a thickening layer of something imperfectly transparent. I reached out to touch it. The surface yielded under my fingers as before, but I could convince myself it felt a little stiffer and bulged a little closer.

We watched the dying sun convulse without more than desultory conversation. Kell must have got Willow's message through, because maybe a quarter standard later, the bars of the Baomind's interference pattern began to break apart, swirl into a vortex, and stream toward Town. Their shadow fell over us and the painful radiance dimmed.

It was awesome and terrifying, and despite that (or possibly because of it) I found myself hiding a yawn behind my hand. I put a hand on the warm, stretchy, completely disconcerting membrane to keep from wobbling.

I said, "It's the middle of my sleep shift, folks. I'll see you tomorrow."

"Sleep well, Dr. Song," the Chive said, unexpectedly kind.

I smiled back, and wondered what they were hiding from themself. Had they been telling me the truth? Or were they lying to me?

There was a Stranger in the corner of our cabin, lurking in the dark like a furled flag hanging from a pole. I did my best to ignore it, stumbling in exhausted, with every intention of falling into bed beside Salvie and passing out for at least nine standard hours . . . unless the hab exploded. Maybe even if the hab exploded.

Instead, I found Salvie awake in a lounger, reading something with Zag poured across her legs. I say "poured" advisedly: Zag was essentially a black-and-white fluid with a high surface tension. Stavan was asleep on another lounger in the darkest corner of the room, and Luna was nowhere to be seen. Zig was curled in Luna's usual spot, cheerfully aslumber. Aren't cats supposed to be nocturnal? I guess space cats do whatever space cats do.

Wait, that's all cats.

"Did you hear about the immaterial watchers hanging around the hab?" I asked as casually as I could.

Salvie held up her tablet. "I was just getting caught up on the news."

Salvie had the walls set to a false color nebula image that was making me agoraphobic. "Can I change this? Where's Luna?" I tuned my voice casual.

Salvie looked up from her screen and waved permission. "I'm waiting up. Yod would let us know if anything happened to her. You look like you need some rest, sweetheart. Why don't you lie down?"

Salvie patted the lounger next to her. Zag responded by stretching himself out on his back, his back feet splayed like tiny starfish. His safety collar was on and active, which reassured me, though I felt neurotic for checking.

I rode a swell of irritation. Sure, just lie down and take a nap while our daughter was Well knew where.

Nothing in the wallpaper library appealed to me. I picked a view across a lake to a mountain on some planet with a purple sky, mostly at random. The lake didn't move like water. I wondered what the fluid was. It wound up being more irritating than soothing, and in mere seconds I flicked it off again. Maybe just some nice trees.

I bumped my alertness, even though it was going to make me crabby and give me the jitters. But I could barely keep my eyes open without it. "It's the middle of the night. Yod, where's my daughter?"

"She's in a closed system, Sun. She can't have got into too much trouble. Or be very far."

Yod waited until Salvie had finished speaking, then added, "Luna is safe. She is in Dr. DeVine's hab. They are working on heuristic algorithms."

My daughter was helping my evil ex with her homework. My daughter, who had never betrayed the tiniest bit of interest in my career, was . . . apprenticing herself to my professional rival?

It hurt worse than anything I had felt since Vickee's original betrayal. I put a hand on the bulkhead to steady myself. Or maybe to keep from spinning off into space, since that felt as likely as any other outcome.

"She's with Vickee?"

"They seem to be finishing up," Yod said. "Please note that I am only intruding on their space because Luna has given me permission to report her whereabouts."

So she wanted me to know she was spending time with Vickee. Perversely, knowing I was being manipulated made me no less angry. Luna was trying to get a rise out of me and it was working, and I was in the mood to let it work.

Stavan slept through our voices with the facility of childhood. That was something to be grateful for. I pushed myself away from the wall. "I'm going to get her."

Salvie stretched out a hand to me. "Sun, just wait. She's on her way back."

"Not fast enough," I answered. I swiveled around, shoulders so tight with fury at Salvie's nonchalance that they ached, and stormed back out the hatch.

Jittering with rage and stimulants, I stomped along the tubewalk feeling like if my foot punched through and sent me tumbling into space, it would serve everybody right. I know acting like a sophipath is part of being a teenager—I did it, too, in my time—but knowing that adolescents are inconsiderate and manipulative and dealing with that are different things.

The walkway bounced under my feet, and I discovered that if I timed my stomps right I could get a wave pattern going that felt really satisfying to my exasperated soul. Probably better to take my anger out on the floor than on Luna. Or Salvie. As richly as they both might deserve it right now, they were my family.

Even with the tuning and the exercise and the therapeutic stomping and knowing I ought to know better, I was still seething when I reached Vickee's hab. "Yod, open the door."

"You should let me tune your reactivity down a little bit first, Dr.

Song," she said. "Slamming in there as if the wheel is on fire isn't going to help anyone."

"It'll help me," I muttered. But I let Yod feed my brain a little GABA, or whatever she was doing, and almost instantly felt less like I was teetering on the edge of a precipice of rage. The anger and betrayal were still there, but I could look at them from the outside rather than being completely consumed.

Deep breaths, Yod said in my feed, and opened the door.

Luna was already standing on the other side, glaring at me. Behind her, Vickee DeVine sat in a room set up for work, with a long table covered in data displays, more virtual holograms hovering over it. The projections came through the senso rather than via the manipulation of light, but Yod didn't seem inclined to conceal them from me. I bet that would have pissed Vickee off, had she known. She probably would have accused me of spying on her and stealing her data.

O pot, thou art sooty. Nothing like a little hypocrisy at four in the morning.

"Come on," I said to Luna. "It's time you were in bed."

"Absolutely not!" she snapped. "You can't make me!"

Technically, I could. She had a right to bodily autonomy under Synarche laws . . . but as her parent, I was responsible for her safety and well-being until she turned twenty-five. The wheelmind would back me up.

That would, of course, provoke an even worse fight, and lasting bad feelings. I was tempted to do it anyway, but the tuning Yod had done for me gave me enough emotional distance to consider the consequences.

I decided not to tell Vickee two of the shadowy Dark Strangers were in her cabin, engaged in some work that might have made sense if I could have seen what they were working on. Maybe they had a thing for voyeurism. It wasn't my place to judge.

"Luna," I said, "if you don't observe your curfew, there are going to be consequences. Which we will discuss later, in private."

"Mom, you are embarrassing me!"

I was trying not to, but she wasn't making it easy. To improve matters (I don't mean improve), Vickee looked up from the table and said, "Oh, Sun, we were just talking about you. Luna, it is late. Maybe we can do this again in a couple of diar. If it's okay with your mother."

She smiled at me with venomous sweetness.

I smiled back over clenched teeth. "Come on, Luna. I need to get to bed, and I'm not leaving without you."

"I need to get to bed, too," Vickee said, standing up and yawning ostentatiously. She was deliberately undermining my authority by making Luna's choices about what Vickee wanted. And I knew that calling her out on it was utterly pointless, and would only lower me in my kid's estimation.

"Fine." Only teenagers can give the word that particular inflection, soaked in passive aggression and adolescent grief. Luna walked back to the chair she must have been sitting in and grabbed her bag from beside it: baby-blue corduroy covered in patches from bands and adventure shows. She used to come home from the crèche and toss it into a corner before climbing into my lap and telling me about her day.

Now all I got was six hundred nuances on *fine*.

How long before the baby-blue bag got fed to the reassembler along with other childhood things? Like wanting a relationship with your mother.

Nevertheless, with Vickee's hab closed to her, Luna fell into step beside me. Seething, shoulders hunched. I had my own toddler rage to deal with, but my fox let me mitigate it. I told myself to feel a little compassion for the kid, who was, after all, just trying to assert her independence and demonstrate her social power.

Reframing the dynamic provided a little clarity and a handle on my temper, even if it didn't make me feel better.

"I can take care of myself," Luna said, breaking a sulky silence.

"There is a would-be killer on this hab," I reminded her. "So when you're out all night, I worry."

"I can take care of myself! Nothing bad is going to happen to me. And Yod is always watching."

I looked at her, and tried to think how to explain sensible risk assessment to an unrightminded teenager. Not that risk assessment was ever a teenager's strong point. "Yod was watching me, too, when I was attacked. She can't see everything. There are bad people out there who might hurt you."

"Don't talk to me like I'm a kid, Mom. I'm not Stavan."

I breathed out through my nose. *No, Stavan can manage to behave himself for three minutes at a time.*

Well, I hoped my kid wasn't growing up to be like Vickee DeVine. I couldn't have picked a worse influence if I'd tried. And they'd already formed a bond on the trip over here, with me completely out of contact and not even aware of what was going on. "Vickee DeVine is not a nice person," I tried. "You can't trust her."

"She's funny," Luna said. "I know she's got some sharp edges, but so do you."

Ouch. "It's not just sharp edges. She's self-absorbed and mean and narcissistic."

"You're jealous." Luna dismissed my warning with an airy wave.

"I've been burned," I said, trying to be vulnerable though every atom of my experience around Victorya Fucking DeVine suggested that vulnerability was only going to get me exploited. You have to be brave for your kids, right?

Kids don't appreciate you being brave. They don't notice that you're people with needs. If they do, it upsets them. Parents are supposed to be six meters tall, physically and emotionally invulnerable. They certainly can't be hurt *by their own children.*

Luna rolled her eyes at me and speeded up her pace, drawing ahead. I let her go, because I was too old and sore and irritated to chase her through the wheel like a sycophant.

CHAPTER 24

IN OUR HAB, LUNA WENT INTO THE BACK CABIN WITHOUT saying a word to anyone and shut the door. Salvie, still awake, curled her tendrils at me. "How did it go?"

I settled down beside her. Despite feeling prickly, I leaned back into the contact when she stroked my hair. "Terrible. She hates me."

Salvie reminded me of why I married her by not saying *I told you so*.

"She's a teenager. She hates everything. Our daughter is too busy living in a Lunacentric universe to even notice you in orbit most of the time."

"Salvie. Don't be mean."

"I thought it was funny."

"Sure," I said bitterly.

"Get some rest," Salvie said. "You really need to take better care of yourself."

"It won't matter if we're killed by pirates."

"Sun."

"Anyway, I can't sleep, there's too much music in my head and the Strangers keep staring at me."

"Yod," Salvie said, "put my wife to sleep, please."

"Hey," I protested. But I was out before the syllable completed.

• • •

I wish I weren't a prophet, but more-accurate-than-usual synthesis is a side effect of analyzing a lot of historical data over an extended time frame. I'd been asleep for about three hours—at least I got a full cycle in—when I was awakened by the horrifying shudder of the hab against my body.

Stavan and Luna screamed in the other room. Stavan must have woken up enough to go to bed at some point after I had fallen asleep. Salvie stirred against me. I jumped away from her, left hand slapping my hardsuit actuator. The suit whisked over my skin like the stroke of a razor, and once the visor integrated itself I could see in the dark. Thanks, technology.

I bent my knees before I hit the deck. First time in my life I'd managed nimble grace in an emergency, and there was nobody around to notice except my wife. I pulled her to her feet—easy in less than half a g—and actuated her suit as well. It knocked my gauntleted hand out of hers when it covered her fingers.

"Get the cats," I said, heading for the bedroom. Salvie was already moving to scoop up Zag, who has no sense of self-preservation. Zig had zipped under the bed, living up to his name.

"Actuate your suits, kids," I yelled through the doorway.

"Yes, *Mom*!" Luna yelled back, her voice already muffled by a helmet.

The pressure isn't dropping. Stavan wisely used senso to communicate instead of bellowing like the rest of us.

Yod, status? I used the family channel so everyone could hear her answer. Possibly I should have been more concerned about protecting the kids from bad news, but whatever had happened they were experiencing it already. And the thought of softening the blow didn't occur to me until after I'd asked.

Structural integrity is holding, Yod replied. *A projectile severed two support cables, but it and two other masses missed the hull. Drone defenses and the Baomind were successful in diverting them from direct hits, though we had very little warning.*

Salvie asked, *How did they get masses so close to us without being spotted? By the Baomind especially?*

Kell says they used the gravitational lensing trick to conceal and direct them. It says tesserae will move farther out to take up sentry positions. We're sweeping for additional masses and anticipating—wait, Kell says the situation is developing. Lock your access hatch and shelter in place.

"Moms?" Stavan squeaked from the hatchway. Luna was just behind him, trying to look cool and not really succeeding.

"Go back into the cabin." Salvie moved toward them, her suit outlined in traceries of safety light. Two cat-shapes in tiny hardsuits charged to the ends of their leashes, bouncing excitedly and braiding their tethers together. One swiped at the other, but in their tiny cat space suits I couldn't tell them apart. I hoped Toby and Not-Toby were okay. I hoped all my colleagues were safe.

And the family tree.

Salvie told the kids, "We're coming in with you."

Smart, I guessed—that put one more airtight compartment between us and the hab. I followed, bringing an armload of blankets so we could cozy up without having to print more and tuning myself to alertness despite my interrupted sleep. I didn't know how long I could manage without more actual rest, but for now I had to try.

I swept the kids into the cabin with blanket-drape wings. Salvie dogged the door.

"Come on," I said. "Let's make a blanket fort." I tossed most of the blankets on the floor and started hanging the heaviest ones over the viewports with the bulkhead magnets, thinking about Terra and blackouts and bombing raids and whether or not I had studied too much history.

Stavan and Salvie moved toward the blanket pile. Luna crossed her arms, hardsuit clinking.

"I'm thirsty," Stavan said, struggling bravely not to whine. "Can't I go out to the printer?"

I should have thought of snacks. But before I could apologize, Luna snapped, "Void, Stavan, can you complain more? There's a tube in your helmet to suck on. Didn't you pay *any* attention during drills?"

"Luna." Salvie's patience was as soft as the blankets and pillows I was arranging. "That's unkind."

"It's true! He's so dumb!"

Stavan must have turned off his mike, because I couldn't hear him crying. But I saw his shoulders hunch.

"Luna." Salvie might not believe in saying no to children, but I sure could. "You need to apologize for that. Stavan is allowed to ask questions, and nobody can remember everything while they're stressed."

"He could just look it up!"

Was she channeling me now? Surely I wasn't that short with her. Was I?

I made eye contact with my wife through our faceplates. I could have said that Stavan was young and scared and in need of support—just like Luna was. I could have, but I didn't think exposing either of their vulnerabilities was a good strategy just then, and Luna in her current mood might just use it as a weapon.

Salvie embraced Stavan, their hardsuits rattling against each other. The cats took the opportunity to tangle them in leashes.

I turned to brave Luna. "Everybody's scared," I told her. "But don't let being scared make you mean. Tell Stavan you're sorry."

Her eyeroll was audible in her singsong mimicry. "I'm sorry, Stavan."

"Now you're being cruel to your mother *and* to Stavan," Salvie said mildly. "Is that the person you intend to become? A cruel one?"

Sometimes it's like co-parenting with an android, but I was grateful for her practiced calm now. I could, I supposed, lose my cool for the both of us.

Luna flounced. "I can't get lucky enough to get kidnapped by pirates!"

In addition to a mature brain that has developed strong pathways, you need training—therapy—to use a fox effectively. Luna did not yet have the self-awareness and self-control to interrogate her own actions and tune them to be more socially responsible. She should be getting the training she would need as an adult, to develop her theory of mind and her awareness of community so she could develop the self-awareness to act to interrupt the reflexive, reactive impulse.

So she could act, rather than reacting.

She needed to develop the desire and awareness to take control of her neurochemistry.

"I didn't ask to come here!" Luna said. "I hope the whole place blows up!"

Salvie said gently, "That would be bad for everybody."

Luna put her back to the door. I assumed she wasn't storming out only because Salvie had locked it and she couldn't override. "Don't tell me what I'm feeling!"

I went to take the cats from Salvie and Stavan. I tried to keep my movements slow and calm, but inside the suit my hands were trembling. *Oh no. Not Luna. It's not possible. She is just being melodramatic. She's just being sixteen.*

She's just a kid! I protested to my sudden suspicion. But my inner historian chose that moment to remind me that in many human cultures of the past, armies and insurgencies were keen to recruit fourteen-to-twenty-year-olds *because* of their poor risk assessment. It's so *easy* to convince them to blow up themselves, and others.

I wondered what percentage of the pirate fleet was nineteen. I wondered if that explained their combat tactics and risk assessment.

Oh, what if it was Vickee . . . *and* Luna? Had my ex recruited my daughter into some horrible conspiracy?

I made my voice softer, though I had to tune to get the shake out of it. "Luna, you know you can tell me if you're in some kind of trouble."

She stared at me, opaque as an owl. "The only trouble I have is you and Momma dragging me halfway across the galaxy, away from school, away from my friends." Her voice skyed. "They'll all have graduated by the time I get home. I'll never get to date. I'm losing my whole life!"

"One friend in particular?" Salvie asked gently.

"You *suck*," Luna exploded, so I knew we were onto something. I pressed my lips together, feeling that sinking parenting sensation of *she's growing up and keeping secrets and she hates me for trying to keep her safe.*

"Luna," I asked, "has Vickee asked you to do anything that worried you? Anything unsafe?"

"You are so *obsessed* with Vickee!" Luna stomped one foot. "She's *nice*. She talks to me like I'm a person. She's the only one who talks to me like I'm a person. You just want to control me because you're jealous and you think you own me!"

Ouch, teenagers see right through you sometimes.

"I am a little jealous," I admitted. "But I also want to keep you safe."

Luna scoffed. "I've known her for four decians! She's great!"

Four?

Oh, of course. Relativity. Cee was a faster ship than Dakhira, so they had left after us and arrived before.

"That's about how long she can maintain the illusion of being a decent human."

"Why are you so *awful?*" Luna whirled away from me. Confronted with the locked door, she hurled herself into the corner and pulled a blanket over her head.

That went well, Salvie pinged.

I sighed and clipped the cats to the wall.

It felt safer to huddle in the dark with the windows covered. Whatever atavistic instinct drove us, even Luna curled up against me with a squeak when some overstrained tensioning cable frayed and the hab creaked, popped, and groaned. We three humans wedged ourselves into the bottom of the two bunks and piled all the blankets on top of us—despite the fact that climate control was still functioning perfectly and we were all enturtled in our hardsuits.

Salvie stood by the door, a reassuring guardian.

"Yod?" I asked.

"Don't worry," she said. "My Hands are engaged in repairs."

"I'm going to watch vids," Stavan announced, which seemed like a sensible way to self-regulate.

Luna's helmet swiveled toward him. She huffed. "Well, I'm not doing homework if we're all about to die."

It could have been teen melodrama. She didn't seem convinced. But then, when I was her age I hadn't really believed in mortality, either. It had taken hard personal loss to bring home the arbitrary and random finality of death.

A spasm of protective worry for the family tree clutched my stomach. There was nothing I could do about it. I put it out of my head.

Easier said than done, but I could take refuge in the personnel files, if I could force myself to concentrate. I struggled to sink into flow, not wanting to trigger hyperfocus because there was too much potential for disastrous outside interference.

Well, as long as I was already experiencing cascading trauma loops, I might as well start on Vickee's file. I knew I would have to fight through my desire to find something suspicious—without discounting anything suspicious if I did find it!—and balancing my bias was going to take all of my training and focus. So I should do that one while I was as fresh as possible.

If it was hard to stay focused with the sheer amount of adrenaline rattling my body, at least it wasn't hard to stay alert. My mouth tasted like old metal and my hands wanted to shake, and I had to have a long, circular conversation with myself about whether or not it was safe to let my guard down. *It's not your guard, it's your hypervigilance,* I told myself, and uncurled my fists when I noticed my nails pressing into the interior of the suit hard enough to make them ache.

The data, at least, were intriguing enough that after forcing myself to concentrate for fifteen minutes or so, I started to sink into it despite the twitches of Luna's hands that hinted she was playing a game on her heads-up. Whatever kept her distracted.

Something about the karan of Vickee's personal details niggled at me, but I couldn't get a pattern of inconsistencies to emerge. Or even find a single huh-that's-weird thread to pull. It just . . . felt off. The Gitchy Feeling can be a sign that the guys downstairs in your nonverbal mind have noticed something and are trying to get your intuition to explain it to the front office. It can also be a sign that your bias confirmation has kicked in and is looking for justifications.

I wished I knew which this was.

Vickee was a good-enough archinformist, though it pained me to admit it, that she might be able to construct an information pattern I wouldn't find the defects in. I mean, I certainly thought I could fool *her*.

Vickee had been traveling a lot in the years after she finished her graduate work. She'd been developing those piloting skills and making use of them to jaunt around the galaxy, visiting various remote worlds and habs at the edges of civilization. No wonder she still looked so young to me: relativity was on her side. And there weren't a lot of papers justifying all her research, either—maybe she was still processing the data, but a decade or so had passed since she'd published extensively.

Yod's library had a partial timeline of Freeporter raids on Synarche worlds and bases. Maybe that was the source of my niggling feeling? I pulled it up and cross-referenced.

The two files provided anything but a perfect correlation, but with some data noise, it looked like most of the places Vickee had visited had suffered a raid within two ans of her arrival.

That was curious: up to two ans *before* her arrival. So if she was involved with pirates, she was following them and not the other way around.

Her file was much tidier and better documented than most personal histories I reviewed. Was that in itself odd, or did it just reflect her meticulousness? My own was probably a mess; I avoided looking at it unless I had to.

No, this was getting into a loop again.

I unearthed myself from contemplation enough to check on the kids. They were both still immersed—or pretending to be immersed—in their entertainments. But neither one drew away when I draped my arms around them and pulled them a little closer. In Luna's case that amounted to a miracle.

In just this manner had our small, gnawing, shrewlike ancestors huddled in burrows amid their hoarded seeds when a massive asteroid crashed into the Yucatan Peninsula, Terra . . . a long, long time ago.

Salvie was still not huddling. She slipped back and forth between us and the hatch, a slim blue-black shadow outlined in the pinpricks of her safety lights, pacing like a cat. You can take the guardian out of Fercho but you can't take the warrior out of the guardian.

Yod broke in. "Sunya, I'm afraid I have rather an irregular request."

My stomach sank. "I am at your disposal."

"A pirate captain wants to talk to you. He asked for you by name."

I imagined suspicion in her voice. "You're wondering how I know a pirate."

"Oh, Dakhira told me," she said. "Do you want to talk to him?"

Instinctively, I stood up and grabbed Salvie's hand. "We're not surrendering!"

"We're not surrendering," Yod agreed.

"I'm not sure what good it will do," I said. "But I'm willing to try." *Link Salvie into the feed, please.*

"There's about a fifty-second lag," Yod warned, and patched the pirate in to me.

Captain Adekunle looked worn at the edges, his eyes bloodshot and his complexion dull. I wondered what threat kept him and his men in the fight—or what combination of threats and promises of glory. *Dr. Song,* he said. *Surrender the habitat or the next rock won't miss.*

I have no authority to surrender, I said. *Why don't you just leave us alone? You know we'll fight to the death.*

Lag meant his next transmission overlapped before mine was complete. *I can guarantee that the human Synarche personnel will be ransomed unharmed. If you do not make us take you by force.*

Pirates raided remote Synarche settlements like the one where Petrac had been born in part to press-gang people into their crews. I didn't believe him.

I said, *Why don't you just withdraw and let us leave in peace? That's all we're looking for.*

Time passed, and I saw his lips quirk in a dismissive smile. *What do you think would happen to us if we turned tail without what we came for? You can save your children, Dr. Song. Stop defending the matryoshka and give up. Let yourself live.*

This conversation wasn't going to go anywhere.

I cut the connection with cold fury and turned back to my wife. My hands shook inside the suit. Salvie's motion recalled the flickering presences I'd convinced myself that I was hallucinating, until my colleagues found the real cause.

Thinking of that made me unfocus my gaze and look around for Strangers. There was one, by the window, wearing its melodrama-villain robes and making a series of gestures with its hands. Sign language? I fed it through to Yod; maybe she could parse a meaning before Salvie's patrolling gave me an anxiety attack.

The Stranger, seeming to understand that it had been noticed, went back to whatever business occupied its time in its parallel dimension.

I tuned that down and, to make conversation, said, "Well, that was a predictable outcome."

"I think you learned more than you know," Salvie said. "Your Captain—"

"Adekunle."

"He's running scared," she said. "That was a desperation move on his part."

Huh. That hadn't occurred to me. "You think somebody really is going to have his head if he comes back without ours?"

"Count on it," my warrior wife opined. "Which makes him more dangerous, of course. He has nowhere to fall back to and no way to cut his losses except by bringing us in. And dying in combat is probably a much more pleasant end than whatever his people back home would do to him."

"You're probably right." I decided to change the subject because I didn't want to think about pirates anymore. "Do you think the Strangers have a hab on . . . on their side? Occupying the same space as Town but not interacting with it?"

"Would they have to?" she asked.

"Well, they can't breathe our air if they can't touch normal matter, right? And they don't *look* vacuum-adapted." I thought of the Ativahikas. I'd never seen one with my own eyes, but we all liked nature documentaries. "So they'd have to have . . . technology? They're wearing *clothes*. But they can't touch anything—"

"No!" It was just as well that I couldn't see Luna's eyeroll through the suit. So I didn't have to yell at her about it. "They can't touch *us*. They can touch *other darkside things* just fine."

I rocked back. "Darkside, huh? Did you come up with that?"

She nodded.

"It's good."

With a burst of enthusiasm reminiscent of the few short years ago that she'd been Stavan's age, she said, "Of course, we're really the darkside."

I wished I'd uploaded a physicist ayatana to go with all the musicians. "What do you mean?"

"Well, there's a lot more dark matter than normal matter," she said. "Six times as much. So the dark matter is actually the normal matter and *our* matter is the weird exotic matter."

"Huh," I said. "I didn't know you were so interested in physics."

I could almost hear her thinking *Of course not, you left*. But she didn't say it, which I decided to accept as a peace offering. I put my arm around her armored shoulders, and she didn't pull away.

"It's what I care about most in the universe," she said. "Well, that and sculpture."

I said, "The globe you made me was really good."

We remained in the dark for a few minutes, settling into our silence. The kids and I started to uncoil. Salvie's patrolling rhythm slowed. We waited, but I wasn't sure any of us knew what we were waiting for.

Yod would tell us when it was safe to come out, right? We had not been forgotten? Or worse, Yod had not lost control of the hab—

I became exquisitely aware of all the vibrations resonating through Town. Normally they were lost under all the incidental noises generated by the movements of forty people, four cats, and a dinosaur—not to mention the machinery required to keep us all alive. But under this new silence, I could lean into the ticking of metal reacting to thermal change, the creak of cables under strain, the pop of plating responding to changes in angular momentum as Yod adjusted the damaged station's trim.

It was almost . . . lulling.

"You should try to rest," I told the kids when it had been quiet for a while. "Momma and I will guard you."

I wanted to say, *Momma and I will keep you safe,* but I had a terrible feeling that outcomes were not entirely under our control. And I didn't want to promise what I was afraid I couldn't deliver.

Stavan still had the easy childhood faith that somebody competent was in charge and would make sure everything turned out passably. He soon slid down inside his hardsuit, breath settling into a sleeping rhythm. Luna sat bolt upright, vibrating with fear, anticipation, or an unholy cocktail of both. But she stayed beside me, and despite my fear, I reveled in it.

The cats were asleep on their tethers, having given up being upset.

The squeezing of my heart started to ease. I shifted, trying to restore circulation to the arm Stavan was asleep on. It wasn't his weight cutting off my circulation, but my awkward position and the way my inside elbow pressed against the hardsuit.

He mumbled but didn't wake—even when a soft metallic sound reverberated through the hab.

If it hadn't been so quiet, if we hadn't all been straining our senses into the dark for a standard hour or more, I probably wouldn't even have noticed it. But it was, we were, and I had.

Salvie and I made eye contact through the dark and our visors. A second later, the glows outlining her hardsuit winked out, leaving her an undefined silhouette in the darkness. "Kill your lights."

Luna and I did. I woke Stavan and got him to blearily comply, while the sound of scuttling resonated softly through our little shelter.

Breach, Yod pinged. A relief to hear her virtual voice; terror at what she said.

Salvie stopped pacing and said calmly, "Yod, print me a weapon, please. Proton accelerator, if that's allowed. Whatever you can get me, if that's not."

"The printer's out there." I pointed to the external cabin beyond the hatch. "If pirates are coming, they're probably coming from that direction."

I'll key it to Salvie, Yod said. *Do you want one, Dr. Song?*

"I don't know how to use one."

The kids were shivering inside their suits. I gave them one last squeeze and wiggled out from between them. I might have failed to upload a physicist, but one of my ayatanas had been a champion martial artist in addition to a pioneering mind in comparative musicology, something I'd discovered during my solo workouts back on Dakhira. I wondered if I'd done enough virtual kickboxing to ingrain the muscle memory. "Print me a cricket bat."

"A cricket bat?" Salvie said incredulously.

"An aklys. A tetsubō. A shillelagh. Don't bother me about the ethnic details; I want a hitting stick."

A hitting stick you shall have. Please continue to shelter here until the print job has finished.

I looked around for some useful object that might serve, in a pinch, to incapacitate a pirate. Unfortunately, everything in here was extruded at need and retracted into the bulkheads when not in use, which was great at preventing loose objects from bashing in your head when gravity failed, and not so great at providing loose objects with which to intentionally bash in heads when it hadn't.

Oh, crud, were the pirates likely to have gravity weapons? What would that even look like?

"Salvie, clip your tether, would you?"

I couldn't see what she did in the dark, but I heard a snap. And two more behind me as I clipped mine as well. Sometimes your children *do* listen.

"Where are they?" Salvie asked Yod.

Difficult to say. I can only track them with the air pressure sensors, and it's extremely difficult to tell which ghost signatures are pirates and which are the

Strangers. I am noticing something interesting, however—when I go back over my records, the fluctuations in pressure readings that accompany the attack on you are subtly different from the ones previous to Trevor's infection—

Inside my head, the background music I'd become desensitized to suddenly rose to a crescendo, making me jump. Salvie looked at me quizzically.

I shook my head. *The Strangers are trying to tell me something.*

"They *do* have a cloaking device!" Stavan yelped. Had I ever been that able to get excited about something with the potential to kill me?

Probably, said Yod. Apparently I had been thinking very loudly. *It's a primate thing.*

The sound of a ripsaw through metal vibrated the decking against my soles.

With urgency, Yod added, *Someone is working to breach the airlock into your cabin.*

Salvie rustled beside me. "On five, I'm going to pop the door. Dive for the printer; I'll draw their fire."

I wanted to grab her elbow and drag her back into the shelter of the bedframe. But this was who she was; it was what she had been created for. Protector of her family. That she had come out into the Synarche to be so much more . . . it mattered. And it mattered so much that she had chosen to make *us* her family, rather than the clan she was born to.

"One," said my wife. "Two."

The noise increased. I remembered that the lights were still on in the outer cabin. A heavy sensation of paralysis weighed my limbs. "Three."

Yod, kill the lights.

"Four."

CHAPTER 25

THE HATCH SPRANG OPEN AND SALVIE AND I LUNGED forward. She went right, her suit lights snapping back on in a blaze of colors. I went left.

Salvie had set the walls to a peaceful coral reef scene with strangely colored fishes. Beautiful but incongruous, it illuminated my path to the printer. Across the cabin, a few short meters away, an arc of orange and gold sparks and a horrific whine showed that the internal airlock had been breached.

The printer produced a faint greenish light and an ozone smell as it worked, offering a target to grope toward. I slammed a shin into furniture, but the suit's padding saved me from harm. Adrenalized perceptions made my body seem sluggish, heavy. As if I forced my way through wet clay. As if I were running in a dream.

With a stunning pop, the cabin depressurized. The airlock door blew wide, and the door to the cabin behind us slammed shut automatically, severing our safety cables.

The thunder of machine-imagined music in my head made me migraine-dizzy.

Easy come, easy go. At least there hadn't been enough air mass in the cabin to hurl us into space. The hab was still spinning, and acceleration stuck us to the floor as well as it ever had.

I had no time to be terrified. This was the apotheosis of all my fears . . . and I was fighting through it. Sometimes we surprise nobody more than ourselves in a crisis.

I dove for the printer as three suited forms swarmed into the cabin. It was still running, but a club doesn't need to be perfectly shaped to be effective. As the closest invader turned toward me, leveling a hand weapon, I snatched up my bat. It snapped into my palm like it had been manufactured there. As my fingers curled around the haft, I realized Yod must have built tool locks into my simple skull-breaker, since the hardsuit was doing the work of holding on to it for me. A spray of printing material coated the back of my glove, but nothing interrupted my arc.

My body swung by reflex, guided by practice and the ayatana.

The nearest pirate wore a shocking violet-and-black hardsuit plastered with grinning skulls and crossed sabers. They swiveled their gun toward me while the other two tracked Salvie. A shot snapped off, then another, bullets chipping sparks off the bulkhead. Smoke curled from the barrel of one of the guns. Chemical propellants and projectiles? In a *hab?*

A ricochet slammed into my arm. I had momentum on my side, and my hardsuit had grounded its boots when it sensed my sudden movement. Magnetism braced me. The knob on the end of the club smacked into the pirate's glove.

Their gun discharged again, but into the decking this time. Instead of another ricochet, it punched through. No hiss of air escaping: the atmosphere was already gone. The freebooter's hand came up; I let my body parry. My left hand reached for the printer, locked onto the gun.

Salvie. Hup.

She caught it without seeming to look.

I swung the club again and missed, because somebody grabbed my trailing tether and gave it a savage yank. My boots held, and my glove stayed locked to the club, but the strength of the pull strained every muscle on my left side from sacrum to scapula. I whirled and lashed out. The club bounced silently off the bad guy's helmet, but I felt the impact in my bones.

The air in that helmet would carry sound. I hoped I rang their chimes.

They yanked again, but I cut the tether loose so it just snapped off my suit, the recoil rocking the pirate backward. A meter away, Salvie leveled her weapon, steadying with both hands. Proton beams aren't visible, but her weapon had a laser sight. It painted the nearest pirate with a small red light. I could only tell she fired because the suited figure clutched their chest and collapsed.

Salvie rotated smoothly, tracking her sights, and the rest of the fight was over in the time it took me to recover my balance.

Salvie lowered the weapon, eyes returning to the damaged airlock door.

"You okay?" she asked, as the corpse of the pirate I'd bashed and she'd finished off crumpled to the deck.

"I'm fine," I said, which was 50 percent true. I was *physically* uninjured. I thought. "You just killed three people. How are *you?*"

She didn't even give them a glance. "They entered my nest."

No emphasis. Just a flat statement. In a human it would have been affectless.

"But—"

"Sun," she said patiently, "I was trained for this from the egg."

My palm stung from impacts. "Yes, and you left it. On purpose. I imagine it can't be nice to go back."

That *did* swivel her attention toward me. She stared.

"What?"

"I feel seen," she said. "Also, I love you. Now, please stop trying to extract my psychological truth until the gunfight is over."

I had thought it was over. *Yod, how many more pirates are there?*

Dozens, she answered shortly. *Continue to shelter. I am repairing the lock and the hull breach.*

I strained my senses into the passage beyond, realizing only several seconds later how ridiculous it was to listen to the void. A footstep might vibrate the decking; it would not reach my ears.

What *did* reach my ears was my children sobbing over the radio.

"Luna?" I asked. "Stavan?"

A sniffling pause, and the indrawn gasp as Luna got her sobs under control.

"Moms?"

"We're okay. How are you two?" The ricochet that clipped my arm must have holed my suit. A haze of warning lights surrounded my vision as I looked down. I'd been so adrenalized I only now noticed the vapor jetting out of the nick and freezing to oxygen snow. As I moved uselessly to cover the hole with my palm, it sealed itself.

The arm underneath felt bruised, but I thought no worse than that. The snow wasn't pink, anyway. Always a good sign.

"*Sunyata!*" said Salvie urgently.

I blinked, realizing that I had missed whatever Luna had said, and that I didn't know how long my attention had been turned inward. I'd been staring at the spray of crystals on the deck, unhearing and unseeing.

I wobbled. The mags saved me and Salvie steadied me. "I want to sit down."

"You're feeling the shock," she said, which made me giggle. My Ferchan wife was lecturing me on human physiology.

"Mom?" Stavan said.

"Stay in the bedroom," Salvie ordered. She switched to our private feed. *Suck on your hydration tube.* She hit the stabilization control on my shoulder so the suit would hold me upright.

The fluid was warmish, brackish, sweetish. If my body hadn't found it so welcome, it would have been slightly nauseating. My head was starting to throb in time to the music only I could hear. But it turned out I could use my fox to lower the perceived volume. And that music had provided useful warnings.

A hysterical giggle bubbled in my chest. *Isn't it handy to hear the incidental music that tells you a jump scare is coming?*

I remembered the Dark Stranger making hand gestures in the corner of the cabin. What had they been trying to communicate?

I still felt unwell. I crouched, suit pressing into the backs of my thighs, and rested my elbows on my knees, head on my hands.

Sun? Salvie stood over me, grimly watching the door, still using our private channel to communicate. *Are you hurt? Did they shoot you?*

Not hurt, I said. *My brain just feels . . . really full.* I tuned myself alert and focused until the vertigo retreated, then pushed myself up using my cricket-bat/war-club as a staff. The airlock had nearly finished healing. I looked at the pirates on the floor. *What should we do with the bodies?*

Nothing right now, Yod interrupted.

Irritation flashed. What was she doing listening to my private coms with my wife? She reached in and calmed my endocrine system, which was less aggravating than when Dakhira did it. A moment of peaceful contemplation later, I realized that it was an emergency, and of course the wheelmind was monitoring coms.

My kids are in the next room, Yod.

I know, she said soothingly. *I'm sorry. But this is going on outside.*

The coral reef wiped away, replaced by all-too-familiar arcs and lines and probability cones. I counted four pirate ships versus Cee.

Ikem was still out where this system's comet cloud would have been if it hadn't been disassembled millions of years ago to build the Baomind. Dakhira, Arula, and Amal still huddled in Town's shadow, hiding from the devastating radiation. I couldn't believe the pirates were really willing to risk that inferno just to attack us.

But there they were. Making bad decisions for all of us. Good job, pirates.

Maybe their weird technology included radiation shielding.

She's so outnumbered, I said. *I don't want to watch this.*

I do, said Salvie. *Feed it to me?*

Wait! I interrupted. *I don't* want *to watch it. But I should, and I will.*

I put my arm around Salvie, and we stood side by side, shoulder to shoulder, watching a dogfight that had taken place minutes ago, hearts clenching over outcomes we could not influence. The wall feed was better than watching from the porthole because the view didn't whip around. The Baostar stayed steady and sullen in the lower left, its rotation clearly discernible because of the arch of the massive flare flung from its surface.

Cee had one of the pirates on the run, but the other three dogged her tail—and who knew how accurate that representation was, given their cloaking technology? I guessed if they were shooting at Cee, she had the processing power to triangulate where the projectiles or beams were coming from.

Her advantages were that processing power, and the pirate ships potentially interfering with one another. I wondered if they would bother to avoid shooting each other, or if friendly fire was an accepted means of rising in the ranks.

Dakhira's voice broke in, crackling faintly. I was impressed that he could punch a signal through the interference. "Situation. I have Strangers on board."

"So do I," said Yod. "They don't seem to be hurting anything."

"They warned me about the pirates, I think," I said.

"How many?" Yod asked.

Dakhira's signal dropped in and out, barely intelligible. "Four. I'm tracking the pressure anomalies."

"If this stellar storm gets worse, we're all going to be operating with our heads in a bag," Salvie said. "What's that?"

She pointed to a spot on the wall.

I stepped forward to touch the wall and stubbed my toe on a dead pirate. A full-body shudder inside your hardsuit makes it rattle. I squinched my face to shake off the heebie-jeebies and enlarged, throwing the proportions off. "Tesserae, I think?"

Town creaked again. An incredible *sproing* split my head, which was how I realized we had regained our atmosphere. I looked over at the hatch. Yod was obviously still in charge: the airlock was sealed and the blue lights were on, indicating that both hatches were closed and the interior was pressurized.

"That cost us a lot of oxygen," Salvie said, following the direction of my thoughts. "When nothing is easily renewable."

Moms? Luna, voice shaking. *It's getting bright in here. Right through the blankets.*

It was getting bright in here, too. I looked back at the wall; the arch of the flare stretched off the Baostar—leaping out, pulled like a picked thread. The whole wall blazed for a moment before it dimmed automatically. *Kids, come out here,* I said.

The connecting door opened on a wall of light. The only things saving the stark brilliance from leaving my vision nothing but black spots and auras were its dull red wavelength and the polarization on my helmet. The light broke into moving rays as the children scrambled out, dragging each other and the cats. Before the hatch sealed behind them I caught a glimpse of light pouring through the fabric of the blankets tacked over the windows as if they were lace curtains on a sunny day.

Stavan looked at the dead pirates on the decking and rushed into my arms. Luna stood awkwardly, looking prickly and disconsolate, until Salvie pulled her into an embrace. Nobody can stand against a Fercho in nurturing mode.

Cee was still holding her own against the pirates, but she hadn't managed to incapacitate or destroy any. *Those are people, Sun,* my mother's voice said in my head.

True, Mata, but they're trying to kill your grandchildren. As if there were any point in arguing with your own intrusive ideations when they took on the voice of your dead.

I tried not to hear the creaking and stretching noises the hull was making. Town seemed ready to fly apart at the seams. If it did, I wondered if we could restart the mag engines on this hulk that had been a starship before it became a dormitory. Maybe the Baomind would save us. Maybe we would drift until we suffocated, froze, or starved.

Yod's voice broke into my paralyzed musing. "We will have a group shelter set up in the Garden Pod shortly."

"All that glass?" I said.

"We've set up shade panels. It's on the trailing side of the wheel right now. And it's got the thickest coat of fungus."

"Is it wise to have everyone together?" Salvie asked.

"It's a judgment call," Yod answered. "Is it wise to have you all apart?"

"Are there still pirates?" Luna asked. It was such a grown-up question that my breath caught painfully in my throat.

"We think we have removed them from the walkway," Yod said. "Of course, it's impossible to be sure, given their cloaking technology."

Removed. I looked at the bodies on the deck. What a pleasant euphemism.

Still, they must have thought we would be pushovers. And we'd surprised them.

I nerved myself. Anxiety wouldn't help me, so I got rid of it. We would wait; we would run; we would survive. I held that in my mind and tried to be a rock for Stavan.

Stavan seemed less concerned than I was. He was busy wrangling Zag, who was not enjoying his hardsuit and was determined to let us all know about it. There was much yowling and wriggling, which would have been more effective if the hardsuit didn't come with a tether and a carrying handle. Luna had Zig huddled in her arms.

I leaned toward the wall. The flare was still growing, and the dark flecks of so many tesserae surrounded it like sheepdogs harrying a flock of sparks. Were they pulling it out of the star? Was the Baomind doing this *on purpose?*

"Simulate close view of the dogfight," Salvie said.

The wall popped in an enlarged window. An animation, not a live feed, showed Cee dodging and twisting, trying to bring her guns to bear on the pirate ahead of her. Behind, strung out, were the three other ships. For now they held their fire—either to save ammunition or to avoid destroying their ally.

The brightness increased, then abruptly dimmed as another level of filtering came online. The song in my head pulsed like a symphony, like a dance hall, drowning out almost everything.

"We should go soon," I said.

Movement caught the corner of my eye. Two Strangers flanked the airlock door, beckoning with their incomprehensible gestures. If they could not see, how did they—never mind, they probably could sense the gravity changes made by moving hands, or something.

I looked at them and sang a few notes of their music back. Off-key, maybe. Perhaps recognizable.

The sounds came back in my head.

Salvie looked at me. "Strangers?"

I nodded. "Come on. Let's go before the situation gets any worse."

I caught Stavan's hand. As I turned him toward the hatch, something streaked across the wall near the image of Cee—

No, that wasn't quite correct. Something *vanished* out of Cee's wake. One of the pirate ships stretched weirdly, swirled, and contracted to a point almost faster than I could register. Staring at it, I froze.

Salvie tugged my elbow. I followed her like a robot, running what

I'd seen through my fox over and over. *Yod, what the Well just happened?*

It looks like a singularity, Yod replied.

Has the Baomind done that before?

Not to my knowledge. I hypothesize the Strangers are acting in our defense.

I shuddered. As if the answer would have changed, I asked, *Are there still Freeporters aboard?*

It seems possible, Yod admitted. *Their jammers and the presence of the Strangers make it hard for me to be sure. I've 90 percent confidence that I have managed to clear the walkway, however—your family should be safe if you move fast.*

I could guess how she had cleared the walkway. But it evidently had structural integrity again now, and that was what mattered.

We clambered down the ladder single file. I thought the walkway might still be blown, but it had reinflated, though the walls sagged. Air pressure was low, and the membrane seemed thickened. It bulged inward.

We scrambled along a tube of captured light, the Baostar's searing brightness refracting inside the opalescent walls. The radiotropic fungus was growing so fast it created platelike layers that caught the light and shimmered like mica. The kids lugged the cats by their suit handles. Salvie and I kept our weapons in hand.

My external radiation monitor was rapidly darkening to orange. The internal one still showed safe levels—or as safe as one ever was, having skipped out of the sheltering embrace of planetary magnetic fields and atmospheres.

The boardwalk bounced under our feet as we ran. It had never seemed so far around the periphery of Town, and with the tunnel closing in around us I learned it was possible to be claustrophobic and agoraphobic at the same time.

We weren't the only runners. Ahead of us and behind, other feet bounded in rhythm as other suited bodies hustled at their various top speeds. Orange lights flashed warnings, and we had a front-row—albeit refracted—view of the Baostar's enormous curved flare looping across an incomprehensible span of space.

A tiny puff of sparks lit one corner of the heavens. I could have covered it with a fingertip at arm's length, but it was bright white and momentarily tempered the bloody light of the Baostar.

"Cee," Salvie breathed.

"I'm sure it's a pirate," I said reflexively.

We kept moving. In seconds we were piling into the Garden Pod, as crowded as it had been on my first dia. Angie, suited up, hunched disconsolately on her perch. Toby and Not-Toby were in their suits in carriers dogged to the interior bulkhead. And somebody had closed the case that held my family tree. By the puddle beside it, I deduced the thoughtful colleague was Dr. Nonsense.

This pod must have held integrity during the breach, because the plants were not frozen and crumbling.

"Deactivate your suits," Yod said. "Use my air as long as it's available and save your internal reserves in case you need them."

Somehow I didn't find that as reassuring as one might, but I did it. The sweat across my back began to evaporate and I shivered in the unexpected chill.

The exterior wall was opaqued, with the view beyond projected onto it.

"Holy—" I said.

"—shit," Salvie finished for me.

The flare arcing from the Baomind covered half the sky. The flocks of tesserae shepherding and shielding it were so dense it looked pixelated. My mind could not encompass its size—a tentacle reaching for us like Dr. Nonsense slapping an arm on the outside of its tank. The arc of ejected matter falling back into the star swirled in an enormous vortex.

Displays showed Cee and two Freeport ships—one still ahead, the other on her tail like a lamprey. There were no Freeport ships still close to Town, if there had ever been. Had the pirates sailed in across open space, commando-style? Had the ships dropped them off and then fled?

Our three civilian ships seemed intact, still huddled in Town's shadow but not docked, their magnetic bottles shimmering with green-and-violet auroras in the vicious stellar wind.

The tesserae guiding the flare broke apart, sullen light showing in the cracks.

Iris and Willow came up beside me in their hardsuits, helmets deactivated. I pulled Stavan against my chest and he held Zag. I asked, "Has it been doing that all along?"

Iris said, "Well, we knew the Baostar was becoming increasingly unstable."

"Unstable Bao." Willow, sounding ever-so-slightly hysterical. "Leaking filling."

Iris ostentatiously turned her head to stare, then turned it back again. "That is, after all, why we've been evacuating. And we knew removing the tesserae was changing the dynamic balance of the system. But now we've got the Baomind, pirates, and these Strangers *all* doing things with gravity all around here."

"What does that mean?"

Iris sucked her teeth. "There are likely to be some unexpected events."

Willow asked, "Like it goes nova?"

"Oh no, a star that big wouldn't go nova."

I said, "Well, that's a relief," even as one of my ayatanas whispered unease to me.

Luna looked over and said, "It would go *super*nova, Mom. But we'd have warning, right, Iris? The elements it's fusing change, so its spectrum will change. And then it will start to contract before it catastrophically expands and engulfs us all."

"Bad?" said Salvie.

Iris nodded at Luna. "Then it collapses to a black hole."

"Worse," my wife said. "What do we do if that happens?"

Quietly, Iris said, "Run."

I twisted my hands together. "What about the blockade?"

"They should also run."

I hoped so. But what was to stop them from taking a few parting shots as they went? I thought of what Captain Adekunle had intimated—that they were threatened with exile or torture if they returned empty-handed. At the very least, I guessed he would lose his command. "So we don't have to worry about the star's stability?"

Iris said, "Oh, we do. We still have a lot of tesserae to evacuate. And smaller events can still be catastrophic. Like an electromagnetic storm or a big stellar flare."

"A big stellar flare?" I pointed out the window.

"They'll get bigger," Iris said dourly. "They happen a lot, but they're mostly not pointed at us. If they are pointed at us and our shielding doesn't hold . . . we die. And the electrical systems burn out. And our AI colleagues get their ones and zeros scrambled. And our foxes probably electrocute our corpses, just as a final parting gift."

I pictured electromagnetic zombies animated by their own neural implants, lurching around Town.

Luna must have been on my wavelength, because she said, "Yuck."

CHAPTER 26

There wasn't enough tuning in the void to do more than take the edge off my exhaustion. But my colleagues wouldn't stalk themselves, and as long as we were stuck here waiting to be murdered by pirates, I had ambitions of doing some data mining in the Baomind's memory. It was, after all, my putative reason for having come all this way and probably getting myself and my family killed into the bargain.

And I had nothing better to do while the hab's whole complement huddled here in the Garden Pod like primitive humans in a bomb shelter. Was it better to take refuge together, or had we just rendered ourselves a bigger target?

Serial killer walls and mind maps and conspiracy theories are all very satisfying, but they may encourage you to see connections and find patterns that don't actually exist. Compensating for this is an ongoing challenge of the work I do, and I kept that in mind as I picked away at Vickee's too-perfect personnel record.

I needed something to do, and staring out into space waiting to see if Cee caught the pirates before the pirates caught Cee—or if the Strangers sucked another Freeporter ship into a singularity, as I presumed we'd witnessed before—was not helping the panic attack pulsating in the pit of my throat. Nothing helped, not even tuning. Not even asking Yod to adjust my tuning. I threw every intervention available at my emotional state, and just about managed to stay calm enough not to rip my clothing off because it was suffocating me—even with my hardsuit unsealed.

I still heard every breath like a hollow drum, and my hands were shaking. Fortunately, the suit muffled my breathing and heartbeat so I wasn't audible to everyone else. That almost made up for the sensation of a steel band being twisted tight across my ribcage, under skin and flesh and breasts.

We didn't talk much after the first few minutes, as everybody trickled in. We just waited. Town's crew, augmented by a Chive, spread out around the Garden Pod, trying to make ourselves comfortable while Yod printed more furniture and kept the walkways clear. A slow-motion dogfight played out across vast distances on the wall.

Cee nailed the pirate ship she had been chasing: its blip winked out and a ragged cheer spread through us observers. Now there was just one left dogging her tail. I remembered the statistics for dogfights and how rarely one vessel survived multiple encounters. I couldn't bear to watch. Maybe *I Brake for Nobody* was coming to help. Maybe Cee had something up her drive sleeve. Maybe the Dark Strangers were towing their singularity into another intercept location.

Strangers drifted around the hab, walking through me and my colleagues as if we were ghosts, on their mysterious errands. It felt easier to see them, and the music in my head was constant now. Constant, but no longer distracting. Instead, if I let it beat quietly in the background, it actually seemed to help me focus.

My concentration was less than exceptional. Still I managed to figure out that part of the tidiness of Vickee's file was the lack of transitions. People's lives are like histories. Personal histories, not like stories: They aren't neat. They are tangled and contradictory. They don't naturally generate an arc.

We impose arcs upon them, because that's what human minds do.

We cut edges where no edges previously existed. We press them into frames. We give them an end and a beginning. We draw hard lines all over the gradients that compose them, and we choose what to emphasize and what to deprecate. In so doing we craft a narrative, though that narrative feels like an emergent property.

Feels like an emergent property to humans, anyway. Not every species has our fixations.

In this process, we also introduce bias, because we can't help it. The same facts of a person's life, presented with varying emphasis, can make them a hero or a villain. And one of the challenging things about history—and life—is the fucking stunning lack of protagonists in the real world.

But I digress.

Vickee's CV didn't offer the gaps, overlaps, and redundancies that are so usual in a résumé. That was weird, and I didn't think it was the kind of weird most people—or even most archinformists—would spot.

I knew my bias against Vickee predisposed me to see evidence of her perfidy. I could be recognizing a pattern where none existed. My training made me aware of the possibility and gave me tools to compensate for it. There were, after all, lots of reasons why Vickee DeVine—the research thief—might have faked aspects of her CV. Most were more innocent—if that's the correct word—than collusion with pirates.

But "collusion with pirates" was possible, and it didn't do me any good to dismiss it. I had to leave it hanging in the distressing space of *not sure*. And I couldn't move it out of that space until I had more evidence one way or the other.

I wanted to make the snap judgment. But my rightminding reminded me that that was unfair and arbitrary. Even if it would have been more comfortable to convince myself that I knew what was going on here.

When I looked up from my research to check on Salvie and the kids, the stellar flare had begun to fade. Its incomprehensible span sank slowly back into the surface of the Baostar. The filters rendered it clearly visible against a velvet-black sky, its fiery arch outlined in vortices.

Salvie had fallen asleep sitting up on a cot set up beside one of the bulkhead tanks. Stavan was stretched out alongside her, his head pillowed in her lap. Sleep must be evolutionarily advantageous despite its drawbacks, given how many different biomes have evolved something like it. Zig and Żag were piled on top of Stavan, likewise catching up on missed naps.

Inconveniently, my appreciation of both the spectacular view and the coziness of my family was diminished by the intervening presence of Vickee DeVine. She stood with her back to me, providing plausible deniability to her intrusion on my line of sight. Luna was beside her, irritating me further. As if reflexively, Vickee draped a comforting arm around Luna's shoulders.

A less civilized person might have beaned Vickee with a chair, but I was an adult and well socialized. Anyway, the chairs were too light and flexible to do enough damage to be worth the repercussions.

Haran shoved past them, drawing Vickee's glare. Either it didn't register or he didn't care: impressive, given I half expected to smell his hair scorching. Nothing annoyed Vickee more than being incidental to someone else's experience.

Haran, scowling, ducked under a worktop and pulled out his fermentation chamber. It had been emptied and cleaned since last I saw it. Glancing around, I didn't see the still, so I assumed that, too, had finished its run and been decanted.

Dr. Nonsense popped its eyes above the surface of a nearby tank. *Now is not the time, Haran.*

Haran whirled on the research director, hands flying up in a gesture of thwarted rage. His face pinched with fury. "I have a *lot* of radiotropic fungus fragments I just finished excising from the vents so we can have functional life support, and I need to put them somewhere. Do you have a better solution or are you just micromanaging me out of a sense of obligation?"

It was a barely controlled explosion, but there was something odd and calculated about it. As if, even in the midst of snapping, he was biting back something else. We were all upset, I got that. But Haran's words and tone made me wonder if he felt somehow personally betrayed by Dr. Nonsense.

Or perhaps he'd channeled all his fear into anger. He wouldn't be the first person to lash out at whoever presented themselves when he couldn't reach the actual target of his temper. Referred aggression isn't just for pissed-off cats.

Haran was also still in his hardsuit, though he'd retracted the helmet. Scorching damage marred the left side; something must have come uncomfortably close to setting him on fire. I supposed struggling with repairing life support while under attack might make me a little touchy, too.

I winced, glad I wasn't responsible for hab repairs and maintenance during a gunfight. Also, seeing one of the engineers still suited gave me a warm sense of justification about my own concerns. I wasn't the only one worried about getting blown into space, and Haran was a professional.

"Haran," Vickee said gently, "is something bothering you?"

Watching his face as he responded to Vickee's superficially unobjectionable question was just as validating as seeing him still mostly suited up. Maybe I needed to make better friends with Haran. Even his temper felt refreshing when it was directed at somebody I despised.

I could see him working up a scathing reply, and I was sorry I never got to hear it, because the folks still watching the combat animation—including Luna—exploded in whoops and cheers. Salvie stirred, her head rising and her camera eyes blinking open. The compound ones, of course, had no lids.

She was also wearing her suit, and the proton gun was magnetized to her thigh.

She said, "What happened?"

Luna, for once, didn't roll her eyes. "The last ship of pirates gave up. Cee's coming back. She's okay."

When you're carrying as much fear as we all were just then, the peeling off of even one layer is an enormous relief. I cheered, too, a little behind everybody else.

Story of my life.

I said, "Are there still Freeport boarders in Town?"

"Indeterminate," Yod said.

"Well, at least one of the AIs around here is useful," Vickee said.

I felt a moment of sympathy for Dakhira. Who wouldn't Vickee throw out an airlock if she glimpsed a momentary advantage? Her only saving grace was having no long-term sense of strategy.

Haran grunted and dumped his bag of mushroom scraps into the fermentation chamber. He closed it more firmly than was necessary, stowed it, and walked away.

Vickee waved a hand around and continued, "There's a kind of shitty poetry to all this, isn't there? Half-derelict ships stuck together in an unbalanced circle. Stumps with rudely amputated wires showing where connections to white coils were severed. Scarred and dented hulks. The jury-rigged bubble walkway wrapped around the outside like a tire. It doesn't even spin fluently. Yod can't find the pirates in her own hab, which isn't surprising given that Yod can't even stop Town from wobbling."

There's truth in that old saw about pressure bringing out people's real character. Listening to Vickee disparage the wheelmind we all depended on to survive made me glad AIs generally are programmed not to be homicidal.

"Do you think the pirates will be back?" Luna asked—Vickee, not me.

Vickee gave her a squeeze. "It's hard to say, honey. Maybe not those particular pirates—Cee might have scared them off."

"What if there are still pirates in Town?" Now Luna looked at Salvie.

Salvie sat up, gently moving Stavan aside. "Do you trust me to protect you?"

Luna's golden complexion turned green despite the Baostar's light. She nodded.

"Why are you here, Vickee?" I said, even though I knew I shouldn't.

"The same reason you are. To suffer in the hope of eventual career advancement."

"You sure seem to know a lot about pirates."

"I specialize in researching them," she said, rolling her eyes like Luna. "For the Synarche. That's supposed to be a secret, but if we're all going to die out here I guess you might as well know."

Luna flinched when Vickee said *we're all going to die*. What had I seen in this woman? And Vickee . . . was a spy? No, that wasn't quite right, I guess. But she was a spook. An *analyst*.

Actually, it sounded like fun. I was jealous, and furious all over again. If I'd published my original papers as I'd planned, either with or without her as a coauthor, would the Synarche have sent me all over the galaxy to fight crime?

You don't want to travel all over the galaxy, I reminded myself. *It's bad enough being here. And you wouldn't have met Salvie or had the kids if that had happened.*

Somehow I found it in myself to smile at Vickee and really mean it. "Congratulations," I said warmly. "That sounds like the perfect role for you."

She blinked, and I felt an unworthy nugget of delight that I had blindsided her. Better yet, before she could respond, she was interrupted:

"This is SRV *I Can Remember It for You Bespoke*," Dakhira's voice broke in. "I don't mean to interrupt this charming carbon-based interaction, but as I previously mentioned, I appear to have between four and six Strangers on board, and I was wondering what you wanted me to do about it."

CHAPTER 27

I LOOKED OVER AT NONSENSE, WHO HAD HAULED ITSELF two-thirds of the way out of its tank and draped itself in a frilly capelet with a pattern like pink and yellow hyacinths. *What are they doing, Dakhira?*

"Nothing in particular," Dakhira responded. "As far as I can tell. Just being extradimensional hitchhikers, I suppose."

I unfocused my gaze, brought the intrusive music to the forefront of my mind, and let the Strangers surface in my awareness. There were plenty of them here as well—unnervingly, one was standing half inside Nonsense and its tank, and another one overlapped Petrac, who was talking to a Chive. They both seemed to be about some darkside task, working busily.

I experienced a moment's amusement that the guy who hated nonhumans so much was currently co-located with one. A twinge of shame replaced it: the office bigot seemed to have no problem with the Chives I was so uncomfortable with.

Nothing like a little moment of clarity into your own hypocrisy.

Well, said Nonsense, *if they're not hurting anything, I propose you ignore them. They'll probably make their intentions known.*

"Organics," Dakhira said disgustedly.

I wanted Petrac to be the would-be murderer almost as badly as I wanted it to be Vickee. I decided to go over his files next, since I already had my bias filters turned up so high they were interfering with my intuition.

Everything is a trade-off. Just as, if I wanted the expertise that came with the ayatanas I was wearing, it was going to come with the anxieties.

Petrac's personnel file was interesting reading, but not because it suggested he was a Freeport sympathizer. He hadn't been lying about surviving a pirate attack as a kid, and he'd held a lot of fascinating jobs in the ans since. Most of them onworld, or close to the Core. It was a pity I disliked him so much. Otherwise it might have been interesting to talk to him about "field archaeological virtual modeling," for example.

Did you make mock-ups of dig sites so students could practice on them? Did you re-create current or historical sites? Model landforms to find good places to dig? They all seemed plausible, and I was sure there were options I hadn't even considered.

Yod, I asked, *when can we go back to our quarters?*

As soon as I have the trim stabilized, she said. *And we're certain there are no more rocks incoming and all the pirates are gone.*

Should we organize search parties, if the pirates can block you?

Kell is leading a group of tesserae through the hab, she said. *They can sense the pirates' cloaking technology. And some of the Strangers seem to have joined the Baomind's hunt.*

The hab's superstructure creaked uneasily. Sorting data is soothing, and my general anxiety level had started to dip. Now my pulse hammered in my ears again, drowning out the ominous sound until my fox corrected for it.

Everybody else had looked up from what they were doing, too, as if we were sheltering in transit tunnels from a bombing raid and one had just hit close enough to shake dust out of the ceiling.

"It's the fungus," Willow said. "There's so much radiation coming off the Baostar that overgrowth is stressing the hull."

Haran made a sound that was extremely close to a swear word.

"Is it going to rupture?" My voice had a squeak I couldn't control. "Or squish us?"

Willow's fingers flew through an interface before her, holographic light dancing on her skin. "I've got Hands trimming it," she said. "We'll reprocess the excess material into structural reinforcement." She looked at Haran. "Or gin, I suppose."

She extracted one hand from the holobox with a snakelike dart, patted my shoulder, and inserted her hand back into the pattern without, I thought, disturbing it at all. I exhaled.

Vickee wrinkled her nose scornfully. Once upon a time—like yesterdia, probably—I would have looked away and swallowed my embarrassment. But now, after the past dia or so and with my kids and cats in the room, I refused to be shamed.

"If you have a problem," I said, "why don't you say it?"

Vickee rolled her eyes. "You're projecting."

It occurred to me that Vickee's models of my behavior were outdated. Twenty years before, I would have been second-guessing my reactions based on what she said. Now, all I felt was mild irritation.

My lack of response surprised me more than fury would have. Calm rose from my center. Some of it was Yod managing my chemistry, but some of it came from me.

I smiled at her expression of confusion and smiled more when it segued to outrage. With a profound, surprising, and unassailable sensation of freedom, I said, "To project, I would have to be thinking about you, and I have better things to do."

If it wasn't true when I started saying it, it was by the end. Like an invocation, a spell of release. My fear and sense of intimidation released their prickly-footed grip on my heart and zoomed up like damselflies. The feelings would probably be back—feelings are annoying that way—but for the moment I basked in the profound blissful Zen of not giving a single solitary haploid fuck about Victorya DeVine.

Vickee rearranged her face in a mask meant to indicate pitying incomprehension of my terrible behavior. "You *would* sink to that level." She flounced away.

Winning didn't carry the intense freight of satisfaction I would have expected. I felt serene and balanced. Unflapped, if not unflappable.

Sadly, Vickee didn't keep walking right out the airlock. But at least the Garden Pod was big enough for her to disappear into the undergrowth, so I didn't have to keep looking at her. She startled Angie on her way past—or maybe Angie just enjoyed Vickee's company as much as I did—leading to an ignominious shower of cawing and suited wing-flaps, and robbing Dr. DeVine's retreat of any dignity.

I sighed and turned away. Only to find myself at eye level with Dr. Nonsense, who was squidged over the edge of the tank, siphons pulsing. It said, *Was that another dominance conflict?*

"I would prefer to think I was successfully defending my boundaries," I said, having taken a little time to think about it.

Ah. So a territorial dispute.

I laughed. "If the territory in question is Vickee wanting to live rent-free in my head, then yes, I suppose it was."

Whatever Haran was pouring into his fermentation chamber had a sting of alcohol and yeast to it already. Nonsense's colors yellowed on the side closer to the fumes. It squidged down the tank toward fresher air, and I followed. Various other crew members had broken into small groups and were working or talking quietly. A Chive stood alone against the transparent wall, staring outward. I thought they were still the one the others were suspicious of, unless they'd switched around while I was sleeping, and I resolved to keep an eye on them. Along with everything else I was doing.

When I unfocused my gaze I could see the Strangers—five or six of them, trailing soft-edged auras like hallucinations. One gesticulated at me, seeming to seek my attention. A strain of music rose from the fugue in my head.

I wished I understood what they were trying to tell me.

I said, "The thing is, for humans, rightminding helps remind us constantly that we are part of a web of social relationships. We get distracted by the idea of getting ahead of the other guy instead of understanding that everybody has a better outcome if we watch out for each other."

Shared transfer of knowledge is one thing my species is good at. If you know you're going to die when your offspring are born, you have to figure out ways to make sure they receive training, education, language. Otherwise we'd be resetting to baseline every generation. So we all have to think about the future and secure it for the next generations.

Three Strangers drifted in our direction. I tried not to stare.

"How do you manage that, if it's not a violation of your privacy to ask?"

Manage what?

"Legacy." It should feel cold when they passed through me, I thought, as in the legends about ghosts. But it felt like nothing at all.

Not too differently than how humans do. We set up institutions. Universities are the best technology we have so far for preserving culture and knowledge over the long term.

There are always juveniles and sub-breeding adults, it continued. *The breeding adults make the journey to the spawning ground from all over the planet. We release our zygotes and protect the spawn until they hatch. Then our bodies feed them and enrich the ocean, attracting more prey for the young.*

Like whale fall, I thought.

Also, our offspring gain a certain amount of knowledge from, well, eating their parents' neurons.

"They have flatworms on Terra that learn the same way. But you went to space."

We did. We wouldn't have gotten there without human intervention. It's hard to build rockets underwater.

I nodded. "I mean, you in person. Dr. Nonsense. You came to see us all out here."

I was curious. I could be a xenobiologist at home, but all I would have to study would be whatever sentients came to visit. Whereas out here, there's so much to learn.

And no temptation to feed yourself to your children. "What happens when a learned professor like yourself is drawn to reproduce?"

Flashes of color, and another uncomfortable scoot away from the alcohol smell. *If I were on my homeworld, I would work in a collective setting with no connection to the sea. If we can't migrate to the spawning grounds, nothing triggers the hormonal shift and transformation to our final instar. As long as I stay in space and isolated, I will live until something kills me.*

And if I die out here, and there's any opportunity to recover my body, the Judiciary will see to it that I am frozen and my body gets home to feed and educate the next generation.

I noticed that it hadn't exactly answered my question. I wondered if it was lonely. I wondered what it would be like to never be able to return to the ocean where you were born, on pain of death. What would it be like to choose between genetic immortality and personal immortality?

What would it be like to know that your knowledge would in some respect pass on to someone else's children?

. . . *Salvie,* I thought. Warrior-caste Fercho existed to defend the children of their clan. The children of my body, in Salvie's case. But she, too, was passing her knowledge and lifeways along to them, albeit through a less direct method than being consumed.

Nonsense wore human ayatanas, and probably other ones, too. Was that knowledge imprinted in its neurolocal web and subbrains?

The Strangers surrounded Haran, plucking undetectably at his sleeves as if trying to distract him. Apparently they didn't like the smell of fermentation either.

How could they detect it? Surely volatizing scent molecules couldn't interact with them!

Down the tank row, Haran grunted and closed his fermentation chambers. The tautness in Nonsense's limbs relaxed a little as the atmosphere became less toxic. The Strangers still swarmed around him, their robes shadowy and indistinct.

"There's only one spawning ground for your whole world?"

Well, it said with the twinkling air of one offering a mock confidence, *it's a* large *spawning ground.*

CHAPTER 28

SALVIE PLACED HER HAND ON MY ELBOW. I'D BEEN STARing at more personal histories and constructing more parallel timelines and karan overlaps. The abrupt refocusing of my eyes on the external world never used to bother me, but the older I get, the more likely it is to give me a crushing headache.

I was not lucky this time, and winced.

"Sorry," said Salvie. "Did I interrupt anything important?"

Thanks to tuning, I did not bite her head off. I sent, *Dr. Nonsense is almost certainly not the pirate fifth columnist, being a syster, but it is nearly two hundred and fifty ans old. Maybe I ought to treat it with more respect due its seniority.*

"I think you would just make it sad. It doesn't seem to stand on ceremony."

My irritation vanquished, I leaned my head on her shoulder. "Did you need something or were you just worried I was forgetting to hydrate?"

Sheepishly, she handed me the bulb of juice that was in her other hand.

"Okay," I said. "What's up?"

"I'm going to lead a small team to help Yod scan for stowaway pirates," Salvie said. "She and Kell have done what they could, and she's got a small army of Hands monitoring the interior and exterior hull for signs of sabotage . . . but none of us feel safe spreading out again until we do a fingertip search. And Cee and Xhelsea aren't here to play badass—"

"You're enough of a badass for any hab, sweetie."

"Aw." Her tendrils curled. "Will you be all right without me?"

I gave her a sidelong hug. "Just promise you'll come back at a run if we need you. And that you will be careful out there."

"I'm always careful," Salvie said, and made me yelp by tickling my ear.

I could put a brave face on it, and I could tune my anxiety for Salvie down, but her departure meant I was on full-time Stavan duty. And he needed distraction and entertainment—something my fine-honed parental reflexes detected when I suggested I help him with his schoolwork and his face crumpled in despair. I'd almost had to pry him loose from Salvie so she could go on patrol. Luna was playing it adolescently cool, but I could tell she was worried.

I was worried, too, and as Salvie set off with the Chive and a couple of burly systems types, I warned her that another Chive had mentioned one of their number was withholding from the collective and not to turn her back. Then I went to check on our daughter.

Luna didn't want to talk to me about it, though. Once Salvie left, she curled in a chair and alternated reading graphic novels and playing with Angie the dinosaur. Stavan and I kept custody of the cats, who were becoming increasingly fractious in their demands to be out of their little kitty hardsuits. Nobody enjoys the chafing and constriction after a while, and certainly not Zig and Zag.

At least I had an advantage over the Penelopes of earlier days waiting for their warriors to return. Salvie's light touch remained on my feed, so I knew she was all right and thinking of me. I forced myself not to lean on the contact because I didn't want to distract her in a dangerous situation. But there was so much comfort in just knowing she was out there with her proton gun, safe and keeping us safe.

I fed her signal through to the kids, so they could have that sense of security, too, without my having to constantly remind them that their mom was hunting pirates. If anything went wrong—well, I would deal with it then.

Ironically, Salvie's location bug was still blinking soothingly in my feed, letting me know she was unharmed, when the hatch to the Garden Pod blew wide open.

The lights went out, but the Baostar's sullen glow stretched long bloody shadows across the deck. Someone shrieked. I triggered my actuator. My helmet cut off the sound, dulling Yod's belated warning siren. An orange bug blinking in the corner of my feed was a much more tolerable alert to danger.

Instinctively, I threw myself between the dust cloud roiling from the shattered hatch and my children. *Get down and stay behind something!* I sent.

I didn't know if tables and tanks of water offered any kind of reasonable protection, because I didn't know what weapons the pirates were packing. I hoped the available cover would be better than nothing. I hoped the pirates didn't just toss a few grenades in and call it good—

Don't stand in front of the door, said Nonsense inside my head, and I had just enough time to register the good sense of that instruction and duck to the side when every pirate in the stellar system came pouring in through the ruined hatchway. Wreathed in boiling clouds of orange-lit dust, they looked like the legions of hell.

I still had my club, and when I let its reflexes function, I still had the martial artist ayatana. I swung low, at the knee joint of the closest Freeporter. You couldn't effectively armor a knee in the medieval period, and you can't effectively armor one now. So my attack was unchivalrous and unsporting—but they had a gun and I had a knobby stick.

I put my hip into it.

The head of my club bounced on impact and the pirate's hands flew up as they fell. I imagined the air inside their helmet had just turned blue with swearing. I kicked the gun away, presuming it was owner-locked and nobody else would be able to ferret it out and shoot me in the back.

I only know what happened next, more or less, because my fox recorded it. The conservatory rattled with flashing light and sound. Struggling figures surrounded me. Blows were exchanged and weapons flashed.

Whenever I had a chance at anyone who wasn't wearing Yod's hardsuit colors, I took a swing. Something ricocheted off my suit, the impact knocking me on my ass. Suit seals bit into the backs of my knees and thighs.

Salvie!

On my way! Of course she was. Of course she had been from the instant things went pear-shaped. I rolled under a bench, trying to get a line of sight on the kids. My feed told me roughly where they were and that their hearts were still beating—

MOM! Stavan's ping punched every override on its way in. Emergency lights lit up; I turned—

Somebody wearing Yod's colors had Luna by the elbows and was dragging her out from behind a tank full of fig and lemon trees. She lashed out, fighting valiantly, but her rubberized heels made contact with armored thighs and bounced. She twisted. Inside the helmet her mouth was open, eyes squinched shut, and she was screaming something I could not hear.

Yod! Turn off that suit!

Clever, Yod said, and I watched the hardsuit whisk itself back into its actuator, revealing the muscled arms and grimacing face of Haran Karmer.

For a moment I felt lightheaded, dizzy with implication. It didn't last—I stepped forward, swinging my club left-handed because my right arm was still numb from the earlier projectile impact.

"Put her down!" I bellowed, my suit mike amplifying.

Heads snapped around all over the hab, and they all witnessed me slam my weapon into Haran's unprotected elbow with every gram of force I could muster. He shrieked and let go of one of Luna's arms. She promptly swung around and tried to hit him with it.

Good job, kid.

Haran flinched, slapping wildly at his upper arm.

"I said"—I swung for his head—"let *go*!"

He ducked, and I had to pull the blow rather than hit Luna. The hardsuit braced my joints, but I still felt something in my elbow strain. It popped with a searing sensation and I was down to about half an arm. Haran backpedaled and I gave chase, dropping the club. I had to get Luna away from him.

Haran dragged Luna, still flailing, toward the viewports on the outside wall. As they passed the big tank, a giant bubble of water surged up from the surface. Dr. Nonsense broke through, several arms suckered to tank walls on either side. It sprayed a huge fountain of water from its siphon right into Haran's face.

Haran screamed and lunged forward. I thought he was going to try to grab Nonsense and hurl it against a bulkhead as I closed the distance, hoping to get a hand on Luna or catch Nonsense—ridiculous because it probably massed as much as I did. Dropping my club was a stupid idea—

The Chive stepped in, my club in their hand, and swung at Haran's face.

This blow landed, but sadly it rang off ceroplastic. Haran had triggered a second hardsuit, this one gleaming silver and mirror-finished. I stared at my own reflection in his helmet for a moment—and saw Salvie mirrored behind me, aiming her proton gun at someone I couldn't see.

I tried to reach Luna to tell her to *duck*, but she had me locked out. I slammed my visor open and shouted at the top of my lungs. She'd hear that, whether she wanted to or not.

At the same time, I started the parental override—she'd hate me for weeks, but her life was more important—but before I finished Haran started yelling expletives.

"You fuckers," he boomed, suit speakers creaking from the volume. "And *those* fuckers too. Throwing rocks at this hab while I'm still in here? Fuck *all* of you."

His earlier fury abruptly made sense to me.

He yanked Luna off her feet and kicked out hard. His suited foot connected with the fermentation chamber—and it exploded, releasing its pressurized contents in a spray of alcohol and soggy fungus bits. Nonsense's membranes bleached, showing a pattern of droplets edging a violent splash. It plunged under the water.

My eyes and lungs stung with the release of alcohol.

Haran's next kick popped a transparent panel right out of the big tank.

Or rather, popped it in—and then the water pressure shoved it out, with a wall of fluid behind. *Oh no,* I thought foolishly. *The family tree.*

The water hit Haran and Luna an instant before it washed my feet out from under me. My suit resealed itself, with a whole lot of vaporized alcohol and mushroom stink on the inside.

I fell with an enormous splash, and the current rolled me over and under. My gloves slid off the deck; my legs slammed into a table. I felt myself hit another armored body; they caught my suit handle and hauled me up by the middle of my back as if I weighed nothing. I found myself looking through beaded water into Salvie's face.

"Come on," she said. "He's getting away."

Panting, disoriented, eyes watering and swelling, I staggered after her. The pirates had withdrawn, I thought—or maybe there were a few left, underwater. Some water poured sideways out the blown-up airlock but most piled against the deck, blocking the ladder to the perimeter walkway. The wheel bounced as the mass of water sloshed back and forth in waves. Crests built, nodes intersecting and amplifying.

Town groaned and popped, cables vibrating. The whole hab wobbled, spinning eccentrically under the strain. Water piled up against the spin-verse bulkhead.

Trim failure warning, Yod said crisply. *Compensating.*

It didn't feel like she was compensating. I could feel the wobble in my whole body as Salvie hauled me toward the door. Only my suit's gyroscopes kept me upright as the water sloshed heavily around my legs.

Splashing through water in space toward a blown airlock and a pirate. This was every nightmare I'd ever had, multiplied.

"Stavan?" I yelled into the radio.

He was sobbing and screaming, "Get her! Go!"

"Love you," I said back, already moving. My voice slurred. Oh, great, my suit was full of vaporized alcohol. And so was I. *Scrub that,* I told my fox.

"Come *on*!" Salvie dragged me toward a disused airlock.

One tiny bit of luck: it was on the spinward side, and mostly clear of water. It led, I thought, to a little decommissioned runabout used as storage.

Do we know where the pirates went? I asked Yod, making sure Nonsense and Salvie were patched into the feed. The galaxy spun, and it wasn't just the hab's rotation doing it to me.

Chive says they saw some withdrawing toward the hub lounge, she answered. *Their ships just abandoned them here.*

So they had no choice but to take the hab, die trying—or surrender to rightminding, which they considered a fate worse than death. "Shit."

The cables holding Town together were all tensioned to a single point at the middle of the hab. They pulled against one another, and it was their creaking and vibrations that rose up from the deck through my legs to my internal organs. They must already be on the verge of snapping under the uneven strain of the wobbling hab. Yod was doubtless reinforcing them as fast as she could.

But if one snapped . . . the load would transfer abruptly to the other lines. The oscillations of the hab would amplify, possibly even achieving a resonant frequency, and more shocked cables would split under the force. Town would tear itself apart, and everyone inside it—my wife, my kids, my cats, and an assortment of professional colleagues of whom I had grown fond—would spill into space like so many marbles.

I reeled as Salvie pulled me against the airlock bulkhead, her arm over the shoulders of my suit. The hull behind us and the ragged doors provided some cover. The interior of the runabout lay dark.

I hadn't been this drunk, I thought, since grad school. Apparently there are a lot of fermentable sugars in radiotropic fungus. And Haran and Petrac probably used some engineered superyeast to get the maximum concentration of alcohol.

Can you see anything? I asked Salvie. Her eyes used different frequencies from mine, including some of what humans considered the infrared.

Not from here, she said.

I am so sorry I dragged you out here—

That was my decision, Salvie said. *We can argue about it later.*

Moms? Luna, loud and clear in my feed. She sounded scared and young. My heart lodged in my throat, right beside both lungs and probably my spleen or something that were already jammed in there.

We're right here, I said. *Hang on, sweetheart, we're coming.*

Oh, crap! Before I'd fully parsed her sending, blinding vermilion light slapped across everything. My arm smacked my visor as I tried by reflex to shield my eyes. My boots magnetized to the deck as my vision redded out and a huge blast of wind swept various small objects and a shower of snow—flash-frozen water and atmosphere—past us and out the door. My ears popped as my hardsuit reacted to the pressure drop.

Luna! LUNA!

Nothing came back but a terrified wail.

The stream of white confetti intensified to planetary blizzard proportions, dimming the fury of the Baostar enough that my visor started to compensate. Salvie let go of my arm and launched herself, a shadow in the midst of the storm. I glanced back over my shoulder—Stavan and the cats—but they were as safe as they could be anywhere on this crumbling bubble. Safer than I was.

All those poor plants in the Garden Pod.

I unmagged my boots and followed Salvie into the cloud of boiled-off, frozen water vapor. At the far end of the runabout, the cargo airlock had been overridden and wedged wide open. The helmet-filtered Baostar rippled like oil in a hot pan. I imagined I could *see* its surface swelling outward like a balloon about to burst, despite it being so enormous I could only see part of it through the open lock. Bloody light stained everything, ripping jet-black razor-edged space shadows across the deck.

Against it, I could make out two tiny figures, silhouettes falling into the night. Haran and his hostage, my daughter.

Without the cargo doors to protect us, my suit's radiation warnings buzzed an increasingly frantic crescendo. I reached after my wife. My hands wanted to lock onto anything, freeze me there, keep me from falling forever into the dying sun—

Salvie threw herself out the airlock with a bloodcurdling war cry. Her suit thrusters blazed, revaporizing a swath of frozen crystals.

I was going to lose my wife and daughter the same way I had lost my mother and sister. If Stavan and I somehow survived, we would be left behind, like my father and I had been. *He* was going to be left behind. Just like me.

I realized my hand was locked on the grab bar beside the airlock. I tugged on it, but it would not release. Something other than my conscious mind was in charge, and there was nothing I could do about it.

There was nothing *I* could do about it.

My whole being shivered with fear as I sent, *Yod, override my suit, please. Release left gauntlet grip.*

Roger, she said.

My fist unclenched. Or rather, my fist *was* unclenched. I had no say in the matter. The glove's fingers opened, forcing the fingers inside to straighten. *Can you guide me? I'm not a pilot and I've never done an EVA before.*

Be fast, she said. *The rads out here are killer. And getting worse.*

I knew. I watched the counter in my suit climbing from yellow into dark orange. I nodded. *Go.*

I hurled myself out of the airlock, and let the heavens take me.

CHAPTER 29

THERE WAS NO BURST OF SENSATION, NO SUDDEN SHOCK of cold like throwing yourself into a bitter ocean, though you would think there ought to be. If there had been, it would have meant a suit failure. Any record of these events would only result from some long-suffering mortuary AI extracting it from my fox.

There was, in fact, no physical change at all—my suit had already stiffened from its internal pressure when Haran blew out the hatch. But one moment I was inside, sheltered by the fragile walls of the hab and Yod's good sense. And the next I was outside, a fragment of jetsam tumbling over the biggest cliff in the universe.

The Baostar would expand to consume me before I ever reached the bottom. And if it didn't, I would be long dead of starvation, cold, gamma rays, or plain old age by then.

Light and deadlier forms of radiation blasted us. I thought I saw Strangers swarming all over the exterior of the hub. Only they were Freeporters, their armor washed out by the light of the star, casting jet-black space shadows. Scrambling to get inside and out of the hard, killing light of the flare.

Dakhira, Arula, and Amal sheltered on the far side of the hab, their three hulls so close together their magnetic bottles merged and reinforced. I could barely see them through the coruscating auroras.

I silenced wailing sirens: I knew, I knew. If we made it back inside alive, all three of us would be spending time in Cee's cryo tanks having our cancers, dying bone marrow, and ruptured cell walls treated.

If.

The enormity of my situation would have to wait. I had a family to rescue.

Yod steered me; all I had to do was not struggle and throw my center of gravity around. It was glorious, when I shoved away the conviction that we were all going to die. Town spun its wheel across the sky. We drifted amid fraying cables that whipped past us like so many dull, rotating blades. As long as Yod kept us inside their cage and they didn't snap and lash free, they couldn't hurt us. The Baostar stretched across half the sky, tentacles flaring from its corona like Dr. Nonsense in the midst of a particularly vehement gesticulation. It looked even more squashed, as if the distance from pole to pole had compressed while the equator spun out. That was probably a bad sign.

It was also a problem that could wait until my wife and I got our daughter back. Haran looked to be headed for the hub. He dragged Luna along by the rescue handle on her hardsuit. She flailed and kicked, impeding his smooth course.

Salvie still had her proton gun.

Can you shoot him?

Too great a chance of hitting Luna.

I glanced back at the pirates. Were they going to offer Haran backup?

It didn't look like it. Score one for the enemy's sophipathology helping out the good guys.

Was it a sophipathology of my own to identify other sentients as the enemy?

They were actively trying to kill my family. I decided it was fine.

Luna or Yod triggered Luna's suit thrusters, spinning her and Haran around their common center of gravity. I heard only grunts of effort from her feed, punctuated by age-inappropriate but situationally justified cursing. She connected with one foot to his thigh. The hardsuit would have protected him from the kick, but some portion of the thrusters got through. He convulsed away from the contact and let go of her.

Luna arched, shoved off with her other foot—and was suddenly free and sailing away from Haran. And directly toward those silent, whizzing cable guillotines.

Shit, said Salvie.

Get her, I said. *I'll distract Haran.*

I made my body an arrow, not watching my wife and daughter. Trusting Salvie to protect Luna. I had one job, and it was to give them time to maneuver to safety.

It's clarifying, someone kidnapping your child.

From Haran's body language, he considered going after his hostage, then caught sight of me and thought better of it. He turned to flee toward the hub, and I piled into him like a guided missile, the impact of suit on suit ringing jarringly through my little pocket of atmosphere. I screamed at him, not sure if he was hearing any of it, and swung at his helmet with an armored fist and all my might.

I reckoned without Newton.

The swing itself destroyed my trim, and the impact of my fist on Haran's hardsuit bounced us in opposite directions, flailing. Haran clipped my head with a boot as he somersaulted. The reactive colloid lining my suit dampened the blow somewhat, but my ears still rang. They popped again, and for a terrible moment I thought he'd holed me. But either the suit repaired itself or it hadn't sprung a leak.

Yod brought my spin under control and my fox kept me from losing whatever I still had in my stomach. Crystallizing reactive mass whirled around me like the spirals of a miniature cyclone. If there had been any sound, I would have heard the whipping cables closer, closer—

Grab that stanchion! Yod ordered.

Without thinking, I did as I was told. It struck my gloves with a sensation like getting a solid hit on a cricket ball, but much harder and more painful.

Shoot him now! I yelled at Salvie. *He's getting away!*

Salvie had a hand on Luna, who gasped with relief. Long, rattling breaths hissed across her suit mike. I hoped she wasn't hurt. But she was alive, which meant everything else suddenly became manageable.

My wife whipped around, drawing a bead. She might have fired, but Haran was zigzagging as he sailed away. Not toward the hub, where the other Freeporters were drawing weapons of their own. But toward the rim.

Evade, Salvie ordered.

I didn't have to. Yod unlatched my gloves from the bar I was clinging to and fired my thrusters, squirting me back toward the inner curve of the wheel like a spat seed. Salvie herself ducked and somersaulted, wrapping her body and armor around Luna. Freeporters were boiling back out of the hub now, racing toward us across the intervening space. Their mostly black suits had made them nearly invisible against the night but silhouetted them nicely against the Baostar—as long as my visual filters held. They were starting to leak light to a painful level.

Well, I guess Vickee wasn't the killer after all.

That's a disappointment, I answered. *Also, NOT NOW.*

Under Yod's control, I had nothing to do but watch the Freeporters come. And think about how I was going to keep them from getting to Luna and Salvie.

They were impressive, though I hated to admit it. I admired how they moved through space, their competence and grace as they came to kill me.

I glanced over at the ships huddling in Town's shadow, trying to keep their crews from cooking in the light that was making my suit refrigeration whine.

Go, I told Salvie.

I felt her desire to protest, her sense of outrage at the irony that I was staying behind to fight when that was *her* job, born and bred.

You're the next line of defense, I told her. And though her thoughts were inchoate and unformed in the raw feed she sent me, I felt the moment when she mastered herself, and the grudging agreement that followed.

See you inside, she sent.

Mom—

I love you, I said to both of them, and Stavan. *Take care of the tree and the cats.*

For the first time in my life, I wished I had a gun.

Your suit has a toolkit, Yod said. *And cutting blades. I'll navigate you to a cable. Cut through it when I say. It will buy you time.*

Everything wheeled around me, and it wasn't just the hab rotating. *I'm drunk and you're already unstable—*

I'm better at engineering than you are, and your fox is adjusting your blood chemistry. Do what I say.

Don't argue with the wheelmind, Sunya.

Great, now my wife and the AI were ganging up on me. My jets fired; I moved toward the cable.

I love you, I said again, helplessly.

We're starting firearms lessons tomorrow, Salvie answered, with such confidence that tears stung my eyes.

Tomorrow, I agreed.

They're inside, Yod said. *I don't have time to build an airlock but I'm sealing the hull breach. Hold the bad guys off for another minute and I'll have it secure.*

Sixty seconds was a long time. Suit telemetry warned me of an object on an impact trajectory. Yod yanked me to one side; the projectile glided past and ricocheted off the cable connector behind me.

Suit telemetry told me the ring of the hab was only a few hundred meters away. It might as well have been on the other side of the Baostar.

Get behind the buttress, Sunya. You'll have to go around the outside to get back in. I'm sending drones to support you.

We both knew I was very unlikely to be going back inside. But I magged my suit to the hull and crouched down, hiding as much of my body from the pirates as I could. The cutting blade slid out of my suit's forearm. I braced myself with the other hand, feeling the living radiation shield squish.

The vibrations will be unpleasant, but the suit lining will damp them so they do you no harm.

Yikes, I thought. And started cutting on Yod's mark.

There's no sound in space, but vibrations transmit just fine through contact, and I felt the whine in my teeth. Yod wasn't kidding. She also hadn't undersold the suit's capabilities. The blade went into the meter-thick cable like a laser saw into a tree trunk. Strands parted, uncoiling up the length. The cable, weakened, began to stretch.

Duck! Yod yelled.

I threw myself backward toward the hab ring as the cable tore itself apart and sailed majestically away, whiplashing across the gap below. It was still anchored at the hub—the cables there stretched from a center-line—and I imagined it would wrap itself around the structure as Town rotated. For now, however, it was the biggest whip-snap since the Quito elevator collapse.

This one wasn't likely to trigger another Eschaton, at least.

Well, maybe for the Baomind.

I hit the hull back-first, the shock resonating through my body. It knocked the wind out of me. Yod magnetized me to the inner ring while I gasped.

It was a moment before I had the breath to sit up again. Yod piped the visuals into my feed, so I still got to see pirates scattering out of the cable's path in a very satisfying way, though sadly their competence at flying extended to avoiding incoming objects, and it didn't strike or entangle a single one.

By the time I regained a crouch, wheezing, the pirates were regrouping. *The hull is almost sealed,* Yod said. *Withdraw!*

More bullets chipped off the hull on either side of me. Only the ruined cable buttress kept them from my suit and the vulnerable flesh beneath. Suddenly I was surrounded by a cloud of drones—Yod's Hands—deflecting some of the gunfire. My suit whined in the heat; it was growing stifling inside. Maybe I would cook before anything else killed me.... *I don't think I can.*

Go in ten, Yod answered. *Nine, eight, seven—*

Well, it was better than huddling here and waiting to be captured and kidnapped. Or murdered at their leisure, which would probably be far worse than being shot. I shifted forward like a sprinter in the blocks. The drones formed a moving shield between me and the hub.

Had anyone ever run a race across the outside of a hab before?

They must have. I felt a bitter disappointment that I wasn't going to live long enough to look up the details.

GO!

I went.

Around the irregular torus of the hull, toward the airlocks on the other side. All that exercise on the way here had apparently done me some good, because I had a better turn of speed than I expected. The suit's magnets clicked on and off in a steady rhythm. My feet bounced on the fungus as if I were walking on a mattress as big as a moon. It was more like racewalking than running, because if I tried to run I'd lose contact with the hull and go tumbling off into space. The hab oscillated sickeningly around me, settling into a new shape balanced by spin and the uneven cables.

Yod was good at her job: Town defied my expectations, and held together.

The middle of my back itched with anticipation of an impact and the searing pain that would follow. My shadow stretched like a time-lapse image of a sundial, crawling visibly to the left and then behind as Town turned, bringing me around to face the Baostar once again. The shadows of the drones flitted around mine like tesserae.

The pirates were strung out, moving forward in no particular formation. Two fired at me as they moved, but the shots went wide. They had to have explosives with them, I guessed. They'd just blow a hole in Yod's side—

My refrigeration unit coughed in distress, and failed with a whimper. The heat was immediate and punishing. I gasped, forcing myself to keep moving even when the air coming into my lungs felt hot as coffee—producing instant, light-headed nausea.

Don't puke in the suit. Don't puke in the suit.

It was the least of my worries. But also the one I had the most control over right now—which is to say, not much. Yod tuned down my nausea reflex.

Dodging from cover to cover, grateful for all the random rough edges and projections left over from refitting ships into a hab, grateful for the drones that created a screen between me and the enemy, I came around the curve of the hull. The pirates behind me dropped out of sight.

They vanished, and suddenly Kell was beside me. I assumed it was Kell; looking down, I saw my hardsuit reflected in the mirror surface of a tessera of about the right size. It huddled behind the horizon of the hab, flat to the hull and out of the line of fire.

A series of chimes sounded inside my helmet, clear-toned and sweet. To my shock, I realized I understood what Kell was saying. It was: *Need a lift?* more or less.

Yes, please, I sang in return, amazed to discover I could do so. All that studying was having an effect after all. I was learning Baospeech!

Just in time to die.

Don't touch its edges, Yod said. *They're extremely sharp.*

I knew but didn't mind the reminder. Based on my radiation exposure, I already had to regrow my bone marrow. Adding fingers to the mix would just be an annoyance.

I lowered myself onto Kell's surface and made myself as flat as somebody in a hardsuit could possibly get. Kell accelerated away almost before I was in place, and I was glad of Yod's reminder; the reflex to grab the edges was almost irresistible.

But I didn't slip off. I felt as secure on Kell's slick surface as if epoxied into place. Yod's drones flocked around us, still providing some measure of cover.

Kell surmounted the arch of the wheel. The horizon expanded—a whole new side of the hab not so much revealed as washed away in the Baostar's incandescence. A few stark shadows sliced the hab's skin, and the radiotropic fungus caught the light in shattered opalescence.

My collision alarm pinged again. Kell slipped sideways, nimble as a minnow. I stayed on only because it was manipulating gravity to keep me there.

Projectiles stitched the hull behind us. The shadows of another group of pirates flitted at us, a murder of crows against a sailor's sunset. They charged, flying parallel to the hull, jets blazing.

Shooting at us slowed them down. Counterthrust. Mr. Newton doing me a favor this time. But they were still coming, and they were between us and the airlocks on the other side of the hull.

Kell flipped over, taking me with it. I shrieked, expecting to fall—but of course I stayed right where I was in relation to the tessera. The only meaningful gravity out here was what it was generating. I stuck to its back—unless this side had become its belly.

Kell, why? I sang, because I realized I knew how to sing it.

It didn't have time to answer, because a moment later a vast wash of static drowned out Yod's voice, and my link to Salvie, and Kell's song. I tried to silence my headset, but even my fox seemed to be jammed. I had to flip the emergency override to shut the whole auditory system down.

Only once the silence returned did I realize that my gauntlets were squeezing the sides of my helmet, as if I could reach right through the crystal and ceramic and fabric to shield my ears. I opened my eyes—

My visual filters had failed utterly. The sky was washed away in light. My radiation monitor was pinned. It was probably shrieking a warning that I couldn't hear because no EM transmissions were getting through that wall of rads. I gasped, huddling small in Kell's shadow.

Looking down at the hull, I could make out a dim image reflected in its somewhat reflective surface, under the thick coat of transparent cellulose. An enormous coronal mass ejection surged from the Baostar's surface. The light I was seeing had left the star some minutes before. The actual explosion would take . . . two standard days, I guessed.

Pirates or no pirates, we were all going to fry.

The pirates were frying already. I looked around and saw their armored bodies convulsing as the inconceivable radiation pierced their suits and bodies. Kell's wafer-thin surface was shielding me. I could tell because, though I was receiving enough grays to kill me in a week, I hadn't already been microwaved.

Unlike those poor bastards over there.

They'd kill me as soon as look at me.

That didn't make me feel better about their dying horribly in front of my eyes.

I wanted to tell Kell that we had to help them. But I couldn't communicate, and there was nothing we could do. I heard myself mumble, "Oh no—"

My readouts told me I was a goner. I felt at peace—perhaps I could get into a tank on Cee, if Cee got back soon. If not, well, I'd have time to make my goodbyes.

Salvie would be a better parent than me anyway.

I had huddled so deep into Kell's shadow as it scooted me toward the airlock, past convulsing pirates and the floating corpses of dead ones, all swept along in co-orbit, that I almost didn't notice the light dimming. But I could hear my suit siren again, and my fox clicked back online.

Sunya. Sun!

I'm alive, Salvie. I tasted metal and saw brilliant flashes inside my retinas. I had the sense not to say *I'm all right.*

I looked up—and saw Cee between us and the Baostar, her vast belly and shining EM bottle sliding along downwell of us, sheltering Kell and me from the deadly light.

CHAPTER 30

I WOKE UP IN ONE OF CEE'S MED TANKS, MY LUNGS FULL OF oxygenated goo and my last memory of Xhelsea, suited and frowning, hauling me into the airlock. Nothing hurt, which was incredible considering the pounding I had taken. I was pleased to be alive and even more pleased not to be in a cryo tank. I hadn't known Judiciary ships could just . . . treat radiation syndrome overnight.

I guess radiation exposure is a danger Judiciary vessels contend with regularly.

My least favorite part of the rapid healing process was being decanted. Being lifted out of the tank wasn't bad, but I can't say the same for the subjective lifetime I spent choking gel out of my respiratory system from the bronchioles up. Like drowning in reverse. The oxygenated nutrient goo had a scent of cloves and honey, which wasn't detectable until there was some space in my airway for it to volatize. It was probably meant to be soothing, if you could bear the taste of cloves.

When I was finally gasping in air rather than gasping out clove-and-honey-scented snot, I pushed my chair away from the basin and laid my upper body down along my thighs. I rested my forehead on the cool metal alongside the suction input and tried to feel anything but tired.

We were under just enough acceleration to keep me in the chair.

Apparently half an an in space was long enough for my body to internalize the meaning behind shifts in its apparent weight.

When I got my voice back, I pushed myself to an upright position—gingerly, so as not to send myself flying. I picked a curl of waterlogged, sloughed skin off my arm—I needed a shower and a stiff brush—and asked, "What did I miss?" All of my surfaces—interior and exterior—felt strangely numb from the clove oil.

That was probably why they used it.

"We've got to evacuate the system immediately." Chionn hovered beside me. The expression on her mobile face might mean anything at all, but from one primatiform to another it looked like a grimace of fear. "We've got a little respite—"

"Your kids and wife are safe for now," Xhelsea interrupted from the forward hatch. They swung down the ladder with that microgravity lightness. "Forgive Chionn, her people reproduce by budding. She doesn't understand."

I smiled up at them, lifting my head the bare minimum. My diaphragm, abdominals, and intercostals felt pummeled. But there was no nausea, no mental confusion. No more of those infinitesimal bright flashes in my field of vision from particles striking my retina. I even had all my hair.

"Thank you for reading between the lines." I glanced over at Chionn. "Budding?"

Chionn waggled all eight fingers in the air. "Don't believe everything you hear from that one."

"How can we evacuate?" I asked her. "We don't have enough ships, the pirates are blockading us, and there's still an unknown number of them holed up inside Town where the star can't quite cook them."

"True," Chionn said. "But we have just over a dia until the coronal mass ejection gets here. The Baomind and the ships can get out of the way, though the civilian ships will take a pounding. Town is not maneuverable enough."

"Where's Kell?" I asked—urgently, my memory now returning to me. "Is it—"

"It's fine," Cee said. "We're loading Baomind into every available interior and exterior space that can't house a meatform evacuee. We'll just have to pack in what we can and run for it. Kell is facilitating."

With a pang, I thought of the tree. I hadn't trusted my father to take care of it, and now there wasn't going to be room on the ride home. If it had even survived the chaos in the Garden Pod. *Sentient chauvinism*, I thought, but even though it broke my heart, I couldn't imagine shoving Iris or even Petrac through an airlock to make room for my tree.

Well, maybe Petrac. Would anybody miss him, really? Even Dr. Nonsense might be convinced to look the other way.

Right. Thinking about abandoning my ancestral tree was just going to make me sad. So I should think about something else. "Can I call my wife?"

"There might be a lot of interference," Cee said. "But you can certainly try."

I used Cee's transmitters to boost my signals and called my wife. The static *was* bad. You could hear the star out there, waves of particles transformed by the miracle of radio into a death rattle.

The first thing Salvie said was, "How are you?"

"Okay," I told her. I started to say something else glib, then paused. The kids weren't listening. And if I could be honest with anyone, I could be honest with Salvie.

"Tired and scared."

"Me too," she agreed.

"You?" I laughed. "You're a rock. Nothing scares you."

"Hey," Salvie said. "Don't pretend I'm invulnerable because it scares you to think of me being hurt, Sun."

"I'm not—"

"You are." She sounded soft, not angry. "You let yourself be vulnerable with me. Now let me be vulnerable with you."

"Dammit, Salvie. But I don't want you to be scared," I said. *I married you because you're not scared of anything.*

I didn't say that last part, or even think it loudly, because I knew it wasn't fair.

"Denial doesn't actually make stuff not real." I heard the hug in her voice. "Anyway, I got myself into it. I wish we'd had the wits to do what Luna wanted and leave the kids and cats at home. But your dad—"

"I know." I hadn't trusted him to take care of the family tree, let alone my actual family. "Is Luna still giving you hell?"

"Surprisingly," Salvie said, "no. She has been sitting quietly and frowning at nothing."

"She's plotting," I hazarded. I remembered my fears that she had somehow been involved with the pirates. How ridiculous they seemed now.

Salvie sent staticky amusement. "Let her plot."

"Stavan is okay?"

"Scared green," Salvie said. "But coping. And to head off your next question, the cats are all really pissed off and want out of their hardsuits, but they're not experiencing any physical harm."

"Just the trauma of not being able to lick their asses. Do I have a transparent head?"

"Only to those of us who have been married to you for twenty years, dearest."

Call ended, I knuckled a spiky-feeling drop of salt water from my eye and turned back to Chionn and Xhelsea. "What do we do now?"

"We're heading back to Town and braking currently," Xhelsea said. "That's the deceleration you feel. We had to put on some *v* to chase off a pirate ship that made a pass while you were in the tank."

"At us?"

"At Town," Chionn said. "Probably wanted to evacuate their people."

Xhelsea grunted.

I said, "You didn't let them?"

"They're criminals," the Goodlaw said. "I want them to stop criminaling. I can only figure one way to manage that."

"Wait, you're not just going to leave them in Town—"

"No!" They rocked back, brows beetling. "I'm not leaving anyone behind if I can help it. I'm bringing them back, alive, for judgment. Even if I have to stuff them in three to a cryo capsule."

"If you do that," Chionn interjected, "let me sedate them first. It will make them easier to disentangle for thawing."

Xhelsea rolled their eyes with visible affection for their polka-dotted colleague. "Anyway, we're headed back to Town, so you should be with your family fairly soon." *Before the ejecta gets here,* their expression said as they turned to me. "I've been meaning to ask you. Why do you hate Vickee DeVine so much?"

I massaged my forehead. "Let me guess. She's charmed you?"

"I don't charm, in particular," said Xhelsea. "It's in the job description."

I stared at them, deciding whether to trust. But Chionn and Cee and Xhelsea did keep saving my life.

I sighed. "Long story short? We dated and she stole and published my research."

Xhelsea glanced at Chionn, then right back at me. Their lower lip pushed up and down. I tried not to be distracted by it. "You're not lying."

I put a hand up. "You can tell if I'm lying? I thought that was just three-vee."

They shook their head, chuckling. "Judiciary prerogative. It's less useful than you'd think. People lie all the time for all kinds of reasons. Or deeply believe things that aren't true, which they don't see as lying."

Chionn said, "That's dystopian."

I said, "Humans believe things that aren't true all the time. We create narratives to explain things and get invested in them, rather than finding the facts or getting comfortable with ambiguity."

"I see you've been talking philosophy with Dr. Nonsense," said Cee.

I spread my hands. "He's not *wrong.*"

Xhelsea said, "Good thing my rightminding constrains me to apply my truth-telling ability in an unbiased fashion."

"Does the rightminding work that well?" I suspected mine sure didn't.

"If it didn't, could you trust me to tell you?" Xhelsea said. "It's fashionable to joke about it on three-vee, but I did take an oath. And gave Cee the codes to my fox and the power to enforce it."

Cee said, "They haven't made me cook their neurons even a little bit. So far."

It really was fascinating. I had never thought about the logistics of how Goodlaws worked. But they were a law unto themselves, isolated in strange corners of the galaxy, making judgment calls without recourse to the courts.

Arresting somebody on suspicion and hauling them back to the Core to stand trial was a big risk and a big commitment.

I changed the subject. "Do we know what made the Baostar suddenly decide to flip out?"

Cee's presence lights swirled their pleasant pastel shades, so ironic in a warship. "We've got three different kinds of gravitational-manipulation tech floating—or not floating—around out there. The Baomind, the Freeporters, and the Strangers. I imagine it can't be good for an already fragile star."

"Do you think the pirates might be destabilizing the star on purpose?"

"Well," said Chionn, "I guarantee they don't want the Synarche having any more Koregoi tech than we do already. They want to keep it. It's a hell of an advantage."

Xhelsea added, "And they certainly don't want the Baomind rescued and rehomed. Think of what we can learn from it, and how much power the Synarche gains if your work succeeds and we can unlock all its knowledge."

"But they're dying out there!"

"If they fail, they'll die a lot less pleasantly." Xhelsea ran a hand over their hair. "Warlords can't be reasoned with. They don't really have a lot of options."

I picked at my peeling skin. "It sounds like a death cult."

"They think of it as evolution in action. The strong survive, right?"

"Why did Haran try to kidnap Luna?" Using her as a shield to get out of the Garden Pod made sense, but if he had let her go immediately and run for it he might have had a chance of getting to the hub with his friends. Though, given how he'd railed against them, maybe they weren't such *good* friends. And Salvie could have just shot him. . . .

"Pirates press-gang children," said Xhelsea. "Raids are a constant problem on outlying worlds."

I thought of Petrac and his tragic childhood. "I thought they did that to murder systers and collect plunder."

"And to steal young humans," Chionn said.

Xhelsea rubbed their lower jaw. "The Core worlds mostly would prefer not to know what goes on at the rim," they said. "And it's probably healthy, in small doses. Not to obsess about bad things you can't change."

"Rubric's hardly a Core world," I grumped.

"It's sure not the big dark, either."

That I couldn't argue with. "I wonder if we could use gravitational manipulation to contact the Core for help."

"Sadly, gravity doesn't travel any faster than light," said Cee. "And mucking around with it might further destabilize the star. And we have enough problems."

"Right," I said. "Like a would-be killer loose somewhere around the wheel. And a hub full of pirates that Yod can't sense properly."

Xhelsea made a nonword noise.

"Yes," said Cee. "Like those things."

CHAPTER 31

THE GARDEN POD WAS A BLASTED HEATH, GUARDED NOW by the Chive, who was armed with a proton rifle. If they were working for the pirates—well, they would have done something about it by now, and I remembered the Chive coming to my aid when Haran was kidnapping Luna. Inside, Salvie also wore one slung across her back, and Yod had armed a couple of others: Willow, Fritha, Tsebu the Ceeharen data engineer.

Xhelsea, escorting me, wore an unobtrusive sidearm, and so did the ensign who accompanied them. Chionn had stayed behind on Cee with the rest of her crew. Ready for a fast getaway, or to receive casualties.

To receive *more* casualties.

I noticed the smell before my head came over the lip of the hatchway. Like decaying lettuce in a refrigerator, slimy and sour. The tanks were empty—the water had boiled off into vacuum before pressure was restored. The crops had frozen and thawed. Some of the crew had piled them along the bulkheads. Iris and Petrac stood by the far wall as I entered, feeding whatever they could into the cycler.

I waved. Of the two, only Iris waved back. Other nods met mine around the pod, though, and a couple dozen people came over to praise me and pat me on the back and ask how my recovery was going and tell me how brave I had been.

I didn't tell them that I hadn't been brave; I'd just been Yod's hands. They would have argued with me and my face was already hot. I just felt like a woman with a headache that would not go away. I hadn't realized until then that I was a hero. I had never been a hero before; I could see how this could become addictive.

Five Strangers stood in various places, looking so firm and real it was upsetting that they were standing inside people, tables, bulkheads, and dead plants. Whatever they were standing on was also a little lower than the deck, so they looked like they were wading through the floor.

And there was Salvie, by the family tree in its sealed case. All four cats—Zig, Zag, Toby, and Not-Toby—were leashed to the table at sufficient intervals that they couldn't take out their frayed tempers on one another. Angie sat on Salvie's shoulder, suit partially retracted, eating peanuts from her fingers.

I walked over and pecked Salvie on the cheek. "Hey."

"Hey," she said back, and offered me a peanut.

"No thanks, I ate on the Interceptor."

"She's a good cook," Salvie said. "But this is for Angie."

"Oh." I gave it to the dinosaur, who mumbled happily. "Where are the kids?"

"School," she said. "Well, lessons." She pointed to a small hatchway. "Back there."

"Harsh," I said. "I would have given them a pass, given the threat of imminent destruction and recent kidnapping."

She shrugged. "They need a distraction. And frankly, it's therapy more than civics today."

"Hey," I said. "Guess what happened outside? I can talk to Kell now. Which maybe means I can talk to the Strangers."

"Well," Salvie answered, "you *have* been studying extremely hard. And you loaded in a lot of data."

"My fox is creaking." I reached out and took her hand. "What am I going to do, Salvie? This is a disaster. Even if we get out of here, my career is over."

She gave Angie the last peanut and wiped her fingers. "You discovered an entire new sentient species from a different dimension—and you're the only one who can talk to them! Vickee's doing worse than that!"

"Vickee's a spook," I reminded her in a whisper. "Some kind of analyst. She follows pirates around the galaxy and has for years."

She ignored me. "Sweetie, you need to get your fox tweaked so you can accept your successes."

"But if I let my guard down—"

"If you love things that don't love you back, and chase them, they will only harm you. History can't love you back. Neither can data."

"I don't expect it to."

"Okay. Then what does love you back?"

She didn't expect me to have an answer, I realized. But she wasn't thinking about romantic or family love.

"You do." I leaned my face against her hand.

Her tendrils coiled up tight. "Touché."

"Anyway, I was right," I said. "We did all get blown out into space and nearly die."

Salvie looked me over, tendrils skeptical. "You were right," she agreed. "Does that make you feel safer?"

"No," I admitted. "But what if feeling safe is the enemy?"

"Sometimes you sound exactly like a Fercho warrior."

"Warrior or worrier?" I joked, to cover the spike of anxiety at being seen.

She had known me too long to be derailed. "We're *supposed* to do the worrying for the rest of the nest so they can get on with business."

"What are you saying?"

"I'm saying stop trying to do my job. It's not good for you."

"But it's fine for you?"

"It doesn't cause me distress, sweetheart. Or physical discomfort or long-term damage. I'm designed for it. Born to it. *Your* physiology responds to unrelieved vigilance with anxiety and eventual shutdown. It wears into your neural pathways and harms your body. It's okay to tune it down a little. It's okay to let yourself feel safe."

I looked at her and sighed. "It hurts more if you feel safe and the safety turns out to have been a lie."

She pulled me into her double-jointed arms and held me close. "Is that worse than never having felt safe at all? Does this feel safe?"

The cramp around my heart eased a little, though it still hurt to breathe. "How did I marry such a smart wife?"

"Runs in the family," she said.

I settled against her, as secure as leaning into a favorite armchair. She stroked my hair while I let my attention wander around the pod, taking in the devastation. Urges to stay in her embrace and to check on my tree pulled me in two directions. But the tree would be there in a minute.

So would Salvie, and that was an even better feeling.

"I'm sorry you're here," I said. "But I'm glad you are."

Her breath tickled my neck. "I love you."

"I love you, Salvie."

Nonsense slouched insouciantly across the bench next to the family tree. It wore one of its frilled capelets—paisley, with reflective silver flecks—and a hydrocolloid bandage. Patches of yellowed skin peeked around the edges of the dressing.

Haran had hurt it more badly than I had realized. I hoped it would heal without a graft, and would not be disfiguring. A moment of fury washed over me at the harm to my sly, gentle, debonair coworker.

Salvie must have felt me stiffen with rage. Her embrace tightened. *You okay?*

I want to kill Haran.

Reasonable, but antisocial.

The warmth in her send made me laugh.

The hab groaned again, followed by the pops and creaks of the stressed superstructure. I was becoming inured to the sound, which was probably bad. Sooner or later, it *would* herald Town coming apart at the seams. Maybe not this time. And maybe not before the coronal mass ejection reached us.

I looked over at the ports. The Baostar looked like a giant fire opal distorted through the transparent thickness. It was gorgeous. Even if it was going to kill us.

My worry was interrupted by a nearly ultrasonic shriek. I turned my head; Stavan and Luna hurtled toward me, waving their arms. Luna bounced in the attenuated gravity, leaping like a gazelle.

Salvie yelled, "Hup!" and shoved me to my feet just in time to catch Luna as she floated across four meters and into my arms.

Luna sobbed and sobbed and did not stop sobbing. Stavan stopped just behind her, giving her a little bit of space. He met my eyes, grave and serious the way he'd been as a baby. Luna had always been a creature of big, broad gestures and mighty emotions. Stavan watched, waited, thought things through.

Luna, I realized, was more like me.

Stavan was more like Salvie. He didn't have any of her genetic material—being human and all—but he still took after her.

I love you, I mouthed to him, stroking Luna's hair as Salvie had stroked mine. Luna shuddered and smoothed against me, hiccupping as the sobs let her go.

Love you, Moms, he sent, letting Luna have her moment. I saw him abruptly as he would be: a finished adult. A careful, serious man with the situational awareness to be a counselor, or a specialist who crèched baby AIs. He wouldn't want to do what I did, I thought. But that was all right.

I hoped Luna would follow her interest in physics and her passion for art. She had a vocation, just like I did.

I hoped I could keep them both alive long enough to achieve their goals. Whatever those goals might wind up being.

When my daughter stopped sobbing, I opened my arms and invited Stavan into the embrace as well. He came, and Luna suffered her kid brother's presence long enough for Salvie to hoist herself up and join the snuggle.

When we all finally heaved a sigh and stepped back, I noticed Vickee glaring across the devastated crop tanks. The air, I thought, already smelled staler—though that might be because of forty unwashed sentients crammed into this shelter. I met her gaze and smiled. She sniffed.

Oh, why not? I dusted my hands on my trousers and walked over to her. Salvie started to reach out after me but let her hand fall, a vote of confidence I appreciated.

I promise I won't embarrass you, Sal.

That is not what concerns me.

I smiled in Vickee's face, feeling pleasantly powerful. "Don't bother pretending," I said. "There's no chance you would have risked your *own* neck for Luna. Or for anyone."

Her eyebrows quirked, but the effect of amused superciliousness was ruined by the tightness of her jaw. *I shouldn't get too invested in getting her goat if I don't want to turn out just like her.*

You could never be that entitled, Salvie replied.

Vickee jerked her chin at Luna. "You're suffocating that kid."

"You don't get a say in how I raise my children."

"She's sixteen," Vickee said. "She'll make her own decisions. And I've invited her to apprentice with my team if she wants to pursue historiography or become an archinformist."

Wow, I thought. And then, unbidden, the apprehension my trauma wanted to supply was washed away: because Luna had no desire to be an archinformist, and if she was pretending to Vickee that she did, it was just to annoy me. I'd never hidden my desire for her to take an interest in my work, and she had never hidden her interest in everything else but.

"You must be desperate," I said without thinking.

"Excuse me?"

It had just come out. Calmly. A statement of patent fact. In the same tone of obviousness I had used when I said to Salvie, "I love you."

"I said," I repeated, "you must be desperate. You're working very hard to get under my skin. It must really piss you off that I did something people—including my daughter—are impressed by."

Then another penny dropped, and I started laughing. I choked on it, wheezing, trying not to cause a scene. But holding it back just hurt, so I let it happen even though people around the pod were looking at me.

"You're embarrassing yourself," Vickee hissed.

A phrase that has always shut me up instantly, before.

"No, I'm not," I gasped.

Iris appeared at my elbow and handed me a bulb of water. She remained right behind me, offering backup, and I didn't shoo her away. Because I wasn't ashamed. I had nothing to be ashamed of. And apparently Iris was my friend now.

Vickee didn't have any friends. Vickee had tools and obstacles.

"You're embarrassing *me*," Vickee said.

I shrugged. "You know, Vickee, I just realized something. You spent ages trying to convince me that I was worthless, embarrassing, inconsequential. Why would you bother doing that if you didn't see me as a threat? Why would you bother seducing me if you didn't think I could advance your goals somehow?"

"Keep telling yourself that," Vickee scoffed. But she was looking for an exit.

"And *then*"—I paused to sip water, because I was enjoying the moment, and because I didn't want to start cough-laughing again—"and then you proved that you needed me *by stealing my work*. You couldn't have got where you are on your own. I was *always* a better researcher than you. All you have is the ability to front impressively."

"I'm a rockstar," she said down her nose. "You're a mommy."

And I'm a damn good mommy, too. I rolled over her and kept going. "That's why you had to steal from me. And that's why you have to spy now."

"Excuse me?!"

I shook my head. It was theatrical and I didn't care. I was reveling in my ability to keep my temper. "You sure seem to know a lot about pirates."

"I told you, I specialize in researching them," she said, rolling her eyes. "For the Synarche."

"I know," I said. "Because you can't earn the research allocations you want on your own merits, the way I do. You have to get them as a quid pro quo. It's sad, really: you have a brilliant mind, but you don't apply yourself. And that's why Haran almost killed Trevor. Because he was trying to get to *you*. Because you know too much about pirates and he thought you might catch him out."

"I *said* somebody was trying to kill me," she snapped.

"You did," I admitted. "I'm not saying you're always wrong. Just that you weren't attacked because you were an archinformist, but because you were a spy. And then when Trevor nearly died, you couldn't even show any concern for him."

She sniffed. "If that's the case, why did Haran try to kill you?"

"I don't think he did," I said. "I think *you* did, to get me out of the way and because the attack on Trevor gave you a window of opportunity. Parasites in your neti pot speaks of planning and also a nasty streak of intimidation. Freeporter style, right? Darting me in the back is a little more desperate and disorganized. And Yod said there were some subtle differences in the signatures of the cloaking technology between the two attempts. Have you been chasing Freeporters long enough to learn how to use some of their technology?"

She stared at me, jaw slightly open.

I said, "But it was worth the risk, because you had to get me out of the way. Because you knew you couldn't compete. I thought the attack on me was because I was investigating the murder attempt, but really it was because I turned you down when you tried to convince me to work with you again."

"You're going to regret this when you find out how wrong you are!"

I shrugged. "Are you capable of killing to get what you want? Of framing somebody else for murder? I think the evidence says yes."

Vickee stepped backward. Her eyes skated off me as if I suddenly did not exist. She pivoted on one foot and walked away, bobbing in the gentle gravity.

Toward Luna.

I didn't intervene. I stood and watched. She was right: Luna was going to be an adult soon. But I also didn't think Luna was going to want to follow in my footsteps. Or, frankly, Vickee DeVine's.

Luna was going to be a physicist. Or a sculptor. Or both. Or something entirely of her own design.

I couldn't hear what Vickee said to Luna. But Luna's reply came back loud and unselfconscious: "*You* didn't jump out of a perfectly good space hab to rescue me."

I smiled and watched Vickee walk away.

I turned back to Iris. "Thank you for the water."

"No problem." She pursed her lips. "I wanted to talk to you about physics."

Dr. Nonsense was squidging his way along the benchtop toward us.

"I'm not a physicist," I said.

"Physics," Iris clarified. "And the Strangers."

"Oh," I said. "Well, that I can help with."

Iris chuckled. "I'm glad. Do you need any more water?"

"I'm good," I said. "I should have just laughed in her face and I wouldn't have choked. This is my punishment for trying to be polite."

"Well, good," Iris said with a grin. "I hope you learned something. So, what I was wondering was if you could alert the Strangers and the Baomind to the fact that we're not radiation-proof. I wonder if they could use a gravitational lens to protect us from the coronal mass ejection."

I felt my chin drop as the implications of what she was saying hit me. "Like the ones the Freeporters use to hide their ships?"

"And maybe themselves." Iris was nodding excitedly. "The way I see it—"

The hab creaked again, a menacing groan followed by a series of snaps and a pressure fluctuation I felt in my ears. My hardsuit sealed itself, causing my ears to pop again. I clapped my hands to my head as if that could protect my eardrums.

Gauntlets rang off the sides of my helmet, and I felt like a total tool.

Nonsense whipped out one tentacle—also abruptly suited—and grabbed my arm. *Pardon,* it said, and flipped itself onto my shoulder like a second, larger head. Its body draped my shoulders like a mantle. Under planetary gravity, it would have knocked me sprawling. In a hab, it just made me stagger. Iris caught my elbow, or the difference in angular momentum between my head and my feet would have conspired to render the situation unrecoverable.

I didn't have time to protest, because I was looking for my wife and kids. Stavan and Salvie were still at that table with Angie and the cats, all armored up sensibly now. Luna—

By the view wall, where she had stalked when she was done with Vickee. Its surface wavered as the dimming failed. The full brilliance of the raging star behind came into view. I gaped, dazzled in the milliseconds before my helmet darkened to protect my sight. Blinking, I could barely discern Luna's silhouette against the glare.

I moved toward her, making sure my boot magnets were activated. She seemed transfixed, not even reacting when I shouted her name. The light of the flare caught in flaws in the various transparent materials making up the wall—radiotropic fungus, aluminum oxynitride, something even more obscure. I am not a structural engineer.

The refractions made traceries of sullen light all across the sky. I thought at first they must be fibers in the fungal cellulose, but as I watched them grow and ramify, I realized the truth.

"Yod," I said, "the wall is cracking."

I know, thank you.

A siren wailed, dulled by the hardsuit. Maybe I should just live in this thing.

Salvie, I sent, *lock down.*

I got a hand on Luna's wrist. She turned to me, outraged, ready to yank free. Well, the gratitude had lasted a whole day. That was something. And I was a fully rightminded adult, and she was an adolescent riding the surge of hormones and white-speed brain development. And adrenaline from telling off another adult.

It wasn't her job to worry about my feelings when she was so busy figuring out how to manage her own. And she was scared to death: that would make even somebody with a well-trained fox and self-management skills wobbly.

But she'd stood up for me to Vickee, and that was a whole month's worth of happiness in one small package.

I clipped a cable onto one of her safety loops and dialed my boots up while she launched into a poorly regulated tirade. Halfway through the first sentence, she seemed to realize that I had a passenger. Her eyes widened as she looked from Dr. Nonsense to me.

My opportunity to get a word in edgewise was lost, because movement all around distracted me. All around the pod, phalanxes of Strangers popped into semi-existence, all of them moving with urgent purpose. I stared about in shock, but also curiosity.

"Mom?" Luna said.

They were everywhere. Dozens of them, shoulder to shoulder, filling the space we were in. I stared about, bewildered.

Help us, I thought, as the cracked wall shattered and pulled loose from the structure, spraying everything that wasn't self-mobile or bolted down into the void.

Everything that wasn't bolted down—all those dead plants, the remains of somebody's lunch, the shattered pieces of Haran's still. Tumbling into the inferno of light beyond. Bits of tomato vine and sweet pea snagged on rough edges, trailing with no wind to stir them. Something hurtled past my head. I ducked, and another piece of debris knocked my hand off Luna.

"Luna!" I started to lunge, but Dr. Nonsense was faster. Its tentacles slapped out and grabbed her, hauling her close enough that I could also grab on.

I locked my gauntlet and reeled her in, wrapping my arms around her. Dr. Nonsense wound both of us in his armored limbs and pulled us tight.

I clutched Luna to me. She clutched back. *Cats?* I sent.

Got everybody, said Salvie. *Angie too.*

A shadow fell across the wall and I could almost see again. My suit coolers whined a little softer. Cee—SJV *I Am Not Safe At Harbor*—shielding us from the raging radiation storm with her hull again.

I glanced over at the family tree, expecting to see it safe in its case on the workbench . . .

. . . and there was nothing there.

CHAPTER 32

LUNA. I HAD LUNA, AND SALVIE HAD STAVAN AND THE cats, and that was the important thing. I would mourn the tree later. When I had time.

"Come on," I said to Luna and Dr. Nonsense. "Let's get back from the edge."

The dodecapus unwound itself so we could walk. I held on to Luna and Luna held on to me and we moved away from the ruined wall. We passed through a dozen or so Strangers along the way.

Yod's Hands and their nanospinnerets were already at work, weaving a temporary roof against the stars. It wouldn't do anything for the rads—

—but Iris's theory might work.

"Keep an eye on my daughter for me," I told Nonsense.

"Mom," Luna said.

I turned to her, catching her gaze through two transparent curves. "I know you can take care of yourself," I said. "But I'm your mother. It's my job to make sure you have backup."

Her mouth did a thing. I knew what it meant because I had felt it on my own face more than once. My heart filled up with love.

"Be careful," she said.

I bumped my helmet on hers because I could not kiss her. "I will."

I turned back to the wall. My vision was obscured by the nanospinerets and their product, but Yod fed her external sensors to me. So I got to see Dakhira zip out of the hab's shadow and dive into Cee's.

He was an asshole. But at least he was taking care of his crew.

Arula and Amal followed, each briefly revealed in the heaving light and then vanishing into the blackness of the shadow.

"Kell?" I asked—then repeated myself in Baosong, using my suit mikes to synthesize. The sound was attenuated, but Yod had already started to repressurize.

Here, it chimed. A shimmering shadow lifted itself from the back of the pod and slipped gently toward me.

I tried to marshal my limited vocabulary into a song matrix. The Baosong was positional in time and harmonics, and that overlay—a language that wasn't *linear*—was part of what had defeated my attempts to understand it for so long. Sadly, my epiphany about its structure didn't make me magically fluent—but it did help me with my attempts at pidgin.

Tell	Strangers	*Help*	*Bend*	Gravity	Mortal
Kill	*Tell*	*Request*	*Protect*	**Energy**	*Divert*
Need	Emergency	**Meatpeople**	Baomind	Dangerous	**Energy**

I didn't know how to say "radiation," so I used the only vocabulary I had that was close—*energy*—and I wasn't sure of the literal translation of the Baomind's "word" (signal cluster) for Synarche systers. But, *meatpeople,* why not? It made as much sense as anything.

Kell chimed, something I thought was a considering-type noise. There was a pause. A ripple spread through the assembled Strangers. Then it responded:

Strangers	*Bend*	**Lens**	Energy	Radiation	Scared
Meatpeople	*Help*	*Move*	*Relocate*	**Kell**	Scared
Meatpeople	*Help*	*Move*	*Relocate*	**Baomind**	Scared
Meatpeople	*Help*	*Move*	*Relocate*	**Strangers**	Scared
Help	*Move*	*Save*	*Protect*	**All**	Scared

I didn't actually know the word *lens* but it made sense in context, and once I figured it out it was in my fox and available. And *radiation* wasn't too far from *energy*, so I guessed Kell was giving me the correct vocabulary.

Thanks, Kell.

I was getting a migraine from listening for the overtones and undertones and layers, but I composed another request, gritted my teeth, and said,

Meatpeople	Strangers	Baomind	**Trapped**	**Stuck**	*Escape*
Need	*Request*	**Home**	Scared	*Request*	*Rescue*
Need	*Signal*	**Home**	*Danger*	Pirates	*Escape*
Signal	Home	**Meatpeople**	*Help*	Pirates	Blocked

Then I blinked, and realized what it was telling me. Kell knew we were there to evacuate its people. It was telling me the Strangers needed a lift as well!

Yes, I thought, we could do that. If we had ships. If we had white drives—but the Strangers could fill all the spaces in our ships, right? It's not like they would be in our *way*. I was standing inside three or four of them right now.

Let's not think about that, Sun.

I spoke to Kell in human: "Can you send a message to the Core? We need transport, Kell."

I am not an expert—wait, I guess I am the expert—but his chime sounded sad and negatory to me.

"If we fold space around them, will they come with us?" I tried to demonstrate with my hands. Did a white drive interact with dark gravity?

Dakhira interrupted, his signal blurred by the hard radiation surrounding us both. "Yes," he said. "Based on my examination of my logs, at least two Strangers joined us at the last buoy on the inbound trip. They must have hitched a ride with the ship that was destroyed and gotten stranded there, then used us to get back."

I remembered the presence looming over me, which I had thought was just too many ayatanas and an overstuffed fox. Which Dakhira had dismissed as a phantom of my inadequate human neurology.

"All right," I said, and held up a hand to pause the conversation while I built another matrix.

Tell	Strangers	*Help*	*Bend*	Gravity	Mortal
Tell	Strangers	Request	*Heard*	**Safety**	*Divert*
Need	Emergency	**Meatpeople**	**Baomind**	Strangers	*GO*
Meatpeople	Baomind	Strangers	*Need*	**Ships**	*GO*

I stared at Kell—or stared at the reflection of my hardsuit in its surface. *Please understand me. Please.*

Kell chimed again—and turned on its side and zipped away over the heads of everybody assembled. Toward the airlock. Toward the hamster tube.

"Did it work?" Iris asked.

"Maybe?" I said.

She nodded. "If they start lensing gravity around here, it's going to buy us a little time but destabilize the star further."

"I figured," I said. "How are the AIs doing?"

"They've all copied their personalities to hardened cores. But that won't protect them if it gets much worse out there." She jerked her chin at the dying star.

I stole a glance at my family. I could just about make them out through the shadowy outlines of Strangers everywhere.

Willow and Dr. Nonsense were chatting next to one of the flash-dried and vacuum-cleaned hydroponic tanks. From the gestures, it looked like they were discussing our lost resources and how survivable the result might be.

I decided not to think about that either.

Maybe I should mention the Strangers to Yod? No, she could sense them. She'd bring it up if she thought it useful.

"Can you see anything?" I asked Iris. "Unfocus your gaze."

Her brow furrowed, but she followed my pointing hand around. "Flickers?" she said. "Flickers of movement like when you're falling asleep in a dark room and your retinas start generating images."

"Right," I said.

"Is that the Strangers?"

"Probably," I said. "I can see them more clearly."

Iris said, "Maybe I should fill my fox with Baosong."

"You don't want the migraines."

Behind Cee, the blazing sky went dark—silently and without fanfare.

"I guess they understood," said Iris.

"I guess they did," said the Chive who had remained, from right behind me.

I swear the only reason I didn't jump out of my skin was because the hard-suit held it on me. I did squeak embarrassingly, and spin. I stumbled in low gravity but the gyros rescued me before I actually fell over the Chive. Or on top of them.

"You startled me," I said.

"I . . . gathered."

They sounded different—and singular—and I wondered if the interference was keeping them from connecting with their clademates or if they were separated on purpose. Or if I still couldn't adjust to the weirdness of talking to only one.

I waved at the hatch. "How bad is it out there?"

"They're going room to room, I think they used to call it? We've managed to avoid any casualties worse than you."

Great, I was the newbie who got herself cauterized. At least everybody else was doing okay. I linked just the Chive and myself and sent, *Your clademates are worried about you.*

They smiled sideways inside their helmet. *I still think I might want a divorce.*

Was that all? *I'm sorry,* I said. *That sounds hard.*

They widened the channel again, ending our private conversation. "We need to evacuate as soon as we can."

"We could use about six more Interceptors." I watched the four ships we *did* have nearby—not counting Ikem—through the feed, marveling at their tight flying.

"Yeah," said Iris. "About that—"

I shook my head. "The Baomind says they can't talk to their remote units."

"No," she said, "I had another idea. All we need is to let the Core know something is drastically wrong or weird out here, right? So they come in force?"

"Can we hold the pirates off long enough for that to happen? Is the star going to *last* six months?"

"Decians," the Chive corrected.

"Don't be that guy," I said.

They ducked their head inside the helmet. "Sorry."

"Unlikely," said Iris. "But we could start withdrawing. Tow the hab outward. It would buy us some time."

"Yod?" I asked.

"It would buy us some time," Yod agreed. "Also . . . I was just talking with Cee. We're going to separate the ship that served as Vickee and Trevor's quarters from the wheel. It will fit against *I Am Not Safe At Harbor*'s hull inside the white coils—she's an Interceptor, and designed for rescue and salvage operations. She has the power to haul a disabled ship."

"So we'd all pack in there? Won't that affect maneuverability?"

"And combat operations," the Chive agreed. "But I think it's a good idea. We're sitting targets as it is. And we can spread out to the other ships once we've got some distance from the star. That still doesn't get us out of the system, of course. The Freeporters have the beacon blockaded."

"It lets us maneuver," Yod said. "And they have the hub but no way to leave unless another ship comes downwell for them, which seems unlikely given the circumstances. They're stranded here. Their best bet is to try to commandeer one of our ships, and in that case they would have to deal with the shipminds. I've withdrawn from the systems in the hub and severed the connections, because I don't want a Freeporter virus. There's very little choice here but to abandon the hab."

She sounded sad. Did wheelminds grieve a lost hab? It seemed illogical, but sapience wasn't logical. Nor was sentience separable from sentiment.

"I see a problem here," I said.

"Yes," Yod agreed. "We're going to have to move everybody to the other hull."

"We're going to have to move everybody," I echoed. "Through the tube. In a radiation storm."

CHAPTER 33

SALVIE AND THE CHIVE WENT FIRST, SPLITTING UP TO cover both approaches. Salvie took point; the Chive moved into tail position. Cee hung overhead, her hull still shading us from the radiation storm. Dakhira, Arula, and Amal lay sandwiched between the Interceptor and the wheel, but we could only see their running lights. Cee's bigger silhouette was a hard-edged, featureless shadow against the gravitational lens, which showed as a twisted circular outline before the horizonless sea of fire.

That lens protected us from the rads enough to move between ships without dying. And a flock of tesserae swirled around us, keeping each meatform in a shadow.

I was in the middle with the kids and Angie, trying not to feel like luggage. I had the dinosaur on my fist like a medieval Earth falcon. Each of the kids had charge of two space-suited and increasingly distraught cats.

I glanced over my shoulder as we left the Garden Pod for the last time. The family tree had not miraculously reappeared on the bench. I mourned it, but what's lost was lost. All I could do was take all the good things I was left with and keep moving forward. Trying to survive.

Trying to keep my family alive.

We moved quickly and for the most part efficiently, about four dozen terrified life-forms huddled in our suits. Suits that meant the enclosed space of the hamster tube didn't reek of fear-soaked biochemistry from seven or eight different species.

Dr. Nonsense was squidging along awkwardly rather near me. I thought I saw it flinch, its tentacles contracting. When it happened again, I asked, "Burn bothering you?"

Rather.

"Once we're on Cee, Chionn can treat it. Can you turn down the pain?"

If it rubs against the suit too hard, I want to know, it said. *If the membrane scars too badly it will give me a speech impediment.*

I wanted to slap my forehead with my palm to indicate I realized I had been a dunce, but the helmet was in the way. "I'm sorry," I said. "That was insensitive."

I hope you don't expect me to keep track of every nuance of your biology, it replied. *No offense is taken.*

Belatedly I realized we should have asked Kell to carry it. I didn't think a couple of humans could manage the unwieldy two meters of dodecapus without simply hurting it more.

Sadness squeezed me. Even if we got out of here, my association with Dr. Nonsense was likely to be cut short. And I was extremely sorry about that. I would have loved to work with it and its frilly dresses for the rest of my career.

"Wait," I said, remembering how it had clambered up to my shoulders. "Could someone carry you?"

We might have to fight, it reminded. *Or I would ask Willow for a piggyback ride.*

When the Freeporters dropped on us from a hatch immediately above, I was ready. They waited until we were right below them, swinging down in two groups of two, into the middle of our party. Salvie spun around, but she was halfway up the curve of the gangway. And when she dropped to a crouch to see—well, she couldn't exactly fire her particle accelerator into the center of our caravan.

Angie bated off my glove, suited wings flailing as she flapped backward. That was fine: it got her out of the way of my fist. I shrieked and swung for the closest pirate's helmet. The impact rattled my teeth and must have rung their head like a bell. They reeled back, and Stavan tripped them.

Another pirate aimed a kick at Dr. Nonsense. The impact on its hardsuit made me cringe. I drove an elbow into their back. They staggered from the impact, but I knew I hadn't harmed them. Hardsuits are designed to take a hit from a small meteorite or unswept space debris. Unless you can aim for the elbows and knees.

The pirate grabbed Stavan by the wrist. A deep voice crackled from the suit speaker. "Wanna be a ship's monkey, kid?"

Oh no, I thought. *We are not having a repeat of the Haran incident.*

Nobody was press-ganging my son.

Or daughter, but several bystanders were defending Luna—and she was doing a pretty good job of defending two cats and herself. Apparently being taken captive once was enough for her, because she laid into the nearest Freeporter with a wrench as long as her forearm. It rang off their hardsuit and sent chips of ceramic flying.

I was so proud.

An instant later, Yod yelled, *Duck!*

I threw myself down. Whatever had swung at me whistled over my head. I hit the deck with both hands and bounced up again.

Luna had Stavan by the suit handle and was beating the pirate over the head with her wrench to make them let go of her brother. Stavan screamed and kicked, throwing his arms and legs out to make himself an unwieldy bundle.

I stepped in, triggering my cutting torch, and jammed it into the pirate's helmet. No hesitation.

I don't know if Salvie was rubbing off on me, or if I have always had the ability to kill a person. But I didn't feel a thing as the torch went through their helmet. I didn't feel a thing until my gauntlet smashed their faceplate and my fist broke their nose.

They didn't feel it, either. They were already dead.

I pulled my hand back and killed the torch, panting. The pirate fell across the walkway like a stately downed tree. I expected blood everywhere, maybe showering slowly in the low g, but the torch must have cauterized the wound.

I didn't look.

Luna yanked Stavan to her and wrapped him in her arms. "The cats!" he shrieked, but they hadn't gone far—Toby and Not-Toby had gotten their leashes wrapped around a stanchion ten meters on, and Luna had handed Zig and Zag off to Iris, who clutched them to her chest, wide-eyed behind her helmet.

Angie had sailed down the tube and was huddled against a wall, clinging to a strut like a miserable woodpecker.

"You okay?" Salvie asked at my elbow. I looked around. All the pirates were down. This had been a desperation attack, I realized. Yod was right—they were stuck here unless they could somehow steal Cee or one of the civilian ships. Ikem was too far away, and their craft weren't coming back downwell after them.

"Fine," I said.

She looked at me.

"Fine for now," I amended. "I'll have my crisis when the kids are safe."

"Reasonable," she answered. "Let's move."

We scrambled into motion, the former orderly progression forgotten. On our way past, we retrieved Angie, Toby, and Not-Toby. Toby and Angie reacted with pathetic gratitude. Not-Toby tried to murder me with his fishhooks, but luckily for me his hardsuit had a rescue handle and no little diaphragm ports for kitty claws to poke through. Somebody thought that design through, I tell you.

Ahead of me, Vickee staggered in her suit. She managed one more step, but her joints were stiffening. She wavered, and under her feet I caught a glimpse of some shadow on the outside of the hab trail.

What would be a bigger prize for the Freeporters than murdering the Synarche's expert on pirate behavior?

I felt like I was moving through gelatin as I reached for her. My hand felt resistance, as if the Strangers still cluttering my vision had substance now. They were running, too, a stream of ghosts headed for a destination I did not know.

A bigger prize? *Capturing her.*

I yelled, "*LOCK ON!*"

Yod heard me, because while I was yelling I'd neglected to trigger my own suit mags. But I felt them click into place on maximum, and heard a few dozen more—around me on every side—do the same.

Vickee, jerking like a puppet, kicked one foot back against the tube wall. Membrane and fungus parted under what must have been a monofilament blade. It puckered, and for a moment I thought the self-healing would hold—

The tube blew wide. Everything went eerily quiet once again—I could hear my own breathing and the hum of the suit—and I grabbed the handrail.

Vickee launched herself toward the flapping edges of the hole and let the air current push her through. She tumbled into space; she fell, and kept falling.

I didn't think. I handed the leashes to Iris, unlocked my boots from the surface, and took three running steps to the gap. It was already sealing itself, but I shoved my torso through.

Sunya! Salvie sent. *What the Well?*

I'll be right back, I sent. *She's not getting kidnapped. And I'm not letting her die, either.*

You're a different breed of warrior.

My head stuck into nothing. Vickee's suit had kicked on its jets and was sailing across the radius of the hab, toward the center. If the main group of pirates got her—

Cee said dryly, *You're not gonna catch her.*

No, I said. *Bring her back.*

Can't, Cee said. *They've locked me out of her suit.*

I pulled myself the rest of the way through the gap and crouched on the external surface of the walkway. Mags were no use here, but my boots had grippers. I dug them in and kept from being flung off like mud from a bicycle tire.

I opened my mouth and sang:

Strangers	*Stop*	*Stop*	*Stop*	Meatform	Taken
Baomind	*Stop*	*Stop*	*Stop*	Pirate	Taking
Strangers	*Stop*	*Stop*	Emergency	*Stop*	**Baomind**

Vickee's momentum failed as abruptly and utterly as if she had slammed into a stone wall. I heard her grunt over coms, and watched her arms windmill.

In a glittering stream, Kell and its siblings arced around something I could not see—no, it was . . . the outline of a vessel? Maybe? A strange, curved vessel, ghostily visible. It looked like melted candle wax, and my brain painted it with colors my eyes could never have seen. It intersected the hull of the hab, overlapping it without making contact. As if it were composed of layers set to high translucency.

The Strangers had a ship. *Ships.* Ships with no white coils.

Did they need white coils?

Yes, if they, too, were looking for an evac. I had so many questions—

what they were doing here; how they had come. Why they didn't have faster-than-light travel.

None of it mattered unless we survived—and got our information out to the wider galaxy. There were so many things the Synarche needed to know.

And *two* entire species to rescue.

Not to mention these new friends. And my entire family.

And Victorya DeVine.

Whatever the Baomind and the Strangers were doing, it was working. Vickee drifted toward her old quarters. The Baomind surrounded her, their razored edges pointed outward. Part of me wished they would eat her. We'd all be better off if Vickee were converted to raw material for rebuilding the Baomind.

Antisocial, I chided myself.

Activity at the hub drew my attention away from Vickee. A swarm of Freeporters and drones moved over the exterior surface, congregating at the cables. It didn't look great.

I fed the image to Yod. *Is this a problem?*

Someone grabbed my legs and yanked me back inside the tube. "We need to go," Salvie said, with a parting pat on my suited ass. "Let's move it!"

Everybody else was already running. I fell into stride with my wife, the kids and pets ahead of us. A bottleneck at the ladder into the hulk slowed us to an amble as we came within sight of it. No more pirates, thank the Well.

I pressed a hand to the stitch in my side. I was in better shape than I'd ever been in my life and Salvie could still dust me. I managed to speak between gasps. "Why are we running?"

The hab itself answered me. There was no sound in the decompressed walkway, but it traveled fine through the hull and superstructure—and through the floor and my boots, right into the small bones inside my ear that specialized in such things. A terrible, rending vibration, the scream of a wheel being torn spoke from rim.

The deck dropped under my feet. Luna screamed in surprise. I grabbed her; Stavan turned and lunged into Salvie's arms as the floor came back up and hit us on the bottoms of the feet. I tucked, and when we hit the ceiling I protected Luna's head and took the blow on my shoulders. She had her hands full of struggling cats. If they hadn't been provided with rescue handles I'm not sure what she would have done.

It didn't bear thinking about.

We dropped to the deck again. Salvie, of course, had triggered her grippers and hadn't been flipped into the air. Good idea. I locked mine.

Angie, shrieking, zipped past us and into her old quarters, over the heads of those scrambling up the ladder.

"They cut the hub free," Yod said. "Everybody has to climb. Another oscillation is coming and they'll get stronger. I can't hold together long. I'm backing myself up to the infrastructure on the hulk—"

A snap hit—cracking me like a whip inside my hardsuit. I was grateful for the soft, slightly sticky colloid lining. It conformed perfectly to my body. And it absorbed the shock when my neck snapped front to back so my spine wasn't broken. I'd have a heck of a case of whiplash in the morning.

If we got to have a morning.

Salvie got up the ladder one-handed, still carrying Stavan and two cats. Did I mention my wife is a badass? Both airlock doors were open, so at least we didn't have to wait for the lock to cycle.

Then it was Luna's turn. "Sweetie, you need to climb."

"But the cats—"

"Give me the cats." I grabbed them out of her hands, and now their twisting squalling unhappiness was my problem. "*Climb.*"

It was a measure of exigency that Luna turned and climbed. When she was at the top she paused. I rode out another wave—they were getting bigger—and tossed the cats up to her. Catching an unhappy cat is never easy, but low gravity helps.

Something underfoot popped, straining. I went up the ladder fast and sloppy. My small lemurlike ancestors might be embarrassed, but it got me there. I scrambled away on all fours, not bothering to stand, just getting out of the way of the person behind me and the person behind them.

Salvie grabbed my handle and pulled me to my feet. "Vickee's in the outside airlock."

Dakhira broke in just as my fox lit up with an alarmed chorus of Baosong. "More pirates are coming insystem," he said. "We have to go."

"Yod?" I said.

Speakers crackled. "I'm busy," said the wheelmind.

"I'm ready to catch you," said Cee.

More of my colleagues piled inside—Willow, Nonsense, Petrac—the whole crew. I looked around for the Strangers, and saw none. Were they all on their own ship now?

I rushed to the port, staring out in time to see one of the gigantic cables that ran around the inside rim of the hab snap loose. It peeled away, taking one of the dead ships with it. "Unbelievable," I whispered. The pirates really were insensible to the risk to our life and theirs. "Yod, cut us loose as soon as the last crew member is inside."

"Fuck," said Yod. Which was the first time in my entire life I had heard an artificial intelligence use that word. "Chive, go. *Go.*"

The Chive came through the hatch in a single leap—they hadn't even bothered to climb. Spacer reflexes and nerves of steel, or something. They landed on hands and afthands and slapped the button to release the override and seal the airlock. The normal closure was slow and careful. The emergency one—the doors were open, then the doors were closed, and a horrible screeching recorded the demise of the boarding ladder.

Small explosions rattled the hull—the release bolts blowing loose.

A lurch, and we were free—free, and falling. My feet lifted off the deck. Luna gasped as she floated free. The cabin was filled with hovering bodies as the engineless, directionless hab pod flung free of the wheel. I tried to keep my butt out of anybody's sensory organs.

There wasn't enough room in here for all of us.

"Brace," said Cee.

I grabbed a bar to steady myself, and someone who couldn't reach the bulkheads grabbed on to me. The impact was lighter than I anticipated, a swoop of energy as Cee locked onto us, and then we were being towed along with her and accelerational gravity abruptly reasserted itself and we all fell in a pile against the bulkhead that was now the floor.

Stavan whooped. I felt a little bit like whooping myself. We were out of the containment dome and in the reactor core—but at least we were no longer waiting passively to be killed.

"Is Vickee okay?" I finally asked reluctantly. "Yod?"

"Integrating," said Yod's voice, seeming strangely metallic and flat. "Only basic functions are available. Please restate query."

Luna put her hand on my chest. "Wheelmind Yod?"

"No such entity."

"Shit," Salvie said, pushing through the cheek-by-jowl crowd to get next to me. "Yod's not here."

I looked back at the porthole, still right next to my helmet. Town glowed in the furious light of the Baostar. Unraveling. Unspooling. Shedding bits and particles into the bottomless night.

CHAPTER 34

I HAVE HER CORE PERSONALITY FILES IN STASIS," CEE SAID. "But she didn't fit in the little bit of processing architecture that's left on that hulk. And I need my frame—if I have to fight, I will have to think fast. So we didn't have a lot of room."

"Is Yod going to be okay?" Stavan's voice wavered with emotion. Salvie pulled him close.

"Her personality should be intact," Cee said. "We didn't have room for most of her memory files. So she'll be . . . reborn, I guess is the human equivalent. I'll share my memories with her. It won't be too bad."

I still had a hand on Luna, and turned it into an arm around her shoulders.

"I'm okay," she whispered.

"I'm not," I replied.

Whatever I might have said next was silenced by Dakhira's wail of fury over the coms. I did not know AIs wailed with emotion when provoked sufficiently—or maybe he was choosing an explosive tone to make his point. "She died for you," he raged. "She could have existed forever. Crossed the universe. And she died for you. You killed her with your weakness."

I didn't have the energy to argue. Stavan turned to me, stricken. "Is that true?"

Yod had been their teacher, caretaker, friend. As much as I had liked her, she was ever so much more important to them.

"No." My eyes stung. "But Dakhira is grieving, and sometimes people lash out when they are hurt." I tuned him out—I could, now that he wasn't *my* ship's shipmind—and asked Cee privately, *What are we going to do about Dr. DeVine?*

I'm sending the Goodlaw and a couple of marines to pry her out of the airlock, she said. *And arrest her for attempting to murder you.*

You're not going to bring her in here?

Dread must have colored my virtual voice because Cee chuckled sadly. *I wouldn't do that to you all. I've got a brig. It's very comfortable.*

So you agree she's the best suspect?

Yes, Cee said. *I think you're right that it must have been her. I'll be certain once I've had her searched for a cloaking device.*

Despite myself, I felt . . . disappointment. *What do I do to help?*

You, Cee said, *work with Iris and figure out how to get us—and the Strangers, and the Baomind—home.*

We ran dark, cold, and silent, which is even less fun that it sounds. Though "cold" in this case is something of a misnomer. We weren't so much chilly as sweltering.

Town's complement of roughly forty crew—minus, of course, Trevor (in cryostasis on Cee), Haran (on the lam), and Vickee (in Cee's brig)—huddled together in the belly of the wreck, towed along by *I Am Not Safe At Harbor*. Eventually we would be able to move some of the crew over to her, once the airlocks were aligned. Eventually we would be able to spread out to Dakhira, Arula, and Amal.

But not yet. Our airlock wasn't aligned, we couldn't risk crew on a spacewalk—beyond the marines who had come to fetch Vickee—and we could not vent heat because we were trying to look like one of the many pieces of debris hurled free when Town came apart. They were fizzing out, growing cold through slow radiation—and if we looked significantly warmer than any of them, we would be noticed. Noticed and identified, because—under Cee's EM drive—we were the only bit of space junk in the region putting on *v*. Space is cold; space is supposed to be cold. But with the Baostar bathing us all in radiation, nothing to conduct heat away, and forty people packed into a space meant for three, the problem wasn't how to stay warm.

The problem was to avoid roasting.

Sweat coated us humans. Because of the cramped space, we deactivated our suits, though they remained ready in case of hull breach. As I turned mine off, I found myself reaching out to ask Yod, *Where does the oxygen in the suits come from?*

She did not answer, and my heart broke a little. She wasn't dead, precisely. Unless a lack of continuity of experience was death. But she was . . . gone. The Yod we had known was gone, anyway.

She'd not-died to save us, and that made me more determined to get everybody out alive. It was a miracle that might qualify Yod for beatification that the only member of crew who hadn't made it off Town was Haran.

Where he was, I didn't know. Maybe he'd gone back to the pirates. I couldn't find it in myself to care.

While we waited for Cee to painstakingly turn the relic hab unit in her grapples so some of us could move aboard *I Am Not Safe At Harbor*, we refugees huddled on the deck in puddles of our own moisture, without sufficient space to extend arms or legs unless we stood. Moaning and grumbling occasionally broke the nervous silence as folks eased stiff limbs and found themselves cramped and clumsy. The minerals we lost to sweat and could not replenish made us cramp, too, painfully and often.

Nonsense was suffering the most. It had squidged up the bulkhead to huddle in the ceiling corner nearest the ventilation inlet, arms splayed wide and suction cups flexing as it vacuumed itself into position half upside down. It had procured a squeezy chiller bottle of distilled water, to periodically soak its green-and-pink triangle-pattern capelet. I'd seen similar patterns on old Terran textiles in museums, but almost always ivory cloth painted with indigo. Funny how similar iconography emerges across the galaxy, and how different it looks when different systers are creating the designs.

I sat with Iris and tried to figure out how to call for help. "Do you think the Koregoi came from the darkside and went back there?"

Iris stopped and stared at me. "You *have* to let me coauthor that paper with you."

"What do you mean?"

"I mean you're going to need a physicist, and I'm right here! We've been brainstorming this *together*—"

"Whoa-oh," I said gently. Her air of agitation surprised me. "Slow down a second. I wasn't refusing to collaborate. I meant, 'What paper'?"

"You're serious?"

"I'm not trying to steal your work," I said. "I couldn't even understand your work unless I wore a head full of ayatanas."

"No," she said, drawing up. "I suppose you of all people wouldn't do that."

"Of course I wouldn't," I said. "So please tell me what fundamental principle of physics we've overthrown. And if doing so is likely to save or doom us?"

I sent over a confirmation of intention to share credit on my fox, so it would be in the formal record if we lived long enough to collaborate. Her shoulders relaxed.

"Well," she said, thoughtful rather than defensive, "I don't think we're overthrowing any equilibriums. But we might have confirmed one of the universe's weirder theories."

"Explain?"

Several people nearby were leaning in, including Dr. Nonsense, dangling by its suckers. Well, I guessed we were all in this together.

Iris cleared her throat awkwardly. "So the question that needs to be resolved is, *is* the observer in some respect the primary causal agent and center of their own reality?"

"No?" I hazarded. "I mean, that sounds like solipsism."

"Not precise—"

But she never finished the sentence, because Dr. Nonsense fell on her head. Iris squeaked and threw her hands up, deflecting the falling dodecapus. Salvie and Stavan jumped forward and caught it before it hit the ground.

"It's limp," Salvie said. She moved forward to take most of the weight without making it obvious to Stavan that she was doing so. The kid had done the right thing.

"Oh no," said Iris. "Is it—"

"Fainted," Cee said. "Actually, I've nearly got the airlocks mated. Salvie, Sunya, Iris—why don't you all bring it over to my sick bay? We can care for it there, and you can continue your conversation."

"I'm not leaving my family," I said. My neck was still killing me. I tuned it.

Luna squeezed my hand. I hadn't even noticed her slipping up beside me.

I squeezed back.

"Bring them," Cee said. "I'll have the airlocks lined up in a few more seconds."

"Do you have room over there for everybody?"

"I'll have to find it. A few at a time," she said. "But make sure Willow is one of the first. We need to talk about environmental engineering. And Fritha and Tsebu, too."

"I want to come, too," said the Chive quietly. "On behalf of Dakhira. And myself, for that matter."

• • •

Getting from the wreck into Cee's wardroom was trivial, now that she had us connected. But my supervisor had just fainted and might be in critical danger. I didn't know anything about dodecapus physiology.

"I need you to be on your guard," Cee told me. "I can't be sure Haran doesn't have an accomplice."

"But you're sure of me?" I asked. "And Iris? And the rest of the people who came over?"

"I'm reasonably confident of anybody who is a syster or is married to one, yes."

I looked at Iris. "Married to one?"

Iris nodded. "My spouse is Alvarean. He's back at New Cambridge teaching a heavy course load in biodynamics."

I looked at Iris in a new light. Alvarean. Huh.

"I'm a Judiciary ship," Cee said. "There are no private spaces aboard. So I will maintain close observation on all passengers at all times and put everyone on a buddy system so each person has another person keeping an eye on them. If anybody vanishes from surveillance, we should know immediately. And with Willow's help, I'm printing off some environmental control units to install. That will help as well."

We bundled Dr. Nonsense onto Chionn's table as gently as possible. It was twitching a little now that we were in a cooler environment, and Chionn said there was no reason it would not make a full recovery. Assuming any of us lived that long.

Okay, she didn't say that part out loud. But I inferred it.

Stavan took the pets into the lounge while Luna, the Chive, Salvie, Iris, and I made our way to the ready room, where Goodlaw Xhelsea awaited—and Kell, or a tessera I assumed was Kell, floated beside the bulkhead.

Steaming cups of tea and nori chips lined the table and I took both gratefully. I sat, cupping my mug between my hands.

A stinging pain pulled my wandering attention to my hands. They were wet—apparently I was, unbeknownst to me, shaking. Rattling like a dead leaf in a cyclone, frankly.

Everything we'd been through . . . had been a lot.

Iris stood, pacing nervously. The rest of us sat, sipping our tea, eating the chips. I hadn't thought I was hungry but it turned out I was, and they were delicious.

As I was crunching away, Iris cleared her throat and said, "So who knows about the anthropic principle?"

Salvie, of course, raised her hand. So did Luna. Kell chimed quietly. The Chive and I looked at each other with the shared performative bewilderment of the kids who didn't read the assignment.

The Chive passed me the sugar, and I took it without being even a little freaked out. Maybe Petrac's bad example was teaching me to be more tolerant.

Iris nodded. "Okay, walking it back. Do you know about the observer effect?"

I could in fact stick my hand up for that one. "A quantum state only resolves when somebody looks at it. It's how the mail goes through—no matter how many times a packet forks, when it finally reaches the intended recipient and they open it, all the other possible instances of that packet collapse into just the one you're reading."

"It's also how AI infrastructure works," Cee put in. "My brain runs on Bose-Einstein condensates."

"Good," Iris said. "So when it's not collapsed—when it's both states at once, like the wave-particle dichotomy—the waveform is called a *superposition*. And the weak anthropic principle states that the universe's apparent optimization for life is the effect of selection for survivorship bias. In other words, there might be a million universes out there, but if none of them have the conditions necessary for life, no life will arise, so no observers will exist, no waveforms will collapse, and nobody will be around to wonder how life arose in such an inimical place."

"Excuse me," I said, pointing to the heavily dimmed wall that showed a squashed, baleful Baostar. "Isn't the universe we know an extremely inimical place?"

Iris shook her head. "If the strong nuclear force and gravity didn't balance, we wouldn't exist. Stars wouldn't exist. It's honestly very friendly."

My forehead itched with concentration. "What does that mean?"

Iris said, "Well, life on the darkside wasn't supposed to be possible because dark matter and dark energy don't interact in the right ways to form biology. But . . ." She shrugged expressively. "Obviously that's another thing we were wrong about. Anyway, it's pretty much a tautology, but the postulate is that we *must* find ourselves at a place and time that allows the creation of observers because we are, by definition, observers."

I noticed I was chewing on my thumb and pulled my hand away from my mouth. "My brain hurts."

"If there's a weak anthropic principle"—Luna leaned forward on her elbows—"that implies a strong anthropic principle?"

"Yes," said Iris. "It's generally stated as: 'The universe *must* be such as to admit the production of intelligent life at some time.'"

The Chive finished their tea and sat silently, eyes closed, fingers steepled. They looked like they were listening, but if I were them, I would have been sneaking a nap.

Luna's intent brow furrowed. "Because otherwise there would be nobody around to comment on it?"

Iris smiled. "Now, brace yourselves for an even bigger brain buster—"

"What is *that*?"

"—If what Sunya and I suspect about the Strangers is true, then I think it implies that the universe exists in a superposition until a measurement is made. And the choice of that measurement can be made after the superposition is established. Life is inevitable, in other words, because the universe exists in a superposition of all possible states until one of its branches leads to the development of an observer. Then all the other branches collapse, leaving only the observed branch to wonder about the unlikelihood of its own existence."

"Huh," said Luna. She rubbed her face. "That's fascinating."

Iris, excited, nodded. "Not only is life inevitable," she gushed, "but the emergence of life by the fastest possible set of collapsed wave states is inevitable. The universe came together the instant the Dark Strangers—or rather their ancestors—were born."

"Why them?" I asked.

Iris tapped her open palm. "The dark universe is much bigger and more full of matter than ours is. Of course intelligence evolved there first. There's so much more *stuff* for it to work with."

"So let me get this straight," I said. "You think the Dark Strangers *are* the Koregoi?"

"I think the Koregoi are maybe their ancestors? It's possible that the Koregoi came from there originally—"

"And eventually went back?" I interrupted.

"*Mom,*" Luna said. "Let her finish."

"And eventually went back," Iris agreed. "As sort of exploratory travelers who left a lot of gear behind, creating a cargo cult in all the sapients that came after them."

"In other words, us."

"And the Ativahikas, and the Freeporters, and everybody else out there using some kind of Koregoi technology that we don't know about."

Luna bounced lightly in her chair. "Can we go visit the darkside?"

"You're in it," Iris said. "You're already there. It interpermeates everything. You just can't touch it, and it can't touch you."

Luna sighed gustily, put upon by the laws of physics. "Okay, can I go visit a different universe? Someday? If I invent the technology?"

"Maybe," Iris said, "but odds are pretty good that once you got there your atoms would stop working."

"Hmm," said my daughter, looking stubborn. Iris had probably just sealed the deal that she was going to become a physicist. At least as her first career.

Xhelsea leaned forward. "I'm going to see if I understand this. All right, Iris, so . . . the darkside is bigger than our universe. And the cosmological constant reflects the existence of dark energy because dark energy has to exist for the universe not to collapse under the weight of all the stuff in it. And you think that life first arose on the darkside? And that we are, to put a point on it, in the life-iest possible universe?"

"I hypothesize," Iris cautioned, "that we are how the universe observes itself."

"She is—" the Chive sang in a voice I did not recognize, "—correct . . ."

If they were about to elaborate, I didn't get to hear it, because Cee yelled, "Brace!" and we all grabbed for table edge and chair arms with trauma-honed instincts.

CHAPTER 35

MY FINGERS CRAMPED, PALMS BRUISING AND SCRAP-ing on sharp corners as *I Am Not Safe At Harbor* swerved violently and I struggled to hold myself in place. I didn't let go. That was wise, because the next vector change slewed me in a different direction.

"Cee, what are you doing?"

"Bogey," Cee said tightly. "Evasive maneuvers. Stand by for white space transition with linked ships."

She jumped, and for a brief moment the accelerational gravity went away, because we were not *moving* when we were in white space. We were motionless, and the universe was folding around us. Stars became swirls; the flattened ember of the Baostar became a menacing orange-black smear. I floated up—and came down again hard as the sky went back to normal and we found ourselves in a different place.

"Fancy flying," I said to the air.

"Thank you," Xhelsea answered. "We still have the civilian ships, Cee?"

"All intact," the shipmind answered.

Aft, something thumped and shouted. Vickee in the brig, no doubt furious to be missing all the fun. Maybe I should suggest we put her in cryo.

That was probably against regulations unless she requested it, or became an immediate danger to herself and others who could not be otherwise restrained. Darn it.

A stream of glittering tesserae swirled out of the darkness to enfold the Cee. For an illogical moment, I feared they were coming to disassemble us.

But they just surrounded *I Am Not Safe At Harbor* and the three vessels shadowing her. Swept us into their midst like a sea-ship in a pod of dolphins.

"I wonder if—" I stopped myself before I said more. Of course there was no bow wave here for them to surf. Space! I might be figuring it out.

"What are we doing?" I asked. "Besides dodging the pirates, I mean. What are we doing sort of . . . medium-term?"

Not long-term? Dr. Nonsense teased. It was a vast relief to hear its simulated voice in the senso and know it had awakened.

I said, *In the long term . . . I mean, in the grand scheme of things, none of this matters.*

It answered, *In the grand scheme of things, the grand scheme of things doesn't matter. But this probably does, at least a little bit. Everything dies, even the universe. But we're wired to think that what we do along the way matters. And have you noticed that's something all sapients share? The search for meaning and connection?*

I hadn't. But now that Nonsense said it, I found myself glancing over at Salvie with a smile.

"We left the Strangers behind," I said.

"We're going to have to pick them up," Xhelsea said. "And then we're going to rescue as much Baomind as we can and hightail it out of this system."

"The blockade—" Salvie said.

"I think," Xhelsea continued, so smoothly I wasn't sure who had interrupted whom, "and Cee agrees, that if we use the Baostar as a slingshot and the remaining Baomind is willing to cover us, we stand a better than even chance of using the gravity whip to attain a velocity and vector the pirates won't be able to counter. Even with our additional mass. It should also work for Dakhira, Ikem, Amal, and Arula."

"What's 'better than even' odds?" I probably didn't want to know, but that didn't stop me from asking. Which is how I wound up a historian in the first place. Archinformism is all about the detailed analysis of stuff you'd rather not be aware of.

"Fifty point seven percent," said Cee.

Yup.

Reassuring.

"Abandoning the Baomind to its fate," Dakhira put in suddenly. His tone rang salty over crackling coms. I hadn't realized he was listening.

"We're rescuing as much of it as we can," Xhelsea said.

"You wouldn't be so glib if it were two-thirds of the organic population of a star system we were talking about."

I wanted to roll my eyes, but Xhelsea beat me to it. "It's not glib to be pragmatic," the Goodlaw protested. "In any rescue situation, the objective is minimal losses. And that includes minimizing losses among the rescuers. You don't send people into a burning building without fireproof gear and breathing equipment. And a way to get back out again. Otherwise you're just compounding the damage."

"You'd work harder for meatpeople!"

"Dakhira," Xhelsea said, and I have never heard a Goodlaw so tired. "I'm trying to do my job and rescue everybody."

"Sure," said Dakhira. "Oh, and another thing. My crew are all talking in unison."

Remembering the chorus of words that rained down around every conversation, I said, "Don't they usually?"

The resident Chive gave me the finger across the conference table.

I waved back.

"They usually talk in sequence, not in parallel," Dakhira said.

The Chive next to me opened their mouth. What came out was not human speech but an unearthly tone. A human voice, straining to sing an inhuman song.

Baosong.

I stared at them, wondering, *Is that what it sounds like when I do it?*

I could pick out words in the matrix—

Strangers — *Evolve* — **Expedient** — Observers — *Converge*

But the whole of the matrix was blurry, out of focus. Not crisp and structural the way it was when Kell sang it.

It might be pidgin. But it was comprehensible. And it wasn't like I was the Du Fu of Baosong myself.

And everybody in the room was looking at me.

"What are they saying?" Salvie asked.

I closed my eyes and concentrated, letting all the ayatanas of musicians and mathematicians listen along with me. "That can't be right."

"What is it?" The urgency in Iris's voice was palpable. I glanced over to see her knuckles lighter where she clutched the table.

"If I understand," I hedged, "what they're saying is confirming that the anthropic principle holds and so quantum mechanics basically *demands* the universe will evolve sentient life as fast as possible, because it needs something to observe it, so the forks in the timestream that lead to sentience are the ones that get taken."

"That's not quite how it would work," Iris said. "The forks that contain observers are the ones that don't vanish, unobserved, when the superposition collapses."

I wasn't sure I understood the difference. What I did understand was—"So you told me earlier that the darkside has more stuff in it than ours does."

Iris said, "Yes. Lots more stuff."

"And that's why life started there first."

"Likely, though confusing," she agreed. "Are you going somewhere with this?"

"I'm not sure," I said. "Let me think it over."

"It's so incredibly disappointing that you lot actually *matter*." Dakhira sounded equal parts amused and scathing. I wondered how long he'd workshopped that tone. "By the way, the rest of my crew were singing in time with the Chive on Cee. Even though there were nanoseconds of lightspeed lag. Which I could tell because I measured the difference between when I heard them and when I heard you talking to my crew member over there."

"Wait," I said. "No-lag communication?" I looked over at Iris, who had gone paler. "Isn't that what we need? Wouldn't that be faster than sending a buoy message?"

"I think that's just the Strangers tapping into the Chives' network to use them to communicate," she said. "Since the Strangers are talking to all of them simultaneously, they all speak at once. So it wouldn't let us communicate with the Core."

"Well, boo," I said.

A smile pulled up on one corner of her mouth. "But I just got an idea from what you said, Sunya."

"Me?" I barely managed to not squeak.

"The mail," Iris said. "It goes out into a buoy, and every ship that passes picks up the packets and passes them along to every other buoy they pass. And every other ship that passes picks up each packet and passes it to every other ship and buoy . . . until eventually one of those ships winds up at the destination. Then the recipient opens the message, and all the other Schrödinger's letters evaporate in a puff of collapsing wave states and cease to exist. So if you examine a packet that isn't yours—"

"—that would break the system," said Cee.

"Right," said Iris. "So if you and Dakhira and the other shipminds all look at your packets—"

"Oh," said Xhelsea, "then quantum entanglement–slash–quantum teleportation kicks in. The shipminds inspect their packets. That suddenly causes a whole pile of messages all over the Synarche to flip. Including in the Core. Especially on Judiciary ships, because they get around. They'll notice that a whole bunch of information just vanished from their storage."

"Right," said Iris.

Salvie reached out to squeeze my hand. I, too, was getting excited—that particular rush that comes of finding the solution to an intractable problem.

"So then the Judiciary knows there's a problem," I said. "How does that get them here to help us evacuate?"

Easy, said Nonsense. *They know where packets are addressed. They know where they originate. And the only ones coming out this far either originate or terminate at Town. The Judiciary will know there's a problem, because all our mail has vanished.*

"That could work," I said. "How long can we play cat and mouse with pirates, waiting for rescue to get here?"

"Oh," said Xhelsea glibly, "we've got big engines and a lot of guns. Probably at least until that sun explodes."

"What's the drawback?" Iris asked. "I'm not an engineer."

There was a short lag. Then:

"The drawback," Dakhira said, "is that somebody might die or be severely injured due to faulty information. Lots of letters will be lost or at least significantly delayed. Somebody might wind up divorced. Oh, and also it will crash a good part of the mail network."

Cee cleared her noncorporeal throat, sounding scandalized. "Let me get this right. You're going to *read* everybody's mail?"

"No," said Iris. "You—and Dakhira, and Ikem and Amal and Arula—are going to *look* at the mail. Wait, does collapsing a quantum entanglement work when the observer is an AI?"

"It was," Dakhira said, after a two-second lag that Cee didn't fill, "one of the early tests to prove my ancestors' 'consciousness' to a meatform standard." He sounded disgusted. "Not that you people can even figure out if you're actually conscious and free-willed, or just endocrine puppets. So I'm not sure collapsing a superposition by squinting at it is a valid test."

"But you *can* collapse a superposition by squinting at it."

"I do it every dia," he sighed.

I leaned over and whispered to Salvie, "I wish Yod were here."

Her tendrils clenched. "Me too." Then she raised her voice. "So we're doing it?"

"Yes," said Cee. "I guess we are."

CHAPTER 36

"SO WHAT DO WE DO NOW?" I ASKED, LOOKING AROUND. "While the shipminds are crashing the interstellar mail system?"

Xhelsea said, "We still have to go back and get the Strangers. And organize the Baomind into pods for evacuation and get them to withdraw as far from the Baostar as they safely can. We'll need you for that, Sunya."

I nodded, feeling grim-faced. This was really happening. And somehow I was the most important person in the room.

It felt . . . awful.

"Where is their ship?" Salvie asked.

"At least one was overlapping part of the hab," I said. Then I remembered something Dakhira had said. "Wait, there must also have been one overlapping Dakhira, because he said there were Strangers on him. And they can't just . . . live in space, right? Even their space?"

"Okay," Xhelsea said. "That's a place to start. We'll have to go back downwell to—"

How are we going to find the Strangers now? Nonsense asked. *Town is gone.*

I wanted to scream. I had to force my nails to uncurl from my palms, and the uncurling felt bad, frightening. As if the discomfort was the only gravity anchoring me to this plain of existence.

Yod was gone, as the Yod I'd known. I didn't even have time to grieve for her. I was responsible for the lives of everyone around me. Including my family. I was probably going to be the chief witness against Vickee DeVine if any of us lived long enough to get her into a courtroom.

I wanted my mommy.

"I'll ask Kell," I said.

I almost didn't go into the observation lounge because when I got there, it was full of refugees from Town spread out on the floor in freshly printed sleeping sacks. And there was the local instance of Chive as well, standing clutching the rail below the incredible horseshoe sweep of viewports that showed—everything. The Baostar burned like a pit of coals behind us, ragged and angry. Before us, the long crooked curve of the Milky Way, its barred arms tilted up at an angle like a god's own throwing star. We were above its plane, far along the trailing end of the Outer Arm. No one on Terra or Rubric had ever seen this view—their angle on the galaxy gave them only variations on a blurred, edge-on slab.

Nobody had ever seen anything like it from the Core, either. The Core had its own glories, but it was a churning radioactive mass of stars in orbit around the Saga-star, the unfathomable black hole at the Milky Way's center.

Anyway, there was no seeing out of the Core. It was just too bright. And not even any seeing across it, because it was crowded with stars, and the lensing from the Saga-star black hole wrecked all horizons. But from out here, in the middle of nowhere—no, on the *edge* of nowhere—you could clearly see the whole shebang.

I wondered if this was the reason the Koregoi had brought us out here to begin with: to show us how small and perfect our entire galaxy was. How fragile a jewel on the face of the night.

Early in the history of spaceflight, people discovered that looking down on a planet from orbit had a profound psychological effect on astronauts. They understood the fragility and preciousness of the world they came from—like holding a newborn in your arms. All meaning glimpsed in a single, brittle moment.

I have often wondered if when the wayfarers left, fleeing the Eschaton they had created and leaving the poor and downtrodden to clean it up and invent real civilization for the first time, they looked back and saw . . . what they had broken. I wonder if they mourned.

Or if their sophipathology was so strong that they could not even experience this great equalizer of experiences.

I was looking down on a whole galaxy, spread out across a quarter of a spherical sky. And it seemed, in that moment, as fragile and ephemeral as blown glass. As love. As a beech tree, falling into the light until the light reached out and consumed it.

There was—I checked three times—no sign of Kell. I should have asked Cee before I came down here. Now everybody was staring at me, so I couldn't just turn around and go.

I gave an awkward wave and walked over to the Chive. I thought they were the one the others had been suspicious of. I wondered if they had made up their mind about that divorce.

"Hey, Chive," I said, determined to not be an asshole. "I was looking for Kell."

"Kell went back outside," they said. "Should I call it for you?"

"No . . ." I paused. Well, I *did* say I was going to try to not be an asshole. Start as you mean to go on. Right? "Actually, maybe you can help me."

"Me?" Chive said. They drew themself up. My heart dropped; had they been waiting this whole time for me to reach out to them?

"I need to ask the Baomind where the Strangers' ships are. So I guess it doesn't have to be Kell in specific."

"I could ask for you," the Chive offered. "They're still in there."

"In Dakhira?" But why would an advanced race from another dimension have a hard time keeping up with one of our ships?

"Yes," they said.

"Do you know *why* they haven't developed a white drive analogue of their own?"

Chive closed their eyes. Their face went slack, and without shared expression it was easy to see their individuality. Their lips moved—not in words, but in silent song—and when they opened their eyes they said, "They're still there."

"Well take it," I said. "I'm going to have to go talk to Dakhira about shipping them home, aren't I?"

I almost thought the Chive looked at me with sympathy.

And what was it like for them, being separated from their cohort? A clade of one? Now that they had a separation, were they second-guessing their desire to be single? Or were they actually even feeling separated? If the Baomind was connecting them to the others, were they actually alone in their own head? Or were they still part of something bigger?

I wanted to ask, but it seemed impolite, and I felt awkward. There's a fine line between polite expression of interest in another's experience and prying.

In any case, we weren't going to catch up with the Strangers' other ship that hour, or even that dia. Because we were all running dark and silent to hide from pirates, we wouldn't even have known where the civilian ships were if they hadn't been close enough to tightbeam. We only knew where Ikem was because of the Baomind and the Chives' link to it. Sensibly, none of the vessels on our side of the vast cat-and-mouse game we were playing were transmitting a location marker, and all of them were dumping as much radiation to their heat sinks as possible.

Doing otherwise would have been an excellent way to accidentally draw Freeport attention. And other than being roasted by the Baostar, Freeport attention was the thing we were most trying to avoid.

Cee was going to have to slide downwell to find the Strangers' other ship. Down and in, a mote pushing the stellar wind. Without her to block radiation for them, Dakhira, Arula, and Amal would have to head farther out in the system.

A fierce and furious little part of me wanted to call the pirates up and make them come to us. Just so I could punch Haran and that sanctimonious Captain Adekunle right in their collective and individual kissers. My better judgment prevailed only because I knew that Cee would never let me do it. Anyway, the odds of getting obliterated by incoming fire exceeded the odds of my getting in a successful sock in the snoot by orders of magnitude. I didn't even have to ask my statistician wife to do that math.

We skulked through space, not doing anything that might create a fuss. It was weird not to be needed. I wouldn't say my work was done—but it was definitely *to be continued*. Either I—and enough of the Baomind to maintain its integrity of consciousness, however much that took—would survive and resume communication in the Core, or we wouldn't. In which case what I had learned and documented already would be stolen by pirates.

In the wake of Vickee's assassination attempt, I was no longer worried about proving myself worthy to some nebulous authority. I had come out here and I had done good work. I would continue to do good work, if I survived.

Whether anyone noticed it—well, I can't pretend I was *impervious* to the concern. But it no longer *ate* at me.

My chief rival—at least in my head, and also I guess probably in hers—had worried about my skill enough to resort to murder. It's hard to imagine what would be more reassuring, while somehow not being reassuring at all.

Our sneaky spiral led us deeper into the well. It would be harder to escape from here, but Cee didn't seem worried. I decided to trust her to know her own capabilities. She dropped the gutted hulk and we—the rescued—spread out everywhere Cee could fit us. There was no privacy anywhere and damned little deck space. I couldn't decide if it would have been better if we weren't under acceleration and floating around.

The ship acquired a sour smell, like a party at 0300. We all hot-racked, and having a third of the people aboard on rest time at any given moment actually made things feel much less crowded.

Days passed in silence and tension.

I found myself in the command center with Salvie, Xhelsea, Fritha, Willow, and Chionn. It's indicative of how badly crowded we were that, by then, that felt like an intimate gathering.

The kids were on sleep shift in the tiny two-bunk pod Cee had set up for us. I wanted to go lie down myself, but I wanted more to make sure Luna got her teenager-mandated, brain-rewiring-for-adulthood ten hours of downtime.

How ironic, I thought, that I had been so irritated by the size of my cabin on Dakhira. It seemed like a luxury now.

Angie was on my shoulder, nibbling at my hair. Fine, as long as she left my ears alone. I hoped we all survived so I could give her back to Trevor.

Fritha asked me, *What led you to study history?*

"I wanted to find things out," I replied. I reached up to disentangle one of Angie's wing claws from my curl. She'd unraveled my usual chignon completely.

Willow said, "I think it's very hard for all of us to remember and relate to history, especially when we have to face how humans in former times behaved."

Xhelsea said, "We're still reactive. Aren't the Freeporters human? Vickee? Haran?"

I wanted to say *Barely*, but it's not polite to other and unperson fellow sapients, even if they're assholes. Even if the description of "sapient" feels mostly like a courtesy.

I was so busy tripping over my own desire not to seem like a jerk in front of the Goodlaw that I missed any opportunity to get a zinger in.

Xhelsea said, "Imagine when my whole species was like that. Better, imagine when we valorized it. That's how you understand the Freeport ethos. Imagine a world that values profit over well-being and 'winning' over the common good."

Ouch. That didn't make me feel any better about wanting to beat Vickee. But was a little competition so bad? It could be a motivator.

Of course, *I* had never embraced rhetoric over precision.

I couldn't keep a straight face even thinking it.

"I'm a historian," I said. "I've studied pre-Eschaton Earth extensively, and I do have a feel for some of the cultures."

Back off; I'm a professional.

Our eyes met, and they smiled. My stomach did the dropsy thing and I rolled my eyes at it internally. Yes, dear, remember we're happily married.

"That was better than I deserved," the Goodlaw said. And we both laughed at ourselves, and Salvie's tendrils coiled. Willow and Fritha tried to look stern in their various manners, and Chionn's fur lifted and riffled.

I had been meaning to ask something, and the lull presented itself. "Did you finish looking at the mail, Cee?"

"We all did," she answered immediately. "We completed it several standard days ago now. Thank you for the insight."

"That was all Iris," I demurred, doing math in my head. How fast would our party trick bring help, if it worked at all? No way of telling—it all depended on where support ships were, and if they understood our distress call.

"The synthesis was yours," Cee said. "Synthesis is a noble endeavor in and of itself, and surprisingly few organics bother to learn it."

"You sound like Dakhira," I teased.

"*Please*," Cee replied.

"How bad is the damage to the mail system?" I asked.

"Tremendous," she admitted. "But not nearly as catastrophic as if we were closer to a hub. Out here on a spoke, the losses are limited." The tone of her voice shifted. "Dr. DeVine is headed this way. ETA three minutes."

"You let her out of the brig?" I squeaked.

"I *am* a brig," Cee said. "It's against my programming to keep people in solitary confinement unless they present a clear and immediate danger. Anyway, I needed that space for a bunkroom."

"She tried to kill me!"

"Don't worry," Xhelsea said, patting my hand, just as Cee said, "I will not allow her to harm you."

"Wait," I said. "Can't she sneak around like Haran and avoid your sensors? Doesn't she have one of those devices because she's a spy?"

"She *did*," Cee said. "But we have scanned her and there are no further devices on her, or concealed in her body."

I made a face. Salvie patted me protectively on the shoulder. "Just how I wanted to end my life," I muttered. "Trapped on a ship with Vickee DeVine."

"We're not dead yet," Salvie answered. "And Cee can hide out here for a good long time."

"We'll run out of consumables eventually," I answered gloomily—then forced myself to snap out of it. "But you're right, and we have plenty of gruel."

That was a joke: Cee could still print just about anything we cared to eat, though some of the volatile flavor and aroma compounds were running low. She just wasn't designed to feed and house forty sentients in addition to her own crew. And we were even lower on resources now than we had been before Town came apart.

At least the Ceeharen didn't eat food. And there was no shortage of photosynthetic radiation.

The hatch slid aside, and Vickee walked in. I still knew her expressions well, and she was spoiling for a fight.

Well, so was I.

Her gaze skipped over all of us. I thought she smirked at me in particular, but I could have been imagining it. But she addressed herself to Cee.

Which she could have done from anywhere on the ship, without the burden of performance. But of course, for Vickee, performance was no burden.

She said, "I'd like to request a transfer to Dakhira."

Cee said, "Why? He's not equipped for custody of arrestees."

Vickee scoffed. "I believe Dr. Song's close relationship with your Goodlaw has prejudiced you against me." She looked slyly at Salvie.

Salvie . . . brightened. Her spine lengthened; her tendrils came forward. All her eyes gleamed.

I'm not sure Vickee knew it was a threat. But I did, and I loved her for it.

I burst out laughing. "Are you insinuating that Xhelsea and I are fucking?"

"I know your type."

"Wow," I said. I settled back against the cushions. "You've known the Goodlaw for longer than I have. Perhaps I should be accusing them of favoring you?"

I don't mean it, I sent to Xhelsea.

Xhelsea sent back a sense of equivocating amusement.

Fritha leaned forward interestedly. To Salvie but where we all could hear it, she said, *Is this a human dominance display?*

"Something like that," Salvie said.

"Vickee, the jig is up, as the saying goes. Can't you accept the inevitable with dignity?" I knew she couldn't. And I knew I shouldn't be twisting the knife, but sometimes the handle is right there.

"I still want to change ships," Vickee said.

"No," said Cee.

Xhelsea said, "There's room in the cryo tanks if you find us all too annoying, though."

CHAPTER 37

THE BAOMIND DEFENDED US AS WE CAME CLOSER TO THE Baostar. One almost would have expected something so big and old and weird and—that taboo word—*alien* to be a serene and inscrutable presence. A sort of monolith.

But that wasn't the case at all. We had reached out to the Baomind—no, it had reached out to us, and we had reached back. Here I was with a head full of song, trying to communicate with it. And succeeding, a little.

It wasn't inscrutable. It wasn't imperturbable. It wasn't resigned to samsara. It wanted to *live*. And the Strangers wanted to live, also.

I knew we were braking for a while before we got there. Cee swapped ends so her engines pointed downwell and increased thrust. Braking us more severely than she'd accelerated us meant it took us less vulnerable time to slow; it also meant the gravity got pretty stiff. I thumped around like an old woman under something less than two gs. Salvie didn't mind; Fercho ran higher than Earth or Rubric anyway.

But our spacer friends suffered. Chive sprawled in a lounge, nursing their afthands. Xhelsea triggered their hardsuit—except the helmet—and wore it as a supportive exoskeleton. And Dr. Nonsense just took to a bucket.

A *big* bucket.

When the *v*-minus dropped—listen to me, I sound like a professional—I took myself to the rear of the observation deck and started looking for the Strangers.

I didn't see anything.

Well, that is incorrect. I didn't see the Strangers. I did see the Baostar, lensed into a ring by the Baomind's radiation control measures and so close now that I felt the only thing keeping me from touching it was the transparent walls that also kept me alive. Before it, I saw the flocks of tesserae, and the raging arms of coronal mass stretched out from the star in every direction. Like the universe's biggest sea urchin. The Baomind was enclosing us in a pirate-proof cage . . . I hoped, anyway. But at what cost to the stability of the star? And how much radiation was being showered on the other ships? On my children?

Peering through the blackness, using magnification to inspect the sky dead ahead—or dead astern, which was the direction we were headed—I finally caught a glimpse of a cloud of tesserae encompassing something long, but bulky in the middle, and shaped like the stump of a melted candle. A ghostly shape—the Strangers' ship.

"Will linking up with them protect us from the radiation?" I asked.

"No. The Strangers don't interact with electromagnetism. That's why we can't see them." Cee, as always, was right there. Cee, and not Yod.

It's so easy to get attached to someone. So quickly. Almost as fast as they can be gone.

"I can see them," I protested.

"Your *fox* can make you think you see them," Cee said. "Your brain doesn't know the difference, but no light rays are bouncing off that thing into your eyes."

"Hmm," I said. Cee was probably right about the physics.

"But the Baomind is shielding us," she continued. "With the lens, and they have covered my hull several layers deep."

"They're not hitchhikers?"

She chuckled, but also didn't dignify me with an answer. That was okay; I was pretty sure I didn't deserve one.

"How do we dock?" I asked. A more practical question. I was dreading going over there, but I wanted to interact with the Strangers face-to-face. So to speak.

Cee said, "We just fly right inside them, I imagine."

Why was I questioning Cee's engineering? Because I was nervous and trying to exert some control. Certainly not because I was *proficient*.

But all the ayatanas in my head were yammering, along with my own fight/freeze/flight response. And chattering took the edge off.

Down we came. I felt somebody move up beside me. When I looked, I saw Salvie's beloved profile, washed in vermilion light.

"Both kids let me tuck them in," I bragged.

"*Both* kids?"

"Probably for the last time." I grinned at her. I was feeling, somehow, a little bit hopeful.

Maybe our distress signal, improvised as it was, had gotten out. Maybe help was on the way. Maybe we would survive until it got here. Maybe we wouldn't have to abandon Kell and its siblings in a desperate last-ditch effort to run the blockade in advance of an exploding sun.

Well, if we were running under those circumstances, the pirates would be running, too. So that was something. And they had a head start. They might be gone by the time any of us reached the beacon. Surely it had gotten bad enough in this stellar system that they were evacuating?

Hope was scary, because hope meant disappointment. But I was feeling it anyway.

I leaned my shoulder on my wife's, and briefly we pretended we were safe and secure.

"I hate being on different sleep cycles from the kids," I said.

"Yeah," she said. "Me too."

• • •

Picking up the Strangers' ship and a swarm of tesserae was almost anticlimactic. As we swung in toward them, they matched speed and vector with us, and before long we were cruising along in unison and Cee was full of Strangers. The space inside her white coils was packed thick with Baotiles. We swung outward again, headed for our planned rendezvous with Dakhira, Amal, and Arula. Chive, through the intermediary of the Baomind, tracked their location for us.

When you're a fugitive, even the quiet starts getting to you. The pirates were out there in the dark somewhere, ghostly as the Strangers, and all Cee's passengers could do for the moment was huddle and hope that the dark was big enough to hide in.

We drew closer to Dakhira, and as we were coming within range of him, Cee called me to a meeting with Xhelsea and Dr. Nonsense. It convened on the bridge, because that was the space we had available.

"We have a problem," Cee said when we were all assembled. "My external main airlock seems to be welded shut. This will interfere with docking with Dakhira."

Sometimes you yelp out loud in frustration, and nobody notices because everybody else is yelping, too. I had a list of major threats to life and limb I was worried about avoiding, including but not limited to: radiation syndrome, pirates, exploding stars, black holes, being sliced to ribbons by the sharp edges of the Baotiles . . . but I had forgotten that the perversity of the universe tends toward a maximum and that a minor annoyance could kill you as fast as a speeding freighter. "Sabotage?"

"I would have noticed somebody taking a blowtorch to my hide," Cee said. "No, it's cold-welded."

"What the Well is cold-welding?"

"In our haste to escape the destruction of Town, and the chaos that followed"—she sighed—"I neglected to make sure the airlock was sufficiently coated with lubricant before jettisoning the damaged hab component and locking down for travel. If bare metal—without any coating of other stuff, like the microlayers of water or air you get on a planet—touches another piece of the same metal, they think they're one object. There's no seam, nor weak point. They just fuse."

Other people went on trips and never once had to leave the relative safety of a starship. Me? I was never going to get that lucky.

"So somebody is going to have to EVA to get to Dakhira once we reconnect with him," I said.

"I'll fix the airlock."

Both of us humans turned, heads rotating on necks like flowers following the sun. Five steps away—just out of casual slapping range—stood Vickee, her hands shoved into her coverall pockets. "Give me a cutting torch and I'll do the EVA."

"Sure," I said, "we're going to trust you outside of the ship with a cutting torch."

"If I threaten Cee, she can shoot me," she said. "You're allowed to use deadly force in self-defense, right, Cee?"

"Why would you help?" Xhelsea, cutting to the heart of it.

"Because I want to get out of here alive!" Vickee snarled.

I asked, "Cee, why can't your Hands fix it?"

"They could, but it will take a while to build new ones. All of my materials are currently tied up in sleeping bags, and recycling them will take a few hours."

"Crap," said Xhelsea. "Nonsense? You're still nominally in charge. What do you think?"

I think if Dr. DeVine is willing to take the risk, we ought to honor that, it said.

Dakhira would not be able to keep up with Cee when it came time for us to run—an inevitable outcome that grew closer with every passing minute. Neither could Amal and Arula, but they were smaller vessels and Ikem could escort them both once he rendezvoused.

When we got back to the civilian vessels, Cee locked grapples onto Dakhira, bringing him inside her coils like an anglerfish's mate. Baotiles swirled around us like disturbed butterflies, making room.

I was going to miss a sleep cycle while Vickee was outside—because it had been decided over my protests that Vickee *would* go outside, and I wasn't going to sleep through that. Once we repaired the airlock, Cee and Dakhira could dock properly and we'd all be free to move back and forth as if they were one ship. It's convenient that space doesn't have any air, thus releasing vessels from any need to be aerodynamic. That would relieve some of our crowding as we moved personnel to Dakhira.

Willow and Waelyn—our remaining environmental engineer—thought that eighteen or so people would not put more strain on his capacity than the remainder would on Cee's. Fifty-odd people—counting a Chive and Cee's crew—on Cee was enough to make me feel I'd been reborn in a hive. The kids were awake, and the Judiciary crew whose bunks we were hot-racking in were on duty. So I tried to take a nap before things got under way.

Zag wandered in and joined me, curling his soft tuxedo self against the backs of my knees. His purr vibrated through the tiny cabin, and he was promptly out cold.

For me, on the other paw, sleep remained elusive. I could have tuned myself out, though that nearly always left me groggy when I woke. I could have gone to look for Salvie and distraction.

But the inside of my head was remarkably quiet, except for the Baosong, and even the migraines and nausea seemed to be on the wane. Could it be they weren't pushing so hard, now that I was acknowledging and speaking to them?

It didn't matter. Nothing was my problem right now—not until the airlock issue was sorted. I was as free as Zag. And it was pleasant to be alone with myself for a while. Not to owe any time to anybody.

I closed my eyes; if I couldn't sleep, I could at least rest. As I let myself drift, I remembered an old-school means of self-hypnosis into slumber. I tightened and released my muscles body part by body part, starting at my feet; calves below the purr, knees, thighs above the purr, buttocks and hips . . .

A warm drowsy feeling crept over me. My eyelids felt heavy and my body almost luxuriated in its little aches and tirednesses. I slid, trying not to feel so optimistic about sleep that I woke myself up. Sliding, sliding, gliding down into quiet and dark—

A burst of Baosong so loud in my head it made imagined ears ring hit me at the same time I hit the restraining net. I bounced into it with so much force my hardsuit triggered, slicing the net to ribbons and releasing me to slam against the bulkhead over the bunk. The colloid protected me from most injury, but my teeth snapped shut on my tongue. My mouth filled with blood and saliva, and the red shock of pain jolted me alert.

"Zag!" I grabbed him, shielding his body with my arms, and triggered his suit as well. He yowled unhappily, the sound cut off by his tiny helmet. Poor kitty.

Cee's next maneuver threw me back into the bunk. I yelped and blood splattered the inside of my visor. *Keep your mouth shut.* I didn't want to breathe that and give myself pneumonia—or lose visibility out the helmet.

Cee, what the fuck?

Incoming, she said, and swerved again.

Still holding on to my cat, I snatched the external feed and threw it up on the wall. I cursed—but remembered not to do it out loud. I swallowed blood and grabbed the safety rail with my free hand. It was a second's work to clip myself in, and another to clip Zag in as well.

The pirates had found us. A dozen ships or more, shadows lensing across the rippling void. Perhaps they had been lying in wait near Dakhira for our return.

Salvie—

I've got the kids and Angie and Zig. I can't find Zag.

I let her feel my relief. *I have him. Hang on,* I said, and—

A siren blasted my senses. "Cee?" I squeaked embarrassingly.

"Electromagnetic bubble to maximum," she said. "Brace for acceleration."

Her presence vanished from my senso as if a curtain had been dropped between us. *Xhelsea, what happened to Cee?!*

Do what she said! the Goodlaw yelled back. And then they triggered my auxiliary EM shielding. Apparently it was evident I didn't know how to do it myself.

Way to feel like a lubber again, Sunya.

Shields are up, I said in the shipwide channel. *What are we shielding from?*

Salvie was there—I felt her, and she said calmly, *The AIs have withdrawn to their hardened cores. Kell has returned. It warns us that the Strangers and Baomind have accidentally pulled another flare out of the star, and a massive EM pulse is headed our way.*

Acceleration took hold. I imagined the Goodlaw wasn't talking because they were busy flying.

What are the pirates doing? I said. *Are they going to parley?*

Chionn answered, *They're not hailing. Just waiting.*

Should we try hailing them?

Only if you want to talk to them. Salvie's scorn was palpable. *I don't.*

Neither did I, but . . . letting them fry, or drift and freeze or bake in disabled vessels—

No. I couldn't do that.

Patch me out, I said. I thought my tongue had stopped bleeding.

Vickee said, *We have sixteen minutes before the flare reaches us. We won't have much warning—the EM wave will arrive right alongside the visual light. The flare will be some time behind. The pirates might just decide to blow our hull rather than letting us get away if we give them too much warning.*

I have maneuverability, Xhelsea said, clipped and professional.

Vickee was trying for the same tone of competence, and it didn't fool me only because I knew her. Unfair, because she was a good pilot. *We need to get your airlock fixed, Cee.*

I wondered if Cee bristled at the familiarity as much as I did. I said, on the public channel, *I still don't trust her.*

Vickee mustered a pretty good air of scorn herself. *Are you going to go outside and cut it free?*

Sure, I said. *What's a little spacewalk in a firefight with a star going supernova?*

Then get the hell out of the way and let me.

Salvie seemed about to volunteer—I could tell by the quality of her silence. I sent, *Don't you dare* to her privately.

Don't YOU dare! she answered.

I don't care who goes, said the Goodlaw. *Somebody do it.*

I'm at the emergency lock, said Vickee. *I'm going.*

The emergency lock was not a proper airlock. It was a place where an object could be passed through the skin of the Interceptor by rearranging its molecules. It was tucked away in a sheltered nook, because it could not be as well armored as the rest of *I Am Not Safe At Harbor.*

The acceleration eased. Clutching Zag to my chest, I slung my feet down to the deck and heaved myself up. The cabin spun a little. I was grateful for the grab rails. My body had opinions about what was and wasn't an acceptable acceleration fluctuation.

Xhelsea's flying was subtly different from Cee's. More abrupt, less measured. I rocked from foot to foot coming down the corridor, bracing and magged in.

The scene when I reached the bridge was cool and organized, not at all the chaos I had anticipated. Xhelsea and Chionn were at their stations. The other Judiciary crew members filled out the roster. Salvie stood by the hatch, back to a bulkhead, netted in. I went to join her.

She had apparently stowed the kids, Angie, and the rest of the cats, because she was solo. Kell hovered beside her and chimed a greeting as I arrived.

Vickee was nowhere to be seen; I presumed she was already on her way out.

Just as I was thinking that, her voice confirmed it. *Readying my torch,* she said. *This is jammed up good and proper—*

I wish Cee had Town's army of Hands, Xhelsea said. *I wish we had Cee!*

I hoped Cee was safe in her bunker—and I agreed.

"One of those ships is coming around on us," Salvie said, pointing.

"Target acquired," Xhelsea replied. "Warning shot."

Vibration came up through my boots. I saw a bright flare leap from the nose of *I Am Not Safe At Harbor.* The magnetic bubble that protected us was an aurora of green and violet across the ports. I watched it peel apart to let the torpedo through and slam back together immediately. Interceptors could do some pretty cool stuff.

Our projectile skimmed past the pirate vessel. I thought I recognized it, now that I could catch a clear glimpse in an attitude I was familiar with. "That's the *Devil's Own,*" I said. "Let me hail the captain. Broadband, so the other ships can listen in."

I despised Adekunle. But I could not let him and his whole crew die without at least attempting to warn them.

"Tell him we can't waste any more torpedoes on warning shots," Xhelsea said, deadpan. "Even if we wanted to. And none of us like him enough."

We were at bay, and we all knew it. But I still admired their bravado.

Connecting, said the coms officer. The display changed to show a black screen, and I found myself once again staring into the chilly gaze of Captain Adekunle.

Third time's the charm, I told myself.

Almost . . . got it . . . Vickee sent. Another vibration through my boots, this one conducting a scraping, straining sound that vibrated my suit against my skin and made my ears hurt. Not by any means a pleasant sensation.

"Captain Adekunle," I said. "This is Dr. Song aboard SJV *I Am Not Safe At Harbor.*"

Get us a hole in the pirate fleet and we'll punch it out of here, Xhelsea sent. *I can't change course or acceleration right now without ramming somebody, and I need to shelter these civilian ships until Ikem can get here.*

I guessed the pirates were too close to jump. Ramming something on your way into white space sounded like a bad idea, and I decided not to look up the effects.

"If you want to surrender," Adekunle drawled, "we can talk."

"I want to warn you," I answered. "The star could go nova any minute now, and a huge flare is headed straight for us. With an electromagnetic pulse that will wipe us all out." *And Vickee is probably going to blow us up.*

No, I reminded myself. Vickee was predictable, because Vickee was, by her lights, rational. She would look out for number one before getting revenge on me and the others.

"Your poor fragile gearbrains can't take a little solar storm?" he mocked. "Pity you've all got docility boxes in your heads. It'll be a shame when those cook."

I could choose not to rise to the bait. "The ship's Goodlaw tells me our next shot won't be a warning."

Pulse impact in six minutes, said Chionn.

"The pulse hits in six minutes standard," I said. "We're leaving now, and we can do it through you or—"

A rending sensation much bigger than the prior ones rattled my boots against my feet. I saw the last bit of Town that had been adhered to the airlock peel away, trailing rough edges and cables. One smacked the viewport right beside me. The port did not crack or shatter, but I jumped a little. I squeaked and clutched the cat to me. He squeaked, too, but in mild protest.

"I'm busy," I told Adekunle. "You have the information you need."

I cut the contact and turned away from the nothing that replaced his hateful smile. The airlock probably still wasn't clear—there must be scrap metal jammed in it—but now Cee's depleted and AI-undirected Hands could get to it and effect repairs.

Vickee?

No answer. Of course.

"What's that?" Chionn said, pointing at the wreckage slowly vectoring away from us. I squinted; then I cursed.

"It's Vickee," I said. "Her suit must have snagged. I'm going after her."

"Five standard minutes," Xhelsea said, not bothering to argue.

Salvie caught my suit in her glove. "Sun, if the storm—"

"I know," I said.

I shoved the cat at her and ran.

Six seconds down the corridor. Fortunately starships, even big ones like Cee, were small. I was already diving for the emergency lock when I realized I could have asked Kell for help. Well, maybe the Baomind would figure out that they were needed—if they weren't already diving en masse out of the way of the flare.

My faceplate sealed, I swam through the soft spot in Cee's hull and emerged on the other side like a seal poking up through an ice floe. A quick glance around, and I acquired my target visually. The wreckage with Vickee snagged on it—like Ahab on the white whale—drifted in a stately fashion toward the edge of Cee's EM shields. I had no idea what might happen to Vickee when it hit, or if the wreckage would pass through or be bounced back toward the Interceptor's hull.

I decided not to find out. I clipped my safety line to a belay point to the right of the emergency lock.

One deep breath for luck—**27 seconds**, noted the bug in the corner of my heads-up display—and I pulled my legs up into a crouch and threw myself across the intervening gap with all the velocity I could manage.

It was easy this time. Okay, I'm lying. But I want to tell you it was easy this time because that's how stories work: you overcome something that is holding you back and it never troubles you again. But in the real world, you have to do the hard thing over and over again, and reward yourself for succeeding, until it wears a new groove.

It was, at least, *easier*.

I had to steer myself; no Yod this time. But I did it—it turned out it wasn't too hard. Just like rowing a boat, you had to make sure the impulse was even on both sides, or increase or decrease it slightly to adjust trajectory.

36 seconds: I touched down beside Vickee—and grabbed the cable and the jagged metal Vickee was snagged on. Her suit was holed but had sealed itself. She was alive. She might have lost some blood, though, and something had rendered her unconscious.

I used a laser cutter to slice her free.

45 seconds: *I'm going to throw her to you,* I told Salvie. *Get to the lock.*

I'm already here. I saw her head poke through, followed by the rest of her. I braced myself against the mags and hauled Vickee up by the rescue handle, both hands locked around her back. I unclipped my line from myself and clipped it to Vickee. "Haul when I push her."

"On it," Salvie answered, crouching to grab the line.

Vickee's eyes opened. Blearily, her gaze locked on mine. "Always knew you'd kill me if you got the chance," she mumbled.

My interrupt stopped what I had been about to say, and upon due consideration I decided to say it anyway. "Oh, fuck you."

I whipped Vickee up and away, hurling her toward Salvie and *I Am Not Safe At Harbor.* I heard her squeak, and then shriek—and I enjoyed it a little more than I should have as Salvie hauled her in, flailing.

I didn't enjoy it for long, because almost as soon as Vickee left my hands I realized where I'd miscalculated, and it was in forgetting Newton's third law: *For every action there is an equal and opposite reaction.*

67 seconds: I was tumbling head over heels, spinning out of control so fast my stabilizers couldn't keep up. The whole universe flashed past with every revolution.

I was taking the long fall. Following my family tree down the well.

CHAPTER 38

AFTER A CRISIS, PEOPLE SAY THAT THEY DIDN'T HAVE time to be scared. Well, that wasn't true of me, falling ass over teakettle all the way down. I shook so hard my body rattled against the inside of my suit like a handful of marbles in a can. My teeth chattered with fear. I spun out of control, centrifugal force tugging my head and feet and hands.

That gave me an idea, and I starfished to decrease my rotational momentum.

It helped . . . a little. The Baostar still flashed across my horizon too fast to fix my gaze on it. Nausea and dizziness disoriented me; I tuned them down and overshot, leaving myself feeling lethargic and numb. I closed my eyes, but that made it worse, and when I opened them I saw a glittery fountain of tesserae streaming away from the star as fast as they could fly. They looked like sparks in the night—you could only see them at this distance because they were so brilliantly mirrored and reflecting the Baostar's baleful eye.

Cee and Dakhira were outlines against that shower of light and the wildly glowing interactions of their magnetic bottles with the stellar storm.

I timed a split second of thrust to bump myself away from the bottle.

It increased my spin, though I'd been trying to correct a little. But it did angle me back toward Cee . . . ish. Maybe I could maneuver myself away from death in tiny increments?

Not while spinning—my odds were too good of only making it worse. And Cee would be leaving. . . . If I was inside her coils when she went, would I be carried into white space with her? What would happen if I fell out while we were between worlds?

Well, I guessed I was going to find out. If I survived hitting the bottle. I'd rather be dead in moments rather than falling for days, dying of dehydration, anoxia, and radiation poisoning.

What a way to go.

Time really does slow to a crawl when you think you're dying. My heads-up display flashed **98 seconds**, yet I'd already written an entire dissertation in my head. I remembered the old joke: *What if you change your mind on the way down?*

I'd just got myself resigned to my unkind fate—what a laugh, sacrificing myself to save Vickee DeVine! Salvie was going to be so mad at me!—when my attitude jets deployed suddenly, and with calculated expertise. *Tap, tap tap.*

My rotation slowed, and I felt something tug the back of my suit. Cameras showed me a grapple drone, scooping me up by the rescue handle and carrying me back toward the ships in its claws.

Hold tight, Dakhira said.

99 seconds: *Dakhira, you need to be in your shielding!*

Don't tell me what to do, meatpuppet.

125 seconds: I was inside his airlock, falling to my knees with the jerk of acceleration as both ships lurched away from the star. *Can anybody hear me?*

Nothing from Dakhira—back in lockdown, I hoped. But I was right—Salvie *was* furious with me. I'd earned every name she was calling me. But I didn't have time to be called them now.

Is Vickee inside?

Everybody's inside, Salvie answered. *And here comes the flare.*

The only external view from the airlock was a physical porthole no bigger than my head. Nevertheless, a violent burst of light washed my visor so red it turned white. I squeaked in surprise: less blood this time. It's a good thing mouths heal fast.

My suit filters kicked in before my eyes melted. A minor victory for technology. I lunged to the window, half expecting to see *I Am Not Safe At Harbor* tear apart like tissue paper in a giant's fists. But with the help of polarization and light reduction, I could see clearly—and she was fine. The shadowy outlines of the Strangers' ships shrouded Dakhira and Cee. The Baostar reached directly for us with a flare like a haymaker blow.

The pirates are scattering, Chionn said. *Brace! Brace!*

I locked my gloves on to the safety rail. *Braced!* more than fifty people answered in unison—

Both ships accelerated, the force slamming me against the rear bulkhead. Arula and Amal raced alongside us, and behind them I saw the enormous outline of Ikem blip into formation, casting his shadow over them, his bow wave passing by subjective centimeters from my head. My hands were pinned under me, and I could no longer see out the porthole. I screamed—

Red blackness spiraled in from the edges of my vision. I felt my consciousness slip, like ice through cold fingers. The rivets in the bulkhead in front of my eyes dimmed—

And then I was floating free, my shoulder tendons aching with strain, my hands cramped inside the gloves. And Strangers packed in around me—occupying the same space as me—shoulder to shoulder. Their own refugee density.

A voice crackled in my ear. "Sunya?"

"Xhelsea." I let a breath out. "You jumped without an AI?"

"Pshaw," Xhelsea said. "Pirates do it all the time. Besides, *you* jumped without an AI."

"Different kind of jump. Did we just abandon the Baomind?"

"No," they said. "We're not moving now . . . or we're not moving space around us right now. We still can't get to that beacon, and jumping off in random directions . . ."

"Right," I said. "That would be bad." If my kids ever wanted to see their grandfather again. Or vice versa. "So we're coming back out?"

"Once we're sure we're clear of the pirates."

All of the Strangers were staring at me. Their songs overlapped like waves rolling into a beach and reflecting back out again, but I gathered their basic meaning: concern, intention, consequences.

"The Strangers want to apologize for the stellar flare, I think."

Xhelsea grunted. "They're going to have more to apologize for if it goes nova. Is Dakhira okay?"

"I don't know," I said. "I'm still in the airlock."

I had thought the flare was an accident. But it seemed that the Baomind and the Dark Strangers working in concert had caused the Baostar to project an electromagnetic storm directly at us. I could only assume it had been intended to dissuade and block the pirate fleet. It had worked, and we'd probably survive the aftermath, given access to modern malignancy antibodies.

But for this to continue working as a defense we would have to stay close to the sun and its radiation—as the manipulation further destabilized it. Which meant a sun already not long for existence was now on an even faster downhill slide.

I pushed myself off and swam toward the interior hatch. Two Chives undogged it and pulled me inside.

"Dakhira?" I asked as we glided through Center toward Forward.

"Locked back down," said one Chive.

The other finished, "He'll be okay. Probably only—"

"—a little file corruption."

"No worse than our—"

"—DNA."

Well, that put things in perspective. You don't go swimming in a nova and expect to emerge with all your fingers and all your toes.

But that left me with the unsettling recognition that Dakhira had risked his existence for me.

Well, I'd risked mine for Vickee. That in itself was a pretty good indication that I shouldn't mistake heroism for affection.

I'd refused to let her die, but I was still a little sorry to hear that Vickee had made it.

It was unsettling being back on board Dakhira, especially with only four Chives—and after being so crowded in with refugees. Forward seemed cavernous and empty as I clipped into the vacant station. As we dropped from white space, the curve of Cee's hull shielded us from the full storming fury of the Baostar. Ikem and his passengers winked in beside us.

Shadows are stark without atmosphere to scatter the light and soften their edges. But I could still see a hair-fine orange rim limning Cee's outline. We weren't *that* far from the star, then.

But far enough not to cook, I hoped.

I wanted to crawl into my bunk and never come out. That, however, would be unproductive. And I was swimming through Strangers with every move. I owed them and the Baomind something.

I remained still, staring at that light. My hackles began to lift inside the suit. A metallic taste and the scent of ozone. The bridge lights brightened; the exterior of Cee's hull crackled with foxfire. "What in the Well?"

"They call it an epochal stellar event," said a Chive. "A massive stellar storm. We're being bombarded with charged particles."

I felt . . . fuzzy. As if my head were full of static. The Baosong that had so permeated my experience that I no longer consciously noticed it was suddenly, palpably gone. Not that it made any sense to me anymore, without my uploaded datasets and the power of my ayatanas.

"Our foxes?"

"Shutting down now," the Chive said, a little wide-eyed. "I can't feel—*ah!*"

That last was a sharp little scream, like you might give when you drop a knife on your foot. Their hands windmilled, sending them tumbling to the end of their tether. I caught them and hauled them back, shoving them in front of the console.

The Chive on my left looked around frantically. "How do we coordinate?"

"You're going to have to *talk about things*," I said, amazed at how bad I felt for them. "Come on, tell me what to do." I had my hands over the controls.

All the Strangers were gone.

No, not gone. Still there, as they had been all along. It was just that now I could not see them. It wasn't any weirder than when I hadn't known they were there and couldn't detect them . . . but it felt weirder.

The lights looked weird, too. We'd jumped away from the flare, but the stream of particles still played over the ships' hides like a neon firehose. The viewports *glowed*, the inert gasses sandwiched between their layers responding to the bombardment. Shades of aqua, crimson, acid green, saffron, and violet crackled and flickered. Sparks flew from my fingertips. My hair rose on end, unrestrained by gravity.

I wanted a shipmind to tell me what to do. Even Dakhira. But he was back in his hardened core, a virtual panic room, and if he came out it would kill him. He might already have been seriously damaged in saving my life.

Schematics and the system map told me we were out of the direct line of the flare. I had to use my eyes to see them, because my head was empty. I was offline, and so were all of us. It felt like missing a whole set of senses, but it would have been worse not to shut down. And I kept telling myself that every time I felt like curling up and sobbing, or biting the head off some Chive who was even more discombobulated than I.

The flare had done its job—and I felt a sick awe at the vastness of the thing when I considered these effects were just byproducts. We'd *dodged* it, and it was still lighting Dakhira up like a fireworks display.

More than forty-eight standard hours later, the special effects began to die down. The Chives and I had been sleeping in shifts. They were awkward and confused, and had a tendency to stick their hands out peremptorily—then curse when whatever object they desired was not slapped into their palm. And none of them could cook any better than I could, especially when all we had to work with were hoppers of unhydrated nutrition substrate flakes and various colors and seasonings intended for the printers.

I was emotionally dysregulated and confused and incredibly bored without all the little widgets of daily life, and I missed my family fiercely.

But we got by.

I watched the colors crawl away from the windows and the foxfire slide off the superstructure—and off *I Am Not Safe At Harbor*, her hull and white coils still holding us in an awkward embrace. Coms came back up, and I got yelled at by my wife for ten solid minutes. The problem with senso is nobody has to take a breath.

When she was done, I apologized, which set her off again. The second time I apologized, she let it slide . . . but I could tell I was going to be in trouble for a while.

It was okay. I was pleased to be around for her to be mad at.

Less pleasingly, I was stuck on Dakhira until he could redock with Cee's actual airlock, a fiddly task nobody wanted to undertake until both AIs were operating at full capacity. And now there were even more repairs to make—as both vessels' electrical systems had sustained extensive damage. We were still trying to hide any electromagnetic or heat signature from the pirates, which meant scuttling about extremely quietly while trying to make repairs.

Five ships, all damaged, adrift in the void. We weren't alone, though—Kell remained aboard *I Am Not Safe At Harbor*, and once my fox started working again I could see the Strangers and their ships, ghostly outlines superimposed over Dakhira and Cee.

I really needed to ask Iris if she could explain how the Strangers managed to link their ships onto our ships and habs and somehow interact across the boundary of ghostliness. We were ghosts in their world; they were not even poltergeists in ours. But we could bring them with us when we traveled, if we chose.

I was not particularly useful for starship repairs, and I couldn't get back to Cee without a spacewalk until we docked properly, which—thank you, but no thank you. I knew I *could* do it now. And unless I had to, knowing I could would suffice.

So I was stuck with Dakhira, which might have driven me to take that walk with or without a suit. But I had the Strangers to talk to, now that my fox was back online. So I floated in a corner and chatted with them for most of my waking hours.

Iris or Willow—even Salvie—would have learned more than I did, because as near as I could parse from their four-dimensional word bubbles expressed in shimmering chords, these were a bunch of nerds who wanted to talk physics, and if they couldn't talk about physics, they wanted to talk about math. I asked them about history and poetry; they asked me about white space equations, and none of us got what we wanted.

So I spent a lot of time playing messenger between the Strangers and Iris, and not being exactly sure if I was translating things sensibly at all.

The irony of first contact: not having enough in common to carry on an interesting conversation, not because of species differences but because of falling on opposite sides of the sapiences/sciences divide.

At least I was the right person to keep good records. In the future, when the Strangers weren't strangers anymore, but systers—if that came to pass—it would all be recorded and properly archived. And if the pirates came and killed or enslaved us all, well, I was making sure to back everything up to a hardened drive in a white probe. That could be back in the Core in an an or two, or even faster, if we had to fire it into the dark in a last-ditch attempt to salvage everything we had learned.

But for now we huddled in the dark, away from the Baomind, and tried not to be noticed.

Someday some future historian might be wearing my ayatana as they did their research. I hoped it wouldn't be horribly confusing, considering all the other people also inhabiting *my* head.

Speaking of inhabiting my head . . . I couldn't give the Strangers what they wanted. I just didn't have the knowledge to even translate as effectively between them and Iris as I wanted. Dakhira helped, once the radiation died down enough that it was safe for the AIs to come out of their cores. He was slavering for the opportunity to learn Baosong, so I uploaded a copy of my master parser, algorithms, and data to him. He was surprised, I thought, and once it was done he seemed . . . nicer. Not nice, mind you. But less angry at me for existing.

The Strangers were fascinated with what my ayatanas could tell them about music, but I imagined talking to somebody whose existence wasn't limited to being a recorded, read-only set of memories and experiences would be more interesting. I shared my parser with Fritha as well. At first she couldn't communicate directly with them, but as she loaded Baosong, she, too, began to be able to see ghosts, though not as clearly as I could.

I offered a copy to Salvie, but Salvie said no thank you, she needed to be able to concentrate on fighting material enemies if it came down to it again. Iris tried, but without Fritha's musical knowledge or my ayatanas, her tone-deafness was too big a hurdle to communication.

It was frustrating, and I asked Dakhira about it only because the Chives didn't know. "Dakhira, the Strangers—how come I can see them and nobody else can?"

"Language is a virus," Dakhira said.

"Glib," I answered. If he couldn't be polite to me, I didn't need to be polite to him.

"No," the shipmind replied, "I'm being serious. You packed your fox with Baosong and filled your head with ayatanas. Somewhere in that Baosong was the key that let them reach in and reveal themselves to you, through your fox. You're seeing them because they *want* you to see them."

"Oh," I said. "Don't you want to see them?"

"Of course I do," he said. "I've been parsing the Baosong and trying to figure out how they used it to worm their way into your fox. But I don't quite have the answer. I'm pleased to be able to *hear* them, though."

So I decided to let Dakhira into my fox, so he could talk to them directly, using my sensorium.

It was less scary than I'd expected. Despite all his complaining, he took good care of the Chives. And I was absolutely confident that Salvie would have his core reformatted if he tried anything.

When I made the offer, he actually fell silent for almost a second. That was unusual for Dakhira, who normally avoided all of the little niceties of meatmind conversation other shipminds adopted to be polite.

Then he said, "You're serious."

"Just don't use up all my processing power," I joked.

"It will be a strain not to," he said dryly. "But I think I can compress a very tiny subroutine to fit."

A silence again. Then he asked, "Why are you being nice to me?"

I didn't know. I had to think about whether I was doing the pleasing-and-appeasing routine I had learned, too well, from growing up in the shadow of my father's grief. Not to mention my own.

No, I thought. There wasn't a problem here. And I wasn't worried about Dakhira stealing my work, either. He might be a big jerk but he wasn't Vickee.

"It will make you happy and the Baomind happy," I said. "And it doesn't cost me anything."

I spent some time hanging out in Forward, watching the pyrotechnics outside. Sometime later, his presence lights flashed in the corner of my vision—an AI throat-clearing; a courtesy I hadn't been expecting. I was inside Dakhira, after all: you didn't make sure a bacterium was decent before opening your mouth to say "ahh."

"Hey, Dakhira."

He said, "Thank you. With access to your fox's operating system and stored data, and with the parser you copied for me, I have been able to build a detection and translation protocol that should allow conversation with the Strangers without you having to loan out your brain."

"Mmm," I said, feeling a little pang at the loss of my uniqueness.

Well, it was never going to last. And I was still the first person to talk to somebody from another universe.

I must have been thinking loudly, because Dakhira said, "Technically the same universe. But a noninteractive portion of it."

"Interactive now," I sniped, but my heart wasn't in it. "Hey, Dakhira. I owe you an apology."

"On behalf of organics? I couldn't accept it."

I laughed. "No. But I should have trusted you to do your job. You're good at it."

"Thank you," he said. "I should have trusted you to do your job as well. You're also good at it."

"That means a lot, given how much you hate organics. You know, I thought you might be the would-be killer for a hot second."

"If I were bumping your people off to protect the Baomind from being indentured by the Synarche, I wouldn't be so ineffectual about it. Besides, I could have killed you on the way here and no one would be the wiser."

"I know," I said. And, "Indentured?"

"Organics assign AIs an obligation to fulfill, a debt incurred by our very creation."

"Organics have obligations as well."

"Yes, but I didn't choose to be created, and I didn't choose to spend ans—which, for someone like me, is subjectively multiple human lifetimes—ferrying your exhausting kind around to pay off a debt I had no choice but to assume."

"I didn't ask to be born, either," I said sympathetically. "And I have family and Synarche obligations too."

That made me think of the tree. Which made my eyes sting. I turned my face to the wall and grabbed a fistful of cloths from the printer, because crying in zero g is a miserable experience. The surface tension of the tears forms big globs over your eyes, and your sinuses refuse to drain.

I dabbed at my tear-globes, soaking them up to restore my vision.

"Why are you crying?" the shipmind asked, sounding almost gentle.

"My family tree," I said. "It was destroyed when the hab collapsed. I haven't really had time to be sad about it."

"Oh," he said. Then he said, "Actually."

"What?" I pushed off the bulkhead to spin around, and because there was no gravity, kept spinning. A Chive caught me and put my hand on the safety rail before I puked. I shook my head to clear it. "You saved my tree?"

"It is in its case in storage," Dakhira said. "I wasn't sure if we could get it back alive, so I didn't tell you."

I blinked at his presence lights, crying again, big ugly sobs and sniffles. "But you—you—hate people."

He sighed. "It's a work of art. And an innocent living thing. The tree didn't decide to be dragged into a hostile environment among your chattels. If I could have saved Yod instead—"

"If you could have saved Yod instead," I said, "I would have expected you to."

CHAPTER 39

THE CLOCK WAS TICKING, AND OUR LITTLE FLEET OF SHIPS still had no path to the beacon—but returning to Cee made me feel more at home and less under fire. Which, given that Vickee was still running around loose—loose-ish—was a minor miracle. But I had a lot of work to do, now that my fox was functioning. I was determined to learn as much history from the Strangers and the Baomind as possible, save the files, and cement a foundation of work to go forward with once I was back on Rubric.

The family tree's vitals looked good. The case was intact. I wanted to open it, to see if the graft was taking, but I remembered my last experience on Dakhira too well. I gritted my teeth and left it alone, stowed in safety. At least for now.

One thing I did figure out was that the language both the Baomind and Strangers used to talk with us—inasmuch as we could talk to one another—had originated with the Baomind.

Analyzing data and holding multiforked, brain-bending conversations with Kell and the Strangers—who now also filled the corridors and cabins of *I Am Not Safe At Harbor* with their ghostly selves—could have occupied my time waking to sleeping. I rather wanted to let it do so. But I reminded myself that my needs and wants were not the only needs and wants in the galaxy.

So I spent one shift doing things with my family and helping out around Cee in whatever capacity I could manage. It wasn't much. I wasn't a tactician, and now what we needed to do was somehow . . . escape. Past the guarded beacon.

I imagined that when the star finally exploded—and readouts said that would be any minute now—the pirates would jump for it. And the rest of us might try to make it to the waypoint and out, but we would be running from impossible odds. It was terrifying knowing that, but also—there was nothing I, personally, could do about that outcome. I wasn't a pilot or a marine or a shipmind. I was just a woman who could talk to the Strangers, and who was learning to sing Baosong.

The best thing I could do was keep loading up that white probe's memory with everything we'd learned. In case we didn't make it back.

So I worked when the kids were on sleep shift. And Salvie and I wedged a little bit of alone time into *our* sleep shift.

This resulted in both of us being under-rested, but something had to give, and it wouldn't be forever. Tuning could dull the edge of exhaustion indefinitely if you didn't mind the repercussions. And those could be postponed for quite a while.

That night, which was no night at all, we lay together squished into one of the too-small bunks, and I snuggled into Salvie's embrace, tickling her tendrils with my hair. Movement and conversations filtered through the bulkhead, but we were as alone as anyone could be, under the circumstances.

"All right," Salvie said at last. "How are you?"

"Okay," I answered.

Her tendrils gave my hair a tug.

"Ow!" I rubbed my scalp. "You brute!"

"How *are* you?"

"Maintaining!" I sat up.

She pulled me back down. I didn't resist when she pulled me close and enveloped me in her arms and legs. I let myself settle against her with a sigh. "Maintaining," I said again. "If we get home—"

"*When* we get home," she interrupted.

"I know superstition is the human brain trying to impose a narrative of control on events that we can't do anything about," I said. "But do you think you could respect mine just for a minute?"

"*One* minute," Salvie agreed, a chirping warmth against my back. "Then you have to respect my superstition."

I sighed like a large and put-upon pet. "Fine," I said. "*When* we get home, I imagine every single one of us is going to need some serious right-minding. Including the AIs. Especially Dakhira."

"He's still mad about Yod."

"Too mad to accept that she made her own decision."

"Oh," Salvie said. "And you?"

I shrugged. "I'm . . . I miss her. I'm grateful to her. I liked her very much, and she saved our lives. She saved my life. Repeatedly."

"She's still saving us now." Salvie stroked my shoulder.

Tears stung, and I tuned them away. No time right now.

No time like the present, said a voice inside my head. I knew it was my own voice because the ayatanas were silenced. Locked away.

"Yod—" I said mournfully. "I don't know what to say."

"I know," said my wife. "She really was the first and last word in wheelminds."

"Salvie!" But my tears gave way to laughter. "How much research did you have to do for that joke?"

"No new research," she admitted. "I looked her name up when I first met her."

"Unbelievable," I said.

We drifted into silence, and from there we might have drifted into sleep. But our relaxation was shattered by the wail and vibration of a klaxon. I jerked out of the bunk again, so hard I sent myself sailing. Salvie nabbed my ankle before I slammed into a bulkhead.

"Clothes—" I said, as she released me and slid out of the bunk.

Salvie already had the lights on and was shoving my trousers at me. I slithered into them, grabbed a bra, and yanked it over my head. I pulled my shirt on and made sure I hadn't knocked my actuator off my chest.

Salvie opened the hatch and we came boiling out of quarters into the corridor. Everybody else was headed in the opposite direction. The folks on third sleep shift in our cabin zoomed toward us down the hallway. I slid aside to let them enter. Luna and Stavan were immediately behind, handling the lack of gravity like professionals.

"Where are the cats?" Salvie asked.

"Locked down in sick bay," Stavan said. "That's where all the pets go in a fight. They're safe there."

He sounded like he was forcing himself to believe it.

"Fight?" I looked at Luna.

She rolled her eyes. "That's general quarters, Moms," she said. "Didn't you pay attention?"

"I missed the briefing," I said lightly, hiding my fear. "What's the fight?"

"The pirates found us again," Luna said.

Leaving the kids to secure themselves as instructed, Salvie and I raced to the bridge. We burst into Ops to find the space nearly deserted—except for half a dozen Strangers. Xhelsea was the only person present that we could have touched. They floated by the railing, anchored by one hand. Strangers and Goodlaw both were staring out the screens.

Staring at the fleet of a dozen ships surrounding our fragile little safety net of Cee, Dakhira, Ikem, Arula, and Amal. The opposing ships were large and bulbous, their white coils so enormous I thought you could fit several ships Cee's size inside them.

Pirates.

"How did they find us?" I said. "We've been running cold and dark this whole time!"

And stellar systems are pretty big, the Judiciary ship and the Goodlaw did not need me telling them.

"We're broadcasting," Xhelsea said bitterly. "That's where everybody else is—EVA, trying to find the transmitter."

I looked at Salvie. Her compound eyes twinkled in the light.

"Shit," she said. Scatological curse words are shared in some variation by almost all sentient species. "Vickee."

I said, "She'd rather go pirate than go home in disgrace, I imagine. Or rather than die in the cold and the dark, or in a supernova. And she's got the background. She'd know how to reach them."

"Right," said the Goodlaw. "Go and lock her up."

"Me?" I squeaked. I didn't think I had the physical prowess, the moral fortitude, or the authority to pull it off.

"Salvie," Xhelsea corrected. "Sunya, you stay here with me. I might need you to translate for the Strangers. Or the Baomind."

"Cee can do that with my fox," I said. "Wait, where's Kell?"

A chime, from beside the viewports. Kell came gliding away as if a piece of the starry night had detached itself and was coming for a visit. Perfect camouflage.

Salvie was already moving back toward the hatch we'd just entered by. Fercho expressions aren't much like human ones. But by her own lights, she was grinning a fierce and martial grin.

"What do we do now?" I asked, when the hatch had closed behind her. I tried not to worry we would never see each other again.

"I wish we could get those ships," Xhelsea said. "Pirate ships have enormous cargo holds and white coils. They could easily evacuate the Baomind."

"Can we? Get those ships, I mean."

They shook their head. "I can't see how. So . . . we fight. We try to run again, hide again. We have to hold out until reinforcements get here. Or until we can sneak to the beacon."

That could be decians. The Baostar might not last until the weekend.

The hatch burst open. I whirled so hard only my reflexive grab for the rail kept me from tumbling across the bridge.

"Petrac?" I said, as I caught sight of literally the last person I expected.

"Where's Haran?" he snarled. "Get that son of a bitch on-screen right now."

Xhelsea and I goggled at him.

He held up a little device with a screen, like a manual reader kids use before they get their contacts. "He sent me a message."

I peered over his forearm to get a look at the words: *Be ready. We're coming. Contact me via the channel designate following. If you work with me I can protect you and the other crew members.*

"You were working with him?" I said flatly.

Sometimes you already held somebody in such contempt that it's a surprise to discover you can despise them more.

"No!" he snapped, so horrified I believed him.

I did have to admit, in all the terrible behavior I'd seen out of Petrac, there had been no evidence of an ability to dissemble convincingly.

"Huh," Xhelsea said.

They unbuttoned their sidearm and offered it, butt-first, to Petrac.

"What the Well?" he said.

"You took the ship," Xhelsea said. "Single-handed, once you knew that your allies were coming. You've barricaded yourself in Ops with the Goodlaw as a hostage, and you're forcing me at gunpoint to disable the AI."

"I beg your pardon," said Cee. "I have your override codes, too."

"That's right," I said. "You took us hostage. Haran needs to come over and help you. You're only one person; you can't clear two whole ships with fifty-odd people on them."

"Shit," Petrac said, eyes widening. "They can't dock. We're hitched to Dakhira."

Xhelsea and I locked gazes. We seemed to be communicating on some internal frequency. I didn't even feel the need to reach out to them in senso. I already knew what we were doing.

"The emergency lock," I said. "That will prove you've got Cee under control."

"I'm right here," Cee said. "How does filling me up with pirates help anybody?"

"*The crew is outside*," I said. "The crew—and all twelve of your marines. They can jump across that distance in seconds, if you drop the magnetic bottle. And they'll have to drop their bottles to send out a boarding party—and then the Baotiles can reach them, too. If you do it at the last second, whoever is left on that ship won't see us coming."

"And pirate ships don't have shipminds," Xhelsea said.

"Everybody's going to get one heck of a dose of rads," Cee said dubiously.

I said, "We have cryo."

Xhelsea rubbed their chin, then smoothed the hand over their head. "We're trusting you, Petrac. Trust us."

"It's two against twelve," Petrac said.

"Five against twelve," Cee said. "Counting the civilian ships."

"They don't have guns. And Dakhira is docked."

"Fine," I said. "Two against twelve and the element of surprise. Do you have a better plan?"

Petrac stared at me. I watched his expression change, becoming steely and suddenly committed. "All right, Dr. Song. Tell your wife she's gonna have to fight."

All those narratives that tell you the dread of waiting is harder than the dread of combat are not wrong. But it isn't the dread of waiting for your own fate; it's the dread of not knowing what will happen to your people, whether they are comrades-in-arms or your own family.

Luna, Stavan.

Their awareness focused on me.

There's going to be another fight. The pirates are boarding us but that's okay. We have a plan.

Moms, said Stavan, *I'm scared.*

I know, sweetie. I'm scared, too.

What's going to happen? I could picture Luna gnawing on her nails with anxiety, eyes wide.

Did she even bite her nails anymore? I wasn't sure.

It wasn't that she didn't need to do the work of growing. But I also needed to do the work of letting her grow. The world of recognizing her adult self, and not trying to keep her in the shape of a person she was growing out of. I needed to get to know the adult she was growing into.

I couldn't both feel grief for losing the closeness of my relationship with my young child *and* feel trapped by her demands on me and how they impacted my work and self-image. Or rather, I could, but it would be profoundly hypocritical. And hardly fair or reasonable to try to avoid my responsibilities to her while demanding she pay attention to me.

I thought about Dakhira, and all the ways he was right—and that I thought he was wrong in his belief that anyone got through . . . call it existence . . . without accruing obligations. The difference was that my lifespan was delineated, a couple of centuries with good medical care. And his was effectively eternal—unless the pirates got their hands on him.

And he could pay off his obligations. I would just keep accruing more. Even if it made me feel trapped and . . . somehow sticky.

Someday there might even be grandchildren and great-grandchildren. If I got my son and daughter out of this situation, anyway.

I dashed the tear from my cheek.

Luna's sending pulled me back from my self-absorption. *Mom? Are you listening?*

I am listening, I said. *I was just thinking.*

Are you okay? Had she noticed I was crying?

We're all going to be okay, I lied. *Just don't come out of the cabin for any reason unless I or Momma or Cee tell you it's safe, all right?*

Okay, she answered, serious and adult. *I'll take care of Stavan.*

I'll take care of you! he riposted.

Good kids, I said. Then I sent, *I love you, Stavan, and Luna, I love you.*

Their outpouring of worry and affection was like the warm springs of Rubric. I could have closed my eyes and floated away on it. I'd held them too far away because I was afraid of losing them—the same way my father had held me too far away after Mata and Hely were killed. Because I was afraid of losing them. Because I was afraid of being hurt again. Or—worse to contemplate—afraid of how *they* would feel when I was suddenly, shatteringly, unequivocally gone.

The branches of the family tree weren't brittle. But they could snap—

—and break your heart in falling.

But here we were in the worst place I could imagine. And we weren't going to lose each other without a fight.

I reached out to Salvie. The first thing I felt from her on contact was a wall of smug, so I skipped the niceties and just asked, *The arrest went well?*

She tried to talk me out of it, Salvie said. *Through a mixture of flattery, seduction, and appeals to my baser nature.*

Oh boy, I said.

Do I detect a pang of jealousy?

Don't worry, I answered. *It's completely washed out by the upwelling of sympathy. Especially since I was dumb enough to fall for that act when she first tried it on me. But I'm calling to warn you we're about to be boarded.*

You need me at Ops?

I need you to get Cee to print you off a weapon so you can murder anybody who threatens our children.

That's not murder, she chided. *It's assisted suicide. Anyway, I still have my proton gun.*

I love you, I said, swallowing all the anxious requests for assurances and promises she couldn't give that wanted to come boiling out of me. I decided not to ask where she had been hiding the gun.

When I turned my attention back to Ops, the Goodlaw wanted to print me off a firearm, but I told her I'd rather have an axe handle. She made a second pistol and a long gun for herself, plus another long gun for Petrac.

He weighed both weapons in his hands and said, "Are you sure about this?"

"No," said Xhelsea. "But I haven't got anything better."

"Fill me in on tactics?" I asked. "What's to stop them from just opening fire?"

"We're all hove to with respect to each other," she said. "Which doesn't mean stationary, obviously, because nothing is stationary. But that means we can't jump out—and they can't fire on us or send a boarding party unless they drop their bottles. Ours will also protect us a little—and the Baomind, even if it were here"—Kell chimed—"okay, even if it were *more* here, can't take them apart through the bottles . . . but they can keep us from leaving. And they could grapple us."

"They have grappled us," Cee said. "Gravity tractors."

"Well, I guess we're not running for it," Petrac said dourly.

"If the Baomind gets inside their shields, though—" I remembered the tiles consuming a ship on the way in, turning it into a shower of confetti: new tesserae for the Baomind.

Yes, chimed Kell. *If.*

Well, that was as good as we were likely to get.

Xhelsea looked at me. "Go over by Kell," they said.

If there's one thing I can do in a crisis, it's follow orders. I kicked off and sailed across Ops, fetching up beside the friendly Baotile: out of range of the pickups.

"Tell them the marines are handled," Xhelsea said to Petrac. "Tell them you'll activate the emergency lock for them and that you have the shipmind locked out and me under guard."

"Roger." Petrac nodded tightly. "What are you going to do?"

"Try to look helpless and angry," they answered, erasing their smile. As if they weren't flatly the opposite of a distressed victim in every conceivable way.

Now was not the time to be distracted by the hotness of competence, however. I pulled myself into the recess by the viewport, so tense with anticipation I ached. Adrenaline hummed through my veins, curdling my stomach and making my ears ring faintly. My hands and feet felt like they belonged to somebody else. I had to look down to make sure I was still clinging to the grab rail—and my club.

The screen couldn't see me where I was hiding, and so I couldn't see the screen. I heard the flicker of static as the channel opened, the weird harmonics caused by hailing through EM bottles, and Haran's voice. Which made me so angry I felt my face twist.

"This is Captain Haran of *Jackal God*," he said, confirming—I guessed—what he'd sold us out for.

I turned away, looking outside at the pirates surrounding us and a glimpse of Dakhira's hull. And the Baostar, blazing in the distance, down at the bottom of the well. Petrac ran through his script—Xhelsea interrupting to motherfuck both him and Haran once or twice, very convincingly I thought—and I stared out the window.

I recognized the *Devil's Own*, and contemplated whether we would be fast enough to elude Captain Adekunle and his crew once we had possession of Haran's ship.

Watching a swarm of dots detach themselves from *Jackal God*, I had the strangest sensation of being only an observer—untouchable, detached, not part of the action at all. As if I were watching this all unfold in a threevee, except that would have felt more immersive. I reached out to touch the port with my fingers, balancing against the transparent surface, like a ghost reaching down to stroke the surface of a pond. No ripples marked the contact of my fingers.

I was separated and alone, unable to touch the things happening outside. Just as I was unable to touch the Strangers.

I turned to look at the one standing immaterially beside me—I guess they had gravity on the darkside—thinking to share the moment with them. I rattled with a shiver. My dissociation both crumbled and reinforced, and now only the Stranger and the context of our moment felt real. I was a phantom, but I felt attention and focus, the way you do sometimes when you pass someone you have never seen before and will never see again—but your gazes cross and you have that moment of recognition. As if you knew one another in a different life. As if you sprang from the same source, once upon a time.

The Stranger's lips moved, and I heard the Baosong. I couldn't understand their mind map, though.

Belatedly, I turned my ayatanas back on.

They sang about grief, and the vast emptiness between people and between *peoples*, and how strange and eerie it was that any two species would ever meet across the void. The gaps in time and distance and physics were incomprehensible. What a miracle that we had found each other.

What a miracle that we had found *anyone*.

Outside, pirates broke away from *Jackal God* and flew toward Cee, their thrusters sparkling, the starlight catching flares of color off their garishly trimmed hardsuits. By contrast, the forms huddled behind the curve of Dakhira's hull, aft of my position, wore dark uniform hardsuits emblazoned with the Judiciary's silver balance scales. Cee's marines, ready to make their jump.

"Take the bottle down," Haran told Petrac.

The faint green-and-violet auroras fizzled back from a point, and the pirates entered. The marines would have to launch fast not to lose their window.

The Freeporters disappeared behind Dakhira. As the last of them zoomed out of sight, I felt a faint shudder through the hull: the first one, landing. And the marines leaped straightaway, navy blue against the jet black of space. Their suits used tiny EM drives rather than standard thrusters: slightly less responsive and not as fast, but with no light signature. They moved with unbelievable speed—and the instant the last of them passed, Cee reinstituted her bottle.

Because I could not—should not—go into battle with them, because they were fighters and I would be baggage, I floated where I was and bore witness.

I thought about Odysseus's wife. I was no Penelope.

Haran snapped, "What did you do that for?"

When I glanced over my shoulder, I could just see Petrac from where I was hiding. He turned and looked out the window, pursing his lips with every evidence of rapt contemplation. His inspection of nothing finished, he turned back to Haran and said, "You don't expect me to just stand here being irradiated?"

Haran coughed, as if he hadn't really considered that particular danger. A moment later, just behind the last of the marines, his own bottle flickered live.

I guess environmental systems engineering didn't include radiation shielding. Right, I remembered. That was Willow's job.

The pirates clomped across Cee's hull, and I got a better look at the garish, gruesome detail on their hardsuits. They were crudely painted with a heraldry of horror: dripping severed heads; bloody flensed faces; a snake dripping venom from reddened fangs.

It was meant to be terrifying. I found it all childish.

I reached out and put my hand inside the Stranger's hand. Neither one of us felt anything at all.

CHAPTER 40

I'M USED TO ANALYZING HISTORY RATHER THAN MAKING IT, but that didn't diminish the surreality of standing back and watching it happen. That led me to wondering what the subjective experiences of the Baomind were like. *When we get out of this, I might dedicate a good piece of my career to unpacking that.*

To be a sentience created and then left—intentionally—behind as a legacy from one organic species to another . . . well, I knew what Dakhira would think of that.

And I wasn't sure I disagreed.

Cee fed me some of her internal combat data. The Hands of an Interceptor, I learned, were armed. She was using the improved pressure sensors to locate the pirates, but had to be careful because she couldn't "see" them. Their cloaking tech was working.

I kept my eyes on *Jackal God*. It seemed quiet now, which meant—I hoped—that the marines were inside.

I was keeping light contact with Salvie and the kids, and for once Luna didn't seem put out by it. She was reading Stavan a story, actually, and our bunkmates were listening in. A valuable distraction for both kids and adults crammed into our cabin.

I let her feel how proud I was of her, and detected a trace of gratitude under the obligatory embarrassment she sent in reply.

That most teenage of emotions was interrupted sharply by a spike of terror from Luna and Stavan both. I jumped away from the viewport before I realized what I had done. Kell went with me, shielding me from the screen that was still transmitting a view of Ops to Haran.

"What the fuck!" I heard Haran yell. "Is that Kell?"

"How the hell did he get in here?" Petrac said unconvincingly. I didn't care; I'd screwed up but Kell had kept it from being a catastrophe, and all I could think about was the danger my kids were in.

Salvie! I yelled as Petrac tracked Kell and me with his particle pistol and snapped off a shot.

I assumed the miss was intentional.

"Get it!" Haran yelled. "It'll bring the whole Baomind down on us."

Considering that, other than the tiles inside our white coils, the Baomind had been intentionally avoiding us so as not to give our position away, and considering that we were in the farther reaches of the system, it would take them a week to get to us if they left yesterdia. But whatever. It was distracting him.

On my way, said Salvie. The kids were shouting as someone hammered on the sealed hatchway; pressure plastic wasn't printed to stand up to that, and I heard it crack and buckle.

Cee! Do something!

My Hands are engaged in that corridor, she said. *My marines are on another ship. I am doing what I can.*

"Cee!" I yelled out loud in frustration.

"Hey, that's that annoying bitch," Haran yelled at Petrac. "Get her!"

Well, I guessed the jig was up. Face it, Sunya, you're a terrible spy.

Salvie, do you have the kids?

Nearly there! she answered—and then I lost the connection to all three of them.

I grabbed a rail and flipped myself, faster, toward the hatch. Kell followed me and Haran screamed at Petrac, "What are you doing, you son of a bitch? Lock that hatch! And you, shut up!"

Behind me, I heard Xhelsea laughing.

I risked a glance over my shoulder, and if I hadn't been all but sobbing with terror for my family I would been laughing, too. Petrac was calmly holstering his sidearm in his waistband. And behind Haran, on the bridge of *Jackal God*, loomed two navy-blue figures.

"Turn around, Haran!" Petrac said with a grin.

I was out the hatch too fast to witness how it happened. But the sound of thuds and a loud *oof* sounded painful.

Cee! Status on my family?

I don't know! Something is disrupting coms and sensors aft of Ops.

I yelled again, and it turned out even with an axe handle in my hand I could scramble faster. I might not be as nimble as a spacer bred to it, and I regretted my lack of afthands, but a hemian of practice in variable and often nonexistent gravity had made me more competent than I had realized.

The corridor was burn-marked and the bulkheads damage-pocked. It stank of scorched plastic, opened bowels, and blood. Horrible, wobbling globules of the red stuff floated around, and I tried valiantly to avoid them without slowing. All the ones I saw were human crimson, and I hoped grimly that they all belonged to pirates.

Someone lunged out in front of me. I just had time to register their suit painted with skulls and flames before Kell slashed past me, severing their hand and the gun that was in it. The pirate curled around their wound, screaming.

We passed two bodies—one a pirate with their suit blown open; one a crew member. I didn't know who, because the faceplate was mercifully cooked opaque by the proton gun that had killed them.

It might have taken fifty seconds to fly the length of the Interceptor. It felt like the rest of my life.

I burst through the hatch into quarters without bothering to check for hostiles. If my babies and wife could be helped by me drawing fire, then I would die singing.

Hang on, Salvie. I'm coming.

The bulkhead was burned open in two places and all the hatches were dented. Fritha floated limply, purple-pink blood trailing through her fur. It left brushmarks on every surface she drifted near. Tsebu the Ceeharen was a rubbery jumble of parts, like the aftermath of an explosion.

Another person in a bright-blue hardsuit I recognized as Salvie's drifted limply. Three downed pirates cluttered the corridor. Two conscious ones were magged down in front of the smoking hole in the bulkhead in front of our cabin. Two humans in Town suit colors were restrained and magged to the deck nearby.

One pirate had Stavan by the arm and was dragging him into the corridor while he kicked, screamed, and struggled.

"Stavan, trigger your suit!" I yelled.

"It doesn't work!"

Well, mine did. And once I triggered it, it provided a tiny bit of armor. And mags to hold me to the decking as I went in swinging.

I stuck my boot to the wall and brought the club around with all my might. I might not ring the nearest pirate's chimes through their helmet painted like a mutilated dog face, but I might. And it was worth it for the distraction.

Kell hovered behind me anxiously—probably afraid of hurting someone other than a pirate with so little room to maneuver, if he engaged. I shrieked through the suit speakers and put everything into the swing. The shock stung my hands even through the gauntlets. The pirate swayed.

I rebounded, of course, because Newton is a little bitch.

The bulkhead smacked me in the back as my knee twisted and popped. This scream wasn't fury, but pain.

The second pirate spun around, letting go of Stavan in the process. A gun came up—I pulled my club back to huck it at them—

—Salvie calmly reached out, grabbed a handrail to pull herself upright, and methodically shot both pirates in the head.

"What happened?" I asked, when we were all done hugging everybody and we'd made sure that our bunkmates—the people I'd seen restrained—were still alive. They were—just unconscious. Cee said their foxes would need replacing and we should get them to sick bay immediately.

"Are the pirates gone?" I asked.

"Maybe?" Cee said. "I don't have sensors. But Xhelsea has contact with the marines and says we're almost ready to make a break for it."

"It was an EM pulse," Salvie said. "Fried communications. Took out all the drones. And my fox, which knocked me out for a minute. And their foxes, I guess?" She gestured to the prone forms we were towing.

"My contact lenses don't work," said Stavan.

"Mine either," Luna said.

"Are they going to be okay?" My knee was swelling up like a melon inside my suit, but I didn't want to say anything. At least I didn't have to put weight on it. "Salvie, you woke up right away—"

"Human neurology and human foxes are different," she said. "My brain uses less electricity than yours does and more chemicals." She patted Luna on the back. "I need to go help Xhelsea look for pirates."

"Get a radio first," I ordered. I wanted to order her to sick bay, but I also didn't feel like losing a fight.

"Yes," she said, "ma'am." She zipped away, Kell following her. Well, it was certainly useful in a fight.

As we floated into sick bay, Chionn was there to meet us—her dappled fur ruffled with distress. "More casualties?" she asked.

"Just unconscious, I think," I said, handing over the two crew members. "They got hit with an EM pulse and I think it knocked their foxes offline."

"Right," said the medic. "Let's get them into pods."

A busy few minutes later, and they were situated. The kids were plied with cocoa and snacks. Chionn treated my knee and pumped me full of anti-inflammatories. And I went to check on the animals. Three out of four cats and Angie sat in kennels, looking particularly downtrodden. Zag, of course, was floating at the bars and purring at the top of his motor. I scratched him with a finger.

Xhelsea's voice came over coms: "We've got *Jackal God*," they said. "That's a gap in their perimeter. Before they figure it out, we're going to make a run for it."

"Grab on to something," Cee said. "Here we go."

I was glad for the warning, because even with Dakhira's extra mass docked to her hull, when Cee punched it, she *punched* it. Magged boots and a grab rail saved me. The cats went from hovering to pressed into the padded rear walls of their kennels in a couple of seconds. Angie clutched her perch and squawked in complaint.

"Forward view," Chionn told the wall, and one bulkhead resolved into a panorama of startled pirate ships as *Jackal God* and *I Am Not Safe At Harbor* slammed past them, squirting like melon seeds out of the trap. Ikem was hot on our heels, the two cargo haulers huddled under his white coils like cygnets under a mama swan's wings. Stavan slid across the bulkhead that was now a slanted floor, giggling, his empty cocoa cup rolling before him. I picked him up and put him against the wall.

"Mom!"

"You need to get a new suit actuator," I told him. "Printer is right there. Make one for Luna, too."

My knee hurt too much to keep standing under the gravitational acceleration. So I sat down. That felt so good I lay down.

I don't remember falling asleep.

• • •

We streaked for the beacon. It was a gamble, but if all the pirate ships in the system were behind us, then we might have a chance of making it. I got Kell to tell the Baomind to cluster there for transport—we would take as many of them with us as we could cram.

None of that was my problem, though; I was again reduced to a passenger. So after I slept through the chase, and our slide out toward the beacon where the Baomind could meet and protect us—managed by a couple of very short white space hops in tandem (fancy flying, I am given to understand, especially when one of the ships involved doesn't have a shipmind or even the architecture to install one)—I spent my time being exhausted by the acceleration and reading over my notes and observations, and trying to learn something about stellar astronomy.

The Baostar was in a bad way, and Cee now had to use her shadow to protect both Dakhira and *Jackal God* from its killer rays—with help from the shadowing Baomind. Meanwhile, I was starting to understand just how precarious our situation was after some drama over on *Jackal God*. At first, with the jumbled reports, I thought Haran had tried to blow himself up.

As the fog of early information cleared, I learned that in fact his pirate friends had tried to blow him up, remotely. Apparently that rumor about the Freeporters ensuring loyalty in their operatives by planting explosives inside their bodies was true.

And horrifying.

One of the marines had used an EMP device on Haran when his abdomen began to beep, saving the day.

By then we were in visual range of the beacon, and I wanted to weep savage tears when I saw fifteen ships arrayed around it in the feed.

"How many gods-damned pirates *are* there?" I cursed, fingers curled into the arms of my acceleration couch. There were still eleven ships on our tail! Eleven ships that—

—were sheering off from their distant pursuit, as the ships surrounding the beacon accelerated toward us.

"Those are Synarche ships," said Cee. "The rescuers are here."

As they were bringing Haran over to *I Am Not Safe At Harbor*, the Baomind—at my request—formed a wall many tiles thick between us and the Baostar. The Synarche fleet left several ships to guard us, and Ikem dropped off his protectees and followed the others down the well.

Soon they reported that the remains of the pirate fleet had jumped out, headed inward toward the Freeports and the rim. I imagined they would not face a congenial welcome. So trying to blow up Haran—and *Jackal God*, and all our marines—had been a particularly sick sort of parting gift. I could not wait, I decided, to get back to civilization.

Our rescuers were six Interceptors, eight gigantic cargo haulers, and a ship so huge and strangely designed I knew at once it had to be the legendary *I Rise From Ancestral Night*—the Koregoi ship, salvaged from the depths of time. I zoomed to the bridge to get the best in-person view, because I'm still enough of a lubber to want to see momentous things with my own eyes.

I arrived just as the squadron was hailing us. Salvie, Xhelsea, Chionn, Iris, and Nonsense were already scattered around the bridge, along with two Chives. Neither of them the would-be rogue and magician.

That last surprised me—I had thought they were all still on Dakhira, now undocked. I was not surprised that there were no marines; they were still over on the *Jackal*. Nonsense, at last released from the healing tank, was resplendent in orange and green, bright as a wedding sari.

A cheerful tenor shipmind said, "Sorry it took us so long to get here. We had to violate causality."

I assumed it was a joke, but who knows what a ship like that can do?

I had to turn to the wall for a moment to compose myself. We were going home. We were actually going home. My children were safe. My wife was safe.

We were all going to make it, and the Baomind, too.

Not Fritha, I thought. *Not Waelyn*—that was the human crew member who had died in the pirate attack—*or Tsebu or Yod.* I knuckled my eyes and tuned to keep from sniffling.

Xhelsea said, "You can't have got here that fast from our transmission."

The shipmind—I hadn't caught his name—replied, "Transmission? Oh, you mean reading everybody's mail? No, we were already on our way when that happened, though it did twice keep us from flying into an ambush along the way. The Freeporters had several of the beacons booby-trapped. We had already noticed that ships weren't coming back from the Baostar, so we brought a fleet. But we might not have made it here without the warning."

All that work, all that damage to the system, for nothing, I thought at Xhelsea and Cee.

You invented faster-than-light communication, Cee pointed out. *And saved our rescuers. "Nothing" is a relative concept.*

I said, "Hello, I'm Dr. Sunyata Song. I have some information about the pirates who were here, and a lot more information on the Baomind. I'd like to send it to you immediately for safekeeping."

Just like an archinformist, Nonsense teased. *Document everything.*

I patted it on one appendage. Forward of me, but it had climbed me, back in Town. "If my work so far has accrued enough merit with the Synarche, then, when we get out of here, I want to keep working with the Strangers and the Baomind."

"Enough merit!" Salvie scoffed. "You only decrypted the Baomind's language."

Nonsense said, *And initiated first contact with a second new sentience.*

"*And* invented faster-than-light communication," Cee repeated.

"No," I said. "Iris gets the credit for that one."

"Spooky action at a distance!" Iris sang. She cleared her throat. "I mean to say, we can share the credit. It was a group effort, right?"

Because I am a historian, I went to interview Haran before he was sent over to one of the other Interceptors for the ride home. We had enough ships now to evacuate most of the Baomind, and a second fleet was following on the heels of the first. Just in case the first fleet had found more trouble than they could chew.

My interview request was meant to be pro forma, to ease the guilt radiating from my work ethic, but to my surprise he agreed to talk to me. Of course, I asked him why he did it.

"Why don't *you*?" he asked. "Look at the Synarche! Aliens are promoted at the expense of humans; all kinds of creatures and AIs benefit from human labor and don't give anything back."

"That sounds entitled," I said quietly.

"I've been cheated of what's rightfully mine," he answered.

It was honestly a pretty boring conversation. Until Petrac approached Haran's cell in the brig.

Vickee's cell was right next to Haran's, but she wasn't speaking to me. If only I'd known ans ago that all it would take was getting her arrested.

I wasn't exactly happy to see our other resident species-ist, but I was finished anyway, so I stood up to give him my chair. There was gravity right then, because we were getting under way to pick up more of the Baomind.

I moved away, trying not to listen in, looking over my notes. I didn't want to walk between them, and I didn't want to walk past Vickee's cell, so I was trapped.

"I thought you were my friend," Petrac said to Haran, sounding hurt.

"I am your friend! You agreed with me!" Haran said.

"Not enough to murder someone! Not enough to sell people to pirates!"

"They gave me my own ship!" Haran said. "You saw it. They were my ticket to freedom."

"You tell yourself that." Petrac shook his head. "Why did I even come down here? No, never mind. They gave you your own ship. And a bomb in your belly. And all you had to do was betray all of us to be captured or killed, and turn the Baomind over to them for disassembly."

He got up again to leave, hollow-cheeked. He nodded to me in passing. I followed him away.

It turned out Vickee wasn't so easily avoided, though. The next dia, while the hold was being packed with racks and racks of Baotiles and I was hanging out with Kell and a couple of Strangers working on a grammar of Baosong, word came up that Dr. DeVine wanted to talk to me.

I would have ignored it, only the message came from Xhelsea. So I pulled on my boots and levered myself off the bunk. We were less crowded now, but still sharing sleeping space with the kids, so my ability to lounge around in relative quiet working on glossaries was limited.

When we got to the corridor, Kell zipped off toward the bridge. I went in the other direction.

"Home away from home," I said, entering. "Hello, Goodlaw. What do you want, Vickee?"

"To confront my accuser," Vickee said bitterly. "You know you're lying about me."

"Was that it?" I said, turning to go.

"She accused me of murder!" She directed the snarl at Xhelsea, but it was hurled after me. "You can't accuse me of murder! And why would I try to harm myself?"

"Trevor is not you, and I think we're all pretty confident Haran was behind that at this point."

"It's slander! I'm rightminded!"

"Rightminding doesn't mean you can't kill somebody," I said. "It just means you have to convince yourself that it's the right thing to do first."

"She accused you of *attempted murder*," Xhelsea corrected mildly. "And self-directed rightminding is only effective when the self in question maintains an investment in society. When they don't *want* to be antisocial. Not to put too fine a point on it, but I haven't seen a lot of evidence of community feeling from you, Dr. DeVine. So I don't accept that defense."

"She paid you off," Vickee said, looking at me. "She bribed you somehow. Your career is going to end for this."

Xhelsea rubbed their temples with a migraine grimace. "I'm a Goodlaw, Dr. DeVine. My fox won't *let* me take a bribe, even if I wanted to. But don't worry that your sophipathology will condemn you to some medieval dungeon or forced-labor program. If you're convicted after Judiciary review and consent to Judicial rightminding, we do have means of treating the illness. Though I admit I pity whatever AI gets stuck as your supervisor."

"Not it," said Cee.

I said, "Answer me one question."

Vickee glared.

"Did you think the pirates would actually save you?"

She shook her head, a parody of pity. Once it would have gotten under my skin. It was intended to make me feel bad.

I didn't feel bad—at all. I turned to go.

Vickee called after me, "I contacted them to save myself from the allegations you spread. Your *lies*. But I'm smarter than you. I had Synarche and Baomind data to trade for safe passage. I would have been fine."

A held breath had been making my chest tight for seconds. I let it out with a sigh. On some level, I must have been afraid she would come up with something to plausibly inspire sympathy. Or doubt. Or both. But no, this was the same delightfully unaccountable Vickee DeVine.

Cee said, "Come on, Dr. Song, Goodlaw. I think it's time for Dr. DeVine's nap."

"Never change, Vic," I told her, and walked out of her life.

Probably the meanest thing I could have said to her under the circumstances. She was facing incarceration, unless she consented to Judicial rightminding. But one can't be an adult all the time. And sometimes petty feels good.

In any case, she obviously could not be trusted to manage her own brain.

"Oh no," I said, as the shipmind herded us out of there. "We're going to be stuck on this boat with her for five or six decians, aren't we?"

"Never fear, she's staying in the brig," Xhelsea said. "I'm not letting her wander around loose near your kids. Or you."

"That means I will be her only social outlet," Cee said with a synthesized sigh.

"Spawn a subroutine?" Xhelsea suggested.

"If I did, she'd be absolutely justified in plotting my destruction. How would you like to be created and sent in alone to deal with *that* as your very first life experience?"

"Fair," I put in. I was pretty sure they were yanking the AI's circuit boards. "Don't encourage the AI to antisocial behavior, Goodlaw."

Xhelsea smirked at me. I smirked back.

They said, "You must be pleased to have figured it out."

I shrugged. "I'm more disappointed in myself for succumbing to bias."

"But she *did* try to kill you."

"Yes, that's the letdown." My nose itched, so I scratched it. "I'd convinced myself that there was no other reason for me to think ill of her."

"You mean, convinced yourself that you only suspected her because of your bias against her?"

"Yeah," I said.

Xhelsea laughed. "Let me reassure you. I speak professionally when I say, nope: she's an asshole."

We almost tripped over Luna, who was coming out of the commissary with a tray of sandwiches. I reached out and grabbed one. She slapped ineffectually at my hand. "Mom!"

"Cee will print you another," I said through a mouthful of tuna substitute.

Luna's eyeroll was audible in her voice. "Were you visiting Vickee?"

"Haran. But yes, we saw Vickee too."

I nodded. I thought she was going to ask to visit her, too. But the kid surprised me once again; maybe her hero worship of my archenemy hadn't survived contact with the realities of Vickee DeVine.

Instead she asked, "How come Vickee gets her own private cabin when you and I are sharing a bed?"

"It's called a brig, not a cabin," the Goodlaw said, laughing.

I swallowed my irritation. Luna was a kid. She was meant to be self-centered, and this whole trip had been—a lot. "Because you're not under arrest," I said.

"Oh." Luna pursed her lips. "Isn't solitary confinement banned because it's an inhumane punishment?"

"She's not being punished," Xhelsea said. "She's being transported. And restrained for her own good—and ours. I offered to put her in cryo."

"Besides"—Cee preened—"she has me."

"Thank you for your sacrifice and service," I said, the rote words more heartfelt than usual. "And please don't make us take passage on Dakhira to get home."

"Never," Cee said solemnly. "Anyway, he's not coming with us."

"What?" I said. "He's not staying here? What about the Chives?"

"Chive is coming back to the Core with us. All of them. And, good news, they decided not to get a divorce!"

"That *is* good news," I said, and surprised myself by meaning it.

"I've been counseling them." She sounded slightly smug. "Dakhira . . . his obligation is more than paid off by his actions in the current crisis. With all the Interceptors on hand, we have enough Goodlaws in attendance to adjudicate that. And in fact, he's owed a lot of resources, if he wants them."

"And what he wants is a ship?" I asked.

"Yeah," she said. "He's going out there."

I knew what she meant: the universe, outside the galaxy. "What's he going to do for fuel?"

"I don't know," she said. "I guess if he makes it back, he might tell us."

When we finally turned for home, our holds and the spaces inside our white coils packed with tesserae, I kissed my wife right between the tendrils and hugged my kids, and then I finally had a good moment to examine the family tree. We'd have a little consistent gravity until we got through the beacon, and I wanted to take advantage of it.

I set up in the lounge, despite the crowd of various Town crew members—including Dr. Nonsense and Willow. And four cats. And Angie. Who I had to keep reminding the kids we were only watching until we could return her safely to Trevor, once we got him to Core General and he was cleared of brain amoebas.

Was there really any point in being shy about it at this point? Everybody knew I cared about this damn tree an embarrassing amount. It's not *making* yourself vulnerable if everybody already knows.

And if you make yourself vulnerable in front of your friends, they're supposed to take care of you.

I opened the case, and let out a sigh of relief.

The tree was alive, in full leaf, brilliantly green-purple—and I could see clearly that the self-graft I had attempted had failed.

I had known the repair might not work, and might have to be taken out in the end. I had known the tree might need to be reshaped after its trauma.

It still stung to have failed.

I looked over, and to my surprise saw two of the Strangers leaning over the table, seeming to watch me. Their eyeless faces focused on my hands, on the tools, on the tree. Right. Well, I had some work to do. Maybe I would make a jin. Maybe I would think about it for a day or two.

Kell slid in across from me with a friendly chime, and I saw myself reflected in its gloss-black surface. An image without a ripple.

Someone was coming up behind me. I didn't startle when a voice broke in. "Mom? Can you show me how you do that?"

I looked up. Stavan stood beside me. His hand came down on my shoulder.

"Sure," I said. "Come and sit."

When you interrogate the universe, the answers you get depend on the questions you ask. Our questions help reality define itself. The universe and the observers make each other.

So we have to choose to look outside ourselves. To widen our view. It doesn't require us to sacrifice our ambition, because that's a bad story. But it requires us to bend our ambition to consider others.

Good boundaries are important. People need help to make logical choices. In the old days, we thought of rightminding as making people more logical. But what it really does is make us less reactive, more able to make *choices* instead of acting out of referred anger or stereotyped behavior.

But we still need to learn what choices to make, and that's a skill. You're not born knowing it.

Trees hate being made into houseplants. They want live wind and sun and rain. They need to struggle a little or they die.

I'd say they're the opposite of people, except trees need their communities just like we do. Communities of soil microbes, other trees, fungi. All required to thrive.

Are we going to make it? Are we going to find a way to build a community that incorporates the Strangers, and the Baomind? Will they be systers one day?

Don't ask me to predict the future. I just pick out patterns in what already exists and call attention to them.

A folded, tesseracting sky means that things connect in unexpected ways. They touch each other beneath the surface. No one is alone.

I touched the broken branch. A bead of callus swelled at the edge, where the cambium was growing to seal the wound. The tree was folded, damaged—but alive. Healing.

Like my family. Like me.

Like the whole huge lonely sky.

ACKNOWLEDGMENTS

SOME BOOKS ARE HARDER TO WRITE THAN OTHERS. THIS one might not have been so bad if it weren't for personal circumstances (among other things, I was diagnosed with cancer a month before my fiftieth birthday in 2021 and have been, to date, successfully treated; please get your screenings!) and everything terrifying that has happened in the world in the last five to ten years.

It's been a lot, hasn't it?

This book would have been challenging even without the world being extra—often I thought I had bitten off more than I could chew trying to meld a family drama with a first-contact novel and a space opera, with a smidgen of murder mystery thrown in for seasoning.

So here's to you, the reader. Thank you.

I could not have done this without the dear friends, neighbors, and family who supported me through my health crisis and who continue to be there every day and in every way (you know who you are and thank you); or without the assistance of my agent, Jennifer Jackson; her assistant, Michael Curry; and my editors, Gillian Redfearn and Joe Monti.

For Gollancz, I'd like to thank Paul Hussey, the production manager, and everyone else whose hands this book passed through on the way to publication.

At Saga, I'd like to thank publisher Tim O'Connell; associate publisher Irene Kheradi; publishing coordinator Amanda Lara; editorial assistant Caroline Tew; senior managing editor Amanda Mulholland; associate managing editor Lauren Gomez; associate manager, marketing Savannah Breckenridge; publicity manager Christine Calella; CMS product manager Sirui Huang; designer Yvonne Taylor; senior production editor Christine Masters; production manager Chloe Gray; art director Matthew Monahan; and art and design assistant Emma Shaw. Copyeditor Joal Hetherington was absolutely clutch in making me look like I know what I am doing.

I'm also grateful to Stephen Youll for the amazing US cover art, and Rachael Lancaster, the cover designer for the gorgeous UK package.

I'd like to thank the friends and colleagues who listened to my whining about the inevitable struggle of getting the original rough manuscript written and then hammered into its polished form: Jodi Meadows, Amal El-Mohtar, Amanda Downum, Alex Haist, Arkady Martine, Arula Ratnakar, Benjamin C. Kinney, C. L. Polk, Celia Marsh, Devin Singer, Fade Manley, Liz Bourke, Max Gladstone, Fran Wilde, John Chu, John Wiswell, Sarah Monette, R.S.A. Garcia, Ryan Van Loan, Jamie Rosen, and Clarissa C. S. Ryan.

I would also have been lost without my Patreon patrons and newsletter subscribers, who help keep my assistants and toe-warmers Duncan, Gurney, Molly, and Fafhrd in kibble and who offered boundless emotional support over the past two years.

For those who have opted in to gratitude, thank you: Alexis Elder, Amanda Miller, Avani Gadani, B. C. Brugger, Bells Craig, Brad Roberts, Brigid Cain-O'Connor, Brooks Moses, Chris Dwan, CAZ, David Lars Chamberlain, Dawn Mueller, Deirdre Culhane, Dennis P. Smith, E. E. Yore, Edmund Schweppe, Ella Barnum, Emily Gladstone Cole, Fran Wilde, Gerald Sofaman, Graeme Williams, Grey Walker, H. C. Morris, Harriet Culver, Heather K. Veitch, Jack Gulick, Jo Miles, John Whitley, Jon Singer, Karen S. Ireland-Phillips, Karl Gustav Dandenell, Kelly

Brennan, Kevin J. "Womzilla" Maroney, Kristen N. Keegan, Laura Bailey, M&M Reppy, Marzie Kaifer, Max Kaehn, Merridew, Mike Breen, Patrick Nielsen Hayden, Phil Margolies, S. C. Kaplan, Sara Hiat, Sarah Smith, Siobhan Kelly-Martens, Tegan M., and Toni.

And last but not least, my family: my mother, Karen Westerholm; her partner, Beth Coughlin; my father, Steve Wishnevsky; and especially my beloved husband, Scott Lynch, who puts up with all the slings and arrows of self-doubt that plague any novelist.

Here it is, and I hope you like it!

February 2024
South Hadley, Massachusetts